HEAVY CROWN

W MILLION

STOMILL BOOKS

Cover Design: Najla Qamber Designs

Model: Matt Z

Photographer: Michelle Lancaster (@lanefotograf)

Editing: Red Adept Editing

To anyone who has ever been faced with an impossible choice.

BELLERIVE ROYALS

All the books in the series are interconnected standalones.

Fake Crown

Scarred Crown

Heavy Crown

Fallen Crown

ONE

ALEX

Whenever I was summoned to my father's—the king's—office as a kid, I expected trouble. As an adult and the first in line to the throne, my father and I meet all the time. Finding the request on my calendar isn't unusual, but given the swirl of controversy surrounding the monarchy right now, I'm uneasy that something else is about to be dropped on me.

When I arrive to his office, the crowd greeting me is a surprise. My younger brothers, Brice and Nick, along with Nick's soon-to-be wife, Julia, are lounging on the couch. My mother is at my father's shoulder, standing at attention. My father's semi-retired secretary, who also happens to be Julia's mother, is also present. Finally, Desmond, the secretary I share with Nick and Brice, is here too. Every person who could either plot against me or rescue me from my own stupidity is in the room. Thankfully, it's a big office.

"This feels ominous," I say. They've left the seat directly in front of my father's desk free.

As a child, standard conversations on etiquette and protocol were had around the dinner table, on our private jet, or in various hotel rooms. If we were called to the office, we were in trouble. Big trouble. My father would be seated across the desk from one or more of us, a reprimand on his lips and suggestions ready for a slew of community service hours. In those instances, he wasn't my father, he was the king.

This crowd, though, is abnormal—whether in celebration or castigation.

"I wanted to make sure everyone was here for this conversation." My father taps a thick book on his desk with his index finger.

Is that the coronation manual? I haven't actually read it. Julia, my younger brother's fiancée and my father's current secretary, is in charge of organizing the exchange of power, both the ceremony and legalities.

I examine each person in the room, and no one meets my gaze. Not unusual—as my brother Nick likes to claim, I'm the asshole in the family. It's a title I don't relish, and one I'm not convinced I always deserve, but I'm not going to deny I can be abrupt and direct. I am who I am.

"Must be a big mess if you needed everyone. Did you invite the butler too?" I check behind me.

"Alexander," my mother admonishes me.

I run my palms along the armrests of the chair. "Who's in charge of delivering the doom and gloom?" Ever since my father was diagnosed with Alzheimer's, I haven't been sure whether he should be leading Bellerive, and he has, for the most part, shared that opinion.

The coronation is almost a year away, but his cognitive decline might not be so predictable.

With the public referendum on legalizing assisted suicide and my father's disease out on social media, our island politics are in disarray. The Advisory Council of Bellerive, our national government, passed a temporary measure to eliminate royal input until I'm king. They cannot risk a political misstep by having my father involved, especially with some of them up for re-election. Cutting us out isn't a problem as long as none of the issues require the tie-breaking vote the sovereign provides.

Fingers crossed the country can make it through the year.

"The page is marked." My father passes the manual across the table to me.

I flip it open to the highlighted section and breathe out a frustrated grunt. "'Prior to the coronation, the heir apparent must be wed,'" I read aloud. "To become king, I need a wife? What kind of archaic bullshit is this?" I glance up, and my gaze connects with my mother's. "Am I interpreting this correctly?"

"You are," my mother confirms. "You'll be the youngest king in hundreds of years, so the marriage rule has never been, as far as we can tell, an issue before. We've had several policy people tear the thing apart. With your father now declared..." She seems to fumble for a kind way to phrase his decline. "Unable to fulfill his duties, we can't even legally change the coronation framework. The line is binding. Of course, once you're king, you can change whatever you wish with the proper public approval process."

I toss the hefty manual back on the desk and rub my face. "I can change the requirement once I'm married, and I'm the king. But to update the rule, I need a wife. The wife rule is the one I'd prefer not to follow in the first place." I give a mirthless chuckle. "It's not as though marriage is going to suddenly turn me into a better ruler and policy maker."

Without thinking, I glance at Julia, but she's avoiding my gaze. Probably for the best. I just promised Nick the other day that I'd stop interfering in their relationship and hoping for something with Jules that will never happen. Old habits die hard.

If the clause about a wife had come out any earlier, we all know I'd have pushed her to assume the royal duty. Asking her wouldn't have been about love. She would have been my best—if most complicated—option.

"Well," I say. "Even if Father can't legislate a change to the coronation, I would think the advisory council could?"

My father shakes his head. "Unfortunately, they cannot. Again, it's another change you are welcome to make once you're king, but as of right now, all royal rule changes, regardless of the circumstances, have to be made by the king and vetted by the royal family as a whole."

"No one actually knows the entire coronation manual." I gesture to what looks like a four- or five-hundred-page tome on his desk. "Is anyone going to notice that page 302 says I should have a wife and I don't?"

At that, Julia perks up. "There's always renewed interest in coronation protocol when one is about to happen. All available manuals have been checked out of the local libraries. Desmond has fielded and fulfilled four requests for the manual in the last week."

Instead of looking at Julia, I glare at Desmond, my shared secretary. "Perhaps you should have run that past me."

"I asked the king," he says. "The requests were approved."

My father sighs. "People are interested. Their interest helps to keep us relevant in a world where monarchies have become mostly obsolete or merely figureheads. There's no getting around the clause, Alex. What we need is a brainstorming session of suitable matches for you."

I smack my lips in displeasure and run a frustrated hand through my hair. "Let's not and say we did. My future wife is not a roundtable discussion."

"Unfortunately," my mother says, "she is now. Whoever she is."

"What about Anna Samuel?" Nick offers from behind me.

"No," I grit out. "I got my fill. Besides, I heard she's married with children now."

Brice passes me his phone. "She's not bad."

I look at the internet address and bark out a laugh. "This is an escort service."

"Is it?" There's a twinkle in Brice's eyes when he takes the phone back. "Wouldn't she be surprised to be escorted down the royal aisle?"

"Whoever Alex marries must either be of royal blood from another country or a native Bellerivian. No celebrities or models or whatever else from wherever else." My father waves a hand. "Bellerivian or royal."

The room falls into an uncomfortable silence.

After telling Nick I wasn't sure I was cut out for romantic love of any sort, I should be grateful to have this obligation thrust upon me. I'll need an heir. My duty to this country never ends. Nothing is ever mine—my privacy, my grief, and now my marriage are public property. There is no division between what I want and what's best for the country. They are melded together, unbreakable. I've known this since I was a child, but sitting in this room having them all contemplate who's doomed to marry me is one indignity I didn't anticipate.

"I'll formulate a short list," Desmond offers. He drags his phone out of his pocket and opens an app. "I can, with permission, put out some feelers to royal families and wealthy Bellerivian nationals."

Perhaps other people would refuse, claim they'll only marry for love, but that's not me. The prosperity of the country comes above all else. Besides, my expectations of marriage are low. I'm not cut out for the all-consuming love that seems to have swept my brother Nick and his fiancée, Julia, into emotional turmoil for years.

"She must be someone I can tolerate and who is good for the country," I say.

"I knew you'd be reasonable about this." My mother gives my father's shoulder a reassuring squeeze.

"With Nick and Julia's wedding just under three months away, it would be best if we could have you debut whoever you intend to marry there," my mother says.

A chill runs through me. Three months to find a woman I can tolerate who is good for the country. Shouldn't be too tall of an order, but I know it will be.

I've casually and secretly dated several of the daughters of the Bellerivian elite already. At diplomatic events in other countries, none of the other available royals have appealed to me. How will I find someone suitable?

"That sounds fine," I agree. My stomach clenches at the reality of what I'm agreeing to.

In three months, I'll be publicly declaring my intention to marry someone and to put up with the match for the rest of my life. Whoever I marry, we'll be stuck with each other forever.

Divorce is outlawed for the royal family.

Two

RORY

When I grab the mail from the box, I riffle through it, looking for anything from my parents. We haven't spoken in months, but it would be like my mother to send a birthday card. While my father can hold a grudge forever, my mother is warmer.

Trailing Derrick, my boyfriend from college, back to Bellerive after graduation seemed like the right choice at the time. We'd been dating for a year, and I loved him. A lot. Maybe even the kind of love where you get married. He asked me to move here with him after we spent a magical week in Bellerive, living in his parent's guesthouse, and musing about the future. The world was full of possibilities.

Bellerive would be an adventure, right?

Who wouldn't want to live on an island that still has castles, palaces, and a prominent royal family? The green landscapes, open fields of animals and produce, and cities with an almost fantastical essence appealed to me.

In some ways, I fell in love with the country as much as I did Derrick.

Bellerive also happens to be one of the most expensive places to live on the planet, which I didn't fully comprehend at the time.

There's no card from anyone I know, let alone my parents. Sometimes choosing the adventure can be pretty isolating. I climb the stairs to the apartment I share with Derrick in the middle of Tucker's Town. His parents own the studio space but make Derrick and I pay full rent. Maybe it's petty of me to think some sort of family discount should be in order, but every month I'm surprised by the exorbitant cost.

We agreed to work for them at their golf club when we moved to the island. So it's a constant exchange of money. They pay us; we pay rent. Round and round we go, and most months, they barely pay us enough to survive. When Derrick suggested getting our feet wet in the country under his parents' guidance, I didn't expect them to treat us like cheap labor.

Us? Who am I kidding? *Me.* They treat *me* like cheap labor.

Any time I've tried to raise the issue with him, he's said we have to "prove our worth" and "earn our keep" and someday the whole empire will be ours.

Though, he hasn't made the "ours" argument in a while.

Since it's my birthday, they let me off my shift early. But that almost didn't happen when a bartender called in sick.

Another thing about becoming part of an extended family business—your life is no longer your own.

I'm the pastry chef, but they slot me into other roles in the restaurant when they're short, and I haven't managed to escape the building. In the year since we moved here, I've covered every imaginable position.

Our apartment is a wide-open, high-ceilinged room on the top floor that has incredible views of the marina. And a sky-high rental price tag to match. The only walls are at the back, and they box in the bathroom and one closet. Our bed lays against the far wall, and it's the first thing anyone sees when they walk in the door. When I suggested to Derrick that we rearrange the layout so our bed wasn't so in your face, he said he liked having the spot where we'd be fucking so accessible. Seemed romantic at the time.

But Derrick has never been much of a true romantic, so when I slot my key into the lock on our apartment door, I'm hoping he's at least remembered today is my birthday. His parents did. They won't remind him because they believe he's highly organized and very efficient. Neither is true.

The door is hard to open, and I grunt as I push against it. Did he drop his shoes in front of the door again? How many times do I have to tell him they get stuck on the mat and make opening the door impossible?

Music blares from the sound system, so he won't even hear me if I shout for help.

With another concerted effort, I get the door to swing wide enough to slip in. On the floor are a pair of heels I've scuffed by forcing the door.

I tilt my head. Heels? Not my heels.

Then my gaze is drawn to the line of discarded clothes leading to the bed. The trail is familiar—usually one I wake up to after Derrick and I have stumbled home drunk and barely made it in the door before stripping each other naked.

The clothes are a tangle of dress pants, shirts, a skirt, panties...

My heart thumps. Reluctantly, I glance at the bed, and sure enough, Derrick's bare ass is pumping away between some other woman's legs. They're both so focused on getting off, they didn't even hear the door open.

"Harder," the woman moans above the music. "Harder!"

"I'm going to come all over your tits," Derrick cries.

My gut twists, and a sinking sensation settles over me. I could turn around and leave, and they'd probably never know. The me from ten minutes ago might have, but there's something about coming home on my *birthday* to find my live-in boyfriend committing adultery that hardens a piece of me I didn't realize was soft.

Instead of leaving, I turn off the device on the kitchen island that's playing the music.

"Happy birthday to me!" I call out. No point in being subtle. It's safe to say Derrick and I are done. I should be gutted, but I'm numb.

Whoever is underneath him screams, and he jumps away from her like she's on fire.

"Rory!" He snags a sheet off the bed and wraps it around his middle, stumbling toward me. As if I'm not well acquainted with what's under the sheet. "You're home early."

I glance behind him and realize it's his ex-girlfriend from high school he's plowing. A lump forms in my throat. She and I couldn't be more different, from the color of our hair—hers dark and mine blond—to the curve of our hips—she has them and I don't. Not to mention our personalities. I'm usually a pleaser, and she is distinctly not.

I have a feeling my pleasing days are over.

How many times have I asked him about her? At every turn he denied what my eyes and heart were telling me. Within months of us moving back to Bellerive, the two of them were magnets at every bar, at every social event, and apparently, even in our shared apartment.

"It's my birthday," I say. "As birthday surprises go, this is a new one." I keep my voice light, but inside I'm dying. We've been together for two years—a year in college and a year here. How long has he been screwing her behind my back?

Derrick runs a hand through his short blond hair and glances over his shoulder at Janessa before turning back to me. "We weren't—I didn't—happy birthday?" He winces.

No apology. No groveling. No regret stamped on his face whatsoever. I don't even bother to drop the mail on the kitchen island before spinning on my heel and racing down the stairs.

"Rory! Wait! We should talk. Come on, babe." Derrick's voice floats along the stairs behind me.

Babe? He has the nerve to call me fucking *babe* when he was just dick-deep in another woman? I toss my purse and the mail on the passenger seat of my compact and roar out of my parking space and down the narrow street.

Where am I going? I have no idea. The only friends I've managed to make are also Derrick's friends or relatives. My life is so intrinsically connected to him that I don't even have anyone to drown my sorrows with.

My parents are back in Canada, but we haven't spoken in almost a year. If I knew for sure my mother would answer the phone, I'd call. Who else could I try? My younger brother is in the military and notoriously hard to reach. With the time change, the few friends I've kept in contact with over the last year will be sleeping.

The reality that I have nowhere to go and no one to call settles over me like a weight. What am I doing here in Bellerive? My adventure doesn't seem daring and cool anymore—it's just lonely.

Dusk falls, and I find myself on roads I don't recognize. There's a cliff near here somewhere, isn't there? This is West Shore Road, isn't it? I don't normally come this way at night. Whenever we venture out of Tucker's Town, Derrick drives.

One of the well-known Bellerivian fog patches rolls across the road in front of me, a wall of white. The fog is dense and thick, and I can barely see the front end of my compact car. Worse than a whiteout in a snowstorm.

My heart thuds so hard in my chest it's all I can hear. If I stop in the middle of the road, I could get plowed into from behind. If I keep going, I could end up tumbling over the cliff.

I scramble for my phone in my purse with one hand, and I grip the steering wheel with the other. Can my GPS guide me? A sweat breaks out across my palms. How many times did Derrick warn me about this road at night?

The thought of Derrick brings a flash of him and Janessa in bed together. A sob lodges in my throat. What am I going to do? I can't go back to the apartment.

I have nowhere else to go.

The bang hits my ears at the same instant the car is propelled forward, a violent surge.

I cry out and clench the steering wheel, but it's no use. My seat snaps, and I fly back. The car is spinning, and spinning, and spinning, until there's nothing but darkness.

THREE

ALEX

My driver and guard, Kane, opens the rear of the black SUV for me after another disastrous arranged-marriage match. This one, Catherine, was Brice's suggestion. Next time, I'll ask more questions. At eighteen, yes, she's legal, and along with the fact she was born in Bellerive, that's the only thing which qualified her to meet me. We had nothing, absolutely nothing, in common. The hour we spent together was painful.

Besides, I'm not having a child bride. I'm thirty-three, and that age gap, among other things, led to the disaster of Charles and Diana's marriage. No thanks. I thought *no child brides* went without having to be said, but I guess I'll need to say those words to Brice.

The reality is I might also need to be more involved. I'm so disinterested in the whole wife-finding affair it's hard to muster any enthusiasm when someone in the royal circle suggests a match.

Kane catches my gaze in the rearview mirror. "Another one bites the dust."

"Do you have any sisters, Kane?" I muse.

"One. But she's already married. We don't qualify anyway."

I sigh and stare out the window as he drives us back to the palace grounds. Not much I can say to that. I already knew, as a first-generation immigrant family from Japan, that no one in his family would fit the narrow criteria.

"What was that process like?" I ask.

"My parents said it was very hard. Bellerive doesn't make it easy to move here permanently. There are other countries that are much easier, but my parents fell in love with this place."

One of the chief complaints of people who come here on a work visa are the strict rules limiting their length of stay. I've never agreed with them, but I understand it's a form of population control. We're an island. There's only so much room to grow. We do let people stay beyond the limits sometimes, but it's unusual for a family to achieve permanency, like Kane's family has, without a clear connection to a native Bellerivian.

"Why, Your Highness? Are you considering chucking it in and immigrating elsewhere?" Kane's expression is lit with mischief.

"Should I? Would save me having to explain an NDA and its consequences to an eighteen-year-old over a bottle of wine she's barely legal to drink while in the back room of a restaurant so no one sees us together." Out loud, the evening sounds like the farce it was.

"That's a mouthful," Kane agrees. "The one the other night was all right."

He's referring to Anna Samuel's younger sister, who has just come back to the island from law school. We did have an okay time considering I fucked her sister on the regular in my early twenties. Seems a bit awkward to me, but Kara glossed over the connection as a nonissue. The family is happy to chase the Crown any way they can.

"I'm on an international wife-finding tour starting next week," I say.

"Bit of a whirlwind, isn't it?" Kane agrees. "Seven countries in seven days."

"Royal speed dating. A high tea here, a royal ball there." We're nearing the point where Kane either continues our well-worn path home or takes the West Shore Road. On impulse, I lean forward. "Let's take the long way home. I'm not keen to get back to Brice's intrusive questions."

"There's fog," Kane says, his hesitation clear.

The sensible thing is to tell him never mind and carry on the normal way. But I can't ignore the sensation in the pit of my stomach. Any time I've tried to quiet an instinct this strong, I've regretted it.

"Take it anyway," I say.

Kane grimaces and makes the turn. As we drive, there's a thick fog, but it's sitting at the surface of the road and no match for the SUV, which is higher and has excellent fog lights. Anyone in a compact or vehicle low to the ground would struggle. Despite our advantages, we still can't see very far ahead of us, and I'm sure Kane is cursing me under his breath.

There are intermittent streetlights, and one glints off something metal up ahead. "What is that?" I ask. The fog is thicker here, making it harder to decipher what's in the middle of the road.

It takes Kane a moment to answer. "Better call for an ambulance," he says. "There's a wreck of some sort."

The closer we get, the more the scene comes into focus. At his suggestion, I've called the emergency services number, and I keep my phone glued to my ear, rattling off details as we inch toward the accident. In the middle of the road is a crumpled sports car, but it's the compact hanging at the edge of the cliff that sets my pulse racing.

I hang up on the operator even as she's warning me to stay on the line, and I open my door.

"Your Highness!" Kane calls from the driver's seat. "The fog is thick. Stay in the vehicle."

Remaining in the SUV isn't an option. I'm at the driver's side door of the compact in an instant. The seat is broken, and a young woman with blond hair has been knocked flat onto her back. She's unconscious, and there's a gash on her head leaking an alarming amount of blood.

Kane has thrown on the hazards in the SUV, and he's at my side now. "Seriously, sir. You could get hit by some other idiot taking this road in such thick fog."

I ignore the implication that I'm an idiot for insisting we take this road and walk around the car, trying to determine whether opening the driver's side door could tip the balance of the vehicle in the wrong direction.

"We need to get her out," I say.

"We need to wait for the professionals." Kane shadows my examination. "If we get this wrong, the car is over the cliff."

Is he right?

There's an aura around the woman in the driver's seat that's tugging at something inside me I don't recognize. I need to get to her, and I can't ignore it or tamp down the protectiveness swirling in my belly. Whatever feeling this is, it's primal, not something I can switch off.

A wind kicks up around us off the ocean, and the car groans. If I stand here and do nothing, and the car goes over the edge, I'll never forgive myself.

"Right," I say. "I'm getting her out."

"Your Highness—"

"Help me or watch me, but I've decided." There are a thousand valid reasons for leaving her in the car, not the least of which is that I could do more damage by dragging her out than leaving her there. None of them matters. An instinct is driving me, so deeply ingrained I can't articulate it. Can't understand it. But I'm not disregarding it either.

I grab the door handle, and Kane's hand settles over mine.

"You're sure about this?" he asks.

"Yes." I've never been more certain of anything. Whoever she is, I need to get her out of the car.

"I'll open the door," Kane says. "You undo her seat belt and scoop her out. Slow and steady, yeah?"

I step to the side of the door, and my pulse races. Kane eases the door open, and the car sways slightly. I suck in a sharp breath, but as soon as the door is wide enough, I'm reaching in, clicking the seat belt open, and lifting her into my arms. She's heavier than that she looks, and I grunt as I maneuver her. The car shifts around us, rocking and tilting.

"It's moving!" Kane hollers in a panic.

He tugs on my suit jacket, but I'm not leaving her. The car might take me down into the watery abyss, too, but I *can't* leave her. "Almost," I mutter and readjust my grip.

She moans and curls into me, still unconscious. The movement is enough to steady my grip while the car shudders underneath her, tipping more. Gravel crunches under the tires. Kane yanks on my suit jacket, dragging me back, and I've got her in my arms and out the car door as the car falls away from us, tumbling over the cliff. The three of us hit the ground with an *oomph*, and if Kane hadn't grabbed my jacket, altering my center of gravity, we might have gone over too.

"Fucking hell," Kane says from behind me. "Too close. Way, way too close."

Sirens blare in the distance, but I can't formulate a coherent thought. I'm staring down at the pale blonde in my arms, and the tightness across my chest is unbearable, as though I can't quite get a full breath. She almost died.

"I think I cracked a rib," I mumble. Is that what this feeling is?

"I'll take her." Kane gets to his feet and tries to accept her weight, but I tighten my grip.

"I've got her," I say. "Check the other vehicle."

Kane surveys the road and then jogs to the middle where the sports car is a mess of metal. "Doesn't look good," he calls back. "Can't find a pulse on this guy."

One dead, and she almost went over a cliff. Her breathing is shallow, but it's there. The fact that she's still unconscious can't be good. There's blood all over my suit, staining my white shirt a deep red.

The ambulance screams down the road, followed by the police and fire trucks. Then it's a swarm of people surrounding me, taking her from my arms, and doing rapid assessments while they wheel her off.

Kane tries to mention my broken ribs, and I shake my head at him. He frowns but doesn't contradict me.

"You're a hero tonight, Prince Alexander," one of the police officers says when we recount getting the girl out of the car.

During the brief conversation, I've been too distracted. Half of me is in the ambulance wondering whether she's going to be okay.

"May I—" I start toward the ambulance. "I'm just going to check on her."

When I get there, they're about to shut the back doors.

While I don't understand what's driving me, I'm not in the mood to fight myself. "I'm along for the ride," I say to the attendant.

Her eyes widen in surprise and then narrow. "Do you know her, Your Highness? I understand her ID and everything else went over the cliff."

"I don't know her," I say. "But no one should be alone after something like this."

The paramedic's gaze softens. "Technically you can ride. Hop in."

When I climb into the back and see the blond woman again, my gut twists, and the pain in my ribs returns. *So odd.* I give my head a little shake and settle onto the bench across from the other paramedic monitoring vitals.

"She going to be okay?" Without thinking, I take one of her pale hands in mine.

The medic is flicking machines and checking readings but glances in my direction. "Head injury is concerning. Won't know much more till we get to the hospital. She's alive. Might not have been if you'd waited for us before getting her out."

I stare at the unconscious woman and the mantra *open your eyes* plays in my head. My surge of protectiveness for this woman is the most curious thing I've ever experienced, and I scan her face, searching for a grain of familiarity. That's how it feels—like I've known her for years. A swift and sudden knowing.

My phone buzzes in my pocket, and I take it out.

Shit. I forgot all about Kane. Never even crossed my mind to tell him I was going in the ambulance.

Instead of answering, I ignore the call and shoot him a text to meet me at the hospital.

When was the last time I was distracted to the point of negligence? I've never left my security detail anywhere. I'm not Nick. I don't have the luxury of pretending I'm not famous. My status makes me a prize for someone with sinister motives and a desire for money.

God, where is my head?

I tuck my phone into my pocket and sweep her hand into mine again. Not a single thing I've done since I asked Kane to turn down West Shore Road has been logical or reasonable.

When I glance at the mystery woman on the gurney, a rightness settles over my chest. I might not understand what's happening, but something drew me down that road and into the rear of this ambulance.

For the first time in my life, I feel like I'm exactly where I'm meant to be.

Four

RORY

My right hand is warm, so warm. A comfort seeps into me from the connection—vital and real. I'm tempted to linger here, half-awake and half-asleep, a place where no worries exist. The dull ache in my skull has other ideas.

When I open my eyes, I squint against the brightness of the overhead lights.

"You're awake," a male voice murmurs from beside me.

He appears over me, a mess of midnight hair, and eyes so dark they're almost coal black. His white shirt is covered in blood, and he's pressing a red button next to my other hand. I follow his movements in confusion.

Where am I? A hospital? Who is he?

Then I remember the bang, and I choke out a noise of distress. "Someone hit me."

"Someone did, yeah." He glances down at me, and his brow is furrowed.

"Why do you look so familiar?" I scan his features. There's a tenderness in his expression I can't reconcile, as though we're acquainted with each other. Not that I'm opposed to a gorgeous man looking at me like that. But have we met before? It feels like I know him.

"I've been asking myself the same question." He grimaces, and then he takes in my appearance again for a beat. "You've got such lovely green eyes. Like jade." His voice is gruff and slightly mystified.

"Same as my mother." I can't tear my gaze from his. The intimacy is as if someone tore him out of my dreams and planted him at my side. The reality of what's crossed my mind sinks in.

What a stupid thought. I must have damaged my brain.

A deep throbbing emerges from the dull ache behind my forehead. I touch my temple with my free hand, and there's a bandage covering it.

"Concussion," he says.

Then I realize he's the reason my other hand is so warm. He's holding my hand. When I glance down at our linked fingers, he lets me go and steps back from the bed just as a nurse knocks on the doorframe.

"You're awake," she says with a smile. She gives the man beside me a furtive glance and a wide berth. "How are you feeling?" She leans against the railing and checks the connections to the machines beeping away around me.

Attractive mystery man has stepped into the shadows of the room as though to conceal himself. Obviously the nurse realizes he's here. So strange.

"My head hurts," I admit. My throat is dry, too, but I didn't notice when I was talking before.

"Nasty concussion," the nurse confirms. "The doctor will be in shortly to speak to you."

My skull throbs, and I turn to the guy standing at the side of the bed, where the light isn't as strong. "Are you the one who hit me? You haven't said who you are."

Just then the doctor breezes in the open door. "Aurora Wilson. Happy birthday. You've had quite a lucky escape tonight. Must have had your guardian angel sitting on your shoulder."

"Someone hit me." The stretching ache in my head is making it hard to concentrate. "Did he hit me?" I point to the man beside the bed.

The doctor's eyes widen, and something that sounds like a strangled chuckle escapes. "No, he's the one who pulled you from the car before it fell into the ocean."

Now it's my turn for wide eyes. My brain thumps along to the increased rate of my heart. "You saved me?" I try to turn toward him and wince.

"Can she have more painkillers? She's clearly in pain."

Oh my God. *Drugs.* It's like he read my mind. I press my fingers into my temple. "Is there something to make this better?"

"I'll get the nurse to bring some in, and we'll send you home with a prescription."

"Home?" My stomach rolls when I remember what led me to West Shore Road tonight.

"You've got a concussion, whiplash, and a lot of bruising. You're likely to be very sore for a few days. You'll need to be monitored closely."

Monitored closely? His words wash over me, but I can't make my mind work properly.

The doctor rips off a scribbled note from his pad and hands it to the man beside me. "I understand you're going to get her home and make sure there's someone to watch over her tonight?"

"That's correct," he says.

"My purse." I scan the room. "I need my purse."

"It's at the bottom of the ocean by now," mystery man says.

"Can I at least know your name?" Nothing is making sense to me right now. There's so much pain in my head, and I'm woozy, almost nauseous.

"Alex," he says in a rush, and there's an awkward silence while the doctor narrows his eyes for a beat.

"Well," the doctor says, dragging out the word. "I'll leave you two to sort out the details."

"Thank you," Alex says.

"Wait," I call to the doctor. "I don't know this guy. Are you sure it's safe for him to be... I don't know... arranging things?"

The doctor's eyes fill with amusement. "I suspect there's no one you'd be safer with on the island." When Alex tenses beside me, the doctor continues, "But if there's someone you'd like us to call, we can. There was no emergency contact listed with your visa details."

"Oh my God. My purse. I don't have anything." I was too distracted earlier by Alex to process what he said before. "Do I need to pay?" I touch my forehead again.

"The medication," Alex reminds the doctor.

"Any bills have been taken care of. Not to worry," the doctor says. "I'll send the nurse in with some painkillers."

He's out the door, and the nurse appears at my side while I'm still grimacing from the sharp stabbing that's overtaken the dull throbbing from before.

"Here you go." She passes me a paper cup of pills.

My head hurts too much for me to consider asking what I'm taking, and I place them on my tongue and wash them down without complaint. I hope whatever it is works fast.

Alex is silent beside me for a beat after she leaves. "Is there someone you want me to call? Or I can just deliver you to your flat."

"I can't go back there," I moan.

"What were you doing on West Shore Road after dark?" Alex asks, and his penetrating gaze makes me want to shrink away. His tone implies it was a stupid choice.

"I was just out for a drive."

"Seems odd on your twenty-third birthday not to be out celebrating," he says. "The doctor tells me there was no alcohol in your system."

I pinch the bridge of my nose and take a deep breath. My head hurts so much I'm afraid I might throw up. On top of that, I realize I'm sort of stranded at the hospital. I either go back to Derrick or to a hotel I can't afford because my debit card is at the bottom of the ocean. Since I can't remember that stretch of the evening, my mind can't quite comprehend that my little car along with my purse, keys, and phone are no longer accessible.

Everyone I know on the island exists in my phone's contacts. I don't know anyone's phone number by heart, including Derrick's. There's no way to contact anyone except my parents, who are too far away to help even if they wanted to.

I draw my knees to my chest, and a sob rushes forward before I can contain it. I bury my face in my knees, and my shoulders shake. The crying is only increasing the pressure in my head, but I can't seem to stop.

A firm hand makes a slow circle on my back. "I didn't mean to upset you." His voice has lost its sharp edge.

"I've got no money." I manage to get the garbled words out between sobs. "My boyfriend is cheating on me. I've lost my phone." I'm having trouble catching my breath. "I don't know anyone on the island. My car is in the ocean. My family and friends are back in Canada!" I cry, and then I clutch my chest, desperate to get a deep enough breath between sobs. The pressure in my head has increased to a blinding pain.

"Right." His voice is clipped. "Not the best birthday then." He leans across me and hits the red button.

The nurse appears in the doorway in an instant.

"Have you got something to help Aurora?" he asks. "She's feeling a bit overwhelmed."

Overwhelmed? Is that what I'm feeling? The sharp stabbing in my temple won't recede, then there's a sharp prick in my shoulder.

"What?" I turn to ask, but I'm faint. "Oh," I breathe out. "That's nice. I don't know what that is, but it's nice."

Alex chuckles beside me.

"I don't know where to go, Alex," I whisper, any semblance of a filter long gone.

He smooths my hair off my forehead, and that tenderness I almost thought I imagined earlier is back. "Don't worry. I've got a big house. You can stay there tonight, and we'll sort you in the morning when you're feeling more like yourself."

His accent is strange—Bellerivian but sort of British too.

I scan his chiseled face as my eyelids grow heavy. "Is that my blood on your shirt?" I ask as my gaze drifts downward, and then the world fades to black.

Five

ALEX

My judgement has been questionable tonight. Or bad. Perhaps my judgement has been bad. A blind date with an eighteen-year-old, taking West Shore Road in thick fog, pulling Aurora out of her crashed vehicle, riding in the back of the ambulance, agreeing to be Aurora's responsible adult so she can leave the hospital—the list of my out-of-character decisions has cut a swath across my life.

But in the back seat of the SUV with Aurora's blond head cradled in my lap as we drive to the palace compound, I can't find it in me to consider anything that happened tonight *bad*.

If only my decision-making skills improved once we got to the hospital. When we arrived and realized she didn't have any identification, I used the palace resources and her fingerprints to discover her name, age, and place of birth. Most of Bellerive has free health care as long as you're a taxpayer, and as a pastry chef at McGuinty's Golf Course, she's been paying into our system for just under a year. The few things our health care doesn't cover would have been paid by an insurance provider, but since I couldn't easily access that information, I settled her bill.

The rest of her life—the cheating boyfriend and the lack of close friends—weren't pieces I could determine from paperwork. The revelation about the boyfriend caused an irrational surge of anger. On her birthday, she's out driving around Bellerive on arguably the most dangerous road in the country because her boyfriend is an asshole.

She could have died. As it is, the driver of the sports car wasn't as fortunate as Aurora. The police told me they figure he hit Aurora's car and then smashed into the side of the cliff before spinning out into the center of the road. Died on the second impact. For the damage he caused, the police are sure speed was a factor.

"Where do you want to put her?" Kane asks from the front seat.

"I've called ahead and asked for staff to prepare one of the guest rooms in my wing."

"Is that wise?" Kane raises his eyebrows. "We know very little about her."

"Find out more then." My tone is dismissive. "She's staying in my wing until we can sort out something better for her." I stare out the window while we inch up to the palace gates.

"She'll need close monitoring," Kane says.

"Which I intend to provide." I brush her hair away from her cheek. "I've cancelled my day tomorrow."

Kane frowns in the rearview mirror but doesn't say anything. Everyone knows I never cancel a whole day except in the case of severe or contagious illness. It's not his place to question my choices if they don't pertain to my personal safety. Even then he has to tread lightly.

We pull up to the front entrance, and I climb out before easing Aurora into my arms. "Call Dr. Bennett," I tell Kane. "Have him fill Ms. Wilson's prescription and bring it to my rooms."

He walks me to the front door and ensures I'm inside before he heads to one of the houses on the property where Dr. Bennett and his family have lived for years. Working for the monarchy and being on call at all hours has to have some perks.

Thankfully, I make it to my wing of the house without being seen by any members of my family. How do I explain the unexplainable?

Stella, the maid who manages my part of the palace, is tucking in the sheets in the spare room across from my suite when I arrive.

"Your Highness." She shoves the last section of sheet under the mattress. "Almost done."

"Can you draw back the covers so I can get her into bed?" Aurora is out cold, and I'm carrying her full weight. My muscles strain under the effort.

"Right away." Stella hustles to the side of the bed closest to me and peels back the covers.

The doubled-up hospital gown will have to do for now since her clothes were soiled with blood. Once I've got Aurora settled, I'll grab the stained clothes from the front entrance and take them to the laundry room for them to work their magic.

"Do you know her, sir?" Stella peers at me when I seem reluctant to leave the room.

I shake my head. "No, I don't. Doing a good deed. That's all."

She raises her eyebrows, but she doesn't question my choices. The nice part about being known as straightforward and, perhaps, a little dickish in my response to people is that they don't ask a lot of questions. I'm surprised she asked the one she did.

Brice appears in the doorway. "I heard a rumor you brought a girl home." His face is lit with curiosity.

"And you came running?" I ask dryly.

"Wanted to see if I hit the jackpot with my matchmaking suggestion."

"So, what? You were going to listen at the door for appropriate jackpot sounds?"

Brice laughs. "I will admit my plan to spy was not fully formed." He nods toward Aurora. "That's not Catherine."

"Correct," I say. "That's not Catherine."

"Father says the paper is running a story tomorrow morning about you saving some woman from her car just before it toppled over the edge of the cliff on West Shore Road." He eyes me as though he expects the whole story to come tumbling out of my mouth.

"Seems someone sprung a leak." My voice is tight. "How are so many people still awake and fucking up my life at midnight?"

"In terms of press leaks, this one is a beaut'. The future king being labelled a hero is not exactly a bad thing."

"Even my scandals are top-notch." I draw Brice away from Aurora's door. "I need to get her clothes down to the cleaners, and Dr. Bennett should be coming soon to verify the hospital's assessment."

"Trust you not to trust the hospital." Brice smirks and shakes his head.

"Oh, Alexander!" My mother comes down the hall with her arms flapping. She's in her early sixties but her blond highlights conceal the growing streaks of gray in her brown hair. "I just heard. Are you all right? Saving a woman from a car going off a cliff? Then you brought her here?" She makes a *tsking* noise. "Your father has suppressed that last bit, but the press will want to speak to her."

"She has a severe concussion, so we delay interviews or conversations with anyone until she's feeling better." I make sure to use the tone of voice that doesn't allow for argument.

"Where are you going?" My mother falls into step on my other side.

"She's going to need clothes and other necessities when she wakes up," I say.

"I hear she's been living with Derrick McGuinty," my mother says. "Shouldn't we let him know where she is?"

"No," I say sharply. "She asked that we don't." Not true, but she did say she couldn't go home. "We'll send someone to the apartment to gather her things."

"Alexander." My mother's tone is filled with warning. "She cannot stay here. The optics, especially given what we're doing behind the scenes to find you a wife, are not good."

"I'll move her into a guest house then." I wave a dismissive hand. "She's not going back to her boyfriend or that apartment, so until she knows where she *is* going, she can stay here."

"Alexander." Queen Helen places a hand on my arm. "I don't know what's gone on tonight, but I'm not having you lose your head over some Canadian girl. Do you understand me? Bellerivian or royalty. Not some farm girl from northern Ontario."

That gives me a moment of pause. Either my parents have been doing some very quick background checks or the press knows far more than even I do right now. Perhaps I'll have to read the papers tomorrow to know exactly who's staying in my guest bedroom.

"I don't know her, Mother. No one is losing their head. She needs help, and I intend to provide it. End of." I shrug off her touch. "It almost feels like you don't think I'm capable of a kindness." Except I'm not—not to this level and not for no reason. My priority is always the Crown and the way situations look as much as how they actually are. I've never been one to be ruled by emotion of any type.

At the hospital, I didn't even tell Aurora my complete identity, and I made sure the hospital staff understood I didn't want my "real" name used. They probably assumed I wanted my heroism to go unacknowledged, but that's not why. I'm not sure why. As much as I'd sometimes love to be just *Alex*, that's not who I'll ever be.

"You have to admit, your behavior tonight is unusual," Mother says.

"I second our mother's observation," Brice chimes in.

"It's nothing," I say. "You're both reading more into this than you need to. I had a terrible date with an eighteen-year-old—thank you for that, Brice—and then decided to take the long way home along West Shore Road. We stumbled upon the accident, and seeing the way the car was positioned, Kane and I opted to save her rather than letting her fall to her death." I'm making everything sound like a rational decision, but I have no way to articulate what's been driving me all night. How do I explain what I don't understand? "For various reasons, she didn't feel she could return to her apartment, and since all of her belongings are at the bottom of the ocean, I didn't see the harm in bringing her here."

We're back at the main entrance, and Dr. Bennett is coming through the front door with Kane.

"Kane, can you make sure Ms. Wilson's clothes are taken to the laundry department? Dr. Bennett, you can follow me." I turn to my mother and brother. "As for you two, make yourselves useful and find someone to collect some of Ms. Wilson's things from the McGuinty apartment."

"These are all red flags, Alexander," my mother warns me. "We'd do better to buy her a few new things, and then she can go to her own apartment when she's feeling up to it. Sending a royal representative will spark off a slew of rumors. As much as everyone loves a fairy tale, we don't want to give the public the wrong impression." She gives me a pointed look.

I run a hand across my forehead. She's right. Whatever has dug into me tonight is desperate to ensure I can keep this stranger close to me. A ridiculous thought, but there it is. The idea of Aurora, a woman I do not know and cannot know, returning to her apartment and boyfriend should not send a shot of irrational rage through me. But it's there, nonetheless.

"You're right," I agree. "Call your personal shopper and pick some things a twenty-three-year-old would actually wear."

"Might be better if I call," Brice says. "I can pretend like I'm buying something for a girlfriend."

I snap my fingers and point at him. "Excellent idea. See? It's all coming together. Nothing to worry about."

As I lead Dr. Bennett down the corridor back to Aurora, I hear Brice say, "He's definitely acting weird."

It's that comment that centers me more than anything. Whatever emotion has sprouted in me in regards to this woman can't be allowed to grow.

I need a wife, but it cannot be her.

SIX

RORY

When I wake up, a modern bedside lamp casts a soft glow over the unfamiliar room. In an armchair beside my bed is the man from the hospital. What was his name again?

Alex.

He's not in his blood-stained suit anymore. Instead, he's wearing jeans and a T-shirt that stretches across his wide, firm chest. If I was going to be rescued by anyone, I couldn't have picked a better knight in shining armor. Except this guy looks like a prince.

A prince?

My brain, too addled by injury earlier, clicks with realization.

He *is* a prince.

Prince Alexander.

I gasp, and he stirs in the chair beside me. His eyes open, and in the moment it takes him to focus on me, my chest flutters with an unexpected tenderness. The feeling from the hospital returns, as though I know him, not just from magazines and social media posts, but really *know* him. The blow to my head must have been of epic proportions if I'm hallucinating about being familiar with the first in line to the throne at a soul-deep level. That doesn't happen, not to me, not to anyone.

I have a prince taking care of me. How is *this* my life?

"I know who you are," I say.

"Do you?" He runs a hand through his disheveled hair. "Who am I then?"

"Prince Alexander, first in line to the Bellerive throne." A dull ache persists behind my eyes. My neck is stiff, and my whole body feels like I went too many rounds in a boxing match, but my brain is sort of working now, even if there seems to be a *Prince Alexander* glitch in it. "You took me to your property?"

"To be fair, I did say I had a big house." His lips quirk up into an almost smile.

"Unless I do not actually know where you live, this is not a house—it's a palace."

He peers over my shoulder out the window and glances around the room. "Yeah, it's definitely a palace. I apologize for not meeting your expectations." He places a hand over his heart.

Is he flirting with me? This feels like flirting. I scan his face. My head injury is definitely bad. Must be really bad if I think the future king is flirting with me while I'm dressed in—I peek under the covers—a double layer of hospital gown, no makeup, and a large bandage on my head. It's pity flirting. He's been raised to be such a gentleman that he's flirting with me out of pity.

"What time is it?" I ask.

He flicks his wrist and brings his watch around to examine it. "Six in the morning. Are you hungry?"

I take in the darkness under his eyes and the way he's stretching as though his body is sore. "Did you sleep in that chair all night?"

"I was told you needed to be monitored. I took that responsibility very seriously."

I glance over at the other side of the king-sized bed and wonder why he didn't just stretch out beside me, but even as I think it, I realize waking up to a Bellerivian prince in bed beside me might have induced some screaming. I'm not sure if the scream would have been from surprise, excitement, or fear, but I would have made an ear-piercing noise.

"But why?" I ask.

He rubs his face and leans forward, putting his elbows on his knees. "You needed someone, and I decided to be that someone. End of."

His tone doesn't allow for any argument or rebuttal. He's probably grown up getting his way in almost every conceivable situation.

He rises and lifts his arms over his head in a lengthy stretch.

Concussion or not, I'm not immune to admiring an incredibly fit, gorgeous man when I see one. He catches me staring, and my cheeks light on fire again. A smirk forms on his lips.

Of course he knows he's attractive. The whole family is cover-model material. I'm stunned I didn't realize last night that the reason he seemed so familiar is because I've seen his face staring out from various gossip magazines for the last year.

"Shouldn't you be preparing for a coronation instead of rescuing damsels in distress and then watching over their recovery?"

"What sort of Prince Charming would I be if I only did half a job?" He winks. "Breakfast, yes or no?"

"Yes," I say with a small laugh. "There are people who turn down food?"

"People pretend all sorts of things for all sorts of reasons," Prince Alexander says, and there's a tinge of sadness in his voice before he backs out the door. "I shall return."

Such an odd response, but I guess he was pretending to be *Alex* for some reason last night. Knowing who he is puts all the strange things I witnessed into context—his desire not to be too seen, the doctor's comments, and the nurse's reaction to him each time she entered. They were responding to their future king.

I have an urge to text someone about this incredible turn of events, but when I turn to grab my phone from the nightstand, I remember it's at the bottom of the ocean, along with my purse, my keys, and what feels like my entire life. My temples throb at the reminder.

I have a job, but it's working for the parents of the man who was balls deep in another woman on my birthday. If I leave him, I've got nowhere to go, and with the little I'm paid by the McGuintys, I won't be able to locate much in terms of an apartment. That's assuming I can find one. Affordable housing is horrendously hard to secure. How in demand is a pastry chef in Bellerive?

Prince Alexander appears in the doorway again and leans against it. "It's all hitting you smack in the chest?"

"How'd you guess?" I take in his casual pose in the door, and the idea of leaving the bed and seeking solace in the crook of his neck takes me by surprise. I'd slip my arms around him and breathe him in, soak up his warmth and strength so I'm not so alone, so lonely.

"You've got a very expressive face," he says with a hint of a smile.

"Oh, I—" Another blush heats my cheeks. Please tell me he can't really determine the thoughts in my head by the look on my face. Otherwise he knows I've contemplated snuggling into the crook of his neck. Oh God. I just thought it again. Can he read these thoughts?

"It's nice, actually." He doesn't move from the door. "No pretense."

Subject change. Subject change. We need to be talking about something else. "I thought you were getting breakfast." I pick at the pale-blue sheet in my lap and try not to stare at him. His presence is magnetic in the room, in my life. For the first time,

I understand all the girls in high school and college who went weak in the knees over some famous guy.

Or perhaps I'm just weak in the head. I do have a very bad concussion. The likelihood that Prince Alexander is experiencing this same inexplicable pull has to be less than zero. I've seen pictures of the women he's dated—royalty, famous women, Bellerivian elite. Farm girls from Canada aren't on his radar.

"I made a phone call. Breakfast appears. Palace magic." There's a teasing light in his eyes when I glance up.

"Will the mice be turning into people? A pumpkin into a carriage?"

"No pumpkins in Bellerive, I'm afraid. Perhaps a watermelon."

Our gazes meet, and I'm suddenly self-conscious about comparing myself to Cinderella. That's what I just did, right? Of course, he already called himself Prince Charming, so maybe it's not weird? Ugh. Why am I like this?

My head hurts.

He checks his watch and then crosses the room to a pad of paper on the dresser. "Your painkillers must be wearing off. Are you in pain? You winced."

From my own stupidity, but my head also hurts. "I could use something to help with the pain."

He pops open the top of a pill bottle and shakes two out, passing them to me with a glass of water. I take the pills without comment and down the entire glass of water.

It's weird he's playing nursemaid, isn't it? Couldn't he afford to pass the job to a literal nurse or maid? Hell, he could probably afford to have both of them in here fussing over me.

Someone knocks on the doorframe and wheels in a cart with an extravagant setup. Of course breakfast is served on fancy china with tiny tea cups.

This has to be a hallucination.

Or a dream. Maybe I'm still in the hospital knocked out.

Prince Alexander checks under the various covered plates and narrows his gaze. "I probably ordered too much." He eyes me. "What's your favorite breakfast?"

"Shouldn't you have asked before you ordered?" I let out a little laugh and then wince at how the sound reverberates in my skull. "I'm a no-fuss person. Bacon, eggs, fried potatoes, and toast."

He lifts the covered plates again. "Found it," he says. Then he takes a little folded table from under the cart and attempts to set it up, but it keeps collapsing.

"Do you need some help?" If he tries to set a plate on that before it's locked in place, we'll have food everywhere. "There are probably metal or wooden fasteners underneath that slide in place to keep the table upright."

He ignores me for another moment and then calls, "Stella!"

A tiny woman with graying hair appears at the doorway almost instantly. It makes me realize we're never truly alone together. What must it be like to always have someone lurking in the wings?

"Your Highness?"

"Set this up, please." He backs away from the table and the various platters of food. "This one." He taps the stainless-steel lid of the one that must hold my preferred breakfast.

Stella sets the table across my lap and pushes the metal fasteners up to secure the legs. She places the covered food on the top and arranges a napkin and silverware for me.

"Anything else, Your Highness?"

"That's all for now." Prince Alexander nods his head toward the door. "Thank you."

"You've never set up a tray before?" I ask with a barely concealed smile.

"When would I ever need to do that?" Prince Alexander plucks the lids off the other silver dishes until he finds one he likes.

"You've never looked after someone else before? Never looked after yourself?"

Prince Alexander glances over at me, and his expression is hard to read. "I repeat—when would I ever need to do that?"

"You're doing it now, for some reason."

Prince Alexander takes his dish from the cart, but he doesn't bother opening a tray for himself. Instead, he grabs silverware and a napkin and sits down in the armchair to eat from his lap. "It's good to acquire new skills, Aurora," he says.

"It's Rory. You can just call me Rory."

He searches my face while he chews. There's another beat after he swallows before he says anything. "You can call me Alex. At least around here. My parents call me Alexander."

"What do your brothers call you?" I pile a piece of egg onto my toast and take a bite. The drugs Alex gave me have taken hold, and the pounding in my head is receding.

"Alex or Asshole—depends on which brother you're talking about."

I sputter around my piece of toast and stifle a laugh. "Asshole?"

He shakes his head and takes another bite of food. "I probably shouldn't be telling you these things. I hardly know you."

"You saved me from dropping off a cliff last night, so you've definitely earned *my* secrets even if I don't get yours." I search my tray for a drink and then stare longingly at the coffee and tea still on the cart.

Alex chuckles. "Need a drink?"

"I would kill for a coffee." My gaze darts toward the door. "But not actually kill." I raise my voice. "I wouldn't kill anyone."

He sets his plate on the nightstand and goes to the cart. "How do you take it?"

"You're not going to call Stella?"

He shoots me a withering glare. "I'm capable of mixing and stirring."

"Skills you've already acquired," I tease.

"Indeed. If you'd like to see them in action, you need to tell me what you want."

Desire swirls in my belly at the pitch of his voice. Is it weird for me to find an attractive prince attractive? No. But I recognize my attraction to him is fueled, at least in part, by the hint of annoyance in his voice. I like getting a reaction from him, and the last relationship I had where I enjoyed getting a rise out of my boyfriend led to a lot of great sex and almost no effective communication. For me, Prince Alexander would be a great lay but a terrible boyfriend.

Which is likely just fine since there's no way he wants to do either with me.

"One cream and one sugar," I say.

"Ah, that's a regular, right?" He pours the cream and sugar and then stirs it before bringing it over to set it on my tray.

"It is," I admit. "But only at—"

"Tim Horton's." He mixes his own coffee and then makes eye contact over the steaming rim. "I get around, you know."

I'm tempted to banter back, but now that my mind is clearing, I'm realizing a crush on a member of the royal family isn't wise. After today, I'll probably never see him again. He's done me a tremendous kindness, and this event will be a great story to tell at parties for the rest of my life, but the wings beating in the pit of my stomach can't take flight.

Instead of replying, I sip my coffee. "You probably have a busy day. When I'm done eating, I'll get out of your way."

"And go where?" He raises his eyebrows before he sets his coffee on the nightstand and picks up his plate of food again.

"Well, go on then. Tell me the plan you've worked out while dealing with a massive concussion."

"I don't have a plan," I admit. In fact, the idea of leaving here and trying to face my life is terrifying. Nowhere to go. No one to lean on. I like my job, but I hate who I work for. Now that Derrick and I are done, I can admit that to myself. "I appreciate everything you've done for me," I say. "But my very screwed up life in Bellerive is not your problem to solve."

He eats in silence for a moment, and thinking the subject is settled, I polish off the rest of my breakfast as well.

"But I *could* solve it for you," Alex says. "I could rent you an apartment on the property, and I could secure you a job in our kitchen."

The offer takes me by surprise, and I almost choke on my coffee. "You're offering me a job?"

Alex smirks. "I'm offering you a different life. Much better than a simple job."

SEVEN

ALEX

My family is going to have a fit when they realize what I've suggested to Rory. Nothing I've done in the last twelve hours has been in character for me, and in a weird way, I'm enjoying the change. Doing what's expected of me for the last thirty-three years hasn't made me particularly happy. Perhaps taking a minor detour to do what I want will give me one last shot at happiness before I resign myself to an arranged marriage that's good for the country and tolerable for me.

"Alex." Her tone suggests my life-swap comment is utterly ridiculous, but I like how easily my name rolls off her tongue. Lots of people have said *Prince Alexander* or *Alexander* or even *Alex* in frustration, annoyance, or warning before, but Alex has never sounded quite so sweet.

My idea *is* ludicrous, but she can't know that. "Rory," I counter.

"I can't do that. I cannot move to the royal grounds and work here." She places her knife and fork sideways across her plate.

"Why not?" I should accept her refusal, be satisfied I tried to help, and leave it at that. But I've never been good at being denied something I want. "Tell me your other options." I eat the last bite of my food and place my plate on the nightstand and sit back, arms crossed, and wait for her to spew out some bullshit. She doesn't know I spent the night delving into her life. Other than returning to Canada, she doesn't have other options. Her finances are a mess. I'm not even convinced she could afford a plane ticket home.

"I'll figure something out. I'll have to go back to my shared apartment for a while, and if I keep working—"

"You'll never get ahead working for the McGuinty family. Their payment structure is a disgrace. I'm bringing them in front of the employment board this week."

She gapes at me. "What?"

"Mandatory overtime that isn't properly compensated, no holiday pay, denying employees their right to holidays, and I've heard their health and safety measures are lax."

"The kitchen is fine." She bristles.

"That wasn't a direct criticism of you," I say in a gentler voice.

"How do you even know all this?"

"I'm the future king of Bellerive. There's nothing I can't discover about this country or its inhabitants if I want. You didn't wonder how we learned your identity with no passport, driver's license, or anything else that might indicate who you were?"

She frowns. "My brain wasn't exactly firing on all cylinders last night." Her gaze narrows. "This feels illegal."

"You can't go back to your apartment. Derrick McGuinty's affair with Janessa Cook hasn't been discreet."

All the color drains from her flushed cheeks in an instant. "You even know about that?"

"You said he was cheating. A few well-placed phone calls got me everything else."

Her eyes widen. "I told you my boyfriend was cheating on me?"

I purse my lips to avoid letting my smile rise to the surface. "And that you were broke." The lack of friends or family on the island would only rub salt in her wounds.

"Oh my God." She covers her face with her hands. "This is so embarrassing. Why would I tell you that?"

"I suspect it's because you didn't realize I was *Prince Alexander* at the time. But I have good news—I'm just Alex again." I splay my hands out in a ta-da motion.

"But you're not, are you?" She drags her palms down her face.

"Perhaps it's not as simple as I'm making it out to be. The offer stands, though. Roof over your head, a place in the kitchen." A wry grin rises to the surface. "I always thought suggesting a woman's place was in the kitchen would get me in trouble."

"If I was anyone else," she says. "It probably would."

"Yet another reason to keep you around. All my great jokes will finally land."

"I have news for *you*," she says with a hint of a smile. "They're not great jokes."

"Hmm." I pretend to think. "Perhaps that's why they didn't land." No matter what, I don't want her to leave. I've never been so comfortable in a stranger's presence. Like her expressive face, there's no room for pretense between us.

She cocks her head. "You're not what I expected."

"You've thought about me, have you?" The realization spreads a new warmth across my chest.

"Hard not to when you're plastered across every national paper, and even some of the international gossip magazines. Especially..." She scans my face. "You know, with everything going on right now."

"My father being sick, the referendum, me taking over as king." Those are just the things the public knows about. The realization that her interest in me is the same as that of any other citizen of Bellerive stings.

"And your brother getting married."

The reminder of Nick and Jules causes a cloud to descend over my mood. "Yes, that as well."

"You don't seem happy about that?"

I chuckle. "No, it's a joyous experience. Everyone is incredibly pleased for them."

She runs her fingers along her cheekbone and tucks a strand of blond hair behind her ear. "Of course." The tone of her voice suggests she sees more than I'd like.

"What do you say?" I gloss over the awkward topic of Nick and his soon-to-be-wife. "Shall I get you set up in an apartment on the estate?"

"I'm going to wake up tomorrow and the last twelve hours will turn out to be from a medically induced coma because I really did go over the cliff." Her gaze ping-pongs around the room. "Or I'm dead. That's the other explanation."

I laugh. "Those are the only two possibilities?"

"Things like this don't happen to people—my long-term boyfriend cheats on me, sending me fleeing from my shared apartment on my birthday, and I almost go over a cliff. But instead of dying, I'm rescued by a literal prince who then offers me a chance to lead a totally different life."

"Well, when you recap it like that..."

"Right?!" She sits forward in the bed. "I have to be dead." She reaches for me. "I bet my hand will go right through your arm."

Another laugh escapes me. "You just ate a whole meal. Did that go right through you?" Instead of letting her touch me, I lace our fingers together. A shot of awareness races up my arm and across my body. "Not a mirage," I murmur as much for myself as for her, and I raise our linked hands.

She stares at our intertwined fingers and then raises her gaze to mine. Her green eyes are wide, like she's been caught out doing something she shouldn't. "Oh," she breathes out.

The solitary word hits me right in the gut and sends a blaze of desire to my dick. God, what I wouldn't give to hear her say that word, just like that, while more than our fingers were against each other. The picture rises in my mind before I can smother it, and I drop her hand. Sinking into the armchair beside the bed, I rub my face and try to focus on something other than the breathy sound of her voice.

"Yes or no? I have arrangements I need to make if you're taking the job and the apartment." My tone is annoyed, but it's not annoyance at her which drives my change in mood. She's not an option for me, and I'm putting her right in my line of sight. Ten years younger, not a native Bellerivian, and a prominent ex-boyfriend on the island all spell trouble. She can't be a fling, but she can't possibly be more either.

"Do you really think this is a good idea?" she asks.

I avoid her gaze. "It's better than you living on the street or staying with someone who disrespected you so completely." I run a hand through my hair and lean back in the chair, crossing my arms over my chest.

"I don't understand why you're being so nice to me," she whispers.

Me either. "Sounds like a yes to me." I stand and shove my hands in the pockets of my jeans in an effort to conceal how much she affected me only moments ago.

"I'm paying you, right? You pay me to work. I pay you to rent the apartment. This isn't some weird mistress scheme, and I've missed all the cues because I'm not from around here?"

I scratch my stubbled cheek and chuckle. "When I want something or *someone*, I'm up-front about it. No need for games." Our gazes connect, and I let the words sit between us for a beat. Can I resist her? I'm not sure I've got the will to try, but my desire for her isn't tied to my offer. Or not directly tied, anyway. "We'll pay you a fair wage in accordance with your experience, and no, there is no other expectation attached to my offer other than having you barefoot in the kitchen." I smirk.

"Barefoot, huh?" She gives me an amused look. "Sounds like a health and safety infraction."

"Must have heard you were doing that at McGuinty's Golf Course."

She rolls her eyes, and I stifle a laugh. When was the last time a woman amused me so much? A better question is when was the last time I was this relaxed around anyone? It's as though we've known each other forever.

"You don't even know if I'm a decent pastry chef."

"I checked the Yelp reviews. Seemed favorable." I shrug. "Am I doing you a favor? Yes. Does it have to be a big deal? No." Though I am certain my family is not going to see this as a minor inconvenience and another person's wage to pay. They'll be very suspicious of my interest and motives, perhaps rightfully, but I'm not giving anyone an inch. Whatever does or doesn't happen with Rory will be for me to worry about and no one else.

She gives a little shake of her head. "Okay." A smile floats across her face without quite sticking. "Okay."

"I need to go make some arrangements." I tip my head toward the door. "There's a phone there. If you need anything, dial 226, which will take you to the internal phone system operator. Ask to have me paged."

"I can't just bellow 'Stella' at the top of my lungs?" Her lips twist with an almost smile.

"You'd prefer Stella over me?" I press a hand over my heart and pretend injury.

"I'll need someone to dismantle this tray so I can go to the bathroom."

"Ah, right." I raise my eyebrows. "Stella!"

Rory laughs. "After what should have been a terrible night, I'm actually having a pretty great day so far. Thank you, Alex. I mean that."

Another surge of warmth runs through me at her words and the tenderness in her green eyes. "Don't thank me yet." I pause at the doorway. "You haven't seen your apartment or been down to the kitchen."

I head out of her room and down the hall. Now comes the tricky part—ensuring no one in my family ruins whatever is budding between me and Rory before it has a chance to bloom.

EIGHT

RORY

Despite the fun, flirty banter Alex and I engaged in, my body is stiff and sore. After he leaves and Stella takes my tray and the extra food, I waddle to the oversized en suite bathroom. There, I examine my bruised body in the mirror. I could be some sort of alien species with all the blue and purple skin under my double layer of hospital gown. Seeing myself in the mirror also reminds me I don't have any other clothes.

A shower, a change of clothes, and my phone. If it were possible to have three things, those would be at the top of my wish list.

My movements back to the bed are slow and labored. I'm supposed to be working a shift today at the golf course, but I have no way to contact them. I can't remember their phone number, and I don't have access to the internet or a phone book to look it up. Maybe they've heard about my accident? If Prince

Alexander was involved in my rescue, what are the chances no one knows?

There's a knock on my door. "Come in," I call. Since Stella closed my door for privacy, I have no idea who is on the other side of the heavy wood. My stomach flips that it might be Alex.

The door swings open, and Prince Brice is standing there holding a shopping bag. Actually, I think it's several shopping bags.

"Hi," he says with a grin. "Aurora, right?"

"Oh, uh. Rory is fine." I return his smile, and nerves snake through my system. Like Alex, he's attractive, but he doesn't make my stomach go into knots, and I don't have the strange sensation that I've known him all my life. I can't decide if my reaction is a relief or even more worrying. If I reacted to the whole royal family the same way, I could dismiss whatever vibe is between me and Alex, but since I don't...

"I'm Brice. Alex sent me to get you some clothes." He sneaks into the room and sets the bags on the end of the bed before backing up.

"You went to my apartment?" I press my fingers into my temples at the idea of Prince Brice picking out various pieces of clothing for me. I really hope he didn't go into my period underwear drawer. No one should ever go in there.

"Oh, no. And actually, I didn't get those clothes." He waves at the bags. "Personal shopper. She got your size off the items down in the laundry." He leans against the doorframe and stuffs his hands in his pockets. "Not sure if they'll be salvageable or not. Your head wound bled quite a lot."

"Right," I say as I absorb the opulence of a personal shopper. "Thank you. You didn't have to do that."

Prince Brice examines me for a beat. "So, if Alex gets his way, you'll be baking for us and living in an apartment on the estate."

A flush rises to my cheeks. "I didn't ask him for the job or the apartment." Does he think I'm a gold digger? An opportunist trying to take advantage of Alex's good will? This fairy tale could quickly turn into a nightmare if everyone in the royal family hates me.

He grins. "Never even crossed my mind. When Alex gets an idea in his head, it's very hard to put him off it. He is the proverbial bull in the china shop." He peruses me with undisguised curiosity.

The three brothers were born on a gradient. Alex is midnight hair, eyes like coal, and a *don't fuck with me* demeanor.

Prince Nicholas, from the photos I've seen, is dark-brown hair, hazel eyes, and a reputation as the royal playboy. Though the pictures of him and his soon-to-be-wife are the talk of Bellerive now. How much they love each other is so, so clear. Inspiring, actually. The first time I saw their photo on the front page of the national newspaper, I caught my breath, and then I glanced at Derrick. *I'm never going to have that with him* ran through my head for the rest of the day. At the time, the realization should have been a jolt to my system. But I forgot about it until just now.

Then there's Prince Brice, who is still in the doorway taking in the scene. He's the fairest of them all with light-brown hair and golden-brown eyes. There's a buoyancy to him that shines through in photos and, apparently, in person.

"Is Alex going to be in trouble for offering me a place here?" After what I witnessed between Derrick and his parents, and what I've seen from my family, I understand how complicated family businesses tied to family dynamics can be. How much more convoluted can you get than a royal family? If binging *The Crown* has taught me anything, it's that there's an ugly side to upholding public appearances.

Prince Brice chuckles. "Alex doesn't really get into trouble normally. So it's hard to say." His expression softens at whatever he sees on my face. "They'll be pleased he's showing you kindness, of that I'm sure."

I wish I was in a position to turn down Alex's offer, gather my things, and walk out of here with my head held high. But the reality is that I don't have enough money to replace my phone, purse, keys, car, passport, and who knows what else I'm not remembering. Going back to work for Derrick's family, besides being incredibly awkward, will barely keep my head above water in this country. I'll never make enough to thrive. Although we didn't talk about exact dollar amounts, Alex seemed upset enough at how Derrick's family treated me that it should be at least a bit better here.

"He saved my life last night. Doesn't seem right for him to have more problems because of me." If one of us owes the other, I owe him. How do you repay someone for dragging your unconscious body out of a vehicle before it topples over a cliff into the ocean? A thank-you card doesn't seem like nearly enough. Now he's going above and beyond for me again—a total stranger.

Brice grins. "It's nice you're worried about him. You might be the first person in the history of the world to believe Alex's stubborn streak isn't his own fault." He backs out of the doorway. "I'll let you get dressed if you want. Hopefully Tanya came up with something decent. I told her it was for my girlfriend." His grin turns naughty. "So who knows what she bought you." Then he's gone from the doorway.

His footsteps retreat down the hallway, but he's left the door open. While I'm pretty sure it's just Stella out there, I don't need Alex turning up while I'm struggling to get dressed. Gingerly, I climb off the bed and sweep the plastic bags into my hand. I'll have to find out how much was spent and get Alex to take it off my first paycheck... assuming I end up hired. Alex made it sound like a done deal, but Brice seemed less certain.

In the en suite, I riffle through the bags. Everything is from the high-end clothing stores in the center of Tucker's Town. I can't complain about the quality, but the idea of putting on anything constricting with all my bruises makes my body ache.

At the bottom of the second bag is a jersey shift dress, and I breathe a sigh of relief. The various pairs of jeans, skirts, and fitted tops are super cute, but with the way I feel right now, I just cannot face them.

In the shower, I wash my hair as carefully as I can to avoid the waterproof bandage on my forehead. I'm not even sure how deep the cut is or whether the bandage needs changed. Do I have stitches or that glue stuff they use now?

When I get out, I stare at myself in the mirror and cringe. Pale, bruised, and tired are not good looks on anyone. With a guilty feeling in the pit of my stomach, I open the drawers in the vanity. A toothbrush, toothpaste, and a hair tie would make me feel about a thousand times better. It'd be nice to know I'm not going to knock Alex over with my dragon breath when he comes to deliver the news about the potential changes to my life.

It's funny—I wasn't sure I wanted what Alex was offering, but now that it might not be a sure thing, I'm sad at the prospect of leaving here and never seeing him again. If I'm living and working on the property, we might run into each other from time to time, but if I'm scrambling in my old life, I won't have time for anything or anyone. Not that Alex would want to spend time with me. A ball of anxiety forms in my stomach.

I should be sad about Derrick, shouldn't I? We were together for two years. Just last night I was hopeful we'd do something fun to celebrate my birthday, and instead I found him with his ex-girlfriend.

But the last eighteen hours have been a whirlwind of newness, and I'm not sure anything is sinking in.

I open the last drawer, and a solitary toothbrush, still in its package, a small tube of toothpaste, and a comb are laid out in a neat row. Oh, thank God.

Once I'm feeling presentable, I realize the dull ache in my skull is starting up again. I cross to the dresser where I saw Alex make a note in a book before giving me medication earlier. There, I find a detailed record of all the medications I was given throughout the night. I don't remember waking up and getting anything from him. I run my finger across his neat scrawl and marvel that he did all that for me. The only other person who's taken care of me like this is my mother.

Gratitude and confusion mingle in me as I pop the top off the pill bottle and take two as per the instructions. I note the time underneath Alex's last entry.

"Stella!" I call, and my head throbs at the pitch of my own voice.

"Yes, ma'am?" She appears in the doorway, a newspaper under her arm.

"I don't want to bother Prince Alexander, but is it possible to get some lunch?"

"Of course," Stella says. "Whatever you'd like, I can call it into the kitchen."

"Is that the paper?" I try to catch a glimpse of the headline.

"Yes." She tugs it out from under her arm. "Prince Alexander reads the national paper every day."

"Can I read it?" If I'm sitting in this room all day, I'm going to die of boredom. At least if I can read the paper, it'll give me something else to focus on.

Stella hesitates and then passes it over. "It's a very flattering photo of you."

I swallow at the implication. When I open the folded paper, there's a photo of me alongside a picture of the sports car that hit me and another of my car being dragged up the cliff. Apparently, it didn't clear the jagged rocks to land in the ocean after all. But it's so mangled, I'm certain I wouldn't have survived.

Seeing the proof that I could have died, that the man in the sports car did die, creates a vise around my chest. "Thank you," I manage to eke out. "Can I—just a minute." I shut the door gently but very much in Stella's face, and then I collapse on the bed in a puddle of tears.

NINE

ALEX

I should have known I'd end up here when I began making arrangements for Rory to join the royal staff without consulting my parents. In this instance they're more the king and queen than parental figures. While they've been *almost* regular parents to Nick and Brice, my relationship with them is clouded by succession. The pressure on me to be the best, to make the right choices, and to put the country first would crush many. I've never allowed myself to want anything that would compromise even one of those principals. My shoulders are broad enough to withstand the weight of the kingdom, and my place in history was cemented the day I was born.

Still, part of me hoped the king would let Rory's hiring slide or wouldn't notice her new status until it was too late. Today is one of his good short-term memory days, and the addition of Rory to the apartment listing and kitchen staff has not gone unnoticed.

Also, I'm pretty sure our accounting firm called to confirm Rory as a new hire. Missed that one in my scheming.

"You understand what taking the day off means, don't you?" My father reclines in his chair and observes me. My mother is perched on the couch behind me. She's taken to sitting in on meetings where my father needs to be clear and concise. Too many cooks in the kitchen, if you ask me.

"I do." I'm not dressed in my typical suit, and the power dynamic between us is weirder than normal. Usually, I'm his equal, but right now I'm remembering what it was like to be a boy scolded by my father.

"Hmm." His gaze narrows. "Normally, when one takes a day off, one doesn't negotiate contracts for new employees or slot them into empty estate apartments."

"I've always been an overachiever." I give him a smug smile. "You must know that by now."

"Explain to us what's going on here. It seems like you've developed an intense fixation on this girl. Trauma and traumatic experiences can do strange things to the brain," my father says. "You need to be making clear, level-headed decisions right now."

My mind shouldn't be my father's concern; I understand my place in this family. But the stirring in my chest is an issue. That truth will never leave my lips. Instead, I feed him the same series of logical, rational arguments I made to Rory in her room. I can't remember the last time I spun a tale for my father that appeared real but didn't get to the heart of the matter. We tend to be brutally honest with each other, which made his

Alzheimer's diagnosis and the fact Mom had to tell me about it even more surprising. Between the three of us boys, I've always been the one to bear the brunt of hard decisions before everyone else. I'm used to impossible choices. I was raised on them.

Just as he wasn't completely honest with me about his diagnosis, I'm not being totally honest here. The truth, the bare, unvarnished truth, is that I don't know why I'm so keen to help Rory. Is her life a train wreck? Yes. Under normal circumstances I might help her find a new job or make some calls to get her a new position.

But in our kitchen? At our estate? That's mistress territory, and we all realize it. Hell, even Rory called me on it already.

"She's a very attractive girl." My mother makes the observation my father wouldn't dare articulate.

"She's ten years younger than me. I'm not that dumb." I sigh as though they're being dense.

Truthfully, I might be that dumb.

My parents are seeing a big red flashing sign telling them this path with Rory is trouble. Likely because I've never behaved irrationally before and everything I've done since I turned down West Shore Road has been impulsive.

Me? I'm staring down the path, and I'm seeing yellow. Could this path lead somewhere that isn't good for me? Yes. Is that likely? Only if I allow it. At any point, I can back off.

In university when it became clear Jules would never feel for me what I was beginning to feel for her, I reined in my emotions. When Anna Samuels wanted more than casual fucking on holidays, I broke it off. I can make hard, rational decisions even when my heart or my dick are involved.

Rory will be no different.

"I leave next week for my seven-country wife-finding trip. I'm focused on that. Organizing a better life for Rory is the right thing to do. You've got nothing to worry about. I know where my priorities and obligations lie."

My father and mother exchange a long glance over my shoulder.

"Bellerivian or royal," my mother says from behind me. "I just—I don't want you to get your heart set on an outcome that isn't achievable."

I chuckle and turn to her. "My heart has never been involved in any decision I've ever made." Then I rotate around to my father. "I'm giving her the job in the kitchen, and I'm setting her up in the apartment. As far as I'm concerned, this conversation is over."

When I rise, my mother rises with me. "Alexander."

"Look, Mother, if it makes you feel better, her visa is only good for one more year. I understand Derrick McGuinty lured her here with the promise of a marriage eventually. Obviously, that's not going to happen now, so she'll be going back to Canada in a year. Her time in the country is limited." This time my sigh is real. "But none of that actually matters because I know my place and my commitment to the country comes above all else." I ignore the dip in my stomach at the reminder of Rory's ticking clock.

My mother searches my face for a beat longer than necessary before giving a curt nod and stepping out of my way.

Rory has been crying. I'm not sure what set her off, but the Bellerive National is on the bed when I collect her to view the apartment we have available. She won't start in the kitchen until I'm back from my European tour. Dr. Bennett warned with a concussion like hers that she'll need to take it easy—avoid screens, bright lights, listening to loud music, and reading.

I tuck the paper more firmly under my arm as I lead us to the apartments in the far-left corner of the estate. "You heard Dr. Bennett advise you against reading, correct?"

"I didn't read it." Rory's tone is sullen. "I saw the pictures and... and it hit me, like really hit me for the first time, I could have died." She tucks her hair behind her ears. "I almost died."

I can't deny the truth. Would the car have gone over the edge before the paramedics arrived, or did Kane and I disturb the car enough to cause it to shift? We'll never know for sure.

"And then I started thinking about how I almost died because my boyfriend of two years—the reason I moved here, the reason I've been trapped in a shitty go-nowhere job—couldn't keep his hands off his high-school sweetheart. He also had the nerve to say he was so happy I was alive and he couldn't wait to get me home to take care of me."

I eye her and take the newspaper out, flicking it open while we walk. "Thought you said you didn't read it."

Her blush starts at her chest and migrates up into her cheeks. "I might have skimmed it." She glances up at me, and her chin juts out in defiance. "You left me alone for hours. What was I supposed to do?"

"Sleep, take a shower, contemplate what I look like naked—all suitable distractions. Any screens, music, reading, or staring into bright lights are not."

"I did two out of those three things," she says.

"Why didn't you shower?" I feign confusion.

She shoves my shoulder while I speed read through the article. Derrick the Douche is quoted almost ten paragraphs in. I bet she didn't skim it—I bet she read every last word.

"A shower and sleeping weren't enough," she clarifies. "I was bored."

"Should have gone for option number three as well. I guarantee it would have met all your needs." I waggle my eyebrows at her.

She gives a little laugh and then winces before touching her temple.

Up ahead, the apartment building looms. Not many of our employees live on the estate, but whenever someone runs into trouble with rent or splitting up with a partner, or some other life crisis, we often offer to house them for a while.

"These are the apartments?" Rory's skepticism is clear.

"Funny looking, aren't they?" I smile. "They were built at the start of the Spanish Flu to contain and quarantine any infected employees. Each apartment, regardless of the floor, has its own staircase and its own entry door. Nothing communal in the whole thing."

"Lots of privacy." A frown sits between her brows. "If it's been here for over one hundred years…"

"My grandmother updated them about twenty years ago. So I'm not going to pretend the apartment is incredibly modern, but everything works, the rent is cheap, and your privacy is guaranteed."

She takes in the building from the stone terrace. "No one minded that you were doing this for me?"

Her question is a minefield I'm not walking through. "Why don't I show you the apartment?"

"I'm not going to say no, Alex. It could be a dungeon and I'd say yes. I have nowhere else to go, despite Derrick's pretend devotion."

I frown and glance toward the palace. "We *do* have a dungeon, if you'd prefer that," I tease.

She laughs and then winces again.

"Your head's bothering you?" I peer at her and try to remember when she last had some medication.

"Only when I laugh, so stop being funny." She gives me a playful punch in the arm. "Which one is mine?"

"Around the back." I lead her toward the right side of the building. "Ground floor."

I unlock the heavy wooden door and then pass her the key. She steps through into the open-plan, cottagey space with exposed beams, and her hand goes to her heart.

"Wow," she breathes. "It's so cute."

"The ground floor apartments are all studios. If you think you might have anyone coming to visit, I can check if we have any two beds on another floor."

"No, this is perfect. This is…" She searches the space. "This is exactly what I expected to live in when I moved here." Her delighted smile twists into confusion. "I had a dream about a place just like this when I was still in Canada. Isn't that weird?"

I scan her face and try to piece together what it is about her features that are so achingly familiar. When I can't turn up anything, I realize I can't dismiss her dream either. Have I dreamt of her too? What a strange thought.

"This works for you?" I ask. "I'll get someone to stock the fridge and freezer if you give me a list of things you'll want."

"Oh, no. You can't buy my groceries. If I can't go myself, I'll give whoever money." She bites her lip. "Or you can garnish my wages for the food and for the clothes Tanya bought."

We're not getting into who pays who for what. "The press will be all over you the first time you leave here. Obviously, you'll need to collect your things from the McGuinty apartment."

"When should I do that?" She plucks at her lips. "I'm actually supposed to be working right now at the golf course."

I chuckle. "Safe to say the car accident and Derrick's wayward dick served as your two weeks' notice."

"I've spent all this time, you know, trying to make him happy, clinging on to something that didn't even feel right anymore." Her chin trembles. "But it's kind of scary to realize how drastically my life has changed in the last twenty-four hours."

I lean against the wall and watch her try to fend off more tears. "Need a hug?" My voice is husky as though I've been the one crying.

"Would you?" Her expression is full of teary hopefulness. "I could really use one."

"Go on then." I step away from the wall and open my arms. She clutches onto me, and her cheek presses against my heart. "Can't stand to see a woman cry."

She releases a muffled laugh. "Funny. I turn to putty at the sight of men's tears."

"You've inspired men to cry, have you?"

Her shoulders rise and fall in my tight embrace. "I am the creator of my own downfall."

I chuckle, but her words resonate. Standing in this tiny cottage apartment, the yellow I saw ahead of me earlier is morphing into orange on its way to red. There's something about having this girl in my arms that's doing all sorts of funny things to me—desire, protectiveness, and this other deep-seated emotion I can't put my finger on.

Perhaps my mother was right to be worried.

Ten

RORY

I've been housed in my little cottage for the last few hours with my bags of new clothes, my painkillers, and absolutely nothing to do. Since I've come to Bellerive, I've barely had a free moment between trying to please Derrick's parents and fitting in with Derrick's friends. Realizing exactly how deeply entrenched I allowed myself to get into his life is like awakening from a deep slumber. What choice did I have? The golf course consumed any free time Derrick and I didn't already have assigned to something else. There was no room for me to join clubs or activities, to pursue my own passions or make my own friends.

I won't be making that mistake again.

Since Alex didn't leave me any paper, and I'm not sure when I'll have a phone again, I make a mental list in my head of the sorts of things I'll never do again.

    1. I will never work at a boyfriend's family business

2. I won't allow myself to be cut off from friends and family back home for another guy

3. I'm done pleasing men at the expense of my own happiness

I consider going further and listing all the things I learned in my two years with Derrick, but I suspect letting my mind go there will make me bitter. The truth is that I wanted to come here. I wanted to be with him. But I gave up so much of myself in doing that.

There's a knock on the door, and I breathe a sigh of relief I won't be alone staring out the window at the ocean across the fields and recounting all my mistakes.

When I open the door, a tall, dark-skinned man is holding a clipboard and has a slightly annoyed expression marring his otherwise handsome face.

"I'm Desmond—Royal Secretary for the princes. Prince Alexander asked me to collect a shopping list from you?"

It's clear this task is a royal pain in his ass.

"If someone will drive me, I can shop for myself," I say.

"I was under the impression all your worldly possessions were currently in police custody?" Desmond raises his eyebrows and consults his clipboard. "My instructions are to collect a shopping list and a list of anything else you'd like. Prince Alexander has suggested a phone without a data plan for now since Dr. Bennett has limited your screen time."

Is it weird to feel both cared for and imprisoned at the same time? His adherence to Dr. Bennett's rules is sweet and annoying all at once.

"Do you know what the police recovered from my car? I don't have a bank card, credit card, any of my ID... I'd really like my own phone back." I give him a hopeful look.

Desmond narrows his eyes and purses his lips.

That request was not a winner either. I imagine looking after all three of the royal princes is a busy job, and Alex has tasked him with me instead of whatever official things he's supposed to be doing.

He takes a deep breath. "I will discuss the matter with Prince Alexander. I shall return." He grabs the handle on the door and closes it before I can get another word in.

I bite my lip and go back to looking out the window. If everyone is going to act like I'm an inconvenience, I'll have to actively pursue another job and another place to stay.

An hour later, there's another knock on the door. By this point, I'll take Desmond's barely concealed disapproval over my view from the window. I throw open the door, and a woman with a curvy figure and long chestnut hair is in the doorway. I recognize her from the photos in the paper. She has a bag marked Bellerive Police at her side.

"Hi," she says with a fleeting smile. "I'm Julia Jensen. The king's secretary." She holds up the clear plastic bag. "I have your things from the police station."

"Oh, wow. Thank you. Desmond didn't want to deal with me?" I match her quick smile and step back from the doorway. "I really appreciate this."

"I was returning from the airport after dropping some people off for their flight. Stopping in Tucker's Town made me the logical choice to retrieve your things. Desmond takes some getting used to, but he's very good at his job." She gazes around the cottage. "I haven't been in these before. This is cute."

I tear into the clear plastic bag and find my phone. It's dead, but somehow not crushed. I breathe a sigh of relief. My purse is largely intact, and all my ID is present. Did I have cash in my wallet? I can't remember, but there's none now. The weight that was sitting on my shoulders at the thought of trying to organize the replacement of all these pieces of my life lifts.

"You're relieved?" Julia's blue-gray eyes are soft with kindness. "Must have been quite an ordeal."

I scratch my eyebrow and nod. For some reason, the sight of my things has made me a bit choked up. "Thank you for bringing me this."

"Do you need a charger for your phone? I'm sure I can round one up for you."

"You don't mind?" I clasp my hands together against my chest.

"Not at all." Julia leans against the small kitchen island. "How are you feeling?"

"Apart from some monster headaches, not bad." I lay my items on the counter, taking in each piece. "Alex—er—Prince Alexander has been so kind to me."

"Yes," Julia says, drawing out the word. "He can be." Something seems to amuse her, and she shakes her head. "Do you have groceries?"

"No," I admit. "But now that I have my bank card, I can call a cab and go get some." Bellerive only allows official cab companies, none of the start-ups that have blown up all over the world.

This draws a genuine laugh from her. "A cab? To the royal estate? Alex would collapse from an aneurysm if you did that." She straightens. "No, I think I should arrange for either a guard to do your shopping or for you to be accompanied by guards." She purses her lips. "Might be an abuse of my power, but I hate the thought of you cooped up in here trapped by overprotective kindness, however well-meaning he might be."

"I actually enjoy grocery shopping, so if it's not too much trouble..." I am bordering on pleading, but I'm yearning for something familiar. The aisles of food will bring me some comfort.

"No trouble," Julia says. "You're a baker, right?"

"Pastry chef, yes." I pile all my things into my purse and loop it over my arm. "I've been offered a job here."

"I heard." Julia glances at me over her shoulder as she leads the way out the door. "Alex can be very persuasive, so if you don't want the job—"

"Oh, no. I'm super grateful. My life is a mess, and this job and the cottage are a big help. Massive help." I smile and then wonder whether I'm coming across as too eager. "I didn't ask him for the job or the housing."

Julia waves me off. "None of us think that, if that's a concern. We all know Alex."

I'm not sure how I'm supposed to take that, but can I ask? Alex is my rescuer and now my employer, but that's it. I don't exactly have the right to dig into his family dynamics. Despite the familiarity between us, we've only just met.

We walk across the fields, and Julia peppers me with polite, unobtrusive questions about Canada and my college experience. By the time we get to the front entranceway, the anxiety Desmond produced in me earlier is dried up and replaced by affection for Julia Jensen.

"You must be very good at your job," I say when she uses an internal phone line to call for a car and some guards.

She smiles. "Why's that?"

"I've been feeling very, I don't know, out of place? But you're just so warm and kind." My mind is drawn to all the photos of her and Prince Nicholas I've seen the last few months. If *this* is real then *that* must be real too. I'm dying to ask her a bunch of intensely private questions, but they might kick me off the estate if I seem too curious.

"I grew up in this, but I can imagine it's intimidating to stumble into."

Shoes slap against the tiled floor in the entranceway, and Alex appears dressed in a suit that emphasizes his wide shoulders and trim waist. He looks every inch the prince.

"What's this I hear about a trip to the grocery store?" There's a crease in his brow and annoyance radiates off him.

A shot of awareness zips through me, and I scold myself again for being the least bit turned on by his frustration. Yesterday, I was dating and living with someone else, and today my body is responding to my rescuer as though we've been engaged in some hot affair. There's nothing rational about my attraction to him, but I can't deny its existence either. Nothing will come of it, so there's no point in dwelling on whatever is drawing me to him.

"She needs groceries. She'd like to go shopping." Julia gives him a pointed look. "She's not our prisoner, and she's not even an employee yet."

For the first time, the idea of not receiving a paycheck causes a cool sweat to break out under my arms, and the dull throbbing in my temple returns. If Derrick makes me pay my half of this month's rent at the apartment, I'll barely be able to afford groceries until I'm allowed to start work here. Dr. Bennett said it would be a few weeks before he cleared me—minimum.

He searches my face, ignoring Julia, and his gaze narrows. "What's wrong?"

"I just realized Derrick might expect half of this month's rent, and if I'm not working anywhere..." I glance at Julia because even though she's nice, I don't want her thinking I'm begging for money. Alex asked me what was wrong, and for some reason,

I've got no filter with him. He asks, and words just flow out of my mouth.

He grunts and then turns to Julia. "Ask Desmond to clear my afternoon."

"Alex." Jules groans. "You can't keep seesawing today about whether you're working or you're taking the day off. You're half the reason poor Aurora got the brunt of Desmond's frustration."

Alex's gaze pings back to me. "He wasn't nice to you?"

I shift my feet. "He wasn't *not* nice."

"Never mind, Jules. I'll tell Desmond to clear my schedule myself."

"Alex." Julia's voice radiates with caution.

He's already walking away. "Thank you for getting Aurora's things from the police station. Rory, do not leave without me." Then he's gone out of sight down some corridor.

"Is he—"

"Always like this?" Julia chuckles. "Yes, yes, he is. Intense. Focused. It's just usually those things are on work." She eyes me.

"I was going to say *coming grocery shopping with me*." I shift my purse to my other arm. This isn't how he always behaves? Authoritative. Take charge. Does what he wants when he wants?

Julia's phone vibrates in her hand. "I have to run to a meeting about a project I'm putting together in Tanzania. You're okay to wait here until Alex gets back?" She's already walking backward toward the hall Alex disappeared down. "Kane and Torres should be here in a minute—they're your guards."

"Yeah," I say, feeling small and insignificant in the sprawling entranceway. "No problem."

Eleven

ALEX

When I reach the front entrance to meet Rory, I half expect her to have already left. She's proving to not be very good at taking directions. It's no wonder I found her in a car crash on West Shore Road at night when it's famously foggy. Decision-making cannot be a strength.

I waltz through the main foyer and wave my hand toward her. "With me. The car is outside. Kane and Torres are waiting."

She follows wide-eyed without a word.

Once we're settled in the back of the vehicle, I press a button to put up the divide between us and the guards. They don't need to hear Rory and I arguing, and I'm sure that's what's coming.

"I thought we agreed someone else would do your grocery shopping," I say.

"Yeah. We did. But then Desmond seemed..." She bites her lip. "I thought it might be less inconvenient if I just went myself."

"I spoke to Desmond. He'll be more attentive to your needs from now on." Since I'm sure Jules isn't going to stay on as my secretary given her wedding to my brother, I threatened not to promote Desmond if he can't satisfy all my requirements, and right now I require him to be nice to Rory. Disapproval vibrated off him, but he didn't dare disagree. Most of the time we get along well. He knows his place, and I know mine.

"That's not." Rory closes her eyes. "I didn't tell you to get Desmond in trouble."

"He's fine." I stare out the window and watch the greenery of the Bellerive scenery pass me by. "Just in danger of getting fired if he doesn't understand he works for me. Every once in a while, someone needs a reminder."

"It's just groceries," she says in a small voice.

"It's not. You'll see." I purse my lips. "Most of the time the people of Bellerive are very respectful, but what I did last night has set off a feeding frenzy. Stories about me, my life, my family's lives are all over social media today." I glance at her. "Stories about you."

She massages her temples.

"You didn't know?" Julia delivered her phone over an hour ago. Since she doesn't follow instructions, I assumed she'd have been searching her name or mine on every available social media, reading the articles, sharing anything that made her look good.

"How would I know?" She glares at me. "My phone is dead, and you left me in a cottage with literally nothing to do. I spent the whole time making a list in my head—and it's a long one—of all the things I'll never accept again in a relationship."

"A long one?" I eye her in amusement. "Give me a sample."

"No more dating men who require me to join a family business." Her hand is splayed open and she taps on her index finger, but before she continues she seems to think better of it. "You know what? That's all you're getting."

"Presumably no cheating is another one. Or were you okay with that? Just not on your birthday?"

Her gaze narrows. "I liked you better this morning."

That's honest. I liked me better this morning. I went to work after showing her the cottage because I could see the slippery slope rising in front of me. Spending more time with Rory, as my mother suggested earlier, was a disaster waiting to happen.

Yet here I am. Canceling my day for the second time and going to the grocery store, a place I haven't set foot in for years, just so she isn't bored.

Not my job to amuse her. Not my job to accompany her. The fact that I'm going against some of my own inner checks and balances makes me angry, but it hasn't stopped me from doing them.

"It's been a day that feels like a week," I admit.

"For me too," she says. "At least once I have some things from the store I can cook and bake."

"You're not supposed to be reading."

A slow smile spreads across her face. "I bet you've never cooked anything yourself before."

I raise my eyebrows, but for some reason I'm loathe to admit I haven't spent much time in a kitchen. A handful of times I've made myself a sandwich. That's it. Everywhere I go, whatever I want, someone does it for me or makes it for me. "It's not a skill I've needed to acquire."

Her smile turns into a broad grin. "Can I teach you how to bake something? As a thank you for, you know, everything?"

"You want to teach me how to bake?" I'm sure there's disbelief in my expression; it's definitely in my tone. "Or you want me to read the recipe to you while you bake? I'm quite a good reader."

She laughs, a delighted sound. "No, I don't need you to read. All the recipes live up here." She taps her temple. "If you don't want to learn, it's okay. I just thought it might be something I could do for you." She glances out the window, and her lips tug at another smile. "It would at least amuse me for a little while. The days are going to be long until I can start working again. I've never had so much free time."

The orange color flashing in my mind, slopes with a steep, slippery incline. The lovely green shade of her eyes should make my answer obvious. No, she can't teach me how to bake. Getting any closer to her is a mistake. In a few months, I'll be publicly declaring my affections for someone suitable to assume the throne beside me. Rory isn't that person and can never be that person.

"Today," I say. "Since I've taken the day off, you can teach me to bake something today." I may need to start wearing a muzzle in her company to prevent my mouth from saying things my brain understands I shouldn't be doing.

She turns to me with wide eyes and a broad grin. "Seriously? Oh my God. Alex, this is going to be so fun." She taps her lip. "But what to bake?"

"I have no idea."

"You went to university in England, right? What about scones? We could set up a *proper cream tea*." She takes on a mock British accent that almost sounds South African.

"Your accent is ridiculous."

"It was bad? It was supposed to be British."

"Terrible. Unrecognizable."

"Means I need more practice." She stifles a laugh. "Watch out! I'll be doing it every day now."

"Lord help my ears." My gaze runs over her delighted expression, and something stirs in my chest. I've never had conversations with anyone like I'm having with this woman.

I like it far too much.

I shouldn't have gone into the grocery store, or I shouldn't have allowed Rory to come in. But the combination of the two of us wandering the aisles with a cart and two burly guards is drawing a lot of attention.

"Everyone is videotaping us and taking pictures and pretending they're not." Rory speaks out of the side of her mouth while she drops things from the shelves of the baking aisle into the cart.

"I'm aware," I mutter. "Is it possible to go a little faster?"

"Excuse me, Your Highness?" A guy in an apron is behind Kane, and he peeks out around the guard's shoulders.

I nod to Kane, who turns to address the employee. "Is there something we can help you with?"

If he wants a selfie or to know whether he can share our appearance in his store on social media, it's going to be a no, even if several other people seem to be doing it without my permission. Still, it's interesting to be in a grocery store after so many years. Everything in neat, ordered rows. At least Rory seems to be thoroughly enjoying herself. Well, except for her penchant for checking the price and comparing it to other things on the shelf as though we're pinching pennies. The instinct to be cheap is slowing us down.

"I'll pay for everything. No need to price check. Put stuff in the cart." I keep my voice low.

"I can't let you pay," she whispers back. "There's nothing wrong with being thrifty."

"Your Highness," Kane says from behind me.

I rotate to face him. "That was the store manager. There's quite a crowd gathering outside with some reporters arriving just now. Management has locked the doors so you can shop in peace."

I suck in a deep breath. "Essentials only, Rory. Maybe next time you'll listen to me when I say something like this is a bad idea."

"Might not have been a terrible idea if you hadn't come." She purses her lips in annoyance. "You're not exactly anonymous."

"Neither are you," I retort. "You just don't realize it yet." I turn to Torres. "Get bread—"

"I can make my own," Rory says.

"Milk, eggs." I motion to Rory to continue my list. "Now is your chance. We're not staying much longer. What else?"

She rattles off items, and it's longer than I expected, so I send Kane with Torres. Perhaps not the best plan to have both our guards go on a food-finding mission, but the store isn't huge, and the front door is locked to new people.

"If the front door is locked..." Rory's expression turns hopeful.

"If the front door is locked, the store is probably losing customers. Unless we'll be doing enough shopping for several households, our presence here isn't helping this store right now."

She runs a hand through her hair and then sweeps it over her shoulder. "I didn't think of that."

The guards return with their arms full of food before we're out of the baking aisle. I let out a long-suffering sigh, and Rory slides me an amused glance.

"Not used to waiting for people either? Not a skill you've needed to acquire?"

"I enjoy the skill I've acquired where people do as I say."

"That's not a skill." Rory chuckles. "That's a position."

"At the top."

"Well it certainly wouldn't be at the bottom, would it?"

"I'd hate that."

"Would you?" She tries to lift a giant bag of flour, and I grab it from her, sliding it under the cart.

No point in going down the complicated road of my feelings on being the next in line to the throne. "Is that it?"

She surveys the cart with a critical gaze. "Yes."

When we get to the front checkout, I realize the store is deserted apart from employees. The manager is on the till, and he gives us a wide smile. "Find everything you need?"

"You have a great baking aisle," Rory raves. "So well stocked."

"Thank you," he says. "I'll pass that along to our buyer." He slides me a nervous glance. "Um, is it possible to get a picture for our wall of fame?" He gestures to a wall behind him, where a host of pictures of famous people resides—including both my brothers sporting broad grins.

How can I say no to that? As the eldest brother and the next king, I can't seem too good for such a simple request. "Just me?"

"Yes. Yes." The manager gives an emphatic nod.

"All right then."

Kane takes the photo of me and the manager while other people are outside the glass windows snapping pictures of us. Amazing. It's just occurred to me that the king and queen are going to murder me for such a public show of togetherness. We don't do this sort of thing, and I've done it with the woman I rescued from a car accident. I've done exactly what they warned me not to do.

The manager rings through our groceries while Kane and Torres grumble about the logistics of getting the groceries to the car along with protecting me and Rory.

"If you get in the car, I can meet you around the back of the store at the employee entrance. We'll have the groceries loaded before anyone else can get back there."

"We go out the front," I say to Kane and Torres. "Give them the picture op they want, and then we swing around the back for this stuff."

Kane and Torres confer again in low voices.

"Probably the best we're going to do," Kane agrees. "You'll go out the door with me. Torres will shield Ms. Wilson."

"Keep your head down," I say to Rory. "Don't answer any questions. Nothing. We say nothing."

She meets my gaze and worry is etched in hers. "Okay."

At the front, the manager unlocks the doors while two employees wheel our cart toward the back. I keep my head down and partially shield my face as we head to the car.

As soon as we're out, there's a barrage of voices calling our names and shouting questions, cameras clicking, and people trying to grab selfies with us in the frame. I'm in first, and Rory falls in after me.

"Wow," Rory says when the door slams closed behind her. "I never want to do that again. That happens all the time?"

"Not here very often," I say. "In America, yes. Sometimes in England. Depends on what's happening." My phone buzzes in my pocket, but I don't take it out. It'll be one of my parents or Desmond or maybe even Brice asking me what I was thinking. The short answer is that I wasn't, and that's a problem. One slip so close to her accident might not be a big deal, but if we're seen in public again, the narrative my mother warned me about will take hold in the court of public opinion. That's not fair to Rory on so many levels. She might not be able to anticipate the fallout of a simple trip to the grocery store, but I can.

We drive around the rear, and the three store employees get the vehicle loaded in record time. As we're pulling away, people and reporters stream around the side of the building, desperate for another glimpse.

"I can't believe this is your life." Rory gazes out the back window.

Instead of answering her, I stare out the window. This life is all I've ever known. What would it be like not to have to worry about personal safety, public opinions, the fate of an entire country, or finding a *suitable* wife?

I'll never have that life, so there's no point in wishing for anything different.

Twelve

RORY

Prince Alexander, the next in line to the Bellerive throne, is watching me put away my groceries. He hasn't offered to help. Probably isn't a skill he's been *required to learn*. I would laugh except the skills he demonstrated at the grocery store made my heart ache for him. He seemed so thoughtful on the ride, as though he's not entirely happy with his life.

What would it have been like to grow up in this environment? He can't even go to a grocery store, one of my favorite places, without security and a crowd. I would hate it.

He's been quiet since we got back, but it's not an awkward silence, which I might expect. There's an ease between us that can't be faked. This rapport is similar to what I have with long-term friends back home, but I'm baffled how I can experience the same sensation with someone I met yesterday. I want to tell him my whole life story and yet part of me expects he knows everything about me already. I sound unstable—I cannot say these thoughts aloud to anyone, ever.

Within the year he'll be king of Bellerive and the head of their government here.

The trauma of the car accident has hit me hard if I'm creating an unexpected closeness with Prince Alexander in my mind. The loneliness of being in Bellerive by myself has knocked me sideways because I almost died. That's all. I can't read anything into Alex's kindness.

When I try to lift the bag of flour Kane set on the counter, Alex pushes away from his spot by the door and slides it into his arms.

"Where do you want it?" he asks.

I open one of the bottom cupboards, and he heaves it in. When he straightens, we're practically chest to chest in the tiny kitchen. I suck in a sharp breath, and he glances down.

"You all right?" His voice is gruff.

"Yes." I sound like I've run a marathon. What is wrong with me?

There's a knock on the door, and Alex steps around me to answer it. He takes a phone charger from Kane's outstretched hand.

"I'll be close if you need me." Kane withdraws from the cottage and tugs the door shut behind him.

Without saying a word, Alex takes my phone and plugs it into the nearest outlet. The red battery icon pops onto the screen.

"If I let you keep this, are you going to abuse the privilege?" He points to the phone.

"I'm not a child."

"You follow instructions like a child. A brain injury isn't something to ignore."

I roll my eyes and start gathering ingredients and various measuring instruments. "I was bored." I wave my hand over the masterpiece I'm building on the counter. "I've got this now. No need to break the rules."

He makes a non-committal noise and leans against the island.

"Are you going to help?" I ask.

A hint of a smile tugs at the edges of his lips. "Are you going to tell me how?"

I bite my lip and scan his chiseled face. "It'll be easier for you to learn on this side of the island."

He rolls up the sleeves of his dress shirt so they're at his elbows and washes his hands at the sink. While he does that, I preheat the oven.

"Ready?" I ask when his shoulder brushes mine.

He picks up a few of the measuring instruments and then leans down to read the bags of ingredients littering the surface.

"Meet your inspection standards?"

He chuckles, and the sound sends a shot of warmth arrowing into my heart. "You're going to be setting the standard." He raises his eyebrows. "Intimidated?"

"Hardly," I scoff. "If there's one standard I can set with absolute certainty, it's baking." I pass him ingredients and measuring cups to match. "Fill those."

For the next twenty minutes, I order him around the kitchen, and apart from a few teasing remarks, he does everything I ask without complaint.

"Is the dough supposed to be this messy and crumbly?" Alex frowns at the mound on the counter.

I grin. "Yes." I rock into him. "You don't trust the standard I'm setting?"

"It's a mystifying standard. Sort of expected it to look more like bread."

"You know what raw bread dough looks like?"

He chuckles. "We royals do all sorts of things around the world while we travel—for charity, for press, for a laugh at our own expense. I made naan bread in India, but it was stretchy."

When I turn to say something in response, the words die on my lips, and I forget what I was going to say. We're so close our breaths mingle, and his gaze connects with mine.

I dart my gaze from his lips to his eyes, and I long to wrap my arms around him and bend into him, melding our bodies and mouths together.

"What's next?" he asks, and there's a hint of a smile in his voice.

My cheeks heat. Does he realize what I was thinking? *Oh my God. What is wrong with me?* "We need to, um, shape the scones."

With the pastry cutter, I show him how to carve out wedges. Each brush of our hands or scrape of our bodies shoots awareness through me. When we finish, I cover the wedges, put them in the fridge, and set a timer.

"Why are we making them cold?" Alex points at the fridge and then at the preheated oven. "Am I going to get to eat these? I suspect I've been duped."

I laugh and then wince as my headache reemerges. Alex reaches around me, his arm grazing me, and he takes my pill bottle off the counter. He fills a glass of water and passes me everything without a word. With the pen, he notes the time in the notebook.

He might not be much for baking or putting away groceries, but he can read the pain on my face in a second. I hope he can't read anything else.

"Thanks." I take the pills and gesture to the fridge. "They keep their shape better if they're cold when they go in." I glance at him over my shoulder as I head to the couch. "And yes, you'll get to eat them. I promised you a *proper cream tea*." I try out my British accent again.

He grimaces.

"Really? That bad? I don't believe you. I've got to be close. I've watched a lot of British TV shows." I flip my hair over my shoulder and sit on the couch, drawing my knees into my chest.

Alex follows me and sits on the other end in a relaxed sprawl. He runs a hand through his hair. "You need to watch more, clearly. That was truly terrible. I would not lie to you."

"Right," I say, giving my accent another shot. "I reckon it's all gone pear-shaped."

He chuckles. "British expression with a Texan accent. Somewhat impressive that you mixed and matched so fluidly." He eyes me.

I grin and decide to spare him another attempt. "So what were you doing on West Shore Road last night? I was fleeing my cheating boyfriend on my birthday. What were you doing?"

"Headed back here and decided to take the long way."

"Interesting. Didn't you scold me for taking that road in thick fog?"

He slings an arm over the back of the couch. "I did."

He doesn't offer any other explanation, and I get the impression Alex isn't used to justifying himself to anyone about anything. "You were all dressed up."

"Work event. Wasn't particularly enjoyable." He sighs. "What were you supposed to be doing for your birthday? Did Douchey Derrick forget?"

"Have you really nicknamed him that?" A slow smile spreads across my face. Alex doesn't seem like the type to say those things out loud.

"I have. Do you object? I could go with dickwad, dipshit, dumbass—those were all considerations before I settled on douchey."

"I think I'd prefer dumbass. It's more Canadian." I tap my chin. "Dumbass Derrick. I already feel better. Amazing."

Alex chuckles and runs his fingers along the top of the couch. "You didn't answer my question."

He didn't answer mine in great detail either. But I suppose I'm not worried he'll sell stories about me to the newspaper. Broke and desperate isn't a good look, and it's currently the one I'm sporting.

"I have no idea if he forgot. If he didn't, he's a shitty gift giver too because I'll never get that image out of my head." I cover my eyes. "Or does that make him a good gift giver? Certainly memorable."

"In any scenario, it makes him a terrible boyfriend."

I tug my knees tighter against my chest. "He wasn't always. Once we came here, though, he let his parents run our life, and he couldn't seem to stay away from Janessa. Whenever I asked, he denied it."

To come here, I burned a big bridge with my father. My brother's enrollment in the military cemented me as the one to take over the family farm. As the oldest, I'm the rightful inheritor, but I hoped my brother might take an interest since he had little interest in anything except hockey.

Meanwhile, my family had my life all figured out—run my pastry business out of the farm kitchen and help them with the dairy cows. The property has been in the Wilson family for five generations, and in my father's eyes, I'm the heir. I negotiated my college degree as one last hurrah before accepting my fate.

To be fair, before I met Derrick, I hadn't objected to their plan, but I hadn't been part of creating it either. When I told my parents I was moving to Bellerive and might never return to run the farm, my father didn't take it well.

Yet another reason why mixing family and business is never a good idea. If there is anyone who might understand the push-pull of that, he's likely sitting beside me. Any royal family must be the epitome of mixing family and business. Are there lines between the two? Where are they drawn?

"If you could have done anything on your birthday, what would you have done?" Alex asks as the timer goes off for the scones.

I clamber off the couch, and he follows behind me to observe. "My parents have a dairy farm in Canada, and we have a couple horses. I miss riding them. Isn't that silly?" I glance at him over my shoulder as I baste the wedges in butter before sliding the pan into the oven and setting another timer. "There are no horse farms in Bellerive. At least none I could find on the internet."

"Hmm," Alex says with a nod. "A few people own horses, but I don't know anyone who offers riding or lessons to locals."

"Anyway." I wave him off and head for the couch. "Derrick wouldn't have even remembered let alone tried to make it happen. He's not that kind of guy."

"So he's lazy, and he's a cheater." Alex taps his temple. "I'm building a picture here."

Was Derrick lazy? He never hesitated to ask me to take the extra shifts or go above and beyond for his family. Every time I said yes because I wanted them to like me, and I wanted Derrick to love me enough to ask me to marry him. Had I wanted to marry him, or had I just wanted to marry *someone*? Now that I've got a bit of distance from him, I'm having a hard time remembering why I pinned my hopes on them and him.

"He was different when we were in college." I shrug. "Or maybe he was the same, but the situation made him seem different." I wrap my long hair around my hand and pin it up into an almost bun before letting it fall again. "I should go get my stuff tomorrow."

Alex purses his lips. "I can send a plainclothes guard with you, but I can't help you."

I sit up straighter in surprise. He hasn't come back to the couch and instead is leaning against the island. The studio space is small, so there isn't a lot of distance between us. The queen bed and bathroom are tucked around the corner, out of sight from the door.

"I wouldn't have expected you to come. You've already done more than enough for some strange girl you happened to save from death."

His gaze narrows, and he observes me with a searing intensity. "It's not that I don't want to, but I can't feed into a public narrative that you and I are more than we are."

Understanding dawns, and I tuck my hair behind my ears. Alex is the most eligible bachelor on the island. Gossip articles are written about him weekly. With the coronation coming up, there is rampant speculation about who the next queen will be. If we're seen together, people could believe I might be that woman. Heat creeps from my chest up into my face, burning my cheeks.

A hint of a smile tugs at his lips. "I see you've followed the appropriate train of thought." He makes a winding motion with one of his fingers, as though it's journeying down a path.

"I'm a farm girl from Canada you rescued from a car crash. No one is going to jump to *that* kind of conclusion."

"I once got my haircut twice in one month, and the tabloids ran a story that I was involved with my hairdresser."

Curiosity gets the better of me. "Were you?"

"No comment."

"Oh, no. No way. You can't use an example of them getting it right to prove they'll get it wrong." I wag my finger. "You broke a pattern, and they responded to it."

He made a fist and raised a finger. "Put my life in danger to rescue you from a car about to go over a cliff." He raises another finger. "Brought you here to the royal doctor." He raises another finger. "Put you up in an apartment. Offered you a job." He counts both of those as one. "Went to a grocery store for the first time in years." He points to his thumb. "I'm one away, if it hasn't happened already, from the press declaring this a grand affair."

I swallow my unease. "You're being nice. We just met *yesterday*."

"Perhaps, but I can guarantee the public won't see it that way." He takes a deep breath. "I can't be seen with you again or it'll set off all sorts of rumors and conjecture. Or if those have already started, my appearance will feed them."

"I understand," I whisper. While I didn't ask him to go to my apartment with me, it's probably best he laid out all the reasons we'll never be going anywhere public together again. For all I know, this baking experiment in my little cottage will be the last time we're alone together. "You don't owe me an explanation. You've got a complicated life, and I don't want to make it any worse."

He nodded as the timer went off for the scones.

A shot of elation zipped through me, and I clapped my hands, springing off the couch. "Prepare to be amazed." I rush past him to check the oven. They're a beautiful golden brown. With an oven mitt on, I draw them out and place the baking sheet on the top of the stove.

From the fridge, Alex takes out the clotted cream and jam. He grabs the kettle from under the sink and fills it.

"I can do that." I nod to the tea-making station he's setting up.

"Nonsense." He grins. "The one thing I'm confident about after spending four years in England is my tea-making ability." He opens a cupboard. "Even stashed some PG Tips in here earlier." He removes the tea bags.

"PG Tips?" I shut off the oven and get out the cooling racks.

"The most popular tea in England—with good reason." He flicks the switch on the automatic kettle and leans against the counter. "Prepare to be amazed."

Over by the window is a two-person table, and I grab everything I can find from the kitchen to make it an elaborate high-tea setup. When I'm done, I survey the little plates, the silverware, the rack of scones, and the cream and jam I spooned into little bowls.

Alex brings over the teapot brimming with the hot beverage, and I cart over the milk and sugar. In silence, we cut and smear all the fixings on a scone each. Alex pours tea into my teacup and then into his own.

We both lift half our scone at the same time, and our gazes meet.

"Thanks for saving my life," I whisper.

"Thanks for teaching me how to do a *proper cream tea*."

His accent, unlike mine, is spot on, and a grin splits my face. "You'll have to tutor me in accents."

"Seems like a tough job. Not sure I'm cut out for it." His dark eyes are filled with silent laughter.

"You're underestimating your skills as a teacher." I scan his handsome face.

"Not a skill I've been required to learn." He smirks.

"If you ever decide to take up accent tutoring as a side hustle, you know where to find me."

He chuckles. "Noted." He raises his scone a little higher. "Shall we?"

"We shall, and if it isn't the best scone you've ever tasted, I may have to hide my face in shame."

"Don't feel too bad. I've had scones all over England. I'll be hard to impress." One corner of his mouth quirks up.

Instead of answering, I take a bite. They're good. Very, very good. When his teeth clamp over the buttery pastry, and his lips follow, I search his face for any sign of approval.

He chews and closes his eyes before groaning. "These are bloody good."

My scone drops onto my plate, and I throw my hands above my head in victory. "Scale of one to ten?"

He draws the pastry back to examine it, and then his gaze meets mine. "I believe it might be an eleven."

I grin before picking up my scone again and taking another bite. "I'll accept your assessment."

For a beat he stares at me, and there's amusement and confusion on his face.

"What?" I ask. "Is there a weird aftertaste? Did you speak too soon?" They taste almost as good as the ones I used to make in my parents' farm kitchen.

He points at me with what's left of the scone. "You're unexpected, that's all." With a shake of his head, he pops the last bite of his scone into his mouth. He takes a long sip of his tea, and then brushes off his hands. "I should go. I'll arrange for someone to take you to your apartment tomorrow. Is there a time that works best for you?"

The teasing, thoughtful man is gone, and in his place is the business prince. It's not the first time I've seen the abrupt shift in his attitude, but the switch jars me out of our easy camaraderie.

"Whatever works best for you and your staff." I make a swirling gesture around the small apartment. "I'll be here."

"The property is safe to walk around if you're going stir crazy. Stay away from the cliffs—for obvious reasons. I'm in Europe next week, but if you need anything before that, have a staff member, any of them, get in touch with me."

"Right. Yeah. Of course. I'm sure I'll be fine." I rise with him. A ball of sadness is forming in my stomach. I didn't expect us to become best friends, but I didn't realize there'd be this definite cutoff, as though there's no hope of seeing him again unless it's critical. "Did you want to take any of this to go?"

He rolls down his sleeves and grabs his jacket from the back of a chair. "I'll be in touch."

The door opens, and he's gone. If I didn't know better, I'd think I did something wrong.

Thirteen

ALEX

My phone buzzed in my pocket throughout my scone-making experience, but I didn't take it out for fear of what I'd find. As soon as the door to her apartment is closed, I draw out my phone and wince at the sheer number of notifications. My parents. My brothers. Julia. Desmond. Everyone has texted me about the *grocery store incident*.

Desmond's texts are about social media fallout, reporters calling for comments, and the general interest from the public my tiny outing has caused.

My parents are concerned about public appearances and have requested a meeting ASAP.

Julia, unlike my parents, is concerned about the shitstorm I'm dragging Rory into without her understanding.

Brice's text is about how down-to-earth Rory seemed and how I need to be careful not to lead her on.

Nick's text is the most surprising. Instead of taking the piss or railing at me for being stupid, he's offered to be a sounding board if I need to chat about the arranged marriage bullshit. I stop walking to read the text again, but I close my phone without replying to any of them.

I stride across the fields toward the main palace and try to smooth out my features so no one suspects the riot that's started inside me. When was the last time I had so much fun doing something so simple? University, maybe? Back then I was somewhat free of the restrictions my life has now. To spend that much time with a woman and not to sense even a hint of an ulterior motive is rare. As much as I've wanted to be normal, whatever that means, I've never felt like *Alex* around anyone. Rory's easy acceptance of me is startling. She treats me like we're old friends instead of strangers, instead of *royalty*. Sitting across from her enjoying the best cream tea I've ever eaten, a flashing neon *Danger* sign lit up above her head. She's not a possibility for me in any sense, and letting myself sit at her table, potentially leading her to believe otherwise, wasn't something I could tolerate.

So I left. Now, I need to give the performance of my life when I'm sitting across from my parents and explaining my actions (again) in relation to Rory.

No matter what, I can't let myself see her anymore. My predetermined destiny doesn't include an incredible pastry chef from Canada.

After a thorough dressing down from the king and queen, the likes of which I haven't experienced in years, I'm in my suite of rooms on my burner phone scrolling through the social media nonsense I lit on fire earlier by going grocery shopping. The headlines would be laughable if it wasn't my life they were burning down. As the king and queen, rightly, pointed out, any woman on the island looking at these photos of me and Rory would wonder why I'd be there if I wasn't trying to make a statement. None but the most desperate will want to marry a man, future king or not, who appears interested in another woman.

After telling Nick he didn't understand our lives were a series of political maneuvers, my lack of savvy in this instance is cringeworthy. Our social media manager is arranging for Dumbass Derrick to be home tomorrow when Rory collects her things so the media latches onto a different story. Derrick has agreed, which makes me think he either wants Rory back or is genuinely too dumb to realize the media will sniff out his affair lickety-split.

Annoyed, I toss the phone onto the coffee table and sink deeper into the armchair near the gas fireplace.

There's a knock on my door, and although I don't want company, I rarely have a choice. "Come in," I call.

The suite door swings back, and Nick stands in the entrance. As the middle child, Nick's brown hair and hazel eyes are reflective of our father. But none of us are mirror images of our parents—a trait here or there from them, and some from our grandparents too. A mishmash of royal heritage.

He leans his shoulder against the door jam and takes in my décor. Has he been here since we were teenagers? We haven't exactly sought each other out in the past.

"You fuck up with Jules again?" I ask. My grumpiness is showing, as it often does in Nick's presence.

Nick chuckles. "I'm going to pretend you didn't say that since I come in peace at Julia's request."

"Your wife sent you to give me a talking to? You're too late. The king and queen beat you to it."

Nick shakes his head and enters the room, plopping into the chair across from me. "I appreciate that it's hard to believe, but I'm not here to talk at all. I've been advised to listen." His eyebrows rise with the last word.

This makes me laugh. "She's determined we'll be friends, is she?"

"I think she wants us to be brothers." Nick gives me a searching look. "Not opposed to it myself, despite your usual dickish response to my arrival."

"It's just been a fucking day. Sorry about that." I drag my hands down my face and sigh.

He doesn't speak for a minute, and I wonder whether he's going to take Julia's advice a little too literally.

"I wouldn't be happy if I was in your shoes. I'd probably be off doing stupid shit too."

There isn't a doubt in my mind Nick would be out doing "stupid shit" if he was in my shoes. He's never been as good at following the rules and living within the confines of royal life. I've never bucked any of it. My destiny was set at birth, and no one has let me forget it for a moment in thirty-three years.

"Rescuing someone on the brink of death is hardly *stupid shit.*"

"Putting your life at risk would be in that category, wouldn't it?" Nick raises his eyebrows. "Look, I didn't come here to fight." He gives a dark chuckle. "Even if that's our default mode. Are you okay? That's all I came to ask."

"A bit out of sorts," I admit. "I'll be all right. I'm always all right eventually." I cross my arms and stare at the unlit fire. "I'm dreading this whole marriage business."

Nick draws his ankle to rest over his knee, and he taps out an annoying rhythm on his leg. While I appreciate him coming, there's an edge between us. Until everything blew up with Julia, I didn't see the conflict running underneath the surface. Since he returned from Tanzania, I've started to understand our relationship for what it is. He thinks I'm an arrogant asshole, and he's been a careless, carefree man-child in my eyes. Perhaps it's time we both discovered whether we're right about each other.

"What's she like?" Nick asks. "The woman you rescued. Aurora, isn't it?"

"Rory." Her name slips out with an unexpected gentleness. "Probably what you'd expect of someone raised far from the royal shadow." It's not really an answer, but listing all the unexpected qualities I enjoy about Rory says more about me than her. My armor around him is still too firmly in place for me to be completely honest.

Nick's eyes widen. "You *do* like her."

I chuckle. "There's nothing not to like. I won't be seeing her again. Every single conversation I've had since I left her apartment today has clarified why I'm an idiot. Not to worry."

"She's young, isn't she?" Nick cocks his head to the side.

"Twenty-three."

He tilts his head from side to side. "That's young, but it's not *terribly* young."

I laugh. "Okay, but she's Canadian. She's got one year left on her work visa, and then she's gone."

"You probably won't get married until close to the coronation, right? That's about a year from now."

I narrow my eyes. Is he encouraging me to make a bad decision here? Fourteen years ago I went after what I wanted, even though I understood there might be consequences. They stretched far and wide and almost severed my relationship with Nick. While I might be prepared to put myself in a no-win situation for a bit of fun, throwing Rory into that fire with me is immature. Would either of us emerge unscathed?

"Your bad advice is subtle," I say.

Nick's eyes dance with amusement. "Not going to deny it's terrible advice—subtle or otherwise—but you really haven't contemplated it?"

"A passing consideration." Though my version had her as a mistress for years. The Camilla to my un-named Diana. To even be thinking this way after knowing her for twenty-four hours is the scariest part. I'm not the marrying kind or the mistress kind. I go after what I want, and I abandon the impulse when it no longer suits me or my duties.

Clean. Unemotional.

"Not really you, though, is it? A reckless affair," Nick muses. "Figured I'd get the idea out there before Brice could."

His comment causes a genuine laugh to rise in me. He's not wrong about our brother. Peacemaker, comedian, truth teller, but he's also the one who often comes up with outlandish solutions to complicated problems. Without a doubt, he'd suggest Rory could be my mistress.

"Next week I'm in Europe, and if none of the women there seems like a good fit, I didn't mind my conversation with Kara, Anna Samuels's sister."

"Anna Samuels's sister?" Nick frowns. "That wouldn't be weird?"

"The family is intent on climbing the royal tree any way they can." I sigh. Transparency is a gift and a curse. "Neither of us would enter the marriage with any illusions, and she's old enough to understand the risks and the benefits of royal life."

"Very clinical." Nick runs a hand through his hair. "Are you sure that's what you want?"

"I'm on the clock, Nicky. Someone I can tolerate and who is good for the country. I can't afford a higher bar with Dad's sickness and the impending coronation."

"But you can't get divorced if you're wrong."

"Hence the reason why it's probably better to be clinical. From what I've seen, love is volatile, sometimes fleeting. Companionship is a solid foundation. Less likely to shift unexpectedly." Given his fraught and complicated history with Julia, he can't deny the truth.

Nick searches my expression. "We really are very different."

"I realize that," I say. He's proven capable of turning himself inside out for love. Tying himself up into knots. Wrecking anything in his path when he feels betrayed or let down.

Not me. Despite my temper, I seek logic and reason. My anger often arises because unreasonable solutions are posed to logical situations.

"If at any point you change your mind about the clinical approach to your arranged marriage, I'm happy to discuss the emotional bit." Nick stands and thrusts his hands into his pockets. "I understand what it's like to be adrift in a sea of feelings."

I smirk. "I didn't get that strand of DNA."

Nick grins. "Missed a few of the vital strands, I've noticed."

Where that might normally sting, his comment causes an answering smile in me. Perhaps all isn't lost between us. "You'll see," I say. "No one has anything to worry about. Emotion won't rule me."

FOURTEEN

RORY

The next morning I wake up with a dull headache but otherwise more refreshed than I've been since I arrived in Bellerive almost a year ago. There is nowhere to rush off to, no one calling me to work, and no boyfriend poking me in the ass with an erection asking me to "take care of it" before getting out of bed.

We fell so far from my vision of our life on the island so fast. When I agreed to move here, we were in love. I would have followed him anywhere, but Bellerive, a gorgeous island paradise, was a bonus. Imagining what it would be like to live here and being here turned out to be in opposition.

In my mind, we were lying on beaches, taking moonlight walks through Tucker's Town, eating fancy dinners on balconies overlooking the ocean—work was secondary.

In reality, working for his parents stole every spare second of our lives, and we only had a "beach day" three times in the last year. While the picture I painted before we arrived was naïve, the reality wasn't balanced either. Over the last few weeks, I became more disgruntled with our lack of freedom, but I don't know if I would have done anything about it.

Go home to my parents and eat crow? Confront Derrick and his parents about the unfair expectations? Neither response is me. Would anything have broken the Bellerive monotony if I hadn't found Dumbass Derrick with Janessa? There's no comfort in the realization I might have carried on, a sharp edge of unhappiness surrounding my life, forever.

After I've buttered a scone for breakfast, I peek at my phone on the counter. Alex left last night, and I resisted turning it on even though it was fully charged. My mother hasn't called, but she left me a text message saying she's glad I'm all right and to call if I need anything from her. Nothing from my father, and she doesn't mention him either. His grudges are epic.

My parents caught the accident on their local TV station. Alex's involvement has made my escape from the brink of death international news. There are other messages from friends and family, but it's Derrick's that catches my eye. Rather than saying sorry and begging for forgiveness, he says he'll see me after lunch. After lunch? If I'm getting my things from the apartment, I'd rather he wasn't there. At this point, I never want to see him again. There's a hard ball of anger sitting in the pit of my stomach.

Frowning, I click on the reply as there's a knock on my door. My heart kicks. I cross to the door and throw it open without checking the peephole, somewhat expecting Alex on the other side. A silly, useless hope.

Instead, it's Desmond and his clipboard. "Prince Alexander asked me to give you the itinerary for today."

"I have an itinerary?" I frown and take a bite of my scone. "I guess you should come in then so I can hear what this is about?"

Desmond follows me into the cottage and then seems at a loss about where to set his clipboard or where to sit. The couch in front of the gas fireplace is probably too far away, as is the two-person table by the window. My bed would be out of the question, and there are no stools at the island. After a quick scan of the space, he sets his clipboard on the island with a small sigh.

"The Crown requires you to stay at the McGuinty apartment today until we're able to escort you out a rear exit with your things. Given the interest in the car accident, your rescue, and the rather unfortunate trip to the grocery story yesterday, the Crown would prefer the press doesn't realize you're living here now."

I scoop a glop of butter off the dish in front of me and apply it to the last bit of scone. It's going to be an excessive-use-of-butter kind of day. "Would you like a scone? They're the best you'll ever have."

Desmond narrows his gaze at the container beside me. "Clotted cream and jam?"

"Of course." I grin and take everything out of the fridge. Good food can thaw even the hardest hearts. While I would never say anything to anyone again, Desmond still doesn't seem pleased to be here. Not hostile, more resigned. I dress his scone while I consider the implications of the Crown's request. Saying 'no' isn't an option, especially if Alex is asking me to help cool the gossipy fire. If I can put out the deluge of press speculation, I will.

When I pass him the scone, he removes his hands from his clipboard and pen to draw the first half toward his mouth. "Any questions?"

"What do I say to the press?" I ask.

"No comment. Derrick has also been advised not to comment."

Other than the article I read yesterday, I haven't checked social media or other newspapers. "Do they—" I take a deep breath. "Does the press know about Janessa?"

"Yes," Desmond says, and when his gaze meets mine while he chews, there's a hint of sympathy in his dark eyes. "The Crown provided those details to give some context for why Prince Alexander has been protective of you."

I take a sip of my tea and try to digest my humiliation being put on broadcast to keep Alex's reputation intact. "Being attached to me in any romantic way is really that bad?" As soon as the words are out of my mouth, I regret them. It's not that I want to be linked to him romantically, but we're not getting married or anything. We went to the grocery store. Have all his public affairs bothered him this much?

"Right now? Yes." There's no room for argument or debate in Desmond's emphatic response. "The timing could *not* be worse."

"King George's illness, the referendum, the coronation... I guess there's a lot going on," I say.

"Hmm." Desmond takes another bite of scone. "This might be the best cream tea I've ever had. I was skeptical when Prince Alexander suggested you'd be a perfect fit as a pastry chef here, but I'm eating the proof of his theory."

I grin at the compliment. Much like Alex, I doubt he gives them out often. "Thank you. So, what time am I to run the gauntlet today?"

A hint of a smile tugs at Desmond's lips. "Derrick will be at the apartment at one to help escort you in. Kane will be with you, but we'd prefer he doesn't enter the building. He will circle around the back to collect you and your things approximately one hour later."

"You want it to look like Kane's not staying."

"The more distance between you and Prince Alexander, the better." He meets my gaze. "For both of you."

The message is clear. Alex and I won't be a thing—in public or in private. Maybe Alex couldn't bring himself to be this direct last night, but he made it clear the public's impression of our burgeoning friendship matters. Makes sense that the Crown's impression would be important too.

On one hand, these warnings are an overreaction. I met him two days ago, and I have all my things in the apartment I shared with my sort-of boyfriend. While Derrick and I are definitely not getting back together, we haven't officially broken up either. Although I'm dreading seeing him today, clearing the air might be good for both of us. A clean break.

"I appreciate you might have been hoping for a different outcome with Prince Alexander—"

"Me?" I laugh. "Oh, no. I don't have any illusions about dating the prince. Trust me. My life—and even if it wasn't—his life is..." The gibberish falls out unattached to my brain, but even as I ramble, a tiny part of me deflates.

On the other hand, there's something about Alex that draws me in, and it doesn't have anything to do with him being a prince.

But I'm feeling better today. Sore, but not so fuzzy. So perhaps the next time I see him, he won't inspire an intense familiarity I can't shrug off. He'll be Prince Alexander, a man I don't know at all.

Kane catches my gaze in the rearview mirror as we turn onto Ocean Front Drive, where the apartment I share with Derrick is located. It's a narrow street, and one of the first to be established in Bellerive when the island became inhabited hundreds of years ago.

"I'm going to pull up to the door in the emergency services parking. I'll get out and escort you to the glass doors of the building. Derrick will be inside the doors, and he'll take you from there."

"Are you really expecting a crowd?" I try to peer out of the windshield.

"Yes." Kane's voice is tight. "Remember you're not to comment."

"Easy enough. Keep my mouth shut." What would I want to say anyway? Alex has been kind and helpful. Derrick is a dumbass. If the press realize he cheated on me, the majority of my questions are likely to be about him, right?

We draw closer to the apartment building, and anxiety creeps up my throat. The front door isn't visible with the scrum of reporters, cameras, and spectators milling around.

"Take a deep breath," Kane says as he throws the vehicle into park and comes to my rear door. He opens it and helps me out. His body bends around mine, shielding me from the onslaught of camera clicks, questions, and people shouting my name. The question that keeps coming up over and over again is whether I've left Derrick to be with Prince Alexander.

That's the press narrative? After one trip to the grocery store? Seems Alex wasn't exaggerating.

When I reach the front door, Derrick pops out. Kane backs off, and Derrick slings his arm over my shoulders, tucking me into his side. It's a move he made hundreds of times during our relationship, and seeking his comfort is an instinct I forget to curb in the chaos. He's the only familiar person on the island, and I curve into him. There are so many people shouting at us, taking photos, and trying to get a comment that it's overwhelming. How do celebrities do this all the time? How is this their real life?

Kane is gone, and the crowd closes in around us. Instead of going in, Derrick's arm slides down my back so his hand rests on my hip before traveling to my ass in a possessive gesture he hasn't used since college. I glance up at him, surprised. He gazes down at me, and I realize he's not going to take the Crown's advice—or directive—to heart.

"Derrick, are you and Aurora still together?"

"We are. We're working through our issues," Derrick says. "I've let her down—in a big way—but I intend to make it up to her."

Did I hear him correctly? He's telling people we're still together. What happened to *no comment*?

"What about the employment code violation the Advisory Council has lodged against your family?"

"A misunderstanding. The McGuintys work hard, and we expect our employees to work hard, but we're fair. Rory has a concussion, and I'm sure, in her confusion, she misspoke."

I try to draw away from him, but his grip on me tightens.

"She's had a stressful few days, and we'd really appreciate some space."

Instead of everyone backing off, they inch forward, microphones thrust into my face, and a barrage of questions fly at me.

"Rory, are you and Prince Alexander more than friends?"

"Are you hoping to date him?"

"Had you met the prince before the other night?"

"Where have you been since you left the hospital?"

"Was the grocery store trip an indication of a future relationship?"

"No... I—" I'm too stunned over Derrick's outlandish claims and the unending questions for a moment to finish. "No comment. I have no comment."

He opens the door and leads me inside. He's laced his fingers with mine without me realizing he's done it. When his first foot hits the stairs, I tug my hand out of his, and he lets me.

"What was that about?" I ask.

"The truth. We've had a misunderstanding."

"There was no misunderstanding. I walked into our apartment to witness your bare ass pumping into Janessa on my birthday. I can't unsee that, Derrick."

"She came onto me," he says, glancing at me over his shoulder before we reach the landing for our apartment.

"I'm not coming back here to the apartment or to you. I'm getting my things. Prince Alexander has offered me a job as a pastry chef. They're letting me rent one of their estate apartments."

Derrick eyes me as he lets me into the apartment. "He'll use you and discard you, Rory. You're too good to have a man take advantage of you like this."

Heat creeps into my cheeks. "You cheated on me. I can't think of anything worse."

He takes a deep breath and shoves his hands into his pockets. "Why would you tell Prince Alexander we don't treat our employees properly? You know, better than anyone, that's not true."

I take a deep breath and go into the open kitchen, behind the island to get a glass of water from the fridge. What did I tell Alex? My memory of that night isn't as clear as I'd like. Didn't Alex already know the McGuinty family violated employment laws?

"Why would you tell all those people out there that we're getting back together?" Defending myself over something I can't remember is impossible. "We're not getting back together."

Derrick grimaces. "I made a mistake with Janessa. She stuck her hand down my pants and started talking dirty. I just"—he shrugs his shoulders—"fell into an old habit."

"What's the old habit? Fucking your ex-girlfriend on your current girlfriend's bed?" I raise my eyebrows.

"It's not going to happen again."

"You're right," I say, "because we're done." Instead of waiting for a response, I head to the wardrobe and drawers. The suitcases are in the bottom level storage, so I grab some reusable bags from the kitchen and start stuffing my clothes into those. "You couldn't even get my suitcase? You knew I was coming."

"I don't want you to leave. We can work this out. I was hoping we'd talk. One slipup doesn't have to break us. You moved here to be with me. I made a mistake. We can work this out. Come on, Rory. We're going to get married."

I flash my bare ring finger at him as I pack. "No ring. Lucky escape on my part."

He grabs my elbow. "If you need to get back at me, I'll give you a pass on the prince. Okay? If you've fucked him, I don't care. Or if you want to fuck him... I can... I can accept that as your revenge."

My laugh comes out stilted with disbelief. "I almost died. I could have *died*. You haven't asked me how I'm feeling or if I'm okay. You're not worried about me; you're worried about *you*. How you look, how you appear."

He runs a hand through his short hair and says nothing.

"My concussion is serious. The car is totaled."

"Yeah, we'll have to work something out with my parents about the vehicle since it belonged to the golf course. But it'll be fine. I already told them we'd cover the insurance deductible."

I suck in a sharp breath. Was he always this dense? This stubborn? "That's your primary concern? The *car*? An insurance *deductible*? If I went over the cliff with the car, would you be wondering how much you had to *pay*?"

"Look, Rory. You're angry right now. I get it. I do. If I'd walked in on what you saw, I probably would have beat the shit out of the other guy. It must have been awful for you." He splays his hands wide and gives me the puppy-dog eyes that used to make me melt. "Janessa has been all over me since we moved to the island. She's a weakness, but seeing you walk in the door the other day was a moment of absolute clarity. I fucked up, but I love you. I love you. Just you."

Something about the way he says it makes me wonder how many times he succumbed to his *weakness*. My phone beeps in my pocket as I shove more things into my bags. I take it out, and there's a text from a number I don't have in my phone. Puzzled, I stare at it for a second until the words register.

Sent Kane back early. He's coming up the rear staircase to help you pack. Dumbass Derrick proved true to his name. Not sure you should be alone with him.

Relief rushes through me, and I'm heading to the door before the knock sounds. When I tug it open, Kane is there with a bag.

"I understand this is yours?" Kane lifts a large suitcase which isn't mine but is far better than what I'm using.

The urge to hug him is almost overwhelming. Whether I should be hugging Kane or Alex, I'm not sure. When Alex wants something done, it happens. I've never known a man who was able to direct life so smoothly, even from a distance.

"Thank you!" Marching back to Derrick, I sling the suitcase onto the bed. I heave armfuls of clothes into the suitcase while Kane and Derrick look on. From the bathroom, I stuff my toiletries bag with everything essential. Whatever I leave behind doesn't matter at this point. Away from Derrick is my objective.

"Rory, are you really going to leave like this? We're not going to talk this out?" He tries to tug me into his arms, and Kane tenses. "Come on, babe. We've been together for two years."

The *babe* grinds on my memory of the other night, and I grit my teeth. "There's nothing to talk about." Two years of my life, down the drain. The reality of how deeply, how epically, we've failed hits me, and tears sting the back of my eyes. I ruined my relationship with my father for this, for him. I alienated my family and friends for him.

Maybe I *should* go home. Grasp the life my parents planned for me with both hands and hope I never meet another Derrick.

I pause my packing, a T-shirt in my hand, and close my eyes. Was he always like this? So self-absorbed?

Derrick takes my silence as consent, and he drags me against his chest.

"Don't." I shove him and throw the shirt into my suitcase. "Just don't." I press down on the lid of the suitcase, and I try to tug the zipper closed, but there's too much in the case.

Kane comes to my shoulder. "You press down. I'll zip."

Between the two of us, we wrestle the case closed while Derrick does nothing but stare at us with his hands in his pockets.

"I'm not giving up on us, Rory." Derrick follows us to the door. "Whatever I have to do to get you back, I will."

With a sigh, I whirl on him. "All you had to do was keep your dick in your pants. That's it. Cheating is a hard line for me.

Once or a hundred times, it wouldn't matter. We can't come back from this."

I drag my keys out of my pocket and place them in his hand. There's nothing left for me on the ring—every single key, from the apartment, to the car, to the golf course is a string to Derrick.

When I close the door behind me, the last tie between us severs. There's a weird ache in my chest—not heartbreak, but more like disappointment. I had so much faith in us when I moved here, and this is how it ends.

"Follow me." Kane leads us toward an emergency exit door with my suitcase at his side as though it weighs nothing. He must work out. "The car is at the bottom of the stairs."

"Thanks." A deep shuddering breath escapes me.

A weight I didn't allow to settle while I rushed around my former apartment rests on my chest. No matter what happened the last two years, I had Derrick.

Now, I really am on my own.

Fifteen

ALEX

I pause the video and rewind it on my computer. How many times have I done this? I've lost track. How much of my day has been wasted rewatching Dumbass Derrick cock up the one thing he was asked to do? Not something I intend to calculate. I've never been this distracted by a press conference gone wrong.

Who can't remember two words? "No comment" is not a hard phrase to master. My brothers and I have been saying it since we were old enough to speak.

We needed the two of them, together, and for her leave out the back exit while everyone waited for her at the front. Let the press infer what they wanted from the long, limitless visit.

Royal PR was precise on the sequence. Press snaps photos of Derrick and Rory. No comment from both. They disappear upstairs. Kane picks her up at the emergency exit. A perfect diversion from their obtrusive questions about me and Rory.

The narrative would be turned into a discussion about cheating, taking back an ex, and whether Rory and Derrick had reunited and not about what was brewing between me and the Canadian.

To some extent, the reunited exes appear to have become the story, but I hate how it's come about.

In the video I've memorized, Dumbass Derrick has his hands all over her. But the part I keep rewinding is where she curls into him as though he's a life raft in a stormy ocean. The person who almost literally dumped her into the sea isn't a savior. Rory understands that, doesn't she?

My assumption, based on my own ethics and the few conversations I had with her, was that she wouldn't take him back. The Crown was subtly building a false narrative about Rory and Derrick so she could live and work for us largely in peace.

Except now my brain is in overdrive, wondering whether she might reunite with him, whether she wants to take him back. I rewind the video again.

Kane reports to my parents until the coronation, which is a year from now. I couldn't grill him about Rory's trip to the apartment. His text telling me Derrick wasn't following the narrative was him doing his job. The interference I ran after that could raise the king's and queen's eyebrows even farther. Another lecture about royal duties, protocol, tradition, and not leading on vulnerable women isn't on my agenda again for the rest of my life. No way I'm penciling in another diatribe from my parents because I can't prevent this protective instinct from swelling, crowding out everything else in my life.

Desmond knocks on the door before entering. This meeting is on my calendar, but I've done so little today, I lost track of time. Yesterday, I didn't let myself get sucked into Rory's orbit with Desmond and Kane as my buffers.

This morning I couldn't resist seeing what people were saying, and then I took a peek at the press conference. My brief tangent was hours ago, and I've circled back over and over.

"I have not been very productive," I admit.

He takes a seat across from me and flips open a notebook on his lap. "You're fishing for a conversation I do not want to have." Desmond gives me a pointed look. "Tonight, you're meeting Poppy George for drinks at the back of Camden Pub."

I rub my face. "Can I hit pause on this wife bullshit until I return from Europe?"

"Europe is also the *wife bullshit*. Your coronation is less than a year away. Before you can become king, you must be married. Before you can be married, you must have a partner. Before you can have a partner, you must find one. I'm concerned we'll be down to the wire at your brother's wedding with no *suitable* woman in sight."

"There's that word again," I mutter.

We sit in silence for a beat. We both know I'll go to the meeting with Poppy and that I'll make an appropriate effort to gauge her interest and intentions. The monarchy comes before any tantrum I'm tempted to throw. Whoever I decide to offer a marital contract to, they'll understand they aren't getting either of the charming playboy princes, but me. The more serious one. The one with the weight of the country on his shoulders. There will be no illusions about love or romance. Instead, I offer wealth and influence.

"I heard you bought some new luggage." Desmond sighs.

I perk up at the opening he's given me. "I did. Did you happen to hear how that purchase went?"

Desmond flips a page in his notebook. "Yes, I went to see her this morning, as you requested. Yes, she was upset about her visit with her ex-boyfriend yesterday. Yes, she's taking her medication for her concussion. Yes, she's feeling much better today in comparison to the other days." One side of his lips quirk up. "She also makes an excellent cream tea. If I keep visiting her, I'm going to get fat." He levels me with an intense stare. "No, you do not need to see her yourself."

I frown and shift my gaze from his. "Hadn't even crossed my mind. My plate is full, and I don't need to add her drama to it."

"We can all agree on that." Desmond nods. "Do you want the prep material for Poppy?"

I hold out my hand across the desk, and Desmond slides a folder into my palm. "Duty calls."

"Just close your eyes and think of Bellerive." There's a hint of a smirk on Desmond's face before he rises and heads for the door. "I'll have your itinerary for Europe firm for tomorrow. A few appointments needed to be rearranged. We can go through the prospects in the afternoon."

"Before you go," I say, and Desmond turns to face me again. "Your meetings with Rory are between us. Do you understand?" Unlike some of the other employees, Desmond has more to gain by being loyal to me.

Desmond purses his lips. "She's lovely, but you're playing a dangerous game. You shouldn't need me or anyone else to tell you that. I've never given your secrets to anyone before, and I'm not about to start now."

"Is Poppy my last appointment before I leave for Europe?" My working hours are filled with the press tour to give the public accurate information for the referendum and fulfilling coronation items on Julia's list. In four days, I'll be in European countries meeting royalty in hopes of finding a wife. Neither of those brings me any joy. It must be possible to have a single aspect of my life that doesn't feel like work. One piece, one person who has no connection to my duties or the monarchy or being a prince, is all I need. A wedge of normalcy, just for me.

"Poppy is your last matchmaking date until you return from Europe and we decide to dig deeper into Bellerive society or make an offer to a royal," Desmond agrees from the doorway.

While I am prepared to accept my clinical, emotionless marriage, I hate dwelling on the details. "Dr. Bennett is checking on Rory tonight?"

"He went to see her this afternoon. He's pleased with her progress. She went to the concussion assessment center today, and she'll go again before she begins working in the kitchen."

"Excellent. I'm glad to hear we're taking care of her."

A small smile touches Desmond's lips, and he shakes his head. Since we've worked together for the last eight years, we're in tune. His warning about Rory will go unheeded, and we'll both pretend that's not the case.

After all, no matter what he believes or the current king and queen think, I'll be sitting on the throne within the year. They'll bow to me.

My meeting with Poppy proves to be a bust. She's four years older than me, and she came highly recommend by the elder Secretary Jensen. Her family are well-connected and own several wineries here and across the world. In our discussion, she was ambitious in the wrong ways. She kept drawing us toward monetizing the Bellerive Royal brand. Maybe she thought her progressive ideas might win me over, but as far as I'm concerned, the Bellerive Royals are political figures first and tourist attractions second. I want someone seeking to make a difference in the world, not someone who wants to make money off it.

When I returned to the estate, I told Kane I was going for a walk rather than heading to my wing. Now, I'm standing outside Rory's ground-floor cottage door, and there's a knot of anticipation mixed with dread in my belly. Bad idea or not, I'm carving out my slice of life away from the royal obligations.

Before I can second-guess myself, I knock.

"Coming!" Rory calls from inside.

She opens the door, and the sight of her blond hair in a loose braid, her green eyes wide with surprise, and a broad grin on her face causes my heart to kick. I rub my chest with the heel of my hand, and I don't take my gaze off her pleased expression. There's an exuberance to her that creates an answering lightness in me.

"I wasn't sure you'd ever come back."

"I couldn't get the taste of your cream tea out of my head." I gesture behind her. "May I come in?"

"Oh God. Yes. Come in. It's basically your place, isn't it? Are you officially my landlord or is that your dad?"

I scratch the back of my head. "The estate sort of functions as its own entity. Technically, every member of the royal family over the age of eighteen can make decisions about tenants and other equally boring things." Vanilla, butter, and sugar hit me as though she's spent the day baking delicious things. Do these scents seep into her skin like a natural perfume? If I ran my lips across her skin, would she taste like the world's best dessert? I can't remember what she smelled like when I held her in my arms, but if I close my eyes, I can recall the weight and shape of her cradled there.

"I doubt I could ever find any of it boring." Rory takes the scones out of a container and removes the jam and clotted cream from the fridge. "The last one, Your Highness." She presents it to me on a plate with a mock flourish.

I shrug off my suit jacket and roll up my sleeves. "Desmond will be devastated."

Rory chuckles. "He's warming up to me, or maybe he's just warming up to my cream tea. In any event, he seems to like me better when I'm feeding him."

"How are you feeling?" I've been scanning her face for any sign of pain since I arrived, but she has more color in her face, and her expression doesn't have the tightness it did the last time I saw her. Without the dull veneer of discomfort coating her, her youthfulness is startling.

"Much better. I went to the Concussion Clinic today with Dr. Bennett, and they're confident I'll be feeling good in two weeks if I follow the guidelines. You'll be happy to know the only things I've read in the last few days were text messages."

"Isn't there an app to have them read to you?"

"So you want me to read through a list of apps to find one that'll read my texts to me?" She raises her eyebrows.

My lips twitch with holding back a smile. I grab my plate and head to the couch. She drops onto the other end so we're facing each other. At the first bite, I remember why I had to leave so quickly last time. These are delicious, but more than that, there's an ease between us I want to sink into. Two days ago I was intent on fighting our connection, and now I'm here, unwilling to resist her pull.

"Were you still working?" she asks, drawing her knees into her chest. She digs her toes into the space between the cushions and rests her temple on the back of the couch.

"I had a late meeting." The rest of the truth goes down my throat with my scone. Could I trust Rory with royal secrets? Despite the draw I have to her, we've known each other a few days.

The Crown has no intention of revealing why I'll marry. A wedding will happen so a coronation can happen. The press and the public can make their assumptions and draw their conclusions. The only people, as with most aspects of royal business, who'll ever know the truth will be immediate family and employees involved in the process. Rory isn't in either of those categories, and confiding in her is a risk I can't take.

"You had late meetings, and I baked brownies." She glances over her shoulder at another container on the counter. "They're actually a brownie and a cookie combined. I was messing around in the kitchen today because not working is boring." She purses her lips. "Working too much is also boring."

"Are you trying to imply I'm boring?" I take another bite of scone and eye her across the space between us on the couch.

She laughs. "No—maybe that you work too much. You're practically running a country, so I guess that's a dumb thing to say. I'm probably extra sensitive given everything that's happened with Derrick and his family and my family."

"Tell me about it," I say.

She takes my empty plate and goes to the kitchen. "Brownie?"

I pat my stomach and wonder whether Desmond and I will be sporting pastry bellies by the time Rory is done with us. Guess I should follow Nick's lead and schedule workouts into my days. "I'll try one." She must have an amazing metabolism to be so slight with all these calories at her disposal.

She plucks a square off the top for her and me and then reseals the container. "Do you really want to know about me and Derrick and his family?"

"Yes," I say.

She passes me my dessert and settles into the couch across from me. Without further prompting, she opens her life as though it's the most natural thing in the world to tell the Prince of Bellerive her secrets.

Her words flow over me, some hitting harder than others, but the whole time she's speaking, I can't take my gaze off her expressive face. Every emotion she feels is writ large. She must be a terrible high-stakes game player. Her happiness, sadness, and frustration flit across her features unguarded.

"You haven't spoken to your parents in almost a year?" I take another bite of brownie and suppress a groan. This chocolate chip-brownie concoction is sinful.

"My mom sent me a text after my accident." The corners of her mouth turn down, and her chin trembles. "Better than nothing, right?"

My parents, constantly in a tug-of-war with their role as monarchs, would have flown across the world and slain literal dragons for me if I was in serious trouble. Rory almost goes over a cliff and she gets a *text message*? The surge of protectiveness comes again unbidden.

"Nothing from your father?" I raise my eyebrows. While I'm tempted to point out how deeply flawed her parents are for being so obstinate in the face of her almost death, we don't know each other well enough for that. Also, by the wobble in her chin and the thickness of her voice, I suspect she's aware her parents are shitty.

"No." She shakes her head and avoids meeting my gaze.

Rather than digging deeper, I take the hint she's done discussing them. "Derrick thinks he can win you back?"

Her jaw tightens before she faces me again. "So he says. I could never be with someone who thinks cheating isn't a big deal. He tried to brush it off like he ordered an extra dessert at a restaurant. Called her a *weakness*."

"Hmm." I mull over her answer while trying to discern the best way to bring up her body language in front of the press without seeming creepy or jealous. "Do you know many people on the island?"

She laughs. "No. Derrick's family. The employees in every department of the golf course. Some of his friends from high school. No one I would call a friend, unfortunately. That was part of my panic when I left the apartment. I didn't have anywhere to go that wasn't tied to him."

"Everyone who works in the kitchen here is ancient; they've been with my parents forever. But Julia's sister, Posey, is a few years older than you. I can connect the two of you if you want?"

"So," Rory says with a hint of a smile, "you've found me a job, an apartment, and now you're going to get me some friends?"

When she puts it like that, she makes it sound as though I'm running her life. Maybe I am. I spend my days making big decisions for an entire country. Getting her Bellerive experience in order is more pleasure than pain.

I hold up my empty hands, the brownie long gone. "Merely an offer."

She searches my face, and there's a softness around the corners of her eyes. "Who would ever believe that totaling a vehicle and almost falling off a cliff to my death would be the best thing to happen to me since I landed in Bellerive?"

Her candor takes me by surprise, and I shift forward, closing the distance between us. "Is that a yes to meeting Posey?"

"How do I repay you? You don't need my money." She splays her hands out. "Though, I mean, I'm going to pay rent or whatever." She flushes. "And that was not—I'm not suggesting..." The redness in her cheeks deepens.

A slow grin spreads across my face at her discomfort. She's adorable. "I'm not looking for that sort of payment anyway." I wink.

She covers her face. "Oh God. I cannot believe I just implied that you—" She shakes her head. "Why would you ever need—I should stop talking now."

Her embarrassment elicits a genuine laugh from me. She peeks out from between her fingers.

I inch closer to her on the couch, and I tug her hands from her face into mine. "There is one thing I'm in genuine need of," I admit.

She meets my gaze, and I'm struck by the deep-jade shade. How is she so lovely?

"Name it," she says with confidence.

"I have very little in my life that isn't linked to the monarchy in some shape or form. My life is my job, and my job is my life." When the corners of her eyes crinkle, I continue, "Boring, I know."

She presses her lips together, but the edges turn up. "I can't imagine your life is *boring*."

"I'd like a slice of my life which has nothing to do with being the future king. When I'm with you, I'm Alex instead of Alexander, and I haven't felt like him in a very long time." There's a chance she'll turn me down, but my instinct tells me that whatever is stirring in me is in her too. "I'd like us to be friends."

"Just friends?" Her voice is breathy.

Somehow, one of us has inched even closer, and when I breathe out, my breath stirs the tendrils of her blond hair that have fallen against her cheeks. I'm tempted to brush them back, cup her face, and kiss her deeply. The urge is primal, instinct more than thought, but I'm used to suppressing my urges.

"That's all I can offer." Desmond and my mother might be right about this path being dangerous, but if I'm clear from the start, neither of us will want something we can't have.

She keeps focused on me as she leans forward. She kisses my cheek, her lips lingering on my stubble. Everything in me longs to press her back into the couch, to eat up her lips with my own, to test my theory about the way she'll taste.

She draws back, and our gazes meet.

Does she realize how turned on I am? A simple kiss on the cheek has never been so fucking hot.

"I'd be honored to be your normal slice of life." Her voice is husky.

Despite how appalled she has appeared at being my mistress, electricity jumps between us. If I kissed her, would she stop me?

My phone buzzes in my pocket, and reluctantly I put some distance between us. When I remove it, there's a message from Desmond with a schedule change for tomorrow. We're meeting about potential wives first thing in the morning.

The reminder is exactly what I need.

I clear my throat and rise to my feet. "Duty calls." I grab my suit jacket off the island and open her door. "I leave for Europe in a few days, but if it's okay with you, I might stop around at the end of work this week, if it's not too late."

"Something for me to look forward to." She smiles.

Before I can second-guess myself, I brush my lips against her temple, and she curls her fingers around the lapel of my jacket, keeping me close. The action tugs at my heartstrings.

"Rest up," I say. "I need you in the kitchen making the rest of my family fat so they won't notice how round I've gotten."

She seems to realize she's holding onto me, and she lets go with a self-conscious laugh. "You'll give me a big head."

"It's a lovely shaped head. Even twice its size, that wouldn't change." I step backward into the night, and the warm island air closes around me.

"I would look rather strange with a head twice the normal size," she says in her terrible British accent.

I shake my head.

She beams in response. "I sense a side hustle coming on. Two words. Accent lessons."

"Three words." I hold up my fingers while she leans against the open door. "Noise-canceling headphones."

Her delighted giggle follows me down the path as I head to the palace, and I rub a hand across my chest, surprised at the glowing warmth the fading sound inspires.

Sixteen

RORY

Every night since our friendship chat, sometimes late, sometimes early, Alex has sent me a two-word text. Each time the words 'you up?' light up my phone, my heart kicks and then gallops. A cool sweat breaks out under my armpits, and whether I'm in bed or puttering around the kitchen, my response is always 'yes' because any other answer is unfathomable. He is the highlight, the gleaming spot of brightness, in an unending day of semi-boredom.

Walks across the property alone have given me a chance to explore, but I often feel like an intruder in someone else's life. There is a series of barns on the other side of the sprawling palace, but I haven't had the guts to check them out yet. What sorts of things do royals keep? Pets? Livestock?

If I ask Alex, there's a fifty-fifty chance he'll answer. He's capable of evading a direct question like no one I've ever met. Must be the politician in him. He prides himself on being blunt and direct, but I've come to realize he picks and chooses when. He reminds me of a designer puzzle—meant to be solved once by someone special enough to crack him. What will I find inside if I'm lucky enough to pry the door to his inner self open?

Tomorrow, he leaves for Europe, and he told me he wasn't sure he'd have time to stop by tonight. I've picked up my phone a thousand times already even though I realize he's never texted me before dinner. On top of that, he doesn't send random chitchat throughout the day. I get the two words and my chance to head down this path with him that, when he's not around, feels dangerous and exhilarating. But when he's within sight, I'm thrilled and intrigued.

There's a knock on my door, and I answer it, expecting Desmond. Other than my one visit with Julia and Brice, Desmond is my only regular guest. But it's not Desmond, and I don't actually know who it is. There's a cool breeze across the island today, and she's dressed in jeans and a thin pale-pink sweater. Her light-brown hair is secured in a high ponytail.

Is she a worker? Something about her appearance is familiar. She's standing behind a cart laden with flowers, boxes of chocolates, and a larger cardboard box.

"Oh, hey, I'm Posey." She gives an awkward wave. "I think you've met my sister? Julia? Alex sent me. Said you could use a friend."

I close my eyes and suppress a groan. "He *said* that to you?"

"Don't worry," she says with a laugh. "I'm used to Alex. Also—I'm sort of an expert on the royal family and their staff." She winks. "Stick with me, and you'll know who to avoid."

Despite my embarrassment, I can't help returning her exuberant smile. While Julia was kind but serious, Posey possesses the same air as Brice. I realize my impression of Julia isn't complete because I've seen photos of her laughing with Nick in the papers with a joyous teasing similar to what Posey is giving me now.

"I could use some inside information," I admit.

"I'm your girl." Posey points to herself. "But before I'm that girl, I seem to have turned into a delivery person? These were in the front entrance, and after some grumbling, Alex agreed to let me bring them. Apparently, they've been accumulating the last couple of days?"

I cock my head, and I scan the cart again. Flowers. Chocolates. Rollerblades? "It was my birthday a few days ago." Who would possibly send me these gifts to the palace? A few of Derrick's friends texted me, but I haven't responded to anyone. I'm not even sure what to tell people about my current situation. Eventually, I'll be working. For now, I'm living, quite literally, off the royal estate's charity. Better known as *Alex's* charity.

"Maybe that's it," Posey agrees. "Can I wheel this in? I'll take it back when I leave."

I step away from the entrance to let her push the cart into my tiny space. She butts it against the closet. There's a card perched in the first set of flowers, and the seal is unbroken. Why would Alex keep this from me? I'm puzzled as I rip open the card.

Not giving up, babe.

He didn't sign it, but the *babe* makes me sure it's from Derrick. Each card has a similar message. Nothing about my birthday. No direct apology. There are a series of veiled "take me back" and "stop being unreasonable" comments. I sigh.

"Not about your birthday, I take it?" Posey asks from the couch.

"Ah, no. My cheating, non-apologetic boyfriend." I frown. "*Ex*-boyfriend."

"Did he buy those Rollerblades too?" She crosses her legs and angles herself toward the door.

"You know," I say, thinking out loud. "It's weird. He hasn't texted or called me, but he's having things delivered to the palace? Doesn't that seem weird? And why would Alex keep everything from me?"

"Alex holds everyone to a very high moral standard, and he can be very protective of the royal estate. His little tryst with my sister in high school is probably the only time in his life he's taken the road less traveled."

My eyes must be huge because there's no way I'm hiding my surprise. Alex and Julia? "He dated your *sister*?"

"Oh geez." Posey twirls her ponytail around her index finger. "Alex is going to murder me." She chuckles. "Or Julia might murder me. Their relationship was brief. Not well known. But a *total* mistake. I only found out years later when Alex seemed weirdly fixated on her and Jules revealed the truth."

This revelation makes a lot more sense to me than I would have expected. Whenever Julia has come up, he's hesitated in saying her name, as though even speaking about her is uncomfortable. The thought of him with her, of him hooked on her, causes my stomach to dip.

"Anyway, I'm supposed to be here telling you other people's secrets, not *their* secrets." She jumps up and comes to the cart. "He bought you Rollerblades? Who is it again?" She fingers one of the cards without opening it.

The Rollerblades are the only gift that indicate Derrick and I dated for two years. Surprisingly thoughtful. Did someone help him pick these out? They're even the right size.

"Derrick McGuinty," I say.

"Ooo. A McGuinty. Huh." She appraises me again. "The family is weird, but Derrick is hot. I dated a few hot, damaged guys in university." She gets a wistful expression on her face, and then her gaze narrows. "That kind of man is much better in fiction. Know what I mean? It's like tiptoeing through a minefield in real life."

"Hot, damaged guy..." Her label resonates with me. "Derrick is more like a hot, selfish guy."

"That's a form of damage though, isn't it? Something isn't quite right up here." She taps her temple. "To want to treat your partner like shit?" She crosses her arms. "Thank God I outgrew that phase."

"You have a boyfriend?"

"Brent, yeah. He's from Bellerive, but he's in America training for the Olympics."

"Must be hard—long distance."

"It is, yeah." She hesitates. "But I also sort of really enjoy my freedom? Relationships come in all shapes and sizes, and this one fits me best."

"Derrick was a good fit." Months ago I would have said that statement with more conviction. But we've been fading for a while, and I didn't want to face it. The cost of coming here was so great and to fail... was Janessa the problem or were he and I doomed from the start?

"Was he?" She picks up one of the cards and turns it over before wincing at the message. "I mean, I think it's possible to love someone and realize they aren't good for you at the same time. Love isn't rational or reasonable." She points to herself. "Front row seat to the Nick and Julia show, right here."

I laugh. "You don't think they're good for each other?"

She grins. "No, they are. They are. *Now*." She takes a deep breath. "She's definitely going to kill me later if you mention I've been telling royal secrets."

Except she hasn't told me much at all—brothers dating the same woman and a tumultuous relationship. None of that seems too terrible as far as family secrets go. The reminder of Alex and Julia causes my stomach to clench.

"Okay, getting back on the right foot. Give me your Bellerive wish list. Brent is here this week, and I've taken vacation, but he works out four hours a day, sometimes more. Those hours are yours."

"Oh, you don't have to do that. You've probably got things you want to do with your vacation time."

"Yes, I do. I want to amuse you. Play tourist across Bellerive, which I haven't done in forever. Alex said you've spent most of your year working. That's criminal." She's thoughtful for a moment. "Actually, I think that *is* a crime."

I can't help the laugh that slips out. "Alex tells me it is. Several crimes, apparently."

"He'd know." She puts her hands on my shoulders. "What do you say, Rory? I can show you that Bellerive is actually a lot more fun than Dull Derrick led you to believe."

"We're calling him Dumbass Derrick, just for reference."

Posey lets out a hoot of laughter. "Does Alex call him that too?"

"It was *his* suggestion." Somehow I know that's not an Alex thing to do, and the return of the assessing glint in Posey's eyes tells me I'm right.

"Huh. Interesting. This is all *very* interesting." She makes a circular motion with her finger. "You gave me the nickname for the ex, so does that mean you're in for a Bellerive adventure?"

I nod. "Yeah, I'm in. Thanks. This is—this is really kind."

Posey loops her arm around my shoulders and draws me into her side. "We're going to be great friends. I can already sense it."

Turns out, Alex isn't just skilled at running a country, he's also found me someone who already feels like a genuine friend.

The first person, other than him, who I've experienced an instant kinship with.

While Posey continues peppering me with questions about places in Bellerive I have yet to see, my mind strays to Alex.

How did I get so lucky to end up in his orbit?

ALEX

My fingers hover over the keyboard on my phone as though threatening to detach from my brain. Yesterday, I told Rory I wouldn't have time to see her before I left.

I lied.

She agreed to be my friend, but from the moment her lips lingered on my cheek, I haven't been able to stop thinking about her in ways that are anything but friendly. The air around us crackles with sexual tension the instant we're within reach of each other. Despite my efforts to keep distance between us, she's dismantling my walls one question at a time.

How can someone be bad for you and so good for you at the same time?

Even if there wasn't the issue of her being Canadian, she's ten years younger than me. That's an age gap I specifically rejected when we were narrowing my wife criteria. Five years in either direction was the most I was willing to concede. On top of that, our lives have been so different. Me, a prince in charge of a country. Her, a farm girl who bakes.

If I'm honest, that's part of the appeal. She's so open with her life experiences, as though she's never learned to put up any walls or airs or played pretend with anyone. From the routines of a milk cow farm to her college exploits, she's answered every query with unabashed sincerity. She is a joy, an absolute joy to be around, and I'm sucking up every ounce of it. A leech attached to an angelfish.

Tomorrow I leave for Europe, and when I return, I'll be forced to narrow my choices for a wife. We're just over two months out from my brother's wedding, and I agreed to bring my future bride there to let the public and press *ooh* and *aah* over the woman who will be their queen.

Will there still be room in my life for Rory after that? By my calculations, as long as we remain just friends, I can keep her for the year until her visa runs out and my coronation is finalized. My slice of normalcy. A bright, glittering diamond in the drudgery of everything I must do.

There's a knock on my office door, and Brice pokes his head in. "You all set for your whirlwind wife tour?"

"All packed." I gesture to the seat across from my desk and toss my phone onto the surface. Texting Rory is a bad idea in a list of terrible notions where she's concerned. "How are you?"

"Yeah, I'm okay." Brice shrugs.

I search his somber face. "Somehow I don't think that's true. What's really going on?"

He runs a hand down his face, and his shoulders slouch as though weighed down. "I was visiting with Alzheimer's patients today, and I had a round of PR for the referendum. Just a shit day, you know? I used to feel sorry for those families when I went to visit. What would it be like to have someone you loved so much completely forget you? Awful. Abso-fucking-lutely awful. And here we are. If the referendum doesn't succeed, that'll be us. The lucid days become fewer and fewer. A king reduced to a childlike existence. If we're lucky, we won't get the irrational rages, but if we're not, we won't even recognize him. It's fucking terrifying."

I lean back in my chair and run a hand through my hair. Am I surprised he's more afraid of the disease than our father's death? Perhaps not. I haven't spent the same time with patients and families. Of the three of us, Brice is intimately acquainted with what's ahead for us. Most days, I try not to think about it. There are so many pieces we need to slot into place before I can consider our father's mortality. I can't imagine sitting with it on a regular basis. At the moment, I can barely handle the present, let alone the future.

"The referendum will pass," I say. "We're polling at sixty percent. That's a decent margin, even if we're not voting until after Nick and Julia's wedding."

"What if we don't succeed? What if something happens and it all goes to shit?"

"If our father, if the *king*, is adamant about taking control of his... of his death, there are places we can go, things we can do." Despite our father's insistence that he wants to die at home, I wasn't confident in the referendum plan when he laid it out. Yes, the Advisory Council was a split decision on the issue, but we could have broken the tie. Leaving his life-or-death outcome to a public vote seemed foolish to me. We could make the result what he wanted—why chance it? I almost overruled him. But his argument that being the sovereign meant we weren't allowed to be selfish put the issue into perspective.

Beyond my father, there are many people in the country who'll have a view on the subject. As leaders, we give Bellerive our best, and the correct path includes the opportunity for debate and a vote. Love, family, life, and death unite us all, and my father believes an issue tied so closely to those fundamentals deserves an open discussion.

He's a better man than me. I'd have grasped the outcome I wanted. What's the point in having power if I can't exercise it once in a while?

Guess I'll have to work on the instinct to wield my power as I see fit.

"Would he do that?" Brice's voice is thick.

As the youngest, he's been the peacemaker, the comic relief, the one Nick relies on, but our father's disease has rattled him to the core. I'd love to lie to him about our father, and I suspect he wants me to. Truth and reassurance are the only things I can offer.

"He'll follow the will of the people," I say. "He's accepted his role as the center of this referendum. Everyone on the island realizes they're voting as much in regards to their king as they are about a member of their own family."

"I don't understand how anyone can vote no on this."

I chuckle. "Ask Nick. He only recently changed his mind."

Brice shakes his head. "Asking Nick to explain himself might talk him back into his previous point of view. No thank you. I'm enjoying all of us being on the same page for once."

"I can set up a panel, if you want? See about getting a televised debate?" I purse my lips. Not ideal given that a skilled debater could sway people in the wrong direction. "Or we keep going as we are. The press, social media, and local outreach. The more people we can speak to personally, the more connected everyone on the island will feel to our cause, to our situation, to the king himself."

"No." Brice shakes his head. "No public debate. You're right. I got cold feet today when so many people were asking me about the odds of success at the facility." He meets my gaze. "Christ, Alex. All this is going to be yours in a year."

Another reality I try not to dwell on unless it's convenient. While I'm already doing most of the job, I rely on my father for advice and an additional perspective. When he's unable to offer that, I hope I'm ready.

Will I ever be ready?

"Prepared since birth." The response might be glib, but Brice doesn't need to hear my conflicted feelings when he's deep in his own. Though I told Nick I wasn't prepared for the responsibility, that was more to extend an olive branch to him than how I truly feel. There's no doubt in my mind I can do the job. The real conflict resides in what I sacrifice to accept it. Not that I haven't been giving most of those things up my whole life. Freedom, privacy, choice. The other side of the scale is power and influence, and for most of my life I have accepted that those gains must balance the loses.

Brice rises and shoves his hands into his pockets. "It's okay to let your guard down once in a while. Nothing bad will happen if you let a crack of emotion through."

That is where he's wrong. Once a dam breaks, the deluge ruins everything in its path. The fortress I've built around myself protects me, but it shields everyone else too. There are some things in life that can't be changed, and I've learned to accept that faster and better than anyone else. I don't have time for wasted emotions and overblown feelings.

"I'm not built like you and Nick. If I must withstand something, I do. Can't dwell on what cannot be changed."

"For the record, this arranged marriage clause is bullshit. Sorry I haven't offered better options. I find it hard to take the whole thing seriously."

A more classic Brice response. Why take something that'll literally dictate whether I can become king of Bellerive *too* seriously? "Desmond has advised me to close my eyes and think of Bellerive."

Brice chuckles. "That's funny, actually."

"If you want me to keep you up-to-date on polling data, I can ask Desmond to include you in those briefings."

"Would you?" He gives me a hopeful look. "Be nice to sleep better again."

"Consider it done." I rise and clap him on the shoulder. "It'll be all right." Except we both know, ultimately, it won't be. We're losing our father—one way or another.

He nods and heads for the door. "Good luck in Europe. While I realize you aren't after what Nick and Jules have, I hope you find someone who supports you in the right ways."

Then he goes and throws out a tidbit of wisdom, and he grows up right in front of my eyes. He oscillates between being the most helpful and the least helpful on a daily basis. "I'll let you know when I figure out what that looks like."

Brice grins and waggles his eyebrows. "Maybe you'll discover love at first sight."

Rory's image rises in my mind, and I let her linger there before shoving the thought aside. "Sounds a bit too romantic for me. Tolerable to me and good for Bellerive. No point in creating a bar no one can reach."

He searches my face for a beat. "See you when you get back." He draws the door shut behind him, and I turn on my heel, staring at my phone. The right course of action is clear.

I have an early flight.

Rory cannot be anything more than my friend.

Keeping a sliver of distance between us is the right thing to do.

Rory answers the door, and the familiar pleased grin spreads across her face. My willpower not to text her only lasted five minutes after Brice left. When Rory messaged to wish me a good trip to Europe, instead of being consumed by guilt since she doesn't know *why* I'm going, I longed to see her. Could anything keep me away?

"Moonlit walk?" I ask.

Her gaze sweeps over me, and she bites her lower lip. "You're not wearing a suit."

I chuckle. "I do own other clothes."

"You were wearing jeans and a T-shirt the morning I woke up, but otherwise you're always in a suit."

"I usually come from work. Do you want me to go back and change?" I throw my thumb over my shoulder. Who knew dark gray sweatpants and a white tank top would send her into a lust spiral? The sexual tension zips between us. My hands itch with the desire to bury themselves in the blond strands of her hair, and my lips tingle with the need to angle my mouth over hers, to discover how deep vanilla and sugar mingle on her body.

"No, I—" She shakes her head. "A walk sounds good." She closes the door behind her and falls into step beside me. "Posey came to see me today. Turns out your pity friendship might work out all right."

I laugh and examine her profile. "Oh? You liked her?"

"She's honest in all the best ways."

"There are *bad* ways of being honest?"

"Selective honesty." She gives me the side-eye. "Where you give the details you feel like giving and avoid the rest."

"I feel attacked." I clutch my chest in a joke, but my heart speeds at the truth in her words.

"You should."

A hint of a smile tugs at my lips. Posey is the easy conversation. We can save my trust issues for another day. "I've known her all my life. She took up Julia's rebellious mantle when she dropped it. So beware."

"What's that mean?" Amusement spills out of her. "Julia used to be a rebel?"

"A bit. More with Nick than anyone else. Once she took the secretary job, she, I don't know, became more sensible. In high school she and her mother butted heads a lot."

"Posey mentioned you two dated."

I scowl. "She must have misunderstood my explicit instructions on suitable topics of conversation."

Rory hits my arm. "You did not give her a list of conversation topics."

"I did. I don't need her loose lips sinking Bellerive's ships."

"Whatever gets sunk, you suggested Posey as a friend."

"Yes, I may need to reconsider my endorsement. She's clearly a bad influence already."

Rory laughs.

"How's your head?" I ask.

"Better. Much better. I don't have to watch the clock until I can take more painkillers."

We walk in silence for a beat, and then Rory turns so she's walking backward just ahead of me. "How come you didn't tell me Derrick was flooding the front entrance with gifts?"

I purse my lips. When Posey found them and offered to deliver them to Rory, I debated telling her she couldn't. But that would have raised Posey's suspicions even more, so I gave a curt nod and left her to it. "Would you have wanted any of it?"

A smile somewhere between annoyance and delight seesaws across her expression. "The Rollerblades are nice."

"Are they?" I raise my eyebrows. "Don't know anything about Rollerblades."

"You're not going to answer my question?"

"Did you ask a question? I must have missed it." I shove my hands into the pockets of my sweatpants to keep from drawing her closer. The joy she takes in everything, from teasing me to discussing Rollerblades, to baking in her kitchen, is contagious. While I recognize her point about me not giving direct answers to her questions, I don't know how to be open and honest with her and not slide into a relationship we can't have. With her, more than anyone else I've ever known, a crack will lead to a flood. Of that, I'm one hundred percent sure.

My evenings, here with her, are by far my favorite part of any day. To allow myself any further examination of her, of us, would steer us into the red zone. I'm quite happy here in my bright-orange potential circle of doom rather than dipping into full-on hell. Having her, even with the understanding I can't ever *have* her, would be torture. We're not meant to be, and I am no masochist.

"Come on," Rory cajoles. "Give me this one."

The reason I held Derrick's offerings is perhaps the most dangerous. I want him gone from her life. He doesn't deserve her, and he's the type of man, when given an inch, he'll take a mile. "You can do better than Derrick McGuinty."

"He's spending his not-so-hard-earned money on me. I would have liked to know. The only thing he got me for my birthday was infidelity."

"Ah yes, the gift of infidelity. The classic two-year anniversary is cotton, in case you didn't know. Clearly, he did not. Very uncultured. Perhaps he was using cotton sheets on the bed? We could give him the benefit of the doubt. Were those new?"

Instead of hitting me in the chest, which seems to be her favorite move, she laughs and shakes her head. "You're ridiculous. It wasn't our anniversary; it was my birthday."

"I suppose you can consider your cart of gifts from the front entrance his *appropriate* present. I'll have anything else he sends returned unopened."

"A friend normally enjoys seeing a shitty ex-boyfriend groveling."

"Do they? Must have missed that class on friendship etiquette."

"Probably not a skill you were *required* to learn."

"Definitely not." I run a hand through my hair. "To be fair, apart from Julia you're my only female friend. Women tend to grovel differently when they're in trouble with a man." He winks.

"Oh?" Rory says with a smile.

"Friends don't let friends get blowjobs from crazy ex-girlfriends. Tends to be how that works." Even in the sharp overhead lights, her blush is obvious. I'm tempted to say blowjob again to see if her redness deepens. "This notion of flowers, chocolates, and Rollerblades is foreign to me."

"Men apologize with gifts instead of sexual favors," she says.

"Sounds bor-ring."

She slaps my chest and stops walking. When I almost run into her, she stumbles back and loses her footing. As she's going down, I loop my arm around her waist to keep her upright, flush against me. Her breath catches when she glances up, and I'm praying my sweatpants aren't revealing the effect she's having.

During our evenings together, I've avoided close contact. We can talk about anything as long as we're at least the length of the couch apart. But this—right here—is much too close. Just like when I hauled her out of the car, warmth floods my chest at her proximity, and that sharp pain just above my ribs returns. Being near her is equal parts painful and soothing. The strangest sensation.

"Are you all right?" My voice is gruff with need.

"You caught me." She's breathy with desire.

There's another surge of electricity between us. "I'd never let you fall." It's not a line. I mean it with everything in me. If I could shield her from the world, I'd do it in a heartbeat.

She melts into me, and we stare at each other for a beat longer than we should. The air around us hums, and she rises on her toes, her gaze never leaving mine. I should step back or step away. Heading down this path is madness. At the last minute, she shifts the tiniest bit to the right, and her lips brush against my cheek. I close my eyes and breathe her in, savoring the mix of sugar and vanilla that's seeped into her skin, a natural perfume.

"Alex." Her breath skims across my lips, enticing me to take more, to see whether she tastes as she smells.

How can one word have so much need and hope mixed in? She wants me, and God help me, I want her too.

But she's Canadian.

She's ten years younger than me.

Brief or long-term affairs are no longer an option.

I have to find a wife, and she cannot be it.

Leading her to believe otherwise is wrong. She deserves better than Derrick, and she deserves better than I can offer too.

With more willpower than I realized I possessed, I release her and take a step back. Neither of us speaks, and her confusion is written large across her face. What do I tell her?

"You feel it, too, don't you?" she whispers. "Like we've known each other forever. Tell me I'm not crazy."

I run my hands through my hair and entwine my fingers behind my neck. "I don't have the luxury of following every whim or feeling." The pain above my ribs spreads, crowding out the last of the warmth. "Friendship is all I can offer you."

We stare at each other in silence, and then I ease my hands down my cheeks. "I'll walk you back to your apartment."

"No." She shakes her head. "I'll walk myself."

"Rory." When she tries to walk past me, I grab her elbow. "You have to understand—"

"No." Rory places her hand on my chest. "I agreed to be your friend. You told me it couldn't be anything more. I guess I just..." Her fingers curl into my shirt, and I long to lean into the contact. "You've been here every night, and when we're together—it's like nothing I've ever felt before."

Her admission is a vise around my chest. If I were someone, anyone, else, I could seize her with both hands. I could ride this emotion until I figure out what it is without worrying about ruining her future, my future, the *country's* future. "I can only marry someone who is royalty or a native of Bellerive."

She gazes up at me in surprise.

"You're not crazy. I feel it, too, but we can't ever be more than this. For us to be more than this—" I clear my throat because I haven't allowed myself to consider the idea. "I'd have to give up everything else."

"Oh," she breathes out the word, and her surprise turns to shock. "*Oh.*" She releases my shirt, and as she leaves me, I trail my hand from her elbow to her fingertips, desperate to wrench her back. My muscles strain at being held in check.

She walks along the lit path toward her apartment, and an ache forms across my chest. This is all we'll ever be to each other—secret meetings loaded with sexual tension—and I wouldn't be surprised if she wants nothing to do with me when I return from Europe. Why would she want to be around me after my admission? Drawing closer together is foolish.

I take a deep, unsteady breath. Having her refuse my friendship will be for the best, since I'll be choosing a wife.

Even as I consider her rejection and my forced marriage, I realize I'll seek her out when I come home, that I'll do anything to keep the slice of normalcy she provides.

When I turned down West Shore Road a week ago, a hairline crack sprouted under the surface of my life. While sealing it up is the wise choice, I can't make myself do it. Like the night I found her, something deep and unknown propels me closer, demands I take notice.

Right or wrong, I can't leave her alone.

Eighteen

RORY

The engine roars, and my hair whips around my shoulders, my ponytail barely containing my long strands. The few pieces that have managed to escape flick against my cheeks, and I grin at Posey when we hit a small wave and the speed boat hops.

"Isn't this great?" Posey yells.

It *is* great. The sun is shining, and the ocean breeze is warm. Her boyfriend, Brent, is driving the boat to a shipwreck so we can snorkel with the reef fish. I'm slightly terrified of seeing a shark, but in the last six days I have learned I can't say "no" to Posey.

Her initial suggestion that we amuse each other while her boyfriend trained turned into me swept into her circle as though I'd always been there. After snorkeling, we're having drinks at a fancy bar in the middle of Tucker's Town. Brice is coming, so I won't feel like a third wheel. It's the first time I'll be out in public since Alex rescued me from the wreckage of my life, and

Brice's security is meant to protect him and shield me. Time has passed in such a weird bubble the last two weeks that my accident might as well be years ago. It's hard to believe anyone still cares.

Despite the flurry of activity Posey has swept me into this week, each night when I climb into bed, I stare at my phone willing Alex to text from Europe. I haven't heard a word from him, and I'm not sure I will when he returns either. Through Posey, I found out he's there for coronation business, but she didn't get into specifics, and I didn't ask.

I really wanted to pry. How could anything in Europe influence Bellerive's coronation?

Brent cuts the engine and drops the anchor. The rusty hull of the ship juts out from the ocean less than a hundred feet from us. He passes out the snorkeling gear and gives Posey a quick kiss on her temple.

"Know what you're doing, Wilson?" He tugs on the back of his flipper, and places I didn't even know had muscles ripple. He's an Olympic swimmer chasing Michael Phelps's records and medal count. "Since you aren't technically cleared of your concussion, Posey and I will stick close to you."

"Oh," I say, waving a hand. "I'll be fine." I haven't had a headache in a few days, and the bright sun isn't hurting my eyes. Although I'm no expert, I'm confident I'll be cleared tomorrow when Dr. Bennett takes me to the clinic.

"Rory is probably more worried about the sharks." Posey's grin is wicked.

"Sharks?" Brent frowns. "We'll be fine until the chum drops."

"Chum?" I'm sure all the color drains from my face.

Posey laughs. "He's joking. We're not chumming the water. Most of the ones out here are reef sharks. As long as you leave them alone, they're harmless."

"A harmless shark?" I raise my eyebrows before sliding my mask onto my face. "I'll stick with you two." Being around them has been a balm to my bruised, romantic soul. They radiate happiness together. Exactly what I want to have—a partner who brings me joy instead of heartache.

Brent chuckles and tucks his snorkel into his mouth. He runs off the back of the boat, his flippers slapping, and cannonballs into the ocean. Posey shakes her head.

"You can tell he wears fins far too often when he can run in them," she says. "Come on. I'll go over the back with you."

We slip into the ocean, and the minute I put my masked face under water, I try to contain my internal gasp at the sheer number of fish swimming around. While the hull of the ship is quite far away, the reef is only a few feet from us. Colorful fish swim around and slip in and out of holes in the coral. Posey motions with her hand, and I kick my feet to follow her.

We're the only ones here so far, but Posey and Brent said this is a popular place to snorkel. Would this be something the royals do? For some reason, I can't imagine Alex out here, and it makes me sad to think he wouldn't do these things or might not have time for them.

While we swim, I mull over the complexities of Alex. His declaration that he can never marry me should have stunned me because there's nothing overtly romantic going on between us. We've barely known each other a week. But from the minute I woke up in the hospital, there's been an intangible between us. A connection. A string. Pieces of us are woven together in a way I've never experienced with anyone else.

When I came to visit Bellerive with Derrick, this country felt more like home than Canada ever had. I associated my sense of belonging with Derrick and our relationship. So, when he suggested I move here with him after graduation, I was sure *he* was my fate. Bellerive was right, and therefore Derrick must be right too.

Except, when I was a child, I dreamt of the cottage I now live in. Vivid, visceral dreams I never forgot. As foolish as it sounds, I've wondered whether my gut reaction to the island was tied to Alex all along, even before I knew him.

How is that possible?

Such a silly notion.

A few days ago, when my head throbbed at regular intervals, I could pretend these fanciful thoughts were linked to my concussion, my trauma. Of course I wanted to believe a prince who rescued me could be my very own Prince Charming. Who wouldn't?

But the clearer my head gets, the harder it is to justify these notions. They're there whether or not I want them. I keep trying to talk myself out of falling in love with a prince, but it's not his status I crave. If anything, his notoriety is a drawback. Being lured into another family whose personal lives are tied so intimately to their livelihood is my worst nightmare. My family and Derrick's family are proof of the dysfunction. I shouldn't want anything to do with him in a romantic way.

Except when I look at him, I don't see a prince or his family. He's *Alex*. Stern, funny Alex. In my eyes, *Prince Alexander* isn't a real person. Alex is.

When we climb onto the boat later and put away our gear, Posey loops her arm around my shoulders. "Did you like that? You were pretty quiet."

"No, I loved it." I grin. "The massive shark Brent pointed out across the reef near the end almost gave me a heart attack. But it didn't eat me, so I'll put that in the win column."

Brent laughs at the front of the boat as he draws up the anchor. "Always a good day when no one gets eaten."

"Brice and Brent are going to chill out in Brice's wing of the palace while you and I get glammed up at your place. Sound good?"

For the millionth time, it strikes me how much better my life has been since Alex found my car. Many of Derrick's friends were nice, but none of them were ever mine. They were his, and they tolerated me.

Whereas Posey's friendship is a gift, quite literally from Alex, but nothing has been forced between us this week. She's introduced me to her circle of friends, and while every person is wildly different, they all exuded warmth and acceptance, just like Posey. "You are rapidly becoming one of my favorite people," I admit on impulse.

Posey grins and slides her sunglasses onto her face. "I think you're a gem, too, Rory. Honestly. Makes me so sad your year here has been so shit. Done right, nowhere in the world is better than Bellerive."

"I've got one more year, and the bar is set so low, I can't do any worse."

Posey nods. "We'll drink to that later tonight. To a second year that far exceeds the first."

"You ladies ready?" Brent asks over his shoulder, and his hand rests on the throttle.

Posey and I sink into the bench seat at the back of the power boat and give him the thumbs up. We roar away from the shipwreck. I stare out at the ocean, and for the first time in a long while, I'm consumed by contentment. *This* is where I belong.

Being in a group with someone as famous as Brice Summerset is like journeying to an alternate version of reality—similar to grocery shopping with his brother. When we arrive at the wine bar, we enter via a side entrance and an employee who was instructed to meet us there. We slink down narrow hallways until we get to another concealed entrance, which leads into the VIP area for the Wino Wine Bar. While the name isn't classy, the place certainly is. The décor is deep, lush colors, and the lighting is low. The three of them assured me there was no hotter spot in Bellerive for casual, expensive drinking.

We're led to a red leather couch and two black armchairs with a small coffee table between us. Everything in Bellerive is expensive, but when the wine menu we're offered doesn't even have prices listed, we achieve the next level of wealthy. If you have to ask, you can't afford it.

When it's my turn to order, I ask for water. Brice scoffs beside me. "You can't order water at a wine bar. It's illegal."

I peer at Posey for confirmation, and she laughs. "It's not illegal." She searches my face for a beat and then orders me the same wine as her and tells the waiter to put it on her tab.

On day three of our week together, she rooted out my financial troubles over scone making.

"I have my concussion assessment tomorrow," I say. "I shouldn't drink too much."

Brice waves me off. "No such thing as too much. Power through, Wilson."

Posey slaps him on the arm. "She needs to pass her assessment to be allowed to work. You're not going to be a bad influence tonight, or I'll regret inviting you."

"I invited myself." Brice smirks. "My specialty." He sighs. "It's great Nick and Jules are attached at the hip again, but I miss my partner in crime. He would have gotten drunk with me. Brent's training. Rory has a concussion. Posey, you're my only hope."

"We could have invited them," I say. While I've met Julia a few times this week thanks to my new best friend, I haven't seen Nick.

"Wouldn't have come," Brice says, accepting his glass of wine from the waiter. "He and Jules are chest deep in planning their honeymoon back to Tanzania to build a new charity initiative." His expression turns from open to concerned after he takes his first sip of wine. "Wilson, I'm giving you a blanket statement right now—are you ready?"

I meet his light-brown gaze and nod.

"Everything I say is confidential, royal business. You cannot repeat anything I say, ever, to anyone outside our circle. If I have been drinking, do not believe anything I tell you. It's all lies." He purses his lips and turns to Posey and Brent. "What else does she need to know if she's going to run with us?"

"She can't tell Alex what we get up to." Posey sips her wine and raises her eyebrows in mock innocence.

Brent chuckles and shakes his head. I've learned Posey's antics amuse him for the most part, but Posey said they were a source of frustration when they first started dating.

Brice snaps his fingers. "That's a big one. He's going to be king, and as much as he's my brother, he's also the future monarch. I do not need any lectures from him on top of the ones I receive from our parents."

"Alex is my friend," I hedge. The idea of keeping anything from him doesn't sit right with me. He's done more for me in two weeks than most people have done in my entire life.

Brice turns to Posey, but there's a teasing glint in his eyes. "We've got a spy amongst our lot."

Posey laughs, and Brent joins in.

"It's just—he's done a lot for me." While he might be teasing, I want him to like me. My greatest weakness is wanting everyone to like me. If he pushes much harder, I'll probably agree to keep his secrets against my better judgement.

"Don't worry, Wilson. I won't hold your allegiance to my brother against you." Brice takes another sip of his wine, and then he drags a deck of cards out of his jacket pocket. "Who's in?"

Brent groans. "I told you to leave those at home."

"They're my talisman. High card? I won't even make you play Truth and Tequila tonight."

Brent shakes his head but draws a card off the top of the pile.

"That's our cue to visit the ladies' room," Posey says, and she sets down her wine glass.

I follow her lead and slide my glass onto the small coffee table between us. She weaves through the other people seated in the VIP area.

"Rory?" A familiar male voice rises above the din of people talking.

I stall my step and turn in the direction of my name. Derrick is at the edge of a group of men who I recognize as investors in the McGuinty golf empire. A few of them I've met when Derrick brought them into the kitchen to sample "our" famous desserts.

Posey appears at my shoulder, and Derrick makes excuses to his group before striding over. He glances at Posey before grabbing one of my hands and lacing our fingers. Instead of drawing away, I'm stunned at the familiarity. In my mind, we've been broken up for ages, not just a few weeks. When Alex peered over me in the hospital room, a switch flipped, time reset.

"Have you been getting my deliveries?" he asks.

While I did get the things Posey delivered, I haven't gotten anything since Alex left. Did he put a stop to Derrick bribing his way back into my heart?

"Have you sent something recently?" I ask.

"Flowers, yesterday. Orchids." His brow furrows. "Did you get the Rollerblades at least?"

"I did, yeah. That was very thoughtful." A reminder of another time, another place, how we used to be happy together.

"I thought I would have heard from you by now." He stares at me expectantly.

Now it's my turn to frown. "What were you hoping to hear?"

"I've been asking for another shot or at least a chance to talk, face-to-face."

I withdraw my hand from his grasp and glance at Posey. "I don't think that's a good idea."

"Come on, babe. *Two years*. I think we owe it to ourselves to talk things out."

The image of him and Janessa in bed together surfaces. Who owes who? Did I realize our relationship was slipping away? Am I partially responsible for his betrayal?

Posey cups her hand around my ear. "Tell him Café Plutus—dinner. He pays."

She's suggesting the most expensive and exclusive restaurant on the island. It's not in Tucker's Town but instead perched on a cliff in a small town almost a thirty-minute drive from here. Derrick once told me going there was the equivalent of taking a lighter to his salary.

"You really want to make it up to me?" I ask. He'll never agree, but my request might put an end to this ridiculous notion that he cares. "Take me to Café Plutus for dinner to make up for the shittiest birthday on record. You pay, of course."

Derrick's eyes widen. "Café Plutus?"

Posey rests her arm on my shoulder. "*Babe*, you fucked up. It's Plutus or bust."

Derrick's jaw tightens, and he works his mouth as though grinding his teeth. "Their reservation list is long. I may need a few weeks."

"Perfect," Posey says, and she loops her arm with mine. "If you're still interested in making amends in a couple weeks, it'll be easier for us to believe you're serious."

"Us?" Derrick raises his eyebrows. "Since when do you two know each other?"

"Oh." Posey pretends to be offended. "You didn't know we were friends? Wow, Derrick. Just—wow. Clearly you were neglecting Rory far longer than I suspected."

My insides are rioting with the urge to laugh.

His gaze narrows, and then he chuckles. "You're screwing with me. Rory looks as shocked as I feel about your friendship claims." He shakes his head. "You want Café Plutus, Ror, I'll make it happen. I'll text you the details when our reservation is confirmed."

"Oh." There's no way I'm concealing my shock this time either. I expected him to say no. My request was supposed to put an end to his groveling.

"I made a huge mistake, and if Café Plutus is what it takes to make it right, then I guess that's what I'm doing." He shrugs as though it's not a big deal.

Spending that much money *is* a big deal to Derrick, but more importantly, he's fluffing off the emotional side of what he did. Since the minute I ran down those stairs, he's been trying to buy me back. Will he genuinely try to win me back? Or will we have dinner and he'll consider my loyalty paid for?

"Text me," I say, and I let Posey drag me toward the bathrooms.

"At least you'll get a nice dinner," Posey says. "You should take your own car, though. He clearly doesn't get that one expensive dinner or five hundred boxes of chocolates or even a daily delivery of orchids can erase what he did."

"It did seem that way, didn't it?" I say. "Like he expects us to be even after Café Plutus?"

"He's not ready to do the emotional work." She checks her appearance in the oversized restroom mirror. From her purse, she takes out mascara. "Emotional labor is the best gift you can ever give anyone. He's not there yet. But you'll find someone who is, and when you do, they won't need to take you to Café Plutus in place of a genuine apology." She slides the mascara back into her purse and takes out a lip gloss.

"That psych minor with your interior design degree comes in handy, huh?" I chuckle.

"I also really love self-help books." She shrugs and then checks the time on her phone. "All right. We need to go back and rescue Brent."

"Rescue Brent?"

"Brice will have ordered more alcohol by now, and despite his promise, he'll be trying to talk Brent into Truth and Tequila."

"What is that?" I ask.

"A game Nick and Brice play whenever they get sloppy drunk. They either have to answer a tough, intensely personal question, or take a shot of tequila. To say it can get wild is an understatement."

My mind darts to the questions I'd never want to answer truthfully, and I grimace. "Sounds awful."

"Welcome to the royal family, *babe*." She winks at me. "They're two-parts awful and one part amazing."

So far, my experience is three parts amazing. Other than our ill-fated trip to the grocery store, everything has been great. As we leave the restroom, my conversation with Derrick fully clicks.

"Did I agree to go on a date with my cheating ex-boyfriend?"

"You did," Posey says. "Don't worry. It'll take him weeks to get into Café Plutus. By then, he might have given up. Best evil strategy ever. He has to sit with his feelings for weeks—assuming he has any—before he gets to pour out his tiny, concrete heart. Between the money and the wait, Derrick will have to be serious about getting back together."

"Right," I agree as we reach our seats with Brent and Brice. Just as Posey predicted. There's a bottle of tequila in the center of the low table.

"Brice," Posey says with a hint of warning.

He chuckles and splays out his hands. "Brent says he likes you best when you're drunk. Who am I to deny him?"

When I take my seat in the armchair beside him, Brice grins.

"Alex returns tomorrow," Posey reminds him, and my heart kicks. "You're going to greet him with a hangover?"

"I am," Brice says. "He'd expect nothing less from me." He turns to me. "If you get cleared from your concussion tomorrow, when do you start in the kitchen? Desmond has been raving about your pound-packing concoctions."

That makes me smile. Desmond has dropped by to see me a few times this week without a noticeable agenda from Alex.

"Monday," I say. "I can't wait to start." Getting off the royal charity train I've been riding will be a relief.

He pours all of us a shot. "A toast." He raises his glass, and we follow. "To getting fat."

"No, no, no," Posey says, and she waves her hand to stop us. "We need to toast Rory's second year on the island." She raises her glass again. "To new beginnings. May your second year be impossible to forget for all the right reasons."

"Hear, hear," Brent says.

I stare at my shot for a beat before tipping it back. Her toast is already coming true. After almost dying, I predict this will be my happiest year yet.

Nineteen

ALEX

Denmark is a beautiful country, and Princess Simone is a beautiful woman. The soft lighting above us glints off her dark hair as she laughs at something her sister said. As with all the other "dates" I've been on in the seven European countries I've visited, we're surrounded by other people. Since I won't have the luxury of seeing any of these women multiple times before Nick and Julia's wedding, I've had to ensure our interactions are authentic. First we meet alone for drinks or a meal, and then I attend something informal at the palace. The two things that felt important to me were how we gelled in a one-to-one situation and her relationship with her family. Any open tension or hostility was an automatic no. My family doesn't need to inherit the drama. There's no way to know if she's the cause or a victim in such a short span of time.

The women were told I was hoping to make a match before the coronation but not that I *needed* to. No one likes the stench of desperation linked to marital bliss.

While royals are often raised similarly—country over personal wishes—I've been surprised at the warmth that's greeted me. The family dynamics have varied greatly, and some of the women I've had more in common with than others, but it hasn't been the painful experience I expected. Most of my interactions have been pleasant, if businesslike.

Despite the ease with which I've shifted in and out of countries and families, a portion of my attention has been eaten up with thoughts of Rory. Our first meeting has spoiled me for anyone else. I expected the same spark, a similar inherent protectiveness, to settle deep within me at the sight of one of these women. After all, if I'm going to marry one of them, they should at least match my immediate connection with Rory, shouldn't they? I've felt nothing of the sort. A touch of humor or a vague interest, but none of them have lodged themselves into my gut like Rory did the night I saw her through the car window.

Over the last week, I've hovered over my phone's keyboard more times than I can count, desperate to reach out to her and understanding I shouldn't. Will friendship be enough? The question has plagued me.

Marco, my personal assistant for the trip, comes over and whispers in my ear that it's time to take my leave. Before going to the airport to return to Bellerive, I asked to visit a jewelry shop my mother mentioned as a favorite. A gift for my mother—an apology of sorts for my erratic behavior. She and my father have been a team since they were teenagers, and his diagnosis has hit her hard. My recent behavior has added to her load, but I can't let Rory go. I won't. Not yet, anyway. When I have to, I will, but for now, I'm clinging onto her friendship, a lifeline in the roaring current of what I cannot change.

"Excuse me," I say to Simone's family. "I must get going or I'll miss my flight. Thank you so much for your hospitality and your openness in meeting with me."

"I'll walk you to the door," Simone says. She comes to my side, a tall, lithe figure. I imagine we must look good together—dark hair, dark eyes, trim figures—but when I gaze at Simone, I long for blond hair, jade-green eyes, and an open expression I can read like my favorite book.

At the door, she embraces me, and she gives me a kiss on both my cheeks. My heart doesn't skip, and my dick doesn't twitch at the contact.

Tolerable to me and good for the country. I can't afford to set a higher bar. Letting myself believe anything else is possible is foolish.

"It's been wonderful seeing you again," Simone says. "We were just kids last time."

Teenagers. I was nineteen, and she was only fourteen. I barely remember meeting her, but she assures me I left an impression on her. The five years is nothing now. Hell, I've been contemplating a *ten*-year age gap, something I never thought I'd do, for almost two weeks.

"I've enjoyed getting to know you." Not an *untrue* statement. "I'll be in touch."

Before she can say anything more, I let Marco and my guards lead me to the waiting vehicle. We zip along the streets of Copenhagen. Before long, we pull up to a concrete-and-glass store on a side street of the downtown core. My security sweeps the location while I wait in the car.

Since we called ahead, their staff have a back corner of the store ready for me to make my selection. Based on the criteria I gave them, they've pulled appropriate necklaces for my mother, and they're laid out on the glass case. As I peruse the options, I catch a glimpse of green through the glass. *Jade.*

With a frown, I shift the box in front of me aside, and underneath is an entire case of jewelry made with the precious gemstone. The shade reminds me of the prettiest eyes I've ever seen.

Rory.

I shake my head and chuckle. If I was the type of person to believe in fate, this jewelry case would be a sign. Even though that's not me, I'm drawn to a necklace in the back corner. A square of jade is surrounded by white gold and hangs on a matching box chain necklace. Simple but beautiful.

"I'll take this." My voice is husky as though I wasn't speaking to the associate only a moment ago. "And the third one from the left in the top row for my mother."

"Would you like them both gift wrapped?"

Rory's birthday was a couple weeks ago. Friends traditionally give each other presents. "Yes," I say. "Wrap them separately."

My phone vibrates in my pocket, and when I take it out, there's a photo text from Brice. When I open it up, my breath catches. Rory and Brice at Wino Wine Bar. She looks happy and sober, and Brice looks very, very drunk. My heart kicks, and a jealous surge causes my muscles to tense.

While I'm staring at the photo, remembering and then memorizing her face, cursing myself for leaving the country, my phone buzzes again.

Thought I should confess my sin before you came home. Posey, Brent, and I took her out last night. Doc cleared her of the concussion this morning. Maybe you already know.

Did anything else happen between Brice and Rory? If not, will it? He could be with her. Marry her. Give her normalcy and a royal existence. She wouldn't become a slave to the Crown and country like I am, like my wife will be.

Asking what happened between them would be in character for me, but the reason I want to know is not. I'm not preparing for a scandal; I need to ease the panic seizing my chest.

Desmond hasn't called me yet, but I'm sure he's been in touch with Doctor Bennett to confirm Rory can start in the kitchen on Monday.

Just drinks? I text him back before I can lose my nerve.

Drinks for me. Mostly water for her. She's a good girl. A winky face caps the text. Then another rolls in. *We were supervised the whole time, and I kept my hands to myself.*

A classic Brice response—part teasing, part serious—but it does the trick. My heart rate slows, and the cool sweat that had broken out under my armpits recedes. He was being his typical social self last night. Nothing more.

I shouldn't care, and who she chooses to spend time with shouldn't matter. All week, I've avoided making contact with her. But it's not because I don't care and she doesn't matter.

The associate returns with my wrapped gifts in a small, glossy bag emblazoned with the shop's name.

My stomach swirls with excitement at the thought of seeing Rory again. In a few hours I'll be back in Bellerive. After dinner I can sneak away and see her for myself.

Desmond meets me at the front entrance, clipboard in hand. "I trust you had a good trip back and enough time on the plane to formulate your shortlist."

"I don't even get a day to consider?" I fall into step beside him on the way to my office.

"Do you need a day?"

I sigh. The entire flight I made pro and con lists for all the women I've met over the last month. Seventeen women in total. Ten in Bellerive and seven while on tour. From there, I've narrowed it to three whose pros and cons were acceptable to me. As Nick claimed, I've done my best to keep the decision clinical.

"Your mother is already waiting in your office."

Of course she is. The bag from the jewelry store is dangling from my fingers and inside are two necklaces. They labeled them with a *J* for jade and the other with an *R* for ruby, my mother's birthstone. Trying to sort them out without my mother noticing will be a delight I hadn't anticipated. As we walk, I peer into the bag and locate the *R* one, and then I pass the bag with Rory's gift to Desmond.

"Pretend you asked me to pick up something for your wife if my mother asks."

"Your highness?" Desmond's face pinches in confusion before clearing. "Prince Alexander, we're literally picking your wife today."

"I'm aware." I leave it at that and stroll into the office. "Mother! Lovely to see you. I had a chance to stop at the jewelry store you love." I pass her the long, slender box.

"Oh, Alexander, you didn't have to."

I can already tell from her tone that I made the right call. She loves jewelry and is never without rings, earrings, necklaces, or broaches adorning her.

"I realize my behavior recently hasn't been typical, and I wanted to get you something to recognize that." Not an apology, exactly, since I don't intend to stop doing what I'm doing.

She gives me a shrewd glance before ripping off the paper. She unfurls the necklace and lets the light dance off the diamonds and rubies. "It's lovely. Perfect. I'll wear it to dinner tonight. We'll be celebrating your selection, I hope?"

I slide into my desk chair and purse my lips. "I've narrowed my selection to three." My mother hasn't even noticed the bag in Desmond's hand, but she definitely would have noticed it in mine. "You, Desmond, and Father can confer on who seems like the best choice for the country diplomatically and socially. They're equal in my estimation."

My mother drops the necklace into the box and snaps it closed. "There is no divorce. Are you certain you don't want a more active role in this decision?" She searches my face, and her brown eyes are hard with annoyance.

"The three I'm about to name are tolerable to me." I shrug. "Like any arranged marriage, we'll have to come to know each other during our marriage."

"I would think you'd spend time together prior to getting married," my mother says in exasperation.

"Why? What if spending time with her causes me to change my mind? What then? If we're married, I'm forced to make it work. If we're simply engaged, I might decide breaking the engagement is preferable to being married."

My mother's pale face loses its natural color, and she turns to Desmond in surprise. "Did you know of this plan?"

"I did not." Desmond's voice is tight. "It is a shrewd plan, if not a wise one." Over the back of my mother's head, he glares at me.

My plan has nothing to do with whoever I'm doomed to marry and everything to do with Rory. My mother might not have put those pieces together, but Desmond has been privy to conversations and interactions my mother has not.

She sighs. "We'll discuss how much contact you'll need to have with your future bride once we've chosen her and extended an offer. The public needs to believe this is real, and polling shows they much prefer the romantic notion of royalty marrying for love over some political arrangement."

"You married for love." Much like Nick and Jules, my parents fell in love during high school, but they didn't have the fourteen-year separation my younger brother and his intended suffered. My mother and father have always been excellent communicators. Not a skill they passed on to their middle child.

"We were very lucky to find each other young and to be certain of what we'd found. Your grandmother had a long and relatively happy arranged marriage to your grandfather. They can work if you invest in them."

I suck in a deep breath. That's my cue to lay out the three people who are tolerable and good for the country. I'll make the marriage work but not a minute sooner than I have to.

"Kara Samuels is the only woman of the ten I saw from the island who remotely appealed to me. That union would be complicated considering I dated her sister in secret for several non-exclusive years. But we are both open to it, and her parents are keen to land a royal." Since I never told them about Anna at the time, they've probably been playing catch-up on my association with her. "On my European Tour, Princess Simone of Denmark was satisfactory as was Princess Zuzanna of Luxembourg."

My mother taps her lips as her mind ticks. "We won't choose Kara Samuels. While her family is acceptable, we don't need the scandal should it come out you once 'dated' her sister." She makes air quotes around the word "dated" as though people still use those.

I can't help a brief chuckle, and I shake my head.

"Simone or Zuzanna. They're truly exactly the same in your estimation?" She winces. "I can't believe I just uttered that about your future wife. About my daughter-in-law. This conversation never leaves this room." She glares at me and then Desmond.

"Noted," I say. "They're exactly the same to me. Makes no difference."

"I'm not sure if I should be pleased or appalled you're so agreeable."

"Pleased," I say. "The alternative is an all-out revolt."

My mother laughs and then *tsks*. "You're not the sort to revolt. I hoped you might end up with a true preference."

"No preference," I say, and inside a tinge of sadness takes hold. A preference is emerging, but it's not one she'll want to hear, and I don't need to be told again it can't happen. "Whatever is good for the country is good for me."

"All right." My mother rises with her present from me clutched in her hand. "We'll confirm at dinner who we're offering a contract to."

"Excellent," I say, and I ignore the dip in my stomach.

She swishes out the door, leaving Desmond and me alone. He drops the bag in his hand on my desk, and then he leaves without saying a word. His action speaks volumes, but I can't bring myself to be annoyed with him for his silent rebuke. Instead, I rotate my chair so I'm staring out across the fields toward the estate apartments.

Up to now, my friendship with Rory has been ill-advised but not truly dangerous. Tonight when I go to her apartment, I'll have a future wife out in the world. Should I tell Rory? I've already said she and I can't be anything more than friends. It's impossible.

Her apartment and the time I spend with her are my only slivers of normalcy. If I tell her about the arranged marriage, a potential leak springs in the palace. Would she ever tell anyone? I doubt it, but part of the agreement with my future wife is absolute secrecy. As far as everyone else will believe, Simone and I or Zuzanna and I will be in love when we marry.

I press the heels of my hands into my forehead and draw them down my face.

I won't tell her.

For however long I can, I'm keeping her separate from everything royal. For a little while longer, I want to be Alex. Just Alex.

TWENTY

RORY

The day has been excruciatingly long, the sort of day that seems to be weeks in length instead of mere hours. When I went for my afternoon walk, I caught sight of Alex being greeted by Desmond at the front entrance. It's long past dinner, and he hasn't called or texted.

Maybe the night before he left was the end for us. Since we can't be more than friends, maybe he doesn't see the point in spending time with me?

But wouldn't he have understood the limits to our relationship when he offered his friendship?

If Alex never comes around again, he's much smarter than me. After a week away from him, there's a chance I'd follow him to hell if he walked through my door. Thoughts of him have invaded every aspect of my life. Despite Posey's attempts to keep me occupied, Alex is imbedded in the soil of Bellerive. Everywhere we went I wondered if he'd been there, what he thought of the place, the activity, the people. I got so used to picking his brain every night, even if he evaded some of my questions, that I longed to turn to him and ask his opinion. He'd have one—about everything.

I run my hands through my hair and check the clock on the wall again. It's almost midnight. He's never texted me this late. He's not coming. With my hands on my hips, I waffle between getting out my supplies and frustration-baking something or going to bed to toss and turn all night.

Baking.

Screw it. If I'm going to be awake anyway, I might as well make something. Brice told me last night he intends to order a sandwich on French bread on Monday when I start work, and there had better be the best French roll he's ever tasted encasing Joyce's, the head cook's, sandwich artistry. I don't doubt myself, but a trial run wouldn't hurt.

I'm dragging the flour out of the bottom cupboard when there's a crisp knock on my door. Leaving the cupboard open, I practically leap to the door, my heart hammering. There's only one person who'd come here this late and knock with such authority.

Alex.

Without checking the peephole, I throw open the door and melt in a puddle at his feet. "You came," I breathe out.

Each of his hands are braced in the doorway, a small bag dangling from his fingers. He's in a suit again, but his tie is gone, and his hair is disheveled like he's been running his fingers through it over and over.

When I'm done cataloging him, absorbing his appearance, our gazes connect. A zip of awareness shoots down my spine. How is it possible I've longed for him, someone I've known for a week, more than I've missed my ex-boyfriend of two years? Seeing him again releases the tightness harnessed across my chest.

"My memory did not do you justice." His voice is rusty, and the scent of red wine wafts toward me.

Warmth spreads across my body at the tenderness in his gaze. "You thought about me?"

"I bought something for you. May I come in?" He eases off the door to stand upright.

"You bought me something?" My stomach flutters. He thought about me while he was gone, and he bought me a present. Despite what he said before he left, all of this feels like something a boyfriend would do—or someone who wanted to be my boyfriend. This isn't friend territory, but I'm not saying a word. Maybe I can't ever have him forever, but I'll take him for now.

God, will I ever take him for now.

"Do I need to give it to you to gain entrance?" He cocks his eyebrows.

I give a little laugh and step out of the way. "Sorry, I just—I thought you weren't coming since I hadn't heard from you."

He sets the bag on the island and runs his hands along his face. "I'm jet-lagged, and I'm in a pissy mood. Wasn't sure I should come."

"Oh," I say, and I round the island. "I have your favorite brownies, if that'll help."

He chuckles. "Not sure a midnight brownie is going to solve my problems this time." He pushes the bag toward me. "Open it."

"What's this for?" Despite my resolution to take everything in stride, I can't help asking.

"You had a terrible birthday, and when I saw this, it reminded me of you." He shrugs.

I take the long box out of the bag and set it on the island. "My birthday wasn't *that* terrible." While I pry my index finger under the edge of the wrapping paper, I make eye contact with Alex and hope he understands what I'm saying without using the words. Sure my boyfriend cheated on me, and I almost died. But I also met him, and I'll never regret that.

A hint of a smile twists his lips.

There's no doubt it's jewelry, and my heart thumps heavy when I lift the lid. Inside is a jade necklace. "Alex." I clutch my hand to my chest while I suck in a sharp breath. "Oh my God. It's so pretty." I finger the square of jade and try not to dwell on how much it cost.

"Happy belated birthday," he murmurs.

My stomach flips, and when he comes around the island and takes the necklace from the box, I twist my hair in my hand while he secures the clasp. Over my shoulder, our gazes connect, and we stare at each other for a beat. I want to turn in his arms, frame his face, and kiss him long and deep. Then I'd wrap my arms around his neck and drink him in, savor not just this unknown connection between us, but a physical one too. What would he do if I did it?

Reject me?

Meet my hunger with his own?

"Thank you," I whisper.

His fingers linger on the nape of my neck, and I'm about to test my kiss theory when he steps back and clears his throat. "Have you used those Rollerblades you were so excited about?" He nods toward the box by the door.

I touch the necklace at my throat, a concrete reminder that whatever is budding and blooming between me and Alex, we both feel it. This feeling might never become fully realized, but I'm not alone.

"All the paths here are gravel," I say. "I haven't had the guts to go on the narrow roads outside the estate."

Alex frowns. "Agreed. That's not safe." He eyes me for a beat. "Get them. I'll take you somewhere."

"Really?" I circle the island to grab the handle on the box. "You know somewhere close?"

He chuckles. "Very close." He leads us out of the apartment and around the other side of the building. We cut across the fields, and the salty ocean breeze stirs the trees around the edges. "You got cleared of your concussion?"

"I did. Dr. Bennett told you?" Whatever doctor-patient confidentiality is supposed to exist doesn't seem to matter to him. I haven't minded Alex keeping tabs on my progress. It's been nice to have someone care.

"Brice. Texted me." He glances at me. "Sent me a photo of the two of you at the Wino Wine Bar."

I shake my head. "He told me I couldn't tell you any of our exploits and he rats himself out?"

Alex chuckles. "He does it all the time. Asks for forgiveness rather than permission. Such as it is to be the youngest."

There's an edge to his teasing tone. Rather than pressing him for more details, I follow him around the edge of the palace in silence. I haven't been on this side of the estate, preferring the fields and cliffs.

A double tennis court and a full-size basketball court are laid out in front of us, a stone's throw from a side exit to the palace. Smooth asphalt waits for me to cruise along it. Alex hits a button, and the barriers between the courts slide away, leaving a large, open space in its place.

"Wow," I say. "That's incredible."

"You can come here whenever you want. We used these a lot as kids, and Nick still plays tennis a few times a week with his trainer, but otherwise, they don't get much use."

On the bench beside where Alex is standing, I take off my shoes and lace up the Rollerblades. Once I'm set, I push off onto the smooth surface and sail around a few times before attempting some twirls and a little jump.

"Figure skater?" Alex crosses his arms at the edge of the courts when I whizz by.

"Yes!" I come to a stop in front of him. "One of the few activities my parents let me do as a kid. I still love it. I didn't realize Bellerive wouldn't have a rink."

"Only at the Christmas Festival. Did you go last year?"

I grimace. "Working," I admit. "McGuinty's ran a stall in Tucker's Town to drum up memberships."

"They really took advantage of you."

I skate in a slow circle near him, going wider and wider while I contemplate his words. They did take advantage of me, but I let them. "Work always came first in my house growing up. We didn't take vacations like other people because then we needed someone to run the farm. So it took me a long time to figure out Derrick's family was asking too much of me." I skate backward and repeat the circles. "Shouldn't have, looking back on it. They never asked as much from him. Shouldn't they have expected more from him? I mean..." My mind drifts to my own family. "My parents always demanded more of me than they did my younger brother, my friends, or my boyfriends."

Alex chuckles. "Not sure I'm the best one to comment on parental expectations."

"Why not? You have two younger brothers." I come to a stop in front of him.

"Your parents had different expectations for you as opposed to your brother?"

I roll my eyes. "He's a boy, and the youngest. He could have girls in his room. He could go out drinking with his friends. He played hockey at a high level, and they never worried he wouldn't get to his barn chores. They never gave him a hard time about anything. Joined the army right out of high school. The one thing they weren't sexist about was the farm. Oldest is supposed to take over." I point to myself. "Except I fled the country, so they don't speak to me anymore."

"Seems harsh," Alex says with a frown.

"Feels it too." I push off and fly around the perimeter of the courts. The warm ocean breeze presses against my face, and my loose hair trails in a long stream behind me. The speed, the salty taste of the ocean air, and the familiarity of skating bring me such peacefulness, that I don't consider how late it's getting until Alex flicks his watch around to check it.

He covers a yawn with his fist, and I pause in front of him. "You're tired?"

"Jet lag," he says. "You skated a lot as a kid? Compete?"

"Yeah, I competed. Loved it. The rest of my life was basically the farm. My parents even took me to see Stars on Ice."

He squints in confusion. "What's that?"

"Famous skaters performing."

"Who's your favorite?"

"Oh gosh." I roll to the bench and plop onto the seat beside him. "Virtue and Moir. Ice dancing. So fast and precise. And just, like, gorgeous. I was desperate for them to be dating in real life." I laugh. "Who doesn't love a fairy tale?"

"Indeed," Alex says, and his gaze is filled with amusement. "Anyone else?"

While I undo my second Rollerblade, I consider my options. "Kurt Browning. Oldie but a goodie. Excellent storyteller."

"If I come round tomorrow night, will you show me some of your favorites?"

I glance at him in surprise. "Really? You want to watch figure skating with me?"

"You object?" His eyebrows lift, and there's a hint of a smile tugging at his lips.

"No," I say. "Surprised you'd want to watch it."

"My interests are wide and varied." He waves a hand. "And if it's something you love, I'd like to understand it."

Alex wants to understand something I love. He wants to spend time with me watching figure skating because it's one of my passions. Two of the things I love most—baking and skating—and he's willing to try out both. Is he going to buy me a horse next because I mentioned I missed horse riding? The urge to ask him how he's single when he's so freaking awesome rises to my tongue.

"Are you sure I didn't go over the cliff two weeks ago?" I shove my Rollerblades back in the box and seal it up.

"I'm sure. Why do you ask?"

We rise, and Alex hits the button to put the courts back in order. I can't tell him my comment has to do with his perfection. Talk about embarrassing.

"You don't have to walk me home," I say. "If it's safe enough for the future king to walk alone on the estate, I'm sure I'll be fine too."

He shoves his hands into the pockets of his pants and keeps pace with me. "Still, I'd worry. I'll walk you."

We head back to my place, and when we get there, Alex says, "I just realized you don't have a computer. I'll bring my laptop tomorrow night, and you can show me all your favorites."

"Alex," I say on impulse at the door. "I want to know you. The same way you're beginning to know me. Will you show me something you love tomorrow too? Only seems fair."

He searches my face for a beat, but I can't read his expression. "I'll see you tomorrow night." He leans forward, and his lips linger on my temple. He breathes me in, and my fingers, of their own accord, curl into his shirt. Then he steps back, and he runs his hand along the length of my hair before he lets me go to disappear around the corner.

TWENTY-ONE

ALEX

I 'm back in the king's office, but this time I'm not in trouble. Or at least not the kind they're aware of. A marriage contract sits on the edge of my father's desk, and my mother is at his shoulder, reading her own copy. I haven't picked it up—a small act of defiance, which is silly because I agreed to this weeks ago. Didn't have a problem with an arranged marriage. A means to an end. I need a wife to become king, so I'll get a wife. Simple.

I didn't see Rory coming. Had no idea she'd tip everything I used to believe on its head.

Desmond clears his throat beside me as he turns the page of his contract. Not subtle, but effective. I slide the contract off the desk and pretend to read it over. I should care—I should really, really care what's on these pieces of paper. For the rest of my life, I'll be bound by these words and clauses. But I skim over them like they're pebbles in an ocean. I can't force myself to believe in their weight and permanence.

Last night, I was in Rory's cottage apartment watching figure skating videos through the ages until the wee hours of the morning. Sitting next to her on a couch viewing a bunch of men and women in ridiculously tight, sparkly costumes should have been my worst nightmare.

Not even close.

Her enthusiasm and explanations will be added to my life's highlight reel. Listening to her espouse on footwork or a lift or the chemistry between the skaters amused me more than any conversation I had with anyone on my European wife tour.

Once she exhausted her favorite performances, she coaxed me into sharing my passion: cliff jumping. When I told her, she laughed. Not out of malice, but delight. She couldn't believe someone like me would enjoy such a dangerous, often illegal, sport.

Those afternoons Nick, Brice, and I spent at the cliffs as children were some of my best. No one was standing over us telling us to be better or think logically. A freefall over the edge into the clear blue below. I haven't been since I finished university. No time for such infantile pursuits now.

"They added a clause on page three," my mother says. "Did you see that, Alexander?"

I flip to page three and force myself to focus. A mistress clause. If I cheat, she can refuse to bear me an heir, and if an heir has already been conceived, she can cease all sexual contact. Right now, I couldn't care less, but I can't appear uncaring with this audience. The heir part is likely important. But realistically, if

I'm cheating on her, why would I be concerned with whether she refuses to have sex with me? Apparently others are willing, so I can't see how her withdrawal will bother me in the slightest. None of that can be verbalized with my parents present.

"Strike that out. Unless we're adding one about her potential infidelities, I don't like the implication I'll stray."

Desmond shifts beside me, and from the corner of my eye, I see his red pen hovering over the line. "Are we striking or adding a clause about her potential infidelities?"

"Striking," I say.

"Adding," my mother says at the same time.

Our gazes connect across my father's broad desk. She's clever, and I wonder whether she's thinking of Rory like I am.

"Strike it," my father says, overruling my mother. "Alexander isn't the type to cheat."

Oh, but I might become the type, might already be halfway down that path. I squeeze my thigh with one hand while the other grips the contract. The more time I spend with Rory, the less agreeable I am to this arrangement, even though I need it.

Desmond strikes out the clause with finality. The king has spoken.

I'm looking forward to the absolute control my father has. No more bartering with people. I want it. I get it.

"Page five," my mother says. "Her family would like three public meetings, either in Bellerive or Denmark, prior to Prince Nicholas and Julia getting married."

"No," I say. "We agreed we'd debut my intended wife at Nick and Julia's wedding. I'm not dangling her in front of the press before that." I toss the contract on the desk. "Strike it. We're bringing our *secret* romance into the light at the wedding. End of."

"If we're striking that," my mother says, "we need to add something in its place. She's asked for a meeting once a month after the wedding. Increase that to two?" She peers at me over the edge of the contract.

My father and Desmond might as well not even be here. Mother and I are engaged in a battle of wills. Without a doubt, she realizes I'm seeing Rory. Are these clauses Simone's family inserted or were they my mother's?

"If that's a concession you think we need to make, that's fine with me." Inside, I'm cringing. Once Simone and I go public, it will be next to impossible to maintain anything with Rory. Either she'll hate me, I'll hate myself, or I'll be so busy there'll be no room for her.

"Desmond, bump the monthly meetings to two when you remove the dates prior to Prince Nicholas's wedding."

With his red pen, he makes notes in the margin.

"Is that all?" I ask.

"You're not going to go through the contract with your usual thoroughness? This is the rest of your life we're discussing," my father says.

I suppress a sigh. My life up to now has been a series of compromises, so why should my marriage be any different? Whatever they put in the contract, I'll honor.

"I trust you, Mother, and Desmond will catch anything else unsavory. The wedding is a means to an end." I'm also done talking about the marriage I need but don't want. Before I realized we were having this meeting tonight, I promised Rory I'd be at her place for round two of sparkly outfits and high cliffs. She starts work tomorrow in the kitchen and intends to be baking at some ungodly hour in the morning. If I don't leave this meeting soon, I won't be able to see her. She needs her sleep for her debut as the royal pastry chef. I'm not taking the chance a single person will have a valid criticism of her hiring.

"We'll hold off a day to respond," my father says. "Take the contract. If you see anything else you don't like, let us know. It's all a negotiation, son. Don't be afraid to ask for what you want."

I stare at him for a beat, and then my gaze strays to my mother, whose eyes are narrowed. What I want, I can't have. "I'm getting what I want," I say. "A crown on my head." And the power that comes with it.

After a few hours of watching figure skating and cliff jumping, I left Rory's apartment last night. Now, only a few hours later, I'm back outside her apartment door in the dark. She told me she was nervous for her first day, so rather than letting her go to the kitchen alone, I've decided to walk her there.

I knock on the door and listen for her footsteps against the wood floor. When the door opens, her smile is delighted and confused.

"Alex, what are you doing here?" She's dressed all in white.

"Walking you to work."

"You didn't have to do that," she says, tugging the door shut behind her. "It's so early it's still dark out."

"Means I'll get all my work done early enough to hear about your first day later."

"Your work never ends." She loops her arm through mine.

She often tugs me around her tiny apartment from place to place, and I relish the contact. Now, in public, even if it's early and dark, I should discourage her from being so close. But I won't.

"This coming weekend is my father's birthday," I say. "Every year, there's an island-wide celebration."

"I remember." Rory squeezes my arm. "A huge party."

"The biggest and best part of the day takes place here. We have a ball in his honor. Your name will be on the guest list."

She releases my arm and lets out a little laugh. "I can't go. I work here. If I wasn't working, I still couldn't go. I have nothing to wear."

"My father's birthday is catered so the regular staff can attend if they wish." I examine her for a beat, but she won't meet my gaze. "Tanya will bring you a few outfits to choose from."

"I pay for them. Garnish my wages or whatever."

"Consider it a birthday present from me."

"Alex, my birthday was a few weeks ago now, and you already bought me a necklace."

"I meant my father's birthday," I say as though she's being daft.

"Traditionally, you buy a present for the person *celebrating* their birthday."

"Well, yes. But my father buys everything he wants. Instead, he asks that we do a kindness for someone else. This year, you're my recipient."

She stops walking and stares at me in the glow of the pathway lights. "I swear, if I find out you're lying to me..."

"You'll?" I prompt.

"Be *very* angry."

I laugh. "Oooh. *Very* angry. Sounds ominous."

She slaps my chest and resumes walking. "I want to say no, but I have no idea what people wear to royal birthday balls."

"Clothes, typically."

"You are exasperating sometimes." She grins up at me. "Fine. Thank you. I'll take your help and accept your invitation."

We arrive at the kitchen, and I let Rory in the side entrance. Joyce, the head cook, is here this morning to help Rory get settled. Normally, Rory would be here this early by herself. She said last night she covets the quiet and the large kitchen. Her Zen space.

I introduce Rory and Joyce. Despite the thirty-year age difference, the two of them strike up an easy banter over flour, recipes, and substitutes for various dietary concerns. I lean against the island listening to them while Joyce gives Rory a tour around the kitchen and pantry.

When they come out of the pantry again, Rory's lips twist with an amused smile. "I thought you said you were going to get an early start."

"Right, yes," I say. "Just going to make myself a cup of coffee." I wander over to the coffee machine and keep half an ear on their chatter. She seems to be okay, so perhaps it's safe to leave.

Her shoulder brushes mine as the coffee trickles into the pot. "I'm making French bread for Brice for his lunch. Any requests of your new pastry chef?"

I absorb the playful joy emanating from her and press my hands into the counter to stop myself from brushing my knuckles against her cheek. We've gotten used to casual contact in her little apartment—neither of us thinks twice about a graze here, a brush there. I need to keep myself in check.

"Bring me a cream tea at the end of your shift?" I suggest.

"Cream tea for one, coming up."

"Make it for two," I say. "Perhaps I can convince someone to join me." I pour myself a coffee and leave the rest of the pot for them. When I glance at Rory, her cheeks are a lovely shade of pink. My fingers itch to touch her.

"Cream tea for two," Rory whispers.

Not touching her is so much harder than I expected. If I don't get out of this kitchen soon, I'll make a spectacle of myself in front of Joyce, who is kind but prone to palace gossip. "Have a good day, Joyce," I call over my shoulder when I exit the kitchen.

Now to make sure my day is open when Rory's shift comes to an end later. My cream tea will only be satisfying if she's able to join me.

Twenty-Two

RORY

My week passes in a whirlwind of routine. Each morning I go to the palace kitchen before the crack of dawn to spend several hours baking. While the royal family is small, the kitchen feeds the staff members, and there are a lot of them. I'm slowly learning everyone's preferences and favorites.

My afternoons are consumed by cream teas, Rollerblading around the courts, or going for a walk along the cliffs. Alex told me where he used to jump with his brothers, and I've wandered past there a few times. Concealed from the palace, the drop is steep.

As soon as dinner finishes, Alex turns up at my door. Given all the time we've been spending together, the sexual tension between us should be dissipating, shouldn't it? But it's ramping up. A string drawn so tight, one pluck will break it.

His willpower is incredible. If I weren't so afraid of his reaction, I'd have kissed him by now. The obstacles are numerous. Ten years older than me, heir to the throne, and he's made it clear we can't be together. If I make a move and put a strain on our friendship, I'll never forgive myself. From card games to videos to baking to long walks around the property, Alex and I are never at a loss in each other's company. Being with him isn't just natural, it's exhilarating, as though I've won the lottery. I crave his company. He avoids answering many of my more personal questions, but our connection is more profound than words. Two halves of a whole.

The thought, though it's one I've had before, makes me shake my head while I walk to the main palace with my dress slung over my arm and my makeup bag clutched in my hand. Posey and Julia are getting ready for the ball in Nick and Julia's wing, and I'm to meet them there. Brent has gone back to America to resume training, so I am Posey's date tonight, or she's mine. In any event, we've agreed to be each other's plus one. Go girl power! Or something.

Posey drew me a map of the palace corridors and sent it to my phone. There are additional security measures in place, and I'm stopped several times on my way to Prince Nicholas's wing to clarify who I am and where I'm going. Luckily, I'm on some sort of list the royals provide to security, and after checking my ID, I'm allowed to continue onward.

At the door to Prince Nicholas's suite of rooms, another security guard uses an internal phone line to notify whoever answers on the other side. A moment later, Posey pops her head out the door and squeals.

"Oh my God. I can't wait to see what Tanya picked out for you. She has incredible taste." Posey ushers me into the corridor and through to a set of double doors that are thrown open. There's a sitting area, an abundance of empty floor space, and a king-sized bed where Prince Nicholas is gathering his things. Alex, Brice, and Nicholas are getting ready in Brice's wing, which has apparently become a begrudging custom. Alex told me when they were kids they each had rooms on the second floor of the house, but as they returned from university, they were given separate wings on the ground floor. Alex didn't seem excited but rather resigned to their tradition of dressing in the same area of the palace. I haven't quite put my finger on his relationship with his brothers.

"Rory, have you met Nick?" Posey asks.

Nick glances up from organizing what's on the bed, and his lips quirk into an almost smile. He comes forward with his hand outstretched, and as he heads toward me, I'm not sure I'm breathing. While his stint as a model is well-documented, he's ruggedly handsome. Beard. Dark-brown hair that's a touch too long. Tall. Taller than Alex. The kind of guy who looks natural in a suit or standing on top of a mountain. I might be having a fangirl moment.

My dry mouth isn't helped by my envy over how much he loves his soon-to-be-wife. To be loved like *that*. They are #couplegoals to the nth degree. Posey tells me their relationship hasn't been as fairy-tale amazing as the press makes it seem, but I'm unconvinced.

"Nick," he says, taking my hand. "You ready for this, Rory?"

I let out a strangled chuckle. "Oh yeah. Totally. I go to royal balls all the time. I've lost count of how many I've been to. The number has completely slipped my mind." I wave my hand as though this whole situation isn't anxiety producing. Posey is going with me, and Alex will be there. Nothing to worry about, right?

Nick snorts and tips his chin at Posey. "Alex puts up with her sass?" There's a teasing glint in his hazel eyes.

"Not only does he put up with it," Posey says, talking behind her hand, "he seems to *enjoy* it." When she turns to examine me, she must recognize the blush heating my cheeks. "She's refreshing."

"Nick," Julia says from the en suite door. "Are you and Posey ganging up on poor Rory?"

Nick casts a grin over his shoulder.

"Brice already took her out last week and tried to get her drunk when she was suffering from a concussion," Posey says.

"I was cleared the next day," I say. "And I didn't cave to the peer pressure."

Nick sighs. "Didn't cave? Did you hear that, Jules? I need to know what this sorcery is."

Julia emerges from the bathroom and runs her hand along his shoulders. "Speaking of bad influences, isn't Brice waiting for you?"

"Ah," Nick says, and he winks at me. "My cue to leave." He slides his hands along Julia's cheeks and stares into her eyes for a moment. There's that expression again—absolute adoration. Then he kisses her deeply.

I'm not sure where to look because their kiss is not brief, so I nudge Posey and tip my head toward the en suite. She grabs my arm and drags me over, a giggle slipping out.

"They could be at it for hours," she says, and she shuts the en suite door. "Julia can knock when they're done rubbing their sex life in our faces. I'd shout, 'get a room' but we're actually in it."

I sputter out a laugh. Posey claims she's cool with how often and long Brent is missing from her day-to-day life, but a few of her comments make me wonder. It must be hard to be with someone who has such a singular focus. One of the things I've realized in the last few weeks about my relationship with Derrick is that I never came first. His parents' wishes and desires came before mine, and often before his own too.

Never again will I have a relationship with someone like that. I want what Nick and Julia have—the can't-live-without-you, must-have-you-now vibe. Who wouldn't want an epic love story?

Julia returns, and the three of us chatter away while we put on makeup and get ready for the ball. When we're almost ready, Julia leaves to meet Nick and the rest of the royal family.

Earlier when I took my dress out of my bag, both Julia and Posey gasped. It's a floor-length gown in a deep green with a sweetheart neckline and capped sleeves. Tanya showed up at my cottage yesterday with three options. I didn't get to see any of them in a mirror, but Tanya made me try them all on. She picked the green one, but staring at myself in the mirror, I can't fault her taste. I look like I stepped out of a Disney movie thanks to Posey's makeup wizardry, Julia's skill with a curling iron, and this dress.

After a last swish of mascara, Posey grabs my hand and leads me through the corridors toward a side exit.

"Everyone has to arrive through the main doors and go through the king's birthday receiving line. It's tradition. You have to perform a deep curtsey to the king and queen—that's important. But for Nick, Jules, and Brice, you can just do a quick one. Those are more for show, and since we're all friends, no one is going to be picky about them."

I absorb her advice as we join the receiving line. She doesn't mention Alex, and I'm afraid to ask. Deep curtsey or cursory one?

When we get to the king and queen, Posey does a deep curtsey, and I follow her lead.

"And you are?" the queen says.

When I dare to glance up, she's focused on me. "Aurora Wilson."

Her gaze narrows ever so slightly. "I see." She scans me again. "I should have realized. Enjoy the party. Your cheese bread is the best I've ever tasted."

Warmth rushes across my chest at the compliment. "Thank you, Your Majesty." Then I chance a glimpse at the king. "Happy Birthday, Your Highness."

He chuckles. "Thank you, Rory. Don't let Posey get you into trouble." There's a teasing glint in his eyes so similar to Nick's it's uncanny.

Next are Julia, Nick, and Brice. Posey banters easily with them, but when we get to Alex, my breath catches in my throat. I've seen him in suits before, but tonight he's in a tux. In all the time we've spent together, I've never been with him when he's been at "work," and there's a noticeable difference in the air around him. A touch of arrogance, a tightening of his stature as though he could hold up the room by sheer force of will if it were to collapse around us. He's been my protector, my guardian angel, since he rescued me from the car crash, but tonight he's very much the heir to a country.

When our gazes connect before I curtsey, a shiver of awareness races down my spine. As I rise, he takes my hand and kisses the back of it, his lips lingering.

"You look exquisite," he murmurs before releasing me. "Enjoy your evening."

Posey loops her arm through mine and leans close as we hustle away. "The way he looked at you was..." She inhales a deep, exaggerated breath. "Wow."

I shake my head. "No, I—"

"Look back. Is he still looking? I bet he's watching you."

I steal a glance over my shoulder, and despite the person now in front of him, he is staring after us. His expression is impossible to read, but the air between us, even from this distance, hums. Whenever we're in the same room together, the whole world is more alive.

How long can this go on?

His attention is drawn away, and the connection wavers.

"Told you," Posey says, and she leads me to the bar near the back of the ballroom. While we wait for drinks, Posey seems lost in thought, and she keeps glancing at me. "Huh."

"What's that mean?" I take the Bellerive Blue, the local alcoholic specialty, from the bartender and raise my eyebrows.

"I always thought Alex was hung up on my sister. But he *never* looked at her the way he just looked at you."

Her comment makes my gut twist, but I'm not sure if it's from jealousy over the Julia comment or nerves at the realization other people can see what I feel around him. There's something there—something larger than life. Even if I wanted to, I couldn't control it. A splash of technicolor.

I'm becoming convinced we'll never act on it. For the rest of my life, I'll compare every other relationship to *this* feeling and find the sensation absent.

"Don't worry," she says with a laugh. "You say the two of you are just friends." She holds up her hands, her own drink almost sloshing over the edges. "Maybe you are. I'm not going to pry." She releases a low whistle. "But that look..." She takes a long drink. "I miss Brent."

"When do you see him again?"

"A few weeks. He's here for Nick and Julia's wedding at least, which is good. It won't always be like this. He's married to swimming right now, but someday, he'll be married to me."

"You don't mind waiting?" She hasn't given me many openings to question their relationship. I'll take them where I find them.

She shrugs. "It's not like he's Alex. At some point his massive commitment to something else will end. It has to. Age or interest will dictate he's done." She drains her drink and orders another one.

Her point about Alex is valid, and it's a truth I gloss over whenever I long for more of him. He speaks of work so rarely, and we spend so much of our time in isolation, it's easy to forget a whole country is tied to him. Alex is Bellerive. Bellerive is Alex.

"Want another?" Posey asks.

"No," I say with a shake of my head. "I work here, so I can't drink too much. No need to embarrass myself when they've been so good to me." I won't be able to keep up with her. In college, being a cheap drunk was a bonus. Hanging around the royals, being a cheap drunk will get me into trouble.

"Avoid Nick and Brice then," Posey says. "They love their tequila shots."

The rest of the night passes in a blur of dancing, drinking, and Posey introducing me to people I've never met before. Everyone wants to talk about my car accident, but Alex prepped me to make generic comments that say little in response to probing or overly personal questions. When he gave me tips, I never expected I'd have to use them. He understands the way his world works much better than I do.

Throughout the night, wherever I go in the ballroom, I'm aware of my proximity to Alex. Despite the dress, the invitation, and the *look* earlier, he hasn't sought me out. We haven't even made eye contact, and I'm starting to wonder if I've done something wrong. While I realize he doesn't want to fan the flames of gossip, we could be complete strangers.

As the night winds down, there's a deep sadness settling over my shoulders, and I'm sure I'll never attend another one of these if I have to pretend Alex and I are strangers, that I'm not closer to him than most of the people in this room.

Posey is on the dance floor with some of her friends from high school. She tried to drag me with her, but the longer the night goes on, the less enthusiastic I am. My evening has been wasted wishing for something, *someone*, I'll never have. A depressing thought.

I sense his presence beside me and catch a whiff of his expensive sandalwood cologne at the same time.

Finally. Relief rushes over me that he hasn't forgotten me, that's he's going to speak to me before the night is over.

"You're not having a good time?" Alex asks, and when I turn to him, he searches my face, curiosity and concern lighting his gaze. "Why ever not?"

"It's strange to be here and to act as though I don't know you very well," I say.

"Not a fan of playing pretend?"

"Are you?" Everything I've learned about Alex tells me at least some aspects of his behavior tonight are an act, a façade.

He stares at me for a beat, and our eye contact brings me another sliver of reinforcement. Without thinking, my fingers brush the necklace he gave me that's resting against my throat.

"I never used to mind putting on a front until I met you." He hesitates and takes a breath as though he's going to say more. With a shake of his head, he strides over to a nearby table. He tips back the last of his drink before sliding it onto the surface. There's an air of purpose around him when he comes back to my side just as the music changes.

"Let's give them something real then, shall we?" He takes my hand and leads me onto the dance floor. "Last song of the night."

Classical music streams out of the speaker system. The night has been a mixture of classical, current pop, and jazz with the lighting changed to match the tone of the piece playing. Something for everyone, I suppose. This song is definitely not for me.

"I don't know how to dance to this." I've watched enough T.V. shows about dancing to realize I'm out of my depth.

"I do." He gives me a cocky smirk. "A skill I was required to learn. I'm an excellent partner. Keep your frame. Follow my lead." He draws me in close, and I suck in a sharp breath at the contact. While we often touch each other, we rarely allow our bodies quite this much close contact face-to-face.

Then we're moving, gliding around the dance floor as though I have done this with him a million times before. My dress swirls around my legs, and I imagine we look impossibly elegant. Maybe he is an excellent partner, or perhaps some of my old figure skating instincts are surfacing, but the simple three count is easier to pick up than I expected. We move in sync with one another, and the heaviness that settled across my shoulders lifts with each turn around the dance floor. This—right here—is *real*. The connection, the ease, the sense of knowing.

"You're a natural," he murmurs.

"I've got an exceptional partner." A teasing smile rises to the surface.

"I'm sorry I didn't get a chance to spend more time with you," he says. "The job—the life—never ends."

"I understand," I say, even though I've oscillated between understanding and disappointment all night. "No point in feeding the gossip mills."

He gives a dark chuckle and glances around. "Yes, no point."

When he dips me low, I gasp and tighten my hold on his hand and shoulder. He holds me there for a beat, and our gazes are locked. We're so close his breath stirs the loose strands of hair resting against my cheeks. With very little effort, I could kiss him, right here in front of everyone.

But I wouldn't do that to him. My heart is threatening to beat out of my chest, and the awareness between us is so magnetic, I can't catch a full breath.

Slowly, he returns me upright.

There's a burst of applause, and I glance around, conscious of the people taking pictures or videos. Sometimes it's too easy to forget he's not just the Alex who comes to my cottage, but the man who will soon run this country. Tonight has been a glaring reminder several times over.

I give a nervous smile and run my hands along my dress.

"Thank you for the dance," Alex says before releasing my hand.

Then we're enveloped by people, and the heaviness across my shoulders returns.

Part of me thought Alex might knock on my door once the party quieted, but there's been nothing. No brisk knuckles on my door, no text message, and no acknowledgement when I left the ball with Posey.

My phone buzzes on my bedside table. From my position, Posey's name is lit on the screen. The evening, rather than being this amazing experience, was anticlimactic. Other than the five minutes I spent twirling around the dance floor with Alex, nothing else registered. I hated being in the same room as him and not being with him.

I understand that's a problem.

A big problem.

Friends don't feel that way about each other.

I'm not sure Alex and I *are* friends. But if we're not, what are we?

My phone buzzes again. Another text from Posey.

With a sigh, I snatch it off the nightstand.

You're trending. Check out the link.

She attached a series of links, and each one I click on causes my pulse to pound in my ears. Anonymous accounts have posted photos and videos of my dance with Alex. Once I get past the headlines about Disney princesses and fairy-tale romances, I click on the photo someone took of Alex dipping me.

Our gazes are connected, and even through the lens of the camera on social media, we look completely enamored with each other. The look Posey claimed she spotted on Alex's face when he saw me in the receiving line is there in the photo. Unmistakable. There is no doubt I'm important to him. It's not a trick of the light or the right angle. There are dozens of photos splashed across social media of our dance, and in every single one, we're looking at each other as though no one else exists.

He wanted to give them something real. Is *this* what he meant?

My phone buzzes again in my hand.

Derrick.

I click on the message.

Café Plutus. Next Saturday. They just called me with a cancellation. Can't wait to get a chance to explain in person. I miss you, babe.

Explain what? I literally caught him having sex with someone else. Is there a way to explain that? I'm tempted to cancel, but what is brewing between me and Alex is threatening to bubble over. Maybe a meal with Derrick will give me some perspective.

I toss my phone toward the end of my bed. Whatever Derrick wants, a reconciliation won't be in the cards. Wise or not, my heart now beats for someone else.

TWENTY-THREE

ALEX

The evidence of my folly is spread out before me, not that I didn't realize my mistake before I was summoned to this meeting with Desmond, the king, and the queen. As soon as our dance ended and what was left of the crowd applauded, I understood I shouldn't have been led astray by Rory's melancholy in the midst of my father's birthday party. Whether she had a good time wasn't my responsibility. I spent the entire night talking to people about the referendum and the coronation, while keeping half an eye on her. No matter where she was in the room, I could find her with a glance.

Her arrival at the ball in the green dress inspired the most intense sense of déjà vu I've ever experienced. As though she and I had lived the night before. So vivid and disorienting. A dream inside a dream.

The overwhelming sensation led me to avoid her most of the night. When I finally worked up the nerve to sidle up to her,

I couldn't stand how sad she seemed. To realize my avoidance had such an impact on her made me want to change the course of her evening.

If my parents can be believed, I might have changed the course of my life as well.

"It's a gossip rag," I say, and I toss the international magazine onto my father's desk. "Having the press say we're involved with each other doesn't make it so."

"We signed a contract with Denmark last weekend for a wedding in seven months. They called this morning to find out whether we were going back on our deal." The queen is in fine form. "I realize it may not feel like it, but you are engaged to someone else now."

"They should know better," I say. "Gossip and truth share very few markers." The engagement feels like a stretch even though it's true.

"The problem," the king cuts in before my mother can continue to rage, "is that this isn't the only outlet reporting a secret affair between you two. We don't need to know the details, but we need the relationship to cease."

"We're not engaged in an affair." Though, I'm becoming less opposed to that line of thinking when I should be appalled by it. Princess Simone of Denmark will be my wife within the year.

"Son." He holds up the cover of the magazine where Rory and I are locked into a dip, our lips dangerously close together. "This exchange between the two of you says otherwise. Anyone with eyes can see."

I run my hands down my face and sit forward. We aren't engaged in anything, but I can't disagree about the photo. The sentiment behind the picture is accurate. On the dance floor, no one else mattered but her. Her elevated importance is bleeding into the rest of my life, and I understand how dangerous that is—for me, for her, for the country.

"I'll cut off my friendship with her by Nick and Julia's wedding. You can reassure Simone and her family there is nothing happening between me and Rory. A friendship. I swear on my life. I swear on grandmother's grave. Whoever took that photo got lucky and caught something that doesn't represent how we feel. The implication sells magazines and nothing more."

The queen sucks her teeth in distaste. "Alexander, going into a marriage with Simone when she believes this is how you'll behave doesn't bode well for anyone's happiness."

Funny, I didn't realize happiness was the priority. "I'll be more careful. After Simone and I reveal our relationship at Nick and Julia's wedding, this supposed tryst with Rory won't mean anything to anyone." *Except me.* "The public and the press will be too caught up in the notion of Bellerive being linked to Denmark."

"If you lead Aurora on," the king says, "she could go to the press after the fact and claim you treated her poorly. They'll be on her side with the car accident, the apartment, and the job. It'll look as though you instated her as your mistress and then abandoned her. True or not, that can easily be the narrative here."

"I'm not leading her on," I grit out. "She's aware that nothing can happen between us."

"You're headed down a path meant to break your own heart," my mother says. "I can't understand why you would do this."

Because I can't help myself. The thought of no longer having Rory in my life is agony. While I've said I'll cut her out, I'm not sure *how* I'll do that. Maybe she'll abandon me once she realizes I've been keeping all these royal secrets.

"You're overreacting—again." It's not the first time the king and queen have had a fit about how something *looks* in the press or social media where I am concerned. There were literal pictures of Nick's dick circulating when he was in college, and other than some *tsking*, no one seemed to care. I dance with a woman who is my friend, and they lose their ever-loving minds.

"The rules of succession are very clear. A native of Bellerive or a member of a royal family," the queen says. "I understand why you might be attracted to her. She's beautiful."

She's so much more than beautiful.

"But it cannot be." She shakes her head. "You'd have to step down to be with her. Leave the monarchy. Nick or Brice would have to agree to take your place. Is that the road you want to take?"

The thought of either Nick or Brice in my shoes makes me cringe. Brice is too young, and Nick is too fickle. On top of that, I love my country, and I was born to be king. Whatever is happening with Rory doesn't change my birthright.

"The only person who is putting Rory ahead of the country," I say, "is you." On that note, I'm done with being scolded for dancing at my father's birthday party. "If you need me to call Simone personally, please let Desmond know. Otherwise, I'd prefer not to speak to either of you until you get some perspective. It was one dance at a party where everyone was dancing. I'm not sleeping with her. We're not secretly dating. I haven't asked to marry her. There have been no threats from me about stepping down or needing a loophole. I agreed to the arranged marriage and signed the contract. Rory is my *friend*." I say all of it with conviction, but inside I'm less convinced.

Desmond rises with me, a silent witness to the messiness that is my relationship with the king and queen who also happen to be my parents.

On the way out the door, Desmond says, "Well, that went well."

I bark out a laugh. "Now I remember why I don't do impulsive things."

"Didn't *used* to do impulsive things. Been a whole lot of 'screw it, do it anyway' going on with you the last couple of weeks."

"You're right." I enter my office and stop in the doorway so he can't follow. "I've been letting too many people get away with too many things."

"That's not—" Desmond starts.

"Including you. I didn't ask for your opinion on the Rory situation, and I don't want it. Consider her, as a topic, off-limits. You may pass that decree along to my parents as well. I am no longer discussing my friendship with Aurora Wilson with anyone."

"Your Highness," Desmond says.

Then I shut the door in his face.

I haven't left my office all day, and Rory hasn't turned up with my regular cream tea. Instead, Joyce, the head cook, served it to me with a frown creasing her brow. I'm sure my mother believes she's being helpful by telling the staff to no longer allow Rory to serve me, but I won't be putting up with her interference.

My father's diagnosis has caused her to get too big for her britches. Instead of being the voice of reason in the background, she's become the driving force of my displeasure. Whether my father no longer completely trusts his instincts, or she doesn't trust his mind, our mother-son relationship is in danger of fracturing. She used to be the one counselling my father not to be too hard on me, but now they both expect things I may not be able to deliver.

"Knock, knock," Brice says at the door to my office.

I glance at the clock over the door. Dinnertime is long gone, and it's edging toward being too late to message Rory. One dance has undone my life.

An arm comes around the side of Brice, a bottle of tequila clutched in the hand holding it.

"No," I say. That must be Nick, and whenever the two of them play their idiotic Truth and Tequila, stupidity follows. Nick was probably playing it the night he didn't *quite* marry Julia. Trust him to go to Vegas, rushed-wedding capital of the world, and not be able to seal the deal.

"You didn't even let me ask," Brice says. He plops into the chair across from my desk, and Nick follows with the bottle of tequila and three shot glasses.

Nick bangs the bottle onto the desk with authority. "Come on, brother. At this point, I think you could use a bit of Truth and Tequila."

"No," I say again. "My day has gone up shit's creek without a paddle. Adding alcohol to the mix will likely set my life on literal fire."

"Mom and Dad can't be that angry," Nick says. "It's not as though your dick is plastered all over the internet for eternity."

"The king and queen *are* that angry. I'm engaged to someone else."

"Shit," Brice says. "I completely forgot about that."

Of course he did. With the coronation, his life will barely change. Whatever it's going to take for me to become king is of no consequence to him.

"Have you told Rory yet?" Nick asks, and he pours each of us a shot, pushing mine across the wooden surface when I don't reach for it.

Fuck it. I take the shot and wipe my mouth with the back of my hand. "No."

"Are you going to tell Rory?" Brice fills my glass again.

I throw back the second shot. "This is how it works. Correct? If I don't answer, I drink."

Nick chuckles. "Yeah, but you can just drink. No one is stopping you."

"Getting drunk won't solve my problems," I say.

"Might help you get Rory out of your system," Brice suggests.

"Out of my system? Are there men who really believe that line?" I run my finger along the rim of the shot glass, and Nick seems to take my motion as an invitation to fill it again.

"A different argument," Nick says. "You've got six weeks to live however you want until your arrangement becomes public knowledge. I'm not suggesting you dance the waltz with Rory in the center of Tucker's Town, but what's the harm in embracing what's left of your freedom?"

I give him a side glance and tip back the tequila. Are they even drinking? Did they come here to get me drunk? "How have you been embracing your freedom? Only six weeks until you get married for real."

Nick's jaw tightens. "I'm marrying Jules by choice. You're marrying Simone to fulfill some royal family bullshit rules. I'm not losing anything by marrying her—I'm gaining everything I've ever wanted."

"Me too," I say. "The crown on my head."

Brice scoffs. "Come off it. I'm not your idiotic younger brother anymore who can't read a room. Your feelings about taking over as king are a lot more conflicted than you let on."

I rock back in my chair, and Brice refills my glass again. "You're both trying to advise me to go after Rory? To seize the day, so to speak? At what cost? Does that seem fair to Rory?"

"Tell her the truth," Nick says. "You have to marry Simone to take the throne, and then suggest you seize the next few weeks together."

The shot glass is cool between my fingers, and I hesitate before bringing it to my lips. Could I tell Rory the complete truth? She'd never go for a brief affair, would she? Wouldn't I be setting us up for failure, and dare I say it, heartbreak, as my mother suggested?

"Mother said the only way for me to be with Rory would be if I stepped down as the first in line. Either of you up to the job?" I check their reactions, and this time I pour my own shot.

Nick cringes, and Brice's eyes go wide. "I knew you were conflicted," Brice says. "I didn't think that meant you didn't want it."

"I wanted the accolades you got, but I never wanted the responsibility," Nick says. "Still don't, if I'm being honest. Would you really step down?"

"No." It's the truth. No matter how much I care for Rory, she can't come ahead of Bellerive. The country must be above any of my personal wants or desires. Indulging in an affair with her for six weeks is equal to jumping off a cliff when I'm not sure how deep the water is. I could be completely fine, or I could end up broken beyond repair. "I love our country. I want to be king. I just thought if you were encouraging me to be irresponsible, you should understand where that *could* lead if I was a lesser man."

Brice chuckles. "So we're good then? You're the better man, we're the lesser men." He pours a shot for himself. "In all seriousness, you looked happy last night with her. Actually happy. I always say you take your happiness where you can find it because you never know what's coming next."

Except I do know. An arranged marriage to a woman I'll have met a handful of times and the inevitable loss of Rory. Brice's advice *is* how he lives his life. Largely consequence free. It's never been how I've lived mine.

"Let's talk about something else," I say.

"Nick's wedding," Brice says, and he gives our brother the side-eye. "Ask him anything, and I bet he doesn't have a clue."

"Let's talk travel." Nick ignores Brice and pours everyone another drink. "We've been lots of places together and separately. Neutral territory."

We drink our shots, and since no one seems eager to throw out a country, I start. "Tell me where you've been in Canada."

Twenty-Four

RORY

A sound wakes me. I lie in bed, staring at the ceiling, waiting for it to come again. I'm on the cusp of drifting back to sleep when it comes a second time. A knock. Someone is knocking on my door at—I check the bedside clock—one in the morning.

Either it's an emergency or it's Alex.

God, what if something has happened to Alex?

My heart thuds heavy. *Alex.* I spring off the bed and fly to the door, throwing it open without looking through the peephole.

"Did you even check to see who it was?" Alex's words have the faintest hint of a slur, and he rocks on his feet.

The panic gripping my chest eases once I've given him a quick scan. He's not injured, and though he doesn't seem like himself, the relaxation in his stance isn't from illness.

"Are you... drunk?" I narrow my eyes and cock my head. Disheveled suit and smells like tequila. "Oh my God. Did you play Truth and Tequila with Brice?"

"And Nick. 'Twas a short-lived game." He leans into the doorframe, and his gaze travels over my short shorts and tank top. "Not quite what I pictured. But I am *not* disappointed."

My cheeks heat, and I cross my arms over my braless chest.

"Are you going to invite me in or make me stand out here in the cold?" Alex asks.

I suppress a smile. "Oh? Is it cold out there? Your tropical paradise is betraying you tonight?"

"Bloody freezing. Might catch hypothermia at any moment. The best remedy is skin-to-skin contact." His gaze sears me with its intensity.

With his first comment on my nightwear, I wasn't sure if he was hitting on me or merely drunk. Now I'm sure he's flirting with me. Not pity flirting either. This is unabashed interest... in me. There are so many responses rising to the surface, I'm dizzy with them. Banter back, tell him to leave, or invite him in, but make it clear his drunken moves aren't going to win me over.

Except, I'm already won over, aren't I?

Be smart? Or do what I want?

"Maybe I'll let you stand out there for a few more minutes to make my first aid more effective," I say with the hint of a smile tugging at my lips.

A flash of surprise registers on Alex's face. "You're that confident in your first aid skills, are you?"

"No. I'm that confident in my skin-to-skin skills." I give him my cheekiest grin. His unexpected appearance has given me a burst of confidence. Sober Alex would diffuse this conversation and let me down easy. What will drunk Alex do? Anticipation stirs in my belly. Drunk Alex didn't come here to talk.

His gaze heats with an unmistakable flare of desire an instant before he pushes off the doorframe and digs his hands into my long hair, drawing me into a kiss. I rise on my toes to meet it, to welcome him.

His kiss is demanding and sure of itself, exactly how I've longed to be kissed. There are no half measures, no room for uncertainty. We are united in our hunger for each other.

My body is a chorus of *finally*, as though I've been fasting and am now receiving my first taste of food. He's sustenance, strength, *life*. Like everything else between us, we fall into a natural rhythm of tongues and hands and lips. If I didn't know better, I'd think we'd kissed before. So many times before. There's not a hint of awkwardness, just blind passion.

He kicks the door shut with his foot, and he walks us toward the couch, his lips leaving mine only long enough to change the angle. He sheds his suit jacket, and it hits the floor with a thud. One of his hands slides underneath my thin tank top and along my spine. A shiver runs through me at the skin-to-skin contact I've been craving for weeks.

My body is singing *yes, yes, yes*, and I run my fingers through Alex's dark strands, deepening the kiss.

Alex groans into my mouth, and his other hand grips my ass, drawing me tight against him. The depth of his desire is clear through our clothing, and when his lips leave my mouth to trail a line down my neck, a surge of lust like nothing I've experienced before shoots to my core.

How is it possible to have this much instant chemistry with someone? We're only kissing, and I *never* want it to end.

"You were made for me. No one else, just me," Alex murmurs when he nuzzles under my ear, and then he's kissing me again with so much raw emotion my knees go weak, and I drag him down onto the couch with me.

His body rests between my thighs, and I wrap my legs around him to keep him close.

"Please." I don't know what I'm asking for, but there's an escalating need inside me only he can satisfy. "Please, Alex."

He rocks against me, and I gasp, arching my back to meet the contact. The strangest sense of déjà vu hits me, and I cling to his biceps, trying to catch the almost-memory. We've never done this before, but something recognizable has clicked in my brain. The brush of our bodies, the closeness of his breath in my ear, his lips skimming along my neck, are achingly familiar.

His hand slides under my ass, and each time he shifts forward to change the angle of our kiss, his erection rubs against my sensitive core. I've got my hands under his shirt, and with each flex, his muscles ripple.

Is it possible to die from lust?

From the floor, his phone rings. The piercing sound seems to hit Alex like a bucket of ice-cold water. Who would call him at this hour of the night? He freezes over top of me, but he doesn't look me in the eyes. Then he backs off and sits on the edge of the couch, his face in his hands.

An intense silence settles between us, and I'm not sure what I'm supposed to do or say. I want him to come back and finish what he started. He's not going to leave me like this, is he? He came here. He broke our unspoken agreement not to cross this threshold.

He groans. "I'm an idiot. I'm a fucking idiot. Teach me to get drunk and listen to my brothers." He glances at me before looking away. "Shit, Rory. I'm sorry. I shouldn't be doing this. I *really* should *not* be doing this."

I stare at the wooden beam in the ceiling and wonder what it would take to convince him we *should* be doing this. My body is on fire, and I want him to put out the flames. What's the female equivalent of blue balls?

His stupid phone ruined everything.

"Who would be calling you at this hour?" Perhaps none of my business. Despite what just happened, we're supposed to be just friends. But the only phone calls I've ever made or received this late are for exactly what Alex and I were almost doing. Do women call him for booty calls? Does he have women who keep him satisfied? I've never asked, and now I wonder if I should have.

"Could be anyone," he says with a deep sigh. "I usually have my phone off at night. I run a country which is attached to other countries with different time zones. Sometimes people forget to check the clock before they call." He places his hands on his knees and stands. "I should go."

"Alex." I swing my legs off the couch and follow him to the door. He snatches his suit jacket off the floor. "Are we talking about this?"

He lets out a harsh chuckle. "Clearly my judgement is not good. We should discuss what's happened when I'm sober."

"You're being very dismissive of me, and I don't like it." The words tumble out, and I shock myself. While I can be direct, I hate confrontations. This could turn into a fight, and I tend to avoid them.

Alex has the door open, and he's framed in it for a beat with his back to me. I'm not convinced he's going to turn around, that he'll even acknowledge what I just said.

"I shouldn't have come," he says over his shoulder. "I apologize. I'll exercise better judgement next time."

He draws the door closed behind him, and I release my agony in a wail of frustration. His insistence on us not being able to be together because he can never marry me is infuriating. I'm twenty-three. I don't need to *marry* him. Just because every other woman he's dated has been salivating to join the royal family doesn't mean I am.

But I really, really want us to join other things together. My fingers tingle with the memory of running along the hard planes of his body, and my core aches at the reminder of him pushing his stiff length against me. Who tells a woman she was made just for them and doesn't grab that sensation with both hands?

Yes, Alex. Yes, I was made for you. Give me all of you in return.

I climb into bed and beat my pillow before finally throwing it on the floor. How do we back away from what we've done? Before he kissed me, the attraction between us went largely unspoken. Neither of us can deny what almost happened tonight. Poor judgement or not, we were going for it.

How do I ever look at him again and not think of the way his body fit with mine? How his kiss was exactly what I imagined it would be? How every moment between us is a half-forgotten memory, as though we've mapped each other's souls in another life?

How do I go back to pretending we're friends when one look from him sets me on fire? How do I convince myself friendship is enough?

All these questions have no answers in sight because Alex chose to leave me instead of staying to talk this out. Anger rises in me at how dismissive he was.

Maybe he's right. Maybe going down this path with him—wherever it does or doesn't lead—is a fool's errand. Do I want to have sex with him so badly I'd risk *heartbreak*? Who would choose that?

Stolen kisses in my cottage won't be enough. Even if I can fool myself into thinking I wouldn't want to marry Alex, I have no control over how I'd react if we started an affair. No man has ever felt this right, this destined to be mine.

I've never been the kind of girl who could do temporary. Alex can never be my permanent. We'd have an expiration date, whether that was my visa running out or him growing bored of the farmgirl from Canada. In any scenario, I lose.

I grab my pillow off the floor and slide under the covers. There's a heaviness across my chest when I roll onto my side to stare at the clock.

For the next couple of hours, I drift in and out of sleep. When my alarm goes off at four in the morning, I realize what I have to do, but I'm not sure I have the guts to do it.

Twenty-Five

ALEX

When was the last time I couldn't sleep because of a woman? Easy—Jules when I was in university. Not since I shut down my feelings for her has a woman gotten close enough to stir my emotions. Lust? Sure. But what I experienced with Rory last night was indescribable. I wanted her, but underneath that was a wellspring of something more primal. Like the night I found her in the car, I couldn't get close enough. I wanted to take what she was offering and never let her out from underneath me again.

Fucking terrifying.

Those sorts of thoughts have no place in my life.

Bellerive above all else. Anyone else.

My clock turns over to five in the morning. Rory will be entering the kitchen to prepare her baking for the day ahead. She has an hour of solitude before Joyce arrives to cook breakfast for my parents and any other overnight staff.

She won't be getting that hour to herself today.

What happened between us last night can't happen again. As my mother predicted, Rory is a danger I didn't see with enough clarity weeks ago.

Can we go back to how things were before I showed up at her door drunk and desperate?

While I dress, my gut twists with uncertainty, but I'm not one to back down from a confrontation. I shouldn't have gone to her place last night, and I definitely shouldn't have kissed her—a lot. I kissed her a lot, and if my phone hadn't gone off, I might have done more than that.

I flick the lapels of my suit jacket into place and tug my cuffs to straighten the fabric. From the bedside table, I grab my phone. Perhaps texting or calling her would be wise instead of going to see her in the kitchen. But Joyce arrives soon, so there's no hope of our conversation spiraling too out of control.

Brief. To the point. Salvage what I can of our friendship. Get in and get out.

At the door to the kitchen, someone is banging pots and pans, and the shrill clang reminds me I had a few too many shots of tequila last night. Nothing good comes from hanging out with Brice and Nick together. They are a tag team of poor decisions. No wonder they've gotten in so much trouble over the years.

Before I can lose my nerve, I stride into the kitchen to the coffee maker. "Morning," I say with my back to Rory.

"Morning," Rory mumbles in response.

A single word can say a lot. She's not happy with me. That's the least enthusiastic greeting I've ever gotten. While the coffee percolates, I inhale a steadying breath and turn to face her. Her blond hair is in a tight braid, and she's wearing her usual kitchen whites. She looks tired, and I wonder if she had a terrible sleep like me.

I won't be asking.

"I shouldn't have gone to your cottage last night when I'd had so much to drink. My judgement was impaired, and I apologize if my behavior offended you."

"Offended me?" A frown creases her brow. "How would your behavior have offended me?"

There's an edge to her voice, and I'm aware I need to tread lightly, but I'm not sure which direction I should be stepping in. "We're friends, and I value your friendship. I shouldn't have risked that by turning us into something that can't happen. I don't want to lead you on."

"You've made yourself really clear, Alex. Honestly, hearing the same thing over and over again is a bit tiring."

Wow. She's more than irritated with me. I think she's angry? "I want to make sure you understand the parameters of our friendship."

She rolls her eyes. "I'm not a child."

"I never said you were."

"But sometimes you treat me like I can't grasp the simplest concept. We can't be together—check." She grabs the dough in front of her and flips it over and kneads it with an abundance of aggression. "If you're worried about the parameters of our friendship, we should probably spend less time together." She makes eye contact with me, and her green eyes are blazing. "A lot less."

"Are you *mad* at me? I came here to apologize for acting like an idiot. I don't understand how that makes things *worse* between us."

"We're not friends." When I give her a look of incredulity, she continues, "We haven't been *just* friends since you dragged me out of the car. There's something between us, Alex. Something big. We can ignore it, or we can face it. I ignored a lot in my relationship with Derrick, and I'm not doing it again. So, if we're not facing whatever this is, if we're sweeping it under the rug, then I think it's better we don't see each other."

I'm so stunned, I can't speak. The coffee maker beeps to remind me it's ready. The door handle on the side entrance rattles. The short window of time I wanted is working against me.

"We're a bad idea, Alex. Reasonable people don't court heartbreak." She picks up the dough and slams it against the countertop just as Joyce walks into the kitchen.

"Morning, Joyce," I say with an easiness I don't feel. My gut is twisting itself into knots, and there's so much I want to say to Rory, but I don't know where to start. Nowhere, not with someone else in the kitchen now. She got the last word—all the last words.

"Your Highness, you're in here early." Joyce hangs her things on a hook by the pantry.

"Coffee." I hold up my mug. "Can't function without it."

"Joyce will deliver your cream tea today," Rory says, and for the first time when our gazes meet, she's playing a part. My employee, not my friend, not whatever else has really been brewing under the surface.

"I'm going to skip it today, thank you." I smile at Joyce and pat my stomach. "Can't keep indulging in things that are bad for me."

Rory's jaw tightens, and she kneads the dough with more force. "Wouldn't want you to get fat." The edge is back in her voice.

She couldn't hold onto her fake persona for long, and I'm gratified by the return of the Rory I'm familiar with. In my circle of friends and acquaintances, women learn from an early age to pretend, and I've loved Rory's openness. The idea that spending time with me might change that part of her causes an ache to bloom across my chest. Maybe she's right, and we shouldn't be together anymore.

Joyce's gaze zips between me and Rory, and I need to do something to diffuse the tension or she'll pepper Rory with probing questions.

"I'll take your advice to heart next time I'm tempted to call for a cream tea." With that, I grab my coffee and walk out of the kitchen.

The farther I get from Rory, the more the heaviness across my shoulders threatens to crush me. One drunken mistake, and the best part of my life is no more.

The days drift, one into another. Each is more of the same. Referendum preparation and press. Coronation matters. Emailing with Simone about wedding details. Every time I see her name in my inbox, my stomach drops to my toes. After a few cursory exchanges, I managed to pass her off to Merida, the same wedding planner who is coordinating Nick and Julia's nuptials.

The wedding is a necessity to get what I really want—the crown. I'll deal with the marriage when I have to. Until then, there's someone else occupying every second of my thoughts when I'm not tied up in mentally taxing tasks.

Rory.

We haven't spoken all week. No visits to the kitchen for coffee. No cream tea deliveries. No stolen evenings in her cottage. Silence. Brutal, make-my-chest-cave-in silence.

My mother, who must be keeping tabs, will be ecstatic. Crisis averted.

Is it, though? I'm fucking miserable.

While Rory and I have only known each other a matter of weeks, I wove her as tightly as I could into the fabric of my life, the pattern of my thoughts. Trying to rip her out is a task I not only don't like but don't want.

As my paper fiancée reminded me today, there are only four weeks left before the world believes we're going public with our relationship. My stomach sours. Before I met Rory, this wife process would have been another thing I had to "get through" in order to achieve what I wanted. A hassle, but not something tied to any kind of emotion.

I've never loathed anything more than this impending fake marriage I'll be expected to make real. Not a great foundation to start a marriage on. It is what it is.

I stare at the wall in my office, ignoring the memos strewn across my desk.

Four weeks. I've got four weeks left to carve out a sliver of happiness. The countdown is making me contemplate dangerous things.

Rory isn't wrong. Whatever is between us is destined for disaster or heartbreak. Maybe both. What do I know?

I can't let her go, though. I'm not ready. Right or wrong, if she'll have me, I'll cling on as long as I can.

With that thought in mind, I pick up the phone and call an old friend for a favor.

Rory could be out with Posey or doing a thousand other things on a Friday night, but I'm hoping she's home. When I knock on the door just after dinner, I half expect her not to answer. Through the door, I can hear her, and I wonder whether she's debating keeping me locked out of her life. Safer that way. For both of us. A tiny part of me hopes she does. Apparently, I'm not strong enough to resist her, but maybe she's built of better stuff than me.

When the door draws back, my heart hammers at the sight of her blond hair loose around her shoulders and her expression wary, cautious. Her normal exuberant smile is missing.

I did that.

For another second I search her face—sad. She's sad. The realization tightens the vise around my chest.

She says nothing, but she seems to be drinking me in with the same thirst.

"I have a surprise for you," I say, and I thrust my hands into the pockets of my sweatpants to stop myself from reaching for her. "I have to take you there, if you're willing."

Her teeth snag her bottom lip, and when I meet her gaze, I'm sure she'll say no. She maintains eye contact, and I wonder if she's cataloguing all the reasons coming with me is a bad idea the same way I did while I walked over here. Didn't stop me. Will they stop her?

"What do you want from me, Alex?"

Everything. Anything she's willing to give. So many things I can't have for reasons beyond my control.

"I've been miserable for a long time. I'm not even sure I recognized it as misery. But what I do recognize, what I've understood for years, is that I'm fucking lonely, Rory. When I'm with you, I'm not either of those things."

A sheen of tears coats her green eyes. "Alex," she whispers, and she closes the distance between us, drawing me into a hug.

I squeeze her tight and savor the feel of her slight body pressed against mine. "You make me feel less alone," I rasp. "I'm being selfish, but I can't stay away from you."

When she draws back, she frames my face and searches my expression with renewed tenderness. "Show me your surprise."

I lace my fingers with hers and lead her down the path toward the other part of my apology. For however long Rory will let me cling onto her, onto the way I feel when I'm around her, I'm doing it. The heaviness that's dogged me this week has lifted.

We can't have forever, but we've got right now, and that counts for something.

TWENTY-SIX

RORY

After Alex told me he's been lonely and miserable most of his life, he probably could have picked me up, taken me anywhere, and I wouldn't have let out one peep of dissent.

From my doorway, he leads me down a path I haven't walked. The estate is huge, and I tend to stick to familiar routes for fear of getting lost. Nothing quite like texting the future king to tell him I need to be rescued from somewhere on the property.

"Can I ask where we're going?"

Alex chuckles. "You can. But I won't tell you."

We keep walking, and I'm not sure whether I should broach what's going on between us again or let it rest. The truth is I've missed Alex more in the last few days than I've missed Derrick in the last few weeks after two years together. The difference is stunning. Alex is woven into the fabric of my life on the estate. Every inch of this place reminds me of him.

Despite our connection, I'm supposed to be going to Café Plutus tomorrow night as part of Derrick's apology tour. Do I tell Alex about my dinner date? We're in such a tenuous position, I'm not sure of the right move. If he was truly my friend, I'd tell him. If he was my boyfriend, I'd cancel with Derrick.

Alex says we can't be together, even as he does things that make me feel like we're together.

Screw it. I told him we were done if he wasn't willing to face what's between us. *Be bold, Rory.*

"You didn't answer my question back at my cottage," I say. "About what you want from me." His admission of loneliness and misery, though touching and important, didn't exactly define whatever we are. With Derrick, I skirted around issues to avoid confrontations, and my reluctance led me to find him in bed with another woman. Avoidance doesn't make a problem go away.

"Look," Alex says, pointing ahead of us.

Down the path is a horse trailer, and a tingling sensation starts behind my breastbone and spreads to my fingertips. "Is that... you didn't, did you?"

"I called in a favor," Alex says, and he tucks his hands into the pockets of his sweatpants. "Lots of places we can go on the estate, if you want?"

"You know how to ride?" He never mentioned anything before.

He grimaces. "Had to learn polo as a kid to schmooze with the British royals." He gestures toward the trailer. "Edward taught me, and he agreed to bring two of his horses here tonight for us to ride. A sunset ride. Just an hour or so."

"Hockey on a horse," I muse. "I should have known you'd have another skill you'd been required to learn."

"There are many," Alex says with a side glance. "Most of them completely useless."

When we get to Edward at the trailer, he leads the horses out. Alex and Edward exchange a few teasing remarks about the last time Alex was on a horse while we get them ready to ride. Once they're set, Alex and I swing into the saddles, and I sit for a moment, taking in the sweep of green fields, the ocean in the distant background, and Alex at my side.

"I often get this weird sensation when I'm with you," I say. "Déjà vu, sort of. As though we've done these things before."

Alex glances at me before focusing on the horizon ahead of us. "Do you?" he says. "I thought I was the only one. Perhaps we knew each other in another life."

Then he nudges his horse into a trot, leaving me behind. He is both infuriating and fascinating, and I'm never sure which version of him I'll get. The fascinating one is more authentic, I think. He's the lonely, miserable guy who saves me from car crashes, buys me necklaces, arranges for me to ride a horse around the royal estate, and speaks of reincarnation as though it's factual rather than romantic. The infuriating version of him occurs when he tries to keep some part of himself from me. The guy who will not answer a direct question unless I force him to. As though it's possible for him to wedge some distance between us just by wishing it to be so.

I drive my heels into the horse's side, and I catch up to Alex in no time.

"Tomorrow night," Alex says as we ride. "May I see you?"

"Are we going to talk about what this is?"

"I think it's probably best if we leave it unnamed."

I sigh and bite the inside of my cheek. We can name it or not, but it doesn't change the fact this current between us exists. "I can't see you tomorrow night."

He tugs on the reins to slow his horse. "Because I won't name whatever is between us."

"No, because I already have plans. I have a life beyond our friendship." If he asks me, I'll tell him. Otherwise, I'm keeping the Derrick part to myself.

"Tell Posey I said hello." He kicks his horse to move forward again. "So, we've labelled it then, have we? Friendship."

The urge to throttle him is so great that if he were any closer, I'd jump onto his horse and wrap my hands around his neck. "You know what? I'm going to leave this for tonight. You did a really nice thing for me by having Edward bring the horses here, and I want to enjoy my ride."

"What shall we talk about then?"

"In silence. I would like to enjoy my ride in silence."

"This ride was supposed to be an apology."

I bark out a laugh. "I get that. Thank you. But what I actually want from you, you won't give me."

"A label."

I release a groan of frustration. "For someone so smart, you're remarkably stupid." He's not ready to face what's between us, not in any meaningful way. Maybe he'll never be ready. Since, as he's told me several times, nothing can come of this spark between us, we might never explore us the way that I want to. I meant what I said about courting heartbreak, but what I figured out this last week without him is that I'm already there. The deep outline of a heartbreak exists. If I was smart, I'd probably leave it at that. But if I'm going to experience the pain, I want the pleasure too.

He's quiet beside me, and I wonder if he's surprised by my straightforwardness. I am. For some reason with him, I can't hide my emotions or pretend things I don't feel. Whatever I'm thinking or feeling is written large, just for him.

"I can't give you what you want," Alex says. "It wouldn't be fair."

In frustration, I kick my horse into a trot and leave Alex to follow behind.

The restaurant is built into the cliff, a marvel of engineering and expense. I'm half-convinced the reason their prices are astronomical is to pay for the work needed to keep the restaurant from pitching into the ocean.

Instead of letting Derrick pick me up, which would have been fraught with so many potential problems, I agreed to meet him here.

Julia drives into the parking lot and stares at the front entrance. "Are you sure you want to try the food this badly?"

I laugh. "He's paying, so..." I shrug.

A small answering smile tugs at her lips. "I can see why you and Posey have become such good friends."

"Your sister has almost single-handedly saved my stay in Bellerive." I gather my purse from the floor between my feet. "Thanks for driving me when Posey had to bail."

"That's my job," Julia says. "When Brent pops back to the island unexpectedly."

"I thought Posey said something about an overuse injury."

"Yeah," Julia agrees. "Those crop up when Posey calls him crying because she misses him."

I gape at her. "She calls him crying?" Despite a few eyebrow-raising comments, I'm still shocked to hear Julia's claim.

She laughs. "Don't worry. Posey doesn't realize I know that either." She winks at me. "Despite training for the Olympics, he'd do anything to make her happy." Her expression turns pensive. "If she asked him to quit, I think he would. But she'd never do that. You have to protect each other's happiness, don't you?" She nods toward the front door. "Don't forget that when you're in there. It's not what makes him happy. You both have to be okay with whatever you decide."

The sudden urge to confess everything that's happened between me and Alex sits on the tip of my tongue. My instinct tells me Alex wouldn't like me confiding in Julia. I haven't even told Posey what happened between Alex and me last weekend. No matter what happens at dinner tonight, I can't go back to Derrick. Even coming here tonight makes me feel like I'm cheating on Alex.

We're not friends. We'll never be friends. Slapping on an ill-fitting friendship label is as good as not using one at all. Another surge of anger rushes through me at the reminder of our horseback ride. We spent most of it in silence, and while we both spoke to Edward when we returned, it was hardly the relaxing ride I anticipated when I wanted it for my birthday.

"I don't think there's anything Derrick could say that would make what happened between us acceptable." Not to mention that I'm positive I'm completely over him. "I'm here for the food." Truthfully, I was tempted to cancel, but Alex made me so frustrated this week that keeping this date is my unknown eff-you. I'm such a rebel.

"You sure you want to take a cab back?" Julia asks when I open the passenger door.

"I'll ask them to drop me at the gates. The guard who's on tonight knows me, so it should be fine."

Julia grins. "Your cheese bread has been a real hit with the staff."

"It has been a very useful conversation starter." I return her smile. "One of the guards calls me *the bread woman* whenever we cross paths." I climb out of the car and hold the door. "Thanks so much for the ride."

"Any time! If you change your mind about a ride home, just call. Nick and I are being boring tonight."

Derrick's car is a few spaces to the right in the parking lot. One good thing about him—he's always early for everything. I've never had to wait on him. When I enter the restaurant, the tiered tables and seats are a wash of gray, taupe, and white. Every table has a view of the ocean. None of the customers face me at the hostess's stand, which resembles a desk more than a lectern.

A slim brunette slips out a side door, and the delicious smell of grilled steak wafts out with her. "Good evening. Who is your reservation under?"

"Derrick McGuinty." I tug my purse higher onto my shoulder.

"Right this way. The other member of your party is already here." She takes us down the wide staircase to a table at the front with a prime ocean view.

He didn't just get a cancellation. He managed to snag one of the best tables in the restaurant. An unobstructed view of the water stretches out before us, and the sun will set in an hour or so, coating the sky in an orange-pink blush.

Derrick sips his beer at the table, and when he sees me, he grins.

This date might be pointless, but the view is spectacular. Is there anything he could say to earn a second chance? The memory of Alex's lips slanted across mine rises to the surface, and I touch my fingers to my mouth.

Go back to someone bad for me or seize the opportunity for something else, brief though it may be? The choice should be easy, but where I'm sure Derrick can't shatter my heart, I can't say the same for Alex. Derrick might be the bad choice, but he's also the safe one.

Twenty-Seven

ALEX

My burner phone is blowing up with notifications. With Rory busy tonight, I worked later than normal, and then I powered up my second phone and logged into my accounts to check what was new in the social media world. Most of the time, I don't have a spare moment or the interest to scroll through the noise and nonsense. When I do have the time and inclination, I comment on posts as Joe Nobody, a secondary account. Small things amuse me.

I'm not amused right now.

A flood of people are @-ing me on every major platform. I've gone viral before, but I've sensed it coming or been told it would happen. A stupid comment. A big royal reveal. A woman rescued from a car crash.

Said woman is currently cozied up with her ex-boyfriend—Derrick the Dumbass—at Café Plutus, and Bellerive is losing their collective minds.

I'm definitely losing mine.

Dinner with an ex-boyfriend and documenting the occasion on social media is a move I'd expect of many, many women. Not Rory. To be fair, she isn't the one pushing the narrative now, either. The unexpectedness of her date hits me almost as hard as her glowing smile. She's smiling at *him* like that. *Him.* What. The. Fuck.

I'm tagged in photos on gossip posts as a sidenote as though I won't see all their nonsense. There's even a brief video of her laughing at something Derrick says. My chest has never been this tight with a combination of anger and despair.

Isn't she the one @HRH_PrinceAlexander rescued from the car crash?

OMG. She's the one @HRH_PrinceAlexander went grocery shopping with.

UGH. I was shipping her with @HRH_PrinceAlexander. Obviously not smart enough for him. #ALORA

Does @HRH_PrinceAlexander know she's seeing the cheater again? Can he come rescue her from this too?

On and on it goes. #ALORA is trending in Bellerive. If an irrational, raging jealousy wasn't building at Rory's lie of omission some of the comments would likely be funny.

Nothing is funny right now.

I haul myself to the edge of the bed from the middle where I was sprawled, exhausted. Tiredness left me with the first photo. Instead, I'm fighting the urge to go to Café Plutus and drag her out of there. While I realize that's the worst thing I can do, I've never had to wrestle so hard to choose the right course of action.

Desmond's assertion that my new model is "screw it, I'll do it anyway" isn't so far off.

My day-to-day phone pings on the nightstand with a security alert, and I snatch it up. An unknown car is at the gate seeking entrance. I zoom in using the security camera, and there is Rory in the passenger seat. Dumbass Derrick is driving.

She brought him here? She's intending to reconcile with him *here*? Not bloody likely.

I text security to let Rory in but to deny the vehicle entrance. On the screen, Rory purses her lips and shrugs at Derrick before climbing out the passenger side. Derrick also gets out of the car and follows her to the entrance for guards and foot traffic.

He's not parking there, is he? Granted it's a parking lot, but I don't want him on any part of the estate.

I scan the scene and wish I made it clear Derrick isn't allowed anywhere. At the gate, Derrick draws Rory into a hug, and it lasts far longer than I'm comfortable with.

The urge to go out there is surging through me, an unstoppable flood of raw, uncontrollable jealousy. Tossing my normal phone back on the nightstand, I grab my burner.

Fuck it. I'm going to her apartment.

The mantra *this is a bad idea* plays in my head on repeat as I storm along the gravel path to her place. Women like Rory are worthy of more than whatever Dumbass Derrick has promised. Guaranteed.

She might not be able to be with me, but she sure as shit isn't going to be with him either.

When I get to her apartment, instead of my usual knock, I pound on the door. It takes her a minute to answer, but when it swings back, my breath catches at how gorgeous she looks. Normally, she's pretty. She rarely wears much makeup, but whatever she's done to her eyes, they're stunning. Most nights by the time I get here, she's in sweats. Nothing casual about her outfit tonight. The lavender dress she's wearing clings to her in all the right places.

She created this look to impress *him*. Jealousy has gripped me so hard I can barely breathe.

"Is he here?" I growl.

Her cheeks turn pink. "Who?" Her surprised expression morphs into a frown.

"The dumbass. Is he here?" I move past her into the tiny apartment. The only place he could be is in the bathroom.

"No—I—how—I left him at the gate. He wasn't allowed in."

At least security did the right thing without me having to be explicit. "You went on a date with him after he cheated on you?"

The red in her cheeks deepens. "That's not—"

"You lied to me about what you were doing tonight."

"I didn't *lie*."

I'm on one side of the couch, and she's on the other. She's fidgeting like she realizes she's done something wrong. I've never been angry with her before, but I'm livid right now. My temper is barely in check. Have I ever experienced this intense surge of emotion toward anyone in my life?

"You let me believe something that wasn't true. That's a lie."

"How did you find out? I don't understand how you know."

"Bloody hell, Rory. You're not anonymous in Bellerive anymore. People were @-ing me all night with photos and comments on your date like I should care."

Her jaw tightens, and she straightens. "Well, I have great news for you. There's no need for you to care. *I* didn't ask you to care." She points toward the door, and her hand shakes. "You can leave."

"I'm not leaving until you explain to me what tonight was all about."

"I don't owe you an explanation. We can't be together. You've been *very* clear about that."

My heart pounds, and I close the distance between us. "You want me to leave?"

She doesn't meet my gaze.

"Tell me why you went on a date with Derrick. To make me jealous?" I peer down at her, willing her to make eye contact.

When she finally stares up at me, her expression brims with frustration. "What do you want, Alex? You tell me we can't be together, but then you buy me an expensive birthday present. You tell me we can't be together, and then you kiss me. You agree we shouldn't see each other as much anymore, and then you take me horseback riding. You don't want me, but no one else is allowed either?"

"Not him," I grit out. "Anyone but him."

"Really?" She cocks her head and defiance radiates off her. "Anyone?"

We're inches apart, and she's goading me into doing something I'll likely regret. As angry as I am, I've got one last string of sense tethering me.

"You want me to find someone else? *Be* with someone else?" Her voice is husky, but the challenge is there.

"No." The word is ripped out of me, tearing the final tie to common sense. "God help me, no." And then I'm kissing her, long and deep.

She folds into me, and her hands bunch my T-shirt. The scent of vanilla and sugar swirls around me, addictive, delicious.

I can't—I shouldn't. With a superhuman effort, I wrench myself away. "Rory, I—"

She rises onto her toes, draws me toward her, and kisses me again. There's no question I'm kissing her back, willing to take anything she'll give me. A crumb from her is better than a five-course meal with anyone else.

Anyone else. My mind strays to Simone. I can't. I can't. This is wrong. I break away from Rory and stumble back.

"I can't," I say. "We—"

"I swear if you tell me one more time we can't be together, you might as well walk out that door and never come back." She points to the exit, and there's so much passion in the proclamation that I realize she means it. She'll banish me from her life.

The ultimatum is a spray of cold water on the fire between us, and I run my hand through my hair. "You don't understand," I say.

She closes the distance I put between us. "Do you want to be with me?"

The question is torture. If only my life were so simple. "You're twenty-three. You don't know what you're getting yourself into. I'll ruin you. I'll ruin you, and I'll never forgive myself."

She frames my face with her small hands. "I'm old enough to know what I feel. Let us have this. I'm not asking for forever. I'll never ask for what you can't give. I understand our limits. But we can have right now. We can have this."

My heart pounds in my ears. She makes whatever happens next sound so easy. Possible instead of impossible. If I don't ruin her, she'll definitely ruin me. "We're going to destroy each other," I mutter.

"If you're going to drag me to hell, at least give me heaven first," she whispers.

I search her face for one more beat. Wrong. So wrong. But I can't deny the gut feeling urging me to suck this vein of happiness dry. To take this moment and hope the memory of it will be enough for the years to come. She may never speak to me again after Nick and Julia's wedding.

"You're sure this is what you want? Rory, I can't—"

Before the rest of the warning can leave my lips, she kisses me with the same fevered intensity as before. Except this time, there's no hesitation about the direction we're headed. This is our path, to heaven and then to hell. Our course is set. There's no turning back.

My T-shirt comes over my head, and she pushes my sweatpants down to a heap on the floor. I map her body with my palms, and I step out of my sweats. The zipper on her dress is a magnet to my fingers, and as I tug it down, I trail kisses along her exposed neck.

She drops her shoulders, and the dress falls to her waist. With my fingertips, I trace the line of her waist before encouraging the dress over her hips, so it pools at her feet. I draw back to take her in. She's exquisite. There is only one Rory. Whatever this connection is between us, I've been around long enough to understand it's rare. Volcanic lightning. Beautiful and dangerous. My life will never be the same, and instead of stepping away from the edge of disaster, I'm free-falling over, welcoming the chaos with outstretched arms.

Take me, Rory. I'm yours.

"Alex," she breathes out, drawing me out of my head and back into the moment.

Her bra and panties are white lace, and I skim her peaked nipples with my thumbs. Then we're kissing again. Her exploratory hands weave invisible threads of desire into my skin. Once I have her under me, getting over her will be impossible.

I grip her ass and draw her tight against me, and she sighs into my mouth. Our kiss deepens, and I've never wanted anyone the way I want her. Nothing could convince me to let her go now.

She leads me toward the bed, her lips never leaving mine. I unsnap her bra, and she lets it slide down her arms to drop on the floor. When I lift her to set her on the bed, I seek the closest nipple, scraping my teeth against it.

With a gasp, her fingers dig into my hair, and she arches her back to meet the contact. "Yes," she murmurs. "Yes."

She slides her hand inside my boxer briefs, and her warm fingers on my erection elicit a hiss. I'm so hard it's painful, and having her tentative touch is almost too much.

"Too rough?" she murmurs, and her other hand skims along my cheek.

"No." My voice is tight with desire. "No. I just want you so fucking badly."

She grips my shaft, and her hand moves with perfect pressure. I close my eyes at the pleasure and the realization she's the one providing it after weeks of my wild, private thoughts.

"Look at me," she murmurs.

Our foreheads are close, and I gaze down at her, lost in a haze of sensations.

"I want you to," she whispers. "Just you, Alex. Only you."

Warmth spreads across my chest at the sincerity in her gaze. Instead of making my own declaration, one I'll end up regretting later, I kiss her. She slides my boxer briefs over my ass, and I kick them to the floor.

Then I settle between her legs and rock against her. Her soaked panties are the only barrier between us. She meets my motion and clamps her legs around my back, keeping the friction consistent. We kiss and grind, kiss and grind.

When I grip her hip and adjust the angle, she moans. "Please, Alex. Please. I want you. I want you inside me."

There's nothing I crave more than to be buried in her to the hilt, but there's a not-so-small snag in that plan. I press my forehead to her shoulder. "I didn't bring anything," I rasp.

The last thing I expected when I came here was this, but I am not sorry it's happening.

"I'm on the pill," she says, and she's shimmying out of her underwear.

"I've never…" I meet her gaze and shake my head. "I've never trusted anyone enough." Protection is a must for me.

She brushes her knuckles against my cheeks, and she feathers kisses along my jawline. "I'd never trick you, Alex. I'm clean, and we're protected. I promise."

This isn't a gamble I'd take with anyone else, but I trust her. In the past, if I didn't have a condom, that barrier, I walked away. Too risky. But there isn't a conniving bone in Rory's body.

I slide my hand under her ass, and I'm poised at her entrance. "Are you sure?" The question isn't about what she just told me, it's about so much more than that. After this, I don't understand how I pretend she isn't the most important person in any room, how I go back to lying to myself about the depth of my caring. Nothing will ever be the same in me, between us. Tonight cements a change, even if I can't allow my feelings to harden into concrete.

"Yes," she says, and she draws me into a kiss at the same time as I slide into her.

The intensity of our bare skin so intimately connected is matched only by the incredible emotional ache spreading across my chest. She's perfect. She's so fucking perfect.

"Rory," I murmur. "Oh, Rory."

She tightens her grip on me, and in my ear, she whispers, "I've never wanted anyone the way I want you."

I move inside her, and we make eye contact. Sex has always been bodies brushing together seeking pleasure, but what's happening between us is so far beyond what I've experienced in the past. We're physically connected, but it's more profound than that. As though everything inside of me is yearning to be closer to her, to be one with her. How can sex, something I've done so many times before, be so new and unknown?

I bury my face in her neck, and I try to wrangle these feelings into submission. We get this moment together—nothing more. Once, and never again.

"Yes," she says. "Oh, Alex. Yes. Don't stop."

I thread my fingers through her hair and kiss her, maintaining the rhythm that seems to be driving us both closer to the edge.

Don't think. Just feel.

"There," she breathes out, and she arches her back, pressing herself against me with each thrust. "I'm so... so close."

We rock against each other, and she clutches onto my biceps, moaning.

"Oh my God. Oh, Alex." Her words come out in a garbled rush, and her fingers dig into my arms. "I'm coming." She curls into me, around me.

I press myself deeper into her, and while she contracts with her orgasm, I rush to my own release. The cliff is just in sight. No escape. No out. At some point I'll hit the water below, but I don't know if I'll break or drown. These feelings building in me are fathomless. Impossible to determine. *Break or drown. Break or drown.* In either scenario, whatever is awakening in me will have to die. I cannot swim at this depth.

"Rory." My voice is hoarse with need. I'm so close, but I'm keenly aware of the lack of protection.

She tilts her hips to meet me, and I thrust one more time. I grip her waist while I spill into her, overwhelmed by her warmth. We stay like that for a beat, breathing hard.

"Bloody hell," I mutter, my forehead pressed to hers. Never in my life have I experienced anything that all-consuming.

"Yeah," she agrees with a sigh. "Bloody hell."

A chuckle escapes me at the lilt in her voice, which breaks the tension in me. I feather kisses over her face before landing on her lips. "Your accent is no better."

She giggles, and her knuckles graze my stubbled cheek. "Maybe I need a new tutor."

I growl into her ear, and that makes her laugh harder. The sound is an arrow straight to my heart.

God, I should not be here. Shouldn't have done this. What was I thinking? My chest is an aching, painful mess of emotions I can't let myself absorb, or I'll never leave this cottage.

I draw away from her to sit on the edge of the bed, my back to her naked form. I snatch my boxer briefs off the floor and put them on. "I should go."

"Alex." Her tone is full of warning, but she doesn't sit up to look at me.

When I glance at her over my shoulder, she's staring at the ceiling.

"It's ridiculously late. The staff will talk." It's a stupid thing to say. I've been here later than this and never worried about palace gossip.

She rises on her elbows and stares at me. "If you tell me you regret this, I swear to God…"

"I don't regret it." But I do. A lot. Regret is a rising tide in my body, gaining traction one inch at a time. Though it's only on paper, I'm engaged to someone else, and I haven't told Rory. My selective honesty is shameful. She'll hate me, and the fact that's probably for the best causes the vise around my chest to tighten again.

"Are we sneaking around now? Is that what we're doing?" she asks, and there's a tinge of frustration in her tone.

No. We're not doing this again. We shouldn't have done this in the first place. I take a deep breath and force myself to get my emotions under control. Sneaking around is a stupid, horrible idea, but when I catch a glimpse of her downturned expression, the ridiculous ache in my chest comes roaring back. I run my hands down my face and brace myself for how bad this is likely to get between us.

"If you want to be with me, then yes. With the coronation coming and the referendum, Bellerive is in a fragile position. I can't afford a misstep." I tug on my sweatpants and reach for my T-shirt. Not to mention the wedding I'm being forced into. Emotions have no place here. Cold and clinical is what's needed.

"*I'm* a misstep?"

"That's not what I mean," I say, and I yank my shirt over my head. That's exactly what I mean. "This is all I can offer." And it's far more than I should. What I'm offering is emotional suicide. The rational part of my brain realizes the danger—I'm off the cliff, and I still don't know the depth of the water below.

"I get what I get, and I don't get upset." She gives me a wry smile. "Used to be my mom's favorite line when we were kids. Always hated it."

"I don't have the luxury of doing what I want," I say. Even though I am currently doing what I want. Soon, sooner than I'd like, I'll have to allow reason to snap me back to reality.

"I get it," she says, and she flops onto the bed. "Go. Just go."

I understand enough about women to realize I should stay, that leaving is actually the wrong move here. But I can't foster a real relationship with Rory, and insisting on sticking around when she's told me to leave sends another message.

She doesn't meet my gaze, and my chest develops a hairline fracture. Have I hurt her feelings?

Fuck it. I can't leave like this.

Fully dressed, I crawl up her naked body, planting kisses along her skin until I reach her lips. "I'm an insensitive asshole, and I'm sorry."

Instead of laughing or teasing me back, she frames my face and stares at me. "Sometimes." She bites her lip and scans my face. "I wish we were different people."

The crack in my chest widens. "Rory," I murmur.

"It's okay." There's a sheen of tears in her eyes. "It's okay. Don't—you don't have to say anything. I'm being silly."

I smooth the loose strands of hair off her face, and I wish I could ease her mind. This life is all I've ever known, and until I met her, I was content. Country over person. My course was set, and while I've taken this detour with her, eventually the two roads will meet up again, and I'll have no choice but to continue along the path already arranged for me.

I can't feed any narrative that'll break her heart. The situation isn't going to change, and telling her how much I also wish it would does nothing.

"If you don't want to see me anymore…" Getting the words out is a struggle. "If being around me isn't what's best for you…" My voice is husky.

She plants a soft kiss on my lips. "If I was smart, I'd tell you to stop coming." Her thumb brushes my cheekbone. "I'll take what I can get, and I won't get upset."

A lie, but one I long to accept at face value. If only life were as easy as her motto.

TWENTY-EIGHT

RORY

I'm lying to Alex, even after we've been as close as two people can be, even after he offered me a reluctant out of our entanglement. He'll break my heart, and I'll let him do it if it means I get these moments with him.

Take me to heaven and then drag me to hell. He won't hear a peep of complaint out of me. How long will I get before hell comes knocking?

"You should go," I say. "If we're doing this, we shouldn't give people a reason to gossip." I glance at the clock. Just past midnight. Not unusual for him to be leaving my place this late, but it's hard to believe there aren't already whispers about him coming here. I've learned during my limited time in the kitchen that there are eyes and ears everywhere in the palace. Good gossip circulates fast and furious.

He purses his lips and gazes down at me. "You're okay?"

I pat his cheek and do the one thing that's guaranteed to send him off laughing instead of worried about me. "I reckon I'll be all right till it all goes pear-shaped." Having listened to him for weeks now, I find it hard to believe my accent hasn't improved at all. That had to be decent.

His dark eyes light with amusement before he chuckles and drops a kiss on my lips. "Don't quit your day job."

"I happen to like my employer. But my accent coach is a slacker." I scrunch up my face in mock distaste.

He shakes his head with a smile, and he backs off me to stand at the edge of the bed. His gaze runs over me laid out, still naked. "May I just ask that you look exactly like this next time I see you?"

I laugh and throw a pillow at him. "Get out of here."

He chuckles and goes around the corner to the door. A moment later, it clicks closed behind him.

With a sigh, I get up to lock the door. Then I go into the bathroom to get ready for bed. Despite his assertion I should remain in the same place naked until he returns, I work in a few hours. Saturdays and Mondays are my days off. Sundays are my big baking day for the week, and I'm going to be exhausted.

Slipping under the covers, I refuse to let my mind stray to how disastrous this new development with Alex could be. I pushed and prodded him until he caved, and it would be grossly unfair of me to ask him for something he's already told me he can't give. This is what we are—whatever this is.

Embrace the ecstasy. Don't dwell on the inevitable fall from cloud nine.

I close my eyes and will myself to sleep.

An hour later, I wake to my stomach spasming. It's been a long time since I've been sick with some sort of stomach bug, but there's no doubt that's what's starting. The sheets are soaked with my sweat, and I'm light-headed. When my stomach rolls again, I realize I need to get up or I'm going to puke in the bed.

I stumble through the door to the bathroom. I make it to the bowl just in time to lose my very expensive dinner from Café Plutus. It'll be a long time before I can eat shrimp and Caesar salad again.

"Oh God," I mumble when my stomach clenches with another heave. Whatever is left in my stomach lands in the bowl, and then I press my warm cheek to the cold stone floor. Rather than going back to bed, I curl up on the bath mat and wait for the next wave to hit me.

Later, when I try to stand, my legs are wobbly. In the bathroom mirror, my eyes are glassy. I brace myself against walls on my way back to bed. I'm sweating, and there's no doubt I'm running a fever.

On the bedside table is my phone, and I text Joyce with the news of my illness. Tomorrow will have to become my baking day, and I'll have to hope I'm recovered.

Then it occurs to me that stomach bugs can be contagious. *Alex.*

I stare at my phone through blurry eyes. Too exhausted to overthink it, I fire off a quick warning to Alex not to come see me.

I hope I haven't made him ill.

I spent longer in the bathroom than I thought, and the sky outside my windows is lit with pink.

Joyce texts me back and says she can take some of my baking out of the freezer from previous weeks and not to worry. She wishes me well, and after I take a moment to process her messages, I turn off my phone and drift to sleep.

A cool hand is on my forehead, and I release a sigh at the contact.

"Rory, I brought Doctor Bennett to take a look at you," Alex murmurs in my ear.

I roll over to stare at Alex through groggy eyes. "It's just a stomach bug," I say.

Alex shakes his head. "There's been a food poisoning outbreak at Café Plutus. They think the romaine lettuce was contaminated. Did you eat any last night?"

"Food poisoning? Ugh." I cover my eyes with the back of my hand. "Caesar salad. I had the salad."

Dr. Bennett circles the bed and asks me some questions. He takes my temperature and does all my vitals with some portable machines he has in a little bag. Some aspects of royal life make me feel as though I've been transported back in time. House calls by doctors with little black bags of remedies.

Except food poisoning just has to run its course. This isn't my first experience with it.

"I'll be fine," I mumble while Alex and Dr. Bennett confer just out of my earshot. "Sleep. Liquids," I call out.

Alex peers around the corner from the kitchen. "You need someone to help you. I'll take the day off."

The front door opens and closes, and I assume Dr. Bennett has left because Alex is leaning against the corner between the bed and the kitchen.

I've learned Alex's work ethic doesn't take holidays. Weekends are just another day for diplomatic or country-wide tasks for him. He's got boundary issues, but who am I to tell him that? "You can't take the day off to look after me."

"Technically half a day. It's almost noon." He flicks his watch around to confirm. "I would have come sooner, but this is the earliest I could get here after I lost patience waiting for you to reply to my texts."

"I turned my phone off."

"I saw that." He crosses his arms. "You need help. I can help you."

"You also have a bazillion staff members. Someone other than you can help me." After last night, having him cancel his day to look after me is too much like something a boyfriend would do. He doesn't want that role in my life, and I can't let him slip into it. Too confusing.

He searches my face for a moment and then glances toward the unlit fireplace. "I'll tell Stella to spend the rest of her shift here."

Stella is his personal maid and the one who oversees everything that happens in his wing of the house. He trusts her, but she's also the most conspicuous choice he could make.

"People will talk," I say.

"It's me or it's Stella. If you don't want me, you can have her."

"I didn't say I didn't want you, Alex," I huff out, and my stomach stirs. "But if you want to keep us quiet, then having Dr. Bennett come here, having you here, having Stella look after me—not the way to do that."

"You're an expert in royal affairs now, are you?"

My cheeks heat. "I'm sick. Don't be mean."

He covers his face with both hands and drags them down. "You're right. I'm sorry. You sent the text about being ill, and then wouldn't respond about how ill. I was tied up in diplomatic meetings with my parents, and I couldn't get away to check on you. Then I saw on the news about the food poisoning outbreak at Plutus." He shakes his head. "I'm frustrated, and I'm taking it out on you, and I'm sorry."

At his confession, the riot in my stomach returns. "I think I'm going to be—" I cover my mouth with one hand and throw off the covers with the other. When I stumble around the bed, Alex comes to my side and leads me into the bathroom. I kneel over the toilet and shake my head. "Go. Please, go."

He gathers my long hair in his fist as my stomach starts its next revolt. Embarrassment courses through me hot and shameful as I heave into the toilet. It's bad enough to have food poisoning, so much worse to have a literal prince holding back my hair.

When the heaving ends, and I sit back on my heels, I can't meet his gaze. He flushes the toilet and passes me a tissue.

"Water?" he asks, as though I didn't embarrass myself in front of him. "Do you need help back to bed?"

"I don't want you to stay, Alex," I whisper. "I'm a mess."

"You're sick, and you need help." His tone is matter-of-fact. "If you're embarrassed you just lost your very expensive dinner in front of me, I'm not bothered. If you're worried about some palace gossip, I'm doubly unbothered. Your well-being comes before both."

It's both and it's neither. Having him care is a double-edged sword. I want to soak up his attention, but I realize doing so isn't healthy for my long-term sanity. "Stella," I say. With my hand braced on the bathtub, I try to stand. My legs wobble, and Alex is at my elbow in an instant. "I'll accept Stella." I make it to the sink to brush my teeth, and I brace myself on the edge of the vanity.

When I try to walk, and I sway on my feet, Alex lets out a curse and scoops me into his arms. He carries me with ease back to my bed and slides me under the covers. He tucks me in and smooths my hair off my face.

Beside me on the bed is my phone. He reaches across me and presses the power button. Once he's satisfied it's working, he places it on my nightstand, and then he leans over me, one hand on either side of my shoulders.

"Stella will be here within the hour to help keep you hydrated and to hold back your hair."

"I'm surprised you knew about holding back a woman's hair," I say.

He waggles his eyebrows. "I know all sorts of things about women."

A teasing comment about all the women he's studied rises to my lips, but I can't get it past them. The thought of him with anyone else causes my chest to feel as though it might cave in. Last night altered the dynamic between us, and I wanted it to change, but I'm not sure I was prepared for the consequences. We were so connected, so in tune with one another. Having sex with someone for the first time isn't supposed to be *that* good.

"I could stand here all day and watch your thoughts play out across your face," he murmurs.

Warmth creeps up my neck. "Except you can't actually read my thoughts." Please tell me he doesn't have some sort of prince superpower. My thoughts are not a place he should go.

"You're feeling insecure about something. What is it?"

Shockingly accurate. There's no way I'm telling him how vulnerable I'm feeling after we had sex. Nothing like waving a big "Danger! She's far too into you!" flag right in front of him. Neither of us needs that. "Just the things you mentioned before. Puking. Gossip."

A frown creases his brow, and I'm not sure if he's bought what I've said or if I've raised his suspicions. "Within the hour, Stella will be here. I'll make sure of it." He plants a kiss on my temple, and he takes out his phone before heading for the door. "I'll be back when I'm done work to check on you."

The door clicks closed, and a sigh escapes me. A shot of longing for Alex follows. Should I have asked him to stay instead? Would he really have canceled his day again to play nursemaid to me?

Get a grip, Rory.

I'm already longing for things I promised Alex I wouldn't want, that I've tried to fool myself into believing I'll never want from him.

After last night, any brakes I applied to my emotions are cut. I'm full steam ahead to heartbreak station. The only part I'm not sure about is whether I'm alone on the train, or if Alex is right there riding beside me.

Twenty-Nine

ALEX

Since it's Sunday, it's an asshole move to summon Julia and Nick to my office. Doesn't stop me from making the call. Unless they're traveling, they tend to hole up in their wing of the house for the entire day. Used to annoy me beyond belief, but today it's a relief to realize they're both accessible, even if they'd prefer not to be. Truthfully, I'd rather have this conversation with just Julia, but Nick made his thoughts on my friendship with his future wife clear. Besides, it'll make Julia happy I've looped her husband into my emotional turmoil.

Emotional turmoil? What has happened to me? I close my eyes and squeeze the bridge of my nose.

If there's one person who'll understand the kind of longing I'm beginning to suffer, it's Prince Nicholas. Fourteen years of lovesickness. Not an illness I'm keen to experience.

I've got two choices. Get these feelings for Rory wrangled into something I can manage or figure out a way to cancel my arrangement with Princess Simone and convince Rory to become my queen.

Fuck.

How did I let things get this far? How am I even contemplating this?

Not just contemplating it—an obsessive thought pattern over the last few hours. Figuring out a way to be with her is now my top priority. Forget the referendum or the coronation or any of my other duties—her, just her.

Is it idiotic to explore this marriage maneuver without even asking Rory if she'd want to be queen? Last night she wished we could be different people. Not that she could be queen, but that both of us were different. At the time, I brushed off her comment as ludicrous. I had no desire to be someone else, did I?

When I learned of her illness this morning and I couldn't get to her immediately, panic gripped my chest with such ferocity, I feared I might be having a heart attack. Dr. Bennett diagnosed my condition as anxiety when I retrieved him to check on Rory.

Anxiety. *Me?* Anxious? Baffling. While there have been things about my life I haven't liked or enjoyed, I've never been more than a touch nervous about anything. I'm steady. Rock solid. Not prone to panic or uncertainty. Confident—depending on who you talk to—overconfident.

But the racing heart and strangled sensation in my chest didn't ease until I saw Rory in her cottage. When she opened her eyes and stared up at me, the tight grip of panic lessened.

Yes, she was sick, but she'd get better. The overwhelming need to protect her, shelter her, save her, is the same instinct I couldn't fight the night of the car crash. Primal. Undeniable. Weaved into the fabric of my being.

If I can't find a way to marry Rory, I fear my marriage to Simone is doomed. Even I can recognize I'm on the cusp of spiraling out of control. Could I end things with Rory now even if I had to?

Nope. I couldn't. Wouldn't want to. Have no desire to.

Even those thoughts make it seem as though I have a choice, and I don't. My last shred of conviction I could still back out of this vanished this morning. I've fallen too far, too fast—break or drown.

Fuck.

There's a knock on my office door, and I rock back in my chair as Nick enters with Jules behind him.

"You summoned us?" Nick raises his eyebrows and slides into one of the armchairs across from me.

Julia scans my face and sinks into the other chair. "Are you okay? You're very pale. Is Rory okay? I heard about the food poisoning at Café Plutus."

"She's sick," I confirm, and then I swallow to gather my courage. She's sick, but she'll be okay. I can't be away from her, could never tolerate her being ill and not being there beside her. This is my tipping point. "She's what I wanted to talk to you both about." I nod toward the still open door. "Can you close that?"

Julia frowns while Nick closes the door.

"What's going on?" Julia asks.

Nick sits in his chair and rests his elbows on his knees, his expression curious and pensive.

"I would ask Mother this, but she has been the one driving the arranged marriage, and I'm not sure she'd tell me the truth. Maybe she wouldn't even know. But the two of you have been combing the coronation documents." I take a deep breath. "Is it truly a law that I must marry a Bellerivian or a member of a royal family? I couldn't find anything with those specific parameters."

Julia's frown deepens, and she glances at Nick. "I actually don't know the answer to that. It would be in a different document—a royal marriage one, I'm assuming."

"Holy shit," Nick breathes out. "You're in love with Rory?"

I shake my head and chuckle. "No," I say. "I'm not that foolish." Except whatever just happened in my chest when he said that makes me wonder if I *am* that foolish. In *love* with her?

Julia eyes me, and then she and Nick exchange a long glance. "I can look into it, subtly."

"Any—" I clear my throat. "Any potential loopholes you can find, if it *is* a law, would be appreciated."

"To be clear," Nick says, sitting back in the armchair. "I do not want to become king. None of us want you pulling a King Edward VIII. Can we circle Brice into this? Three brains are better than two." He runs his hand down Julia's hair. "Brilliant brains though they may be."

King Edward VIII and his twice-divorced American wife went the distance in the end—till death did them part. Not the worst role model in the world.

"Four," I say. "Four brains. Mine as well."

"Desmond?" Julia asks.

"Five," I relent. He's well versed in my obsession with Rory, and if this doesn't go the way I hope, I'll need a cool head to talk me around to what I must do. No one is more objective than Desmond.

"Have you talked to Queen Helen?" Julia asks. "She's always wanted you, Nick, and Brice to be happy."

"You're right," I agree. "That was when my father wanted what's best for Bellerive, and she seemed to be in charge of figuring out what was best for us. With the king sick, she seems to have slid too far away from the parenting role." I run a hand through my hair. "I'm also thirty-three. This is more a negotiation with an employer than a conversation with my mother."

"Maybe it *should* be a conversation with your mother," Julia says.

Nick purses his lips. "Alex isn't wrong. Mother has been different since Dad was diagnosed. She's got her fingers in every pie. Not in a bad way, mostly. But she's worried he's going to misstep and the monarchy won't recover. That's probably—I mean, that's exactly what's happening right now. She trusts a fellow royal or a Bellerivian to understand the weight of this country, the intricacies of being in charge." He rubs his cheek.

"Rory is lovely, but she's young, she's Canadian, and she's lived here for a year. A *year*. To put her on the throne is…" He raises his eyebrows.

"I didn't ask for any commentary on Rory." I grab a pen off my desk and twirl it in thought. Trust Nick to encourage me into an affair one minute and convince me it was a bad idea the next. "However, those are all valid reasons for not approaching Queen Helen. She'll put a stop to any investigation." I eye Julia. "I've never had to worry about trusting you before."

She sighs. "You can trust me now. We can scrutinize all the documents and laws. We've all assumed the restriction was a law because the king and queen were so insistent, but I don't know if that's true." She glances at Nick. "Do you?"

He shakes his head. "No idea. You're Bellerivian. No issue. Mother was from here. No issue. Grandfather was royalty from Liechtenstein with an arranged marriage. Before that? No idea." His expression turns pensive. "Do we cover that far back in school?"

"Too long ago to remember," Julia says. "Doesn't matter. We'll dig. See what we turn up." She taps her nail on the arm of the chair. "In four weeks, you'll be at our wedding with Princess Simone. Everyone will believe you're announcing your intentions."

"I realize that," I say. My heart skips at having our agreement spoken aloud. I've avoided discussing Princess Simone and my own wedding at every turn.

"If we can't find anything in the next four weeks," Nick says, "leaving Simone in favor of Rory will become a national and international scandal."

The vise around my chest that dissipated at the sight of Rory earlier reappears. "I realize that." There's no scenario they could give me that I haven't considered since I kissed Rory last week. Kissing her opened the floodgates of "what if," and I haven't been able to shut them. Though I would never say it out loud, since the anxiety surfaced this morning, I've been wondering if I'll have to give up my rightful position in the line of succession. In the end, the coronation we're planning might not even be mine.

Would I do that for her?

I shake my head to clear those thoughts. I'm not there yet. Take power and declare divorce legal. Take power and have Rory as a mistress. Take power and forget about Rory. The last thought causes me to groan out loud.

"You okay?" Julia asks, and she glances at Nick in alarm.

"Just get me what I need, and everything will be fine," I say. "No law, or if there is a law, a loophole I can thread."

"Maybe you should pause your wedding planning with Simone while you figure this out?" Julia suggests.

I rise behind my desk, prepared to usher them out. It took me most of the day to decide bringing them to my office was the only course of action. The sooner I get them out, the sooner I can check on Rory, even though I've been in constant contact with Stella.

"I will take your opinion under advisement," I say. Delaying the wedding might mean delaying the coronation. With Father declared incompetent, there is no royal voting power on the Advisory Council, and allowing that to continue too long would be a mistake. Nothing about this situation is simple.

Nick's jaw ticks. "Do you want to talk about this more? I feel like you should be talking about whatever is going on with Rory."

"Nothing to discuss," I say, and I open the door to my office. "Either there's a loophole or there isn't."

"Still? Even now you can be so cut and dry about whatever is going on with you?" Nick asks. "I mean, this is unprecedented behavior for you."

"What choice do I have?" I burst out and slam the door closed again. "To become king, I must be married. Right now, that cannot be with who I'd prefer. If I can't have her, then I have to resign myself to what I can have. Power. Influence. An heir with ties to two kingdoms." The thought of what I'll have to do with Simone to produce an heir isn't remotely appealing. Unfair to her, perhaps. She seems more than amenable to the arrangement. Even claimed to have had a crush on me when she was younger. Makes me an ass on both sides of this equation.

If I must be, I will. My life's motto.

"Alex," Julia murmurs, and she crosses to me to run her hand down my arm.

"Don't," I say, and I withdraw from her touch. "Don't *Alex* me as though this can be fixed with a few kind words. Find me a way out of this fucking hole I've dug for myself."

Nick appears behind Julia. "You're upset, but you can't speak to my wife like that."

"It's fine," Julia says. She scans my face, and there's sadness in her blue eyes. "Nick, Brice, and I will go through every royal document we can get our hands on. We'll get Desmond on it too. If there's a way out, we'll find it."

I nod, unable to get any words out. Julia's kindness has always poked holes in my armor and might have been able to crush it if she'd been so inclined.

"I'd tell you to stay away from her until we know more," Julia says, "but we're beyond that, aren't we?" Her smile is sad. "If you haven't told Rory the whole truth, she deserves it."

"She knows I can never marry her," I say.

"And Simone?" Julia prompts.

"Does Posey know?" I ask. Mitigate the risk. If Posey knows, I'll have to seriously consider telling Rory. They've gotten quite close.

"Royal business isn't something I share with anyone except my mother." Julia chuckles. "And sometimes not even her if I can help it."

"You should tell her," Nick says. "Rory. You don't want her blindsided."

As much as I hate to admit it, Nick has a point. But my fear that we've already gone too far, that she'll stop seeing me before

I'm ready if she realizes, overshadows any logic. A risk I will not take. If there is a chance we can be together, I'm not telling her about Simone. No reason for her to ever know I came so close to betraying her.

"I will take your words under advisement," I say.

Nick sighs and opens the door to my office. He lets Julia exit first, and then he gives me a long look. "Don't make her hate you. Trust me—you don't want to go down that path."

Then he's gone, and I'm alone in my office with my dark thoughts. If I can't marry her, perhaps having her hate me will be a blessing for both of us.

THIRTY

RORY

Alex appears at my door, and even from the couch, I sense his dour mood. He dismisses Stella, and instead of coming to sit with me, he putters around my kitchen, searching for scraps of my baking.

"Midnight brownies on the bottom shelf of the third cupboard on your right," I say.

He glances at me and opens the door I indicated. The top pops off the container. "Thanks," he mutters.

"Not a good day at work for your seventh day in a row?" Apparently I am going to bring up his workaholic tendencies.

"Only seven days in a row?" he asks between brownie bites. "Thought it was more like fourteen or thirty-six or..." He lifts his gaze to the ceiling. "Twelve thousand and forty-five."

That is not a math equation I'm going to attempt, but it sounds like he just calculated his whole life. I adjust the blanket over my shoulders and shake my head. "Most people at least take the occasional day off."

"I am not most people." He dusts off his hands and flicks on the kettle.

"If—or when or however this whole royal thing works—you decide to have a family, you might need to adjust your work-life balance. You know... so it's balanced." I scrape my hair back and settle deeper into the couch.

"Definitely not in the mood to discuss what my life could be like if only I were better at managing it." His shoulders are tense at the kitchen island, and his back is turned to me.

I'm not feeling well, and he's clearly in a pissy mood. No doubt we're going to end up fighting. With other men, I've tended toward docile and pleasing. Confrontation was a big no-no. Whatever they wanted, I rolled over and did. Even when my relationship with my parents was on the line, I didn't argue with Derrick, I gave in. Of course, I never expected them to truly cut me out. Misjudged that one.

However, Alex and I have a strange dynamic. While it feels as though I'm the one pursuing him, I haven't worried he'll stop coming around or cut me off. Even earlier today when he held my hair while I puked, I didn't worry that would repel him enough to stop appearing on my doorstep. Embarrassing? Yes. Doom us? No. I've hidden much of myself from other men in a bid to please them and never realized. Not once have I hidden any aspect of myself from Alex. He gets the unvarnished truth.

"You're in a shitty mood," I say.

"Indeed." Alex glances at me over his shoulder. "How are you feeling?"

"Weak. Queasy. But I've stopped throwing up every hour on the hour. So I'll take that as a win."

He dips his tea bag into his cup at the island. "Tea?"

"Probably the last thing I need is something to keep me awake."

"You've got that terrible chamomile sleep tea in your cupboard too."

"Ooh. Yes. Do I dare try it?"

He shrugs. "Already held your hair back once today. Perhaps we can go for the hat trick by the end of the night."

"Goals," I say. "Gotta have 'em."

A hint of a smile tugs at his lips. "You're in a mood as well. I'll chalk it up to food poisoning."

"I'll risk the tea," I say.

He makes me a cup in silence, and then he sets it on the coffee table beside me. "Your vile-tasting tea."

I leave it to cool beside me. "Tell me why you're in such a terrible mood," I say.

"I'd rather not." He brings his cup to his lips and leans against the edge of the island, facing me.

In between sickness spells today, I worried he'd be distant with me when he appeared again after what happened between us last night. He's angry and frustrated. Not at all what I expected to combat.

"Have I done something wrong?" I ask.

He runs a hand along his brow. "If you could have anything in the world, what would you want?"

You.

My unvarnished truth doesn't include professing my undying love for him. He's made it clear he doesn't want or need it.

"To be loved," I whisper, and I hold his gaze. It's as close as I'll come to admitting what I'm sure I feel.

"You don't feel loved?" Alex's gaze is soft and assessing. He sets down his mug on the island, but he doesn't come to the couch.

"My father chose the farm over me. My mother chose my father over me. I barely speak to my brother—he's chosen the army. Derrick chose Janessa's vagina over me." I tuck my hair behind my ears. "I want someone who loves me enough to put me first. I just want to be someone's first—the person they want above everything."

He abandons his mug and sits on the couch. He draws my legs over his, so I'm partially sprawled across him. He rests his palm on one of my knees, and a tingling sensation spiders out from the contact.

"You deserve that," he says, and his voice is husky. "Did Derrick tell you that last night?"

I let out a startled laugh. "That he chose Janessa's vagina over me?"

He eyes me with a hint of a smile. "I suspect he didn't use those words."

"No. No. He still doesn't want me. He wants something *from* me. He asked me to convince you to rein in the health-and-safety and employment-standards dogs." My dinner with Derrick wasn't a total disaster. When it came down to it, he was more honest than I expected. Our frank discussion at least allowed us to part on semi-good terms. The fact that I'm no longer in love with him made a huge difference in me accepting he's always been self-absorbed and self-centered, and the advice my mother tried to give me before I left for Bellerive might have been more well-meaning than I believed at the time. I didn't want to hear Derrick wasn't the one when Bellerive already felt like home.

"Ah, so Dumbass Derrick was still, ultimately, looking out for Dumbass Derrick." His thumb circles my kneecap through the thin blanket.

"Yeah," I admit. "We had a good chat, though. I don't know. Despite the food poisoning, I'm glad I went. Solidified things I suspected."

"About him?"

I meet Alex's gaze. "About a lot of things."

The air around us hums. He must know. Can he sense it? The depth of my feelings?

"I have no intention of making his life or his family's life easier after the way they treated you."

"I'm not asking you to."

We stare at each other, and he slides his hand under the blanket so we're skin-to-skin. A shiver of awareness races down my spine.

"Dr. Bennett tells me you shouldn't go to work tomorrow either," he says.

"He called me," I say. "Is there anything Dr. Bennett doesn't tell you?"

A slow smile spreads across Alex's face. "He only tells me if I ask."

"You were concerned about me?" A warm glow spreads across my chest. He was alarmed enough to bring Dr. Bennett to see me earlier when I was too out of it to appreciate how sweet the gesture was.

His dark eyes take on a teasing glint. "Merely worried about my staff and the kitchen. At the rate people eat your cheese bread, the whole estate could be compromised."

"I will accept the compliment and ignore the implication my health and safety standards are subpar."

He lets out a soft chuckle.

"Do you really need to work as much as you do? Or are the insane hours what you've become used to instead of being necessary?" He never talks about his royal duties other than giving me a brief rundown of his day when he arrives at night. The intricacies of how long certain things take to plan and execute are lost to me.

He stares at the unlit fireplace and strokes my leg under the blanket. "Interesting question."

"Is it?"

He glances at me. "When I came back from uni, I threw myself into learning everything I could. But my boundaries worsened after my father's illness came to light. Right now, I can turn to him and ask a question if I'm not sure. It's just—I've realized he's not always going to be there." He takes a deep breath. "Of course that's been true all along, but the threat is more imminent. We were supposed to have years." He stares into the distance. "I haven't told Nick and Brice this, but if the referendum passes, I'm not sure how much time my father will let lapse before he files the paperwork to set things in motion for his case."

I'm sure my eyes must be huge. "You think he'll..." How do I phrase my question without sounding crass or insensitive? "You think it'll be that quick?"

He runs a hand through his hair. "Most countries have parameters in their laws about who can seek assisted suicide and when. One of those clauses is often related to cognitive function. In order to agree to your death, you must be aware of what you're agreeing to. As much as I'd love to believe we won't have to say goodbye until much, much later, I don't know what my father will decide or what the law will allow."

I seek his hand under the blanket and clasp it in mine. "That's a lot to sort through."

"I've been working around the clock under this notion that if I get enough knowledge into my brain, I'll never wish I could turn to my father for help when he's no longer there." He huffs out a breath and shakes his head. "A ridiculous notion." His voice catches. "Is there ever a point when a son doesn't need his father?"

My heart squeezes in my chest. Alex isn't one to show a lot of emotion, but it's there in his voice, in the slant of his mouth. "He's been a good father?"

Alex lets out a strangled chuckle. "The only one I've known." He gives me a wry smile. "When he's my father, he's excellent. When he's the king, he's a force to be reckoned with. Two very different people."

"I suppose that's one of the hard things about running a family business. My parents struggled with when to treat me like their child and when to treat me like an employee."

"The lines are very blurry," Alex admits. "I used to be closer to my mother, but lately..." He shrugs. "She knows me well, and that's actually become a drawback instead of a blessing. Never thought I'd say that."

"What about your brothers?"

"They were raised under slightly less restrictive guidelines." His lips twist. "But it's still essentially the same. When you fuck up, you're not letting down a family member, you're letting down and exposing a whole country."

There was never anything worse as a kid than disappointing my parents. I never minded making them angry, but when I disappointed them, that cut like a knife. How would it feel to have that magnified by one hundred thousand disheartened voices?

"I can't even imagine that level of pressure."

"Would you want to?" Alex's voice is gruff. "If circumstances were different…"

My heart pounds in my chest, and my breathing turns shallow. Is he implying if circumstances were different between us? If the rules were different? He picks his words so carefully, there's no chance he's said this by mistake.

"Between us?" I can't keep the hopeful edge out of my voice.

He shakes his head and breaks eye contact. "Forget I said anything. I shouldn't have said anything."

I grip his hand under the blankets, and when he slowly turns to face me, his expression is hooded. No way to read what's going on in that mind of his, but on the off chance he needs to hear it, I'm going to say it. I *want* to say it.

"I would take on the weight of the country for you." I search his face. "I'd take on the weight of the world if it meant I could have you." A dangerous proclamation. He's been clear about what we cannot have. The impossibility of an *us* forever. Unfortunately, it hasn't stopped me from tending a seed of hope. I'm going to seize every inch of ground he gives me.

He leans across my body, and he kisses me, long and deep. When he draws back, our foreheads rest against each other, and he stares down into my eyes. "Sometimes," he says. "I wish we were different people too."

The rough edge of his voice creates an answering pang in my heart. Tears fill my eyes, and warmth floods my chest. My words are clogged by the immediate lump that's formed in my throat.

Instead of speaking, I just nod and kiss him again. I drag him down on top of me.

"You're sick," Alex murmurs into my neck. "I want to take care of you."

I slide my hand along the front of his suit pants. "I'll let you take care of me."

He chuckles and draws away. "That's taking advantage of you. Two very different things." He rearranges my legs again and stretches his own onto the coffee table. "Drink your tea, and I'll tuck you in."

"Yes, Your Highness." I lift the mug to my lips. The water is lukewarm now, and I take a big gulp. Rather than staging a revolt, my stomach accepts the liquid. There may not be a hat trick of hair holding after all.

I drink the rest of it in the comfortable silence nestling between us. One of the things I love the most about my time with Alex is that we don't have to speak to understand each other.

When I slip the cup onto the coffee table, he raises his eyebrows. "Done?"

I throw off the blanket covering me, but before I can get to my feet, Alex slides his arms under me and lifts me into the air, cradling me against his chest. It's a position I've been in several times now, but the sensation never gets old. I could spend the rest of my life in these arms.

He carries me the short distance to the bed, and then he tucks the covers around me.

"You're probably going to say no," I say, "but will you stay until I fall asleep?"

He draws in a deep breath, and his dark eyes search my face. "I should say no." Instead, he comes around the bed and crawls across it beside me. "But I cannot." He lies beside me, and when I curl into him, he tugs me closer.

We lay like that, wrapped in each other in silence. The clock in the kitchen ticks away the minutes, and I'm amazed he's giving me this. Of the two of us, up to now, he's been the one maintaining any semblance of distance. If it was up to me, I'd glue myself to him. Only a slight exaggeration.

He sighs into my hair. "If I could, I'd unmake the world, and when I built it again, I'd live in this moment forever."

The declaration, a hair's breadth from saying he loves me, makes my heart stutter to a stop.

"I'm going to have a lot of regrets, Rory. But my time with you will never be one of them." He kisses the top of my head. "Never."

I'm stunned into silence.

"Get some sleep," he murmurs.

My emotions are jumping all over the place trying to reconcile Alex's normal reserve to this guy in my bed. Not one but two proclamations that are an inch or two from professing his love. Someone like Alex would never say those things if he didn't genuinely mean them.

I lie in his arms, breathing in his sandalwood scent, and although I didn't believe it was possible, the chamomile tea must be working its magic, because I'm drifting into sleep. The last thing I'm conscious of before I'm drawn under are Alex's warm lips pressed against my temple.

In typical Posey fashion, she arrives the next afternoon when she's done work with chicken noodle soup, heavy on the broth, and a slew of local gossip.

As I scarf down the soup, Posey fills me in on all the people across the island hit with food poisoning. Turns out, Café Plutus sourced their lettuce from the same place as a bunch of other restaurants. Derrick must have fallen ill, but he never reached out to me. Despite what I told Alex, we parted on the understanding I'd get Alex to back off his family's company. I didn't agree so much as I didn't protest. With some time and perspective, I can admit no one deserves to be treated so poorly, and I shouldn't have let it happen.

"Kane tells me Alex was worried about you yesterday." Posey lounges on the couch and slings her arm over the back. "I know I said I wouldn't pry, but I'm totally prying. What's going on there?"

"I can't believe Alex's favorite bodyguard fed you gossip." I stir the soup she gave me. Although I didn't go to work today, and I wasn't one hundred percent myself early this morning, I'm back to feeling fine this evening.

"I get the best gossip from all sorts." She waggles her brows. "Now I want yours."

I hold my soup in my mouth while I run through my options. When I've made up my mind, I swallow. "The last time you implied something, there wasn't anything going on."

"Ooh." Posey sits forward. "And now?" Her eyes sparkle with mischief.

"A fling, maybe? I don't know. He's been very clear he has to marry a Bellerivian or someone from royalty. Whatever this is, it's not going anywhere permanent. It's weird to have the parameters of a relationship laid out so concretely so early." Especially when I've never been so certain so early that I long for more than he can give.

"A fling with the future king. Be a great story someday when you're far enough away to tell it."

Hearing her speak the truth is harder than I expected. Someday, Alex will be nothing but a great story. No longer part of my life. No longer my nightly companion. A memory.

"Is that an actual rule?" She frowns and taps her mouth with a manicured nail. "It's a custom for sure. But a rule? I don't know."

She must have glimpsed the disappointment on my face. Her friend collection means she reads people annoyingly well.

"Alex made it sound like a rule." I take another mouthful of soup, and I ignore the hope blooming across my chest. He wouldn't lie to me. The things he's said to me—whatever is in place can't be as simple as him deciding he wants to be with me.

"How is the fling going? Worth it or not so much?" She picks up her midnight brownie from the plate on the coffee table and takes a bite.

"Worth it, no question." The recollection of his lips pressed to my temple last night as I drifted to sleep springs to mind, and he's so much more than that one moment. The tenderness and the caring from someone who isn't prone to those behaviors is astonishingly addictive. "This might be TMI." Nothing ever seems to be too much for Posey. "But have you ever slept with someone, and it was like..." I struggle to describe the almost out-of-body experience of being with Alex.

"This goes two ways—really terrible or next-level amazing."

"Next-level amazing," I say, and I take another spoonful of soup. "But like, and this is going to sound weird, as though we'd been together before?"

Posey scrunches up her face. "Amazing *and* boring?"

I laugh and chuck the crust of bread I planned to dip in my soup at her. "Is this your way of telling me sex with Brent has become boring?"

"Oh, no." She laughs. "Sex with Brent is *never* boring. He's amazingly flexible." She gets a dreamy look on her face. "Has definitely come in handy."

I shake my head. "Forget I said anything."

"Okay, okay," Posey says, and she grins at me. "There's like, two schools of meant-to-be love, right?"

"Soulmates." Everyone knows that one.

"Right, and twin flames. Or twin souls. Can't remember exactly what it's called. The soul is split in two or something. Your perfect connection." She takes a bite of brownie. "If you're into the idea of marrying yourself, it's a good one."

"Alex and I aren't the same."

"More like opposites, I think. You're open. He's closed. You're small town. He's big city. He runs a country. You live in a country."

The last one makes me laugh again. "Alex would never go for some airy-fairy explanation like that." Does he even feel what I feel when we're together? Does either explanation fit the sensation I've been having around him? Wasn't he the one who mentioned reincarnation once?

"Does it really matter?" Posey asks. "When your gut tells you someone is right, that instinct is rarely wrong. Some things can't be explained. They just are."

"Is that what happened with you and Brent?"

"Well, my libido was pretty sure we were destined to mate. Took the rest of me a while to catch up to the *soul* part." She flicks out a hand. "You've seen him, you know."

Muscles galore, and he doesn't seem to mind playing the straight man to Posey's antics. Appears to delight in them, and in her, most of the time.

"None of that matters." I set down my spoon. "We're sort of together for now, I guess? At some point, it's going to end. Has to. He can't marry me. Do I even want to get married? I'm twenty-three."

The scary part is that I would. I would marry Alex. But marrying the royal family is another consideration entirely. I'm not naïve enough to believe Alex is the only person in the equation. A family. A country. If it were possible to be with him forever, would I be capable of giving him everything he needs?

"I will say this." Posey takes her last bite of brownie. "I've never seen Alex look at any other woman the way he looks at you. I've never known him to take a day off or to be so attentive to anyone else in his life. Whatever is going on, he's into it."

"Yeah, I—" None of that is news to me. Obvious, in some ways, that he cares about me deeply. Neither of us is going to escape this unscathed. "He's going to break my heart though, isn't he?"

Posey's exuberance vanishes, and her eyes soften in sympathy. "Just make sure the pleasure is worth the pain. That'd be my criteria. If you're going to feel like crap for months afterward, make these moments count."

I take another mouthful of soup and stare out the window to the ocean in the distance. If I was only worried about months of feeling terrible, what I'm doing wouldn't seem so bad. A few months in a lifetime is nothing. The reality, and what I will not say to Posey, or anyone else for that matter, is that I may *never* get over Alex. That's how it feels right now. That he'll never be a cool story to tell people—my affair with a future king. Instead, memories of him will be stored inside me. A butterfly dead in the cocoon, never able to take flight.

Later that night when there's a knock on my door, I sit on the couch for a beat. Posey's advice has been ringing in my ears since she left after dinner. Soak up the happiness to make the unhappiness worth it. Show me heaven before you drag me to hell. That's what I told Alex the other night, isn't it?

The thing is, sitting alone in my apartment, I've gotten cold feet. Who agrees to spend the rest of their life in hell for a glimpse of heaven? No one. No one in their right mind would agree to those terms.

There's still a chance I can save myself. If I have the strength to turn Alex away tonight, maybe there's a chance I'll experience a month or two of heartbreak. While there is an eventual expiration date on whatever is developing between us, there's no way to know if that's weeks or months from now. I have almost a whole year left on my visa before I'm forced out of the country.

A *year* of sneaking around with Alex. Would I make it that long? Would he tire of me? Would I get over my fascination with him?

Sitting here, both seem impossible. My feelings for him are infinite, all-consuming, rip-my-heart-out, never-the-same-again kind of levels.

I've got one last chance to find the brakes.

Heartbreak is here, on my doorstep. I cannot let it in.

With that thought in my head, I tug open the door. For a beat, I'm dumbfounded. How did I forget *this*? Why does heartbreak have to look so fucking good?

"Alex," I breathe out.

"How are you feeling?" His voice is husky, and he devours me with his dark gaze.

"Like myself," I say. Not exactly true. Right now, my heart is beating so fast and hard there's no way I'm telling him to leave. There are no brakes. Were there ever? Between my sickness and his absence for the last few hours, I underestimated the pull between us.

Whenever this ends I'll have to leave the country. I won't be able to stay when being face-to-face with him dismantles any sort of defense. Seeing him and not being with him will be a thousand tiny cuts across my heart. He is *everything*.

"Good," he says, and then his hands are in my hair, and his lips are on mine.

I sigh into his mouth and bend into him. He lifts me off my feet and sets me on the island before closing and locking the door. He steps between my knees, and he brushes my hair off my face before kissing me tenderly. When he slants his mouth across mine a second time, his tongue dips in, testing and tasting.

I run my thumbs along his cheekbones and lean into the kiss. This isn't close enough. I drag his T-shirt over his head and run my greedy hands along his chiseled torso. He's taken a page out of Nick's book and started scheduling workouts into his long days. He will not hear a word of complaint from me.

My shirt follows his to the ground, and my bra vanishes too. He grazes my nipples with his thumbs, and they pebble under his touch. I lick a line up his neck, and he chuckles.

"Did you know," he murmurs while he feathers kisses along my body, "that you always smell of vanilla and sugar?"

"Sounds delicious." I can't help my smile.

Just before his lips seize mine again, he says, "Fucking addictive."

Like him, I'm also addicted. For the rest of my life, a whiff of sandalwood is going to draw me back to these moments with him. The smell is ruined for anything normal or average when it's so keenly tied to the pinpricks of desire dancing across my skin, the dampness in my panties.

We shed our clothes in a flurry of hasty movements, and when we're both naked, Alex slides his hands under my ass and dips his head between my legs. He teases my core with his tongue in slow, leisurely movements.

I close my eyes at the immediate burst of pleasure, and I splay my fingers on the island to keep me steady. He tips my hips to get better access, and then it's a whirlwind of lips and tongue and the barest graze of his teeth. I shudder, and one of my hands finds its way into his hair, urging him on.

When was the last time a man worshiped my body so completely? Just like the other night, I'm swept away in a haze of sensations I can't filter or compartmentalize. I'm clutching and clinging to him as he drives me to the edge.

"Alex. Oh my God. I can't. I don't." My words are a garbled mess. I want to drown in this feeling forever.

He chuckles against me, and the vibrations send my orgasm ripping through me, shoving me over the edge. The surge is almost violent. I throw my head back on a moan, panting, barely able to catch my breath.

That was on a scale I've never had before.

He trails kisses up my body, and his teeth graze my ear. "You're gorgeous when you come. I could watch you all day."

I'm tempted to inform him that orgasms like the one I just had don't happen every day—have never happened to me before. Whether it's soulmates or twin flames or reincarnation, there's an extra element to the connection I have with Alex which permeates and elevates everything between us.

Dwelling on how unique our fleeting bond is will make me sad, so I toss my hair and seek his lips with mine. Enjoy him. Live in the now.

It's my turn to watch him lose control. Between us, I stroke the hard length of him, my thumb sliding over the silky tip. He swallows and rests his forehead against my shoulder. His breathing turns labored.

"Rory," he groans, and the sound of my name on his lips is unbelievably sexy.

"I want you," I whisper. "I want all of you." So much truth in that statement.

He grabs my hips and tugs me forward to the edge. We make eye contact, and he eases into me. With one hand holding me steady on the edge of the countertop, the other digs into my hair, securing my lips to his. Then we're kissing and moving together in an exquisite push-pull of bodies. The grinding motion causes a flutter in my belly, and I realize there's a chance I might come again.

Before I can be certain, he wraps my legs around him and lifts me off the counter, and he carries me to the bed. There, he lays me down, and my hair fans around me. Soon, our bodies are back brushing together with each thrust, and his hand under my ass maintains the friction between us. Without a doubt I'm climbing the orgasm mountain again. Unheard of for me. Up to now, multiples were unicorns. Mythical, unachievable.

Of their own volition, my fingers dig into his biceps, and I tremble. He stares down at me, searching my face. A hint of a smirk appears.

"You going to come again, Rory?" His voice is rough, and his tone does funny things to my insides. How can my name sound so sexy?

"I think it's—I think it's possible."

"Tell me how to guarantee it."

"Just don't stop. Don't stop." I squeeze his biceps and moan.

"I can do that," he says, and then he kisses me deeply.

While we kiss, I tumble over the edge again, and my orgasm sends a shock wave through me. I gasp, and goose bumps surface across my skin.

He picks up the pace, breathing hard at my ear, and his thrusts extend my orgasm to an almost unbearable length.

"Fuck, Rory," he groans. One hand cradles my head, and he surges inside me with a shudder.

Spent, we lie entwined for a beat, breathing heavily. He strokes my side, and I savor the closeness.

Take it in, Rory. Take it in.

Time is ticking between us. How much? How long? I have no idea, and I'm not sure I want to know. Ignorance is bliss, isn't it?

I run my fingers through the short strands at the back of his head, and even with multiple orgasms, even with him still this close, I want more. Or maybe I just never want these feelings to end.

Last time, he pulled out and tried to leave as though I set the building on fire. He's not in such a hurry tonight, and it makes me feel better about not calling this off.

Who am I kidding?

The minute I opened the door, all rational thought vanished. There was no calling anything off once I laid eyes on him.

Definitely fleeing the country once this is over. Having my heart ripped out on a daily basis isn't a life goal. If I have to see him with someone else, I might die.

He kisses my forehead and my cheek, and then he eases out to lie beside me. Instead of keeping his distance, he tugs me into his arms and sighs into my air.

"You're staying?" I ask.

"You want me to go?" There's amusement in his tone.

I let out a husky laugh and trace letters absently across his chest. He strokes my arm, and a heavy silence fills the cottage.

"At some point you'll have to leave, right?" I whisper. Not just now, but later. We're not built to last.

He takes a deep breath and settles me tight against his side. "I don't want to."

We're tiptoeing around the truth of our tenuous relationship, and I'm not sure I want to dig deep enough to get the facts. Why me? How long can we last? Do you want me forever like I want you? Typically, if he decides to answer my questions, he's unwaveringly honest. I'm not ready to hear any of those answers.

Someday, my heart will break over Alex, but until then, I enjoy having it intact. Questioning what our relationship is won't change the limits of what it can be. We get *this*, whatever that is, and nothing more.

Maybe by the time this is over, I'll be okay with it ending. A great memory. A fun story. My heart squeezes in my chest. I can't imagine it.

"I should probably get some sleep," I say. The urge to wedge some distance between us seizes me out of nowhere.

Alex kisses my temple. "Mind if I stay for a bit?"

I glance up at him, and the tenderness in his gaze undoes any desire for a separation. "Really?"

"It's cold out there," he says, and there's a hint of a teasing glint in his eyes.

"Right." I draw out the word. "Wouldn't want you to get hypothermia."

"Got the remedy right here." He squeezes me against him.

I inch up and kiss a corner of his mouth. Perhaps the trick to being okay at the end of this is to immerse myself so fully in him I get tired. He'll be routine and boring. You can have too much of a good thing, can't you?

He nuzzles my nose with his, and then he kisses me, dragging me across his body. His hand squeezes my ass, and then I'm straddling him.

"I've never had multiples before," I say as I kiss his neck.

"No?" He trails his fingers along my back. "There's only one thing to do then."

I meet his gaze. "What?" I ask.

He grips my hip, and he flips us around so fluidly I let out a delighted squeal. His stubble scrapes along the sensitive hollow of my neck as he settles between my thighs. When he meets my gaze, a fire burns in his depths. "Go for the hat trick."

"You love the hat trick," I say, thinking about his comment the night before.

He chuckles. "This hat trick will be much better than the other one."

"I sure hope so," I say with a laugh.

He stares down at me. "I—" He hesitates and searches my face. "God, I—" He gives almost an imperceptible shake of his head, and then he kisses me.

Whatever he intended to say gets lost in a sea of sighs, moans, and the cry of his name when he scores his hat trick.

325

THIRTY-ONE

ALEX

Rory comes out of the bathroom naked, and she crawls across the bed to me. For the last three weeks, we've spent an abundance of time in this cottage. Without discussing it, we've fallen into the same pattern as before—we work, do our own thing, and at the end of each night, we're together. Exactly the same as before but with a thousand times more sex. We've christened every square inch of this place, and instead of anything feeling routine or boring, we're becoming more connected, more in tune with each other. I have never craved anyone—their company, their body—the way I do hers.

"I should go," I say. "My lunch hour is almost over."

Rory laughs, and she trails kisses up my side until she reaches my cheek. "You could take a five-hour lunch and still work more hours in a day than most people."

"If I took a five-hour lunch, people would notice." Though I'm sure we're already a source of palace gossip. Instead of taking lunch in my office, as I've done for years, I walk to Rory's cottage on her days off. When she's working, I eat in the kitchen at a worktable by the window, talking to her and the other kitchen staff. The distance I should be keeping has been obliterated by my need to be close to her. I've never had someone I see so often take up so much mental space.

I have completely lost the plot, and I can't bring myself to care.

Untangling myself from Rory, I begin putting my suit back together. The day she tore some buttons off my shirt required an explanation in the laundry department. While it was amusing someone so petite could manage to dislodge them, it was less amusing when I had to find a plausible lie for the seamstress on staff. *The pastry chef did it* is grounds for a sexual harassment claim on top of everything else. I am, after all, one of her bosses. Were I speaking to my parents, I'm sure they'd have played that card too.

I button my shirt, and Rory stretches on the bed, enticing me toward one more lunchtime round. It's Saturday, and I could get away with being here all afternoon under normal circumstances. With Nick and Julia's wedding only a week away, things at the palace are not normal. I have a meeting with Desmond in twenty minutes about wedding logistics.

He's begrudgingly kept my parents' questions in check. I've denied all their requests for a private meeting, and neither of them has had the guts to seek me out. The result is that I've had no one to answer to for the last three weeks. Glorious, glorious independence to make terrible, life-changing choices.

I've gotten into the habit of compartmentalizing even more than normal. The things I want to do versus the things I have to do. At first I kept the details of my coronation from Rory because I didn't know her. Then I kept them because there was a chance I could wiggle out of what I'd agreed to. Now I'm not telling her because hurting her feels like stabbing myself in the heart.

In six months, I'm supposed to be marrying someone else. In one week, I'll be walking into the church in Bellerive with Simone on my arm. No loophole has been found.

I'm totally and completely fucked, and when I let myself consider what I've done, what I'm doing, I want to drown in self-loathing. I haven't told Rory about Simone, but I have no doubt word of my affair with Rory has reached Denmark. So many royal households are connected by staff-member friendships and acquaintances. Someone will have warned her.

No one has warned Rory, and although I know it should be me, that I must be the one to tell her the truth, I refuse to do it before I absolutely have to. I'm squeezing out every drop of happiness, even if that joy is tarnished each day by regret, sadness, and a host of other negative emotions I hope she can't sense.

"You okay?" Rory asks, rising on an elbow to examine me. "You just got this really sad, serious expression on your face."

"Wish I didn't have to go," I say, and I box her in with my arms while I give her a quick kiss. When she tries to draw me down, I laugh and step away from the bed. "I have to meet Desmond." I give her another peck, and then I nuzzle her nose before kissing her again. "I'll be back after dinner."

"I won't be here," she says. "Remember I'm going to Wino Wine Bar with Posey, Julia, and some of Julia's other friends? A mini-bachelorette party or whatever."

"Ah, right." I rub the back of my head. "Right." Any time she hangs out with Julia, I get twitchy. While a sober Julia would never give away any secrets, drunk Julia is rife with bad ideas. "After?"

She rises onto her knees and grabs my tie. She tugs me down for a kiss, and her arms snake around my neck. "After," she murmurs against my lips.

If I don't get out of here soon, I'll be late for my meeting with Desmond. "Later." I disentangle myself, and Rory flops back on the bed with a dramatic sigh.

It's enough to make me want to collapse down there with her. I let out a chuckle and draw my hands down my face. After Nick and Julia's wedding, I'm carving out a better work-life balance. On a Saturday, I can't even crawl back into bed with my love.

The thought draws me up short, and I run a hand through my hair. On the way to the door, I chastise myself for letting such dangerous notions creep in. She's not my love. After Nick and Julia's wedding, she may never speak to me again.

I've played my cards too close to my chest, and when I lay them down, she may very well feel cheated.

Believing she is my love is a shortcut to giving up everything here for a chance to be with her. I can't have her and Bellerive.

My impossible choice.

Desmond is waiting for me in my office when I arrive. I slide into my chair, and I survey the printed emails he's laid out for me to read. I don't touch them. I've read them on my computer and on my phone. Dealing with them is another matter.

"Your parents have requested a meeting with you Monday at eight." Desmond flips to a page in his little black book. "There are no conflicts."

I chuckle. "No? Just pencil Rory's name in there, and I'm sure a conflict will arise."

Desmond releases a long-suffering sigh. "Your Highness, if you do not wish to meet with them, I will relay the message."

"At what point do you think they'll show up uninvited and unscheduled?" I muse.

"The king will respect your wishes. The queen is growing weary of your..." He gazes up at the ceiling. "Temper tantrum, I believe that was her phrase."

"Temper tantrum." I scoff.

"To be fair, you know as well as I do, we haven't discovered a single clause in a single royal document that would allow you to marry someone who isn't Bellerivian or royal."

"That's not exactly true," I mutter. There were several clauses various kings slipped in to cover mistresses or other women on the side. Very, very few interferences in the direct line of succession, but they exist. Those exceptions just don't fit my scenario. If Father hadn't been declared incompetent for the purposes of ruling, he could create an amendment to the rules. Unfortunately, one of the clauses we did discover doesn't allow me to write and enforce anything until I've taken the throne. Probably an overzealous heir at some point, but it fucks me over now.

I don't even know if Rory would want to be with me, but I wish more than anything it was a conversation I could have with her. She said she'd take the weight of the country, the weight of the world for me, but pretty words aren't actions. The weight is heavy, sometimes crushing, and no matter what I feel for her, I would never wish this life on her if she didn't truly want it. Before this whole thing started, she said she'd never work for a boyfriend's family business again.

What about a husband's?

Desmond clears his throat. "In front of you, you'll find a series of emails where you were cc'd and did not respond."

I finger them without picking them up.

"I saw you read them," Desmond prods.

I sigh and skim my knuckles against my cheek. "The logistics of Simone's introduction to Bellerive." I work my jaw in annoyance. "I'm at a crossroads, Desmond. A thing I desperately do *not* want to do is at a junction with a thing I desperately *want* to do."

Desmond closes his little black book and sits back in his armchair. He stares at me, and the silence grows heavy around us.

"You're not going to say anything?" I prod.

"This is not my life; it's yours." Desmond crosses his legs.

"So I can just do what I want."

"Well, you have been, haven't you? Consequences be damned." He nods at the papers on my desk. "She's aware of Rory. An open secret. Probably just as you planned."

If only I'd planned any of this. For the first time in my life, since the minute I told Kane to turn down West Shore Road, I've been at the mercy of something much larger than me, than what I *want*. I couldn't have turned my back on Rory if I possessed superhuman willpower. Fate. Destiny. All those notions I believed to be bullshit came knocking, and I answered. I opened the door, and I can't close it again. I don't know how. I don't *want* to.

"Is it worth speaking to my mother?" I ask.

Desmond shakes his head. "No. I would not, if I were you. She's not on your side in this. The king might be swayed."

"The roles are reversed," I muse.

"The king's perspective on quite a few things has changed—subtly or otherwise—since he was diagnosed."

Desmond has never had to tell me how my parents are feeling before. I'm in the eye of any storm—the son they lean on—but I've removed my support. "Normally, that would be a good thing, to have him on my side. But he's powerless now."

"What are you hoping to gain from your obstinance? Your options are to marry someone other than Rory and assume the throne or to step away from the line of succession to have Rory." He balances his hands in the air. "Flaunting your affair only to marry Princess Simone is beneath you."

I huff out a breath and cross my arms. He's rarely so blunt with me, but it's probably about time someone was. We're down to the wire, and I can't get my head in order. My desire for Rory is superseding everything else.

"Is that why Mother is so angry?"

"For perhaps the first time in her life, she doesn't understand you. She may not have agreed with decisions and conclusions you've made in the past, but she understood them. This"—he waves his hand—"whatever this is, isn't logical or rational. It's emotional. Everyone is used to that from Nick and, to an extent, Brice. But you? Never you. Your tagline—emotions don't rule me, I rule them—is notorious."

Suppose I won't be able to make that claim anymore. It isn't my head that's been steering this train straight into heartbreak station.

"I haven't told Rory about Simone." I keep my voice low.

"But she knows you cannot marry *her*. At least you had that much integrity."

"Rory mentioned it?"

"Posey. Asked me if it was true. I confirmed." Desmond meets my gaze. "Obviously, you're a topic of conversation."

I close my eyes and grimace.

"Are Rory's feelings for you as strong as your feelings for her?" Desmond asks. "If you give up the throne, does she want what you want?"

I pinch the bridge of my nose. "I haven't talked to her about it. I don't—I don't even know how to have that conversation when I'm not sure I *can* walk away from being king. That would put Nick on the throne."

"Correct." Desmond opens his little black book again. "The first time a king's cock will be immortalized on the internet. I suppose there are worse things."

"Good God," I mutter. "He doesn't want to be king. Brice says he doesn't want it either."

"If all of you step aside, succession falls on King George's brother's family."

Desmond's cold assertion does nothing to alleviate the anxiety bubbling inside me. Would Nick and Brice really reject the monarchy to that extent? Julia would talk Nick around, wouldn't she? A reluctant king is better than a miserable one, isn't it?

"You think I should talk to Rory?" The path forward is so muddled, I can't see anything ahead of me.

"You choose the Crown, or you choose her. Given how you've been behaving, I think it's reasonable for you to give her the whole picture. In the past, I wouldn't have had to say this, but I'm going to, in case you need to hear it. Don't wait until Friday night to make a decision. You've never been one to shy away from uncomfortable conversations before. Don't be a coward when your happiness is at stake."

He's not pulling any punches today. I suck in a deep breath and gather the emails. "You've made some valid points."

"Had you cared to listen to anyone, you might have heard them weeks ago."

I give him a sharp look. "There's only so much advice and criticism I'll accept."

"Agreed." Desmond rises. "I trust you'll respond to those emails."

When Desmond opens my office door, Nick is there with his hand raised. "I was just about to knock. Alex," he calls to me. "Take a half day. It's my bachelor party. Brent is on the island, and we need to show him a good time."

"Your bachelor party?" I raise my eyebrows. This is the first I'm hearing about a bachelor party.

"Okay, so not exactly. Julia didn't think a real bachelor party with Brice in charge was a good idea." Nick enters my office and gazes around. "Pre-drinking needs to commence soonish."

"You want to start pre-drinking at—" I glance at the clock over his head. "Two in the afternoon?"

"By the time Brent gets here, it'll be more like four or five. He's stopping to see Posey first."

I rock back in my chair. A piece of the picture is missing. "We're hanging out here, drinking?" Last time I did that, I kissed Rory, and now I'm on the cusp of abandoning the monarchy all together. Bellerive can't take another drunken episode from me.

"Here initially, yeah." He gives me a sly smile. "And then we're crashing Jules's bachelorette at Wino Wine Bar."

Thirty-Two

RORY

Last time we were at Wino Wine Bar, Brice and the rest of us were given what I thought was the VIP treatment. Whatever exists above the VIP level is what I'm experiencing now. For Julia, they've cordoned off an entire section and set up screens that allow us to see everyone else, but they can't see us.

Julia made it clear to everyone when we arrived that her bachelorette party—no strippers, loud music, or drunken proclamations—is endorsed and paid for by the Crown.

"There's a male strip club open tonight on the other side of the island," Posey says, loud enough for Julia to hear once we've all had a few drinks.

"Yes, you sent me the link already." Julia shakes her head and laughs. "I can't. I don't even want to. Have you seen my future husband? I have eye candy on demand. If I ask him to, he'll strip for me." Julia gives an exaggerated wink.

Posey shrugs. "I mean, truthfully, probably none of the strippers have a better body than Brent. But it would be fun to compare, maybe rate them, develop a grading scale. See a few packages."

"No! No scandals," Julia says. "The king and queen are already beside themselves because of Alex." Her gaze slips to me, and she snaps her mouth closed. She picks up her wine and turns away from us with the kind of exaggerated caught-out movements only drunk people can pull off.

Julia is on the other side of Posey, so while I heard what she said, it's clear she wishes to believe I didn't. She's already engaged in conversation with someone else.

"Are people upset with me?" I whisper to Posey.

"You wouldn't be here if people were upset with you," Posey says. She eyes my wine glass. "Drink up."

Why would the king and queen be upset with Alex, and why would Julia have that reaction to her slip, if the two weren't tied to *me*? While I keep consistent hours in the kitchen, and I get palace gossip from other workers, they are careful around me. Having Alex turn up most days to eat lunch in there doesn't help my relationship with my colleagues, but I haven't cared to say anything to him. Whether he's there or not, people at the palace are aware we're close. Likely alert to far too much of what's passed between us, if the gossip I hear has any validity.

None of the talk has bothered me, and it hasn't appeared to bother Alex either. Where he was once paranoid about people getting the wrong—and eventually right—impression about us, he never remarks on it now.

Over the last three weeks, since I was ill, he's opened himself up. He answers questions honestly and fully. He's rarely guarded about palace matters. Now that Julia's let something slip, I realize he hasn't mentioned his mother or father at all. No meetings with them alone. The progress on the referendum, bits and pieces of the coronation, wedding preparations for Nick and Jules, incidents that happen across the country where his presence or insight is needed, but never anything about them. His biggest grievance is the lack of voting power on the Advisory Council and the danger of leaving a member of the family absent for too long. His council meetings are a source of frustration since his father is no longer allowed to attend, and Alex has no vote on matters being discussed.

We've talked about so much, but his family dynamics are still a pressure point. Since mine are also a mess, I never push him too hard in those conversations. Those are always the conversations that make *us* feel temporary, anyway, so I've been happy to drop those threads. We'll never truly live in each other's worlds.

Has our... I stutter over the most appropriate word. Has our relationship caused a rift with his parents? I finish my wine, and another is slotted into its place without me having to ask. I know what it's like to be abandoned by my parents, and I wouldn't wish it on anyone. If I'm the reason there's stress between them, would Alex have told me?

We've become extremely close in the last three weeks, but I don't think he'd tell me anything to unsettle the life we've built in the cottage. My tiny apartment is a bubble from the outside world—a place where we make love, tell each other stories, bake together, laugh a lot, and just exist. He's no more Prince Alexander than I'm a farm girl from Canada. We're just Alex and Rory.

Maybe that's the danger. For me. For him. We exist in that cottage but nowhere else.

"You're being very quiet," Posey says from beside me. "Julia's drunken comment threw you off?"

Posey has been holding court with one outrageous story after another. While Julia is warm and outgoing, she's got nothing on her younger sister's ability to make people feel seen. Right now, Posey is peering into my soul with a wine glass in her hand.

"Am I the cause of Alex's rift with his parents?" I ask.

Julia leans across Posey and sets her hand on my arm. She's so drunk I half expect her words to slur. "I shouldn't have said anything about the king and queen." She raises her glass of wine. "Loose lips sink Bellerive's ships."

"But is..." I stare into my glass. "But is Alex fighting with his parents over me?"

Julia shakes her head. "Absolutely not." She chuckles. "Alex doesn't fight with anyone. He stops listening. They're not fighting. They're just not speaking."

"What?" I shift my gaze between Julia and Posey.

One of the other women calls Julia's name, and she turns away from me to answer their question. Instead of coming back to give me more context, she's sucked into a conversation about Nick and Tanzania.

"Alex is fighting with his parents?" I hiss to Posey.

"I'm not telling you anything you don't know," Posey says. "He can't be with you long-term, and from what I understand, the king and queen are concerned he's leading you on."

I frown and shake my head. "He's not. He wouldn't."

"They'll sort it out eventually." She pats my hand. "I wouldn't worry. It's not as though he's talking about stepping aside as king to be with you."

A wave of heat followed by a shot of ice-cold floods my body. He hasn't, and I don't know what I'd do if he did. He loves Bellerive in an old-fashioned, beyond honorable way. For him, the good of the country comes first. In every discussion we have about politics or Bellerivian affairs, he's determined to do what's best for the people, navigate the correct direction for the whole country. Leaving the monarchy to be with me is inconceivable.

"He'd never do that," I say.

Behind the VIP area, there are raised voices, and then the curtain is thrown aside to reveal Nick, Brice, Alex, and Brent.

Julia lets out a squeal and jumps into Nick's arms. You'd think they hadn't seen each other for years. Posey grins and leaves the couch to wrap herself around Brent. Brice settles among a host of women on the other couches to suck up all the female energy, and Alex's drunken gaze finds me.

I expect him to hesitate, to sit elsewhere, but he strides over and drops into the couch beside me. He flings his arm over the back and kisses my temple as though we do this in front of other people all the time.

"Truth and Tequila," he groans beside me. "I'm going to be hungover tomorrow."

Taking my lead from him, I run my thumb along his cheekbone. "Poor Alex."

"Will you hold my hair back if I puke?"

I laugh. "I'll get out my hair clips and give it my best effort."

He grins and tugs me so I'm snug against his side.

"Should we be doing this?" I ask when I realize quite a few people in the group are watching us.

Alex sighs. "Just give me tonight. Can we do that? Say 'fuck it' and do whatever we damn well like?" He gazes down at me, and his dark eyes are glassy.

"I don't know," I whisper. "Is this going to get you into more trouble with your parents?"

Alex barks out a laugh. "Loose fucking lips." His jaw tightens, and he scans the room before focusing on me. "I'm not in trouble with my parents, I'm in trouble with my employers—the king and queen. There is a difference, even if the two of them have lost sight of it."

"So they *are* upset with you?"

He runs a hand along his cheek. "I'm really drunk, Rory." He peers at my wine glass. "Why aren't *you* really drunk? Everyone else seems to be *very* drunk."

The night—the opulence, the secrecy, the sense of decorum—unsettled me before Julia said anything about his parents, and after that, I couldn't get into the spirit of the evening. Any piece of my conflicted emotions is too big of a conversation to have when he's so drunk.

One of Julia's friends has her phone out and appears to be recording the room.

"Kane!" Alex bellows to his chief bodyguard, and he points to Julia's friend.

Without hesitation, Kane steps into the closed off area and takes the woman's phone.

"Julia!" Alex calls. "Why were phones allowed in here?"

"I didn't know you were coming," Julia says from her perch on Nick's knee. "And now everyone is drunk." She runs her finger along Nick's nose before planting a kiss on his lips.

"All the phones," Alex says, making a circular motion with his hand. "Over to Kane. You get them back at the end of the night."

I observe the exchange with a strange fascination. Despite the time Alex and I have spent together, most of it has been in isolation. The few times we've been in public, I've hated it. The grocery store. The king's birthday. Will I hate tonight as well? So easy to forget he's famous. His photo worth money. The two of us sitting together is a story to be sold.

Alex settles deeper into the couch, and he loops his index finger around a strand of my hair. "You look lovely." He kisses my forehead. "Of course, you always look lovely to me."

I shut my eyes to soak in the compliment and the close contact. My fingers curl into his T-shirt.

He places his hand over mine and glances around. "What do you think? Could you live this life?"

"This life?" I take in the scene with him. Alcohol is strewn around the private area of couches and armchairs. Waiters come and go with drink orders, and everyone is absorbed in their own world. A few curious drunken glances are thrown our way. "I don't... I haven't really thought about it." A hint of a smile tugs at my lips. "This isn't really your life either."

He shrugs. "Could be."

His comment, said with such ease, has a dangerous undertone, and a bright caution sign flashes between us. He's drunk, and I shouldn't encourage whatever line of thinking this is. The VIP scene isn't Alex and pretending otherwise is silly. Anything he says while he's had too much to drink might not be exactly what he means during the harsh light of royal life.

"How was Truth and Tequila with Brice, Brent, and Nick?"

"Enlightening," he says, and he gives me an amused smile. "Perhaps I should have been playing those games all along."

All right, he's starting to freak me out. Drunk or not, this light, uncaring Alex is unfamiliar. Teasing, sure. But this?

"Should we go home?" I ask.

He scans my face. "So soon?"

"I'm not sure we should be... like this. With other people."

"I took their phones."

"But unless you're gluing their mouths shut, this is a bad idea, isn't it? I mean, I realize we've got an expiration date, and you've obviously dated lots of other people, but we've been keeping us quiet. Or I thought we were. Aren't we?" Now I'm confused and rambling. Why did we have to keep what's developed between us quiet? At first it was the press narrative. Is it still that?

His expression clouds, and he takes my wine glass from my hand and drains it. "An expiration date. Is that what you think?"

Something is going on with him beyond being drunk. Outright asking sends a shot of anxiety through me. He's not a careless speaker. Do I want him to tell me what's leading him down these tangents?

"Let's go home," I say again, nudging him in the side.

"Home," he muses. "I like that your home is my home."

A wash of warmth envelops me, but the sensation is followed by nerves crawling up my spine. Where is this coming from? "You're freaking me out," I whisper.

He leans closer so his lips are a hair's breadth from mine. "Let's go home." He stands up and grabs my hand, tugging me to my feet. "We're off," he says to Nick and Jules.

Julia and Nick both have furrowed brows when they notice Alex's hand linked with mine. Are we a surprise to them? I assumed they knew. Posey gives me a wink and tells me to have fun.

Once we're in the vehicle, Alex sits in pensive silence, staring out the window while Kane drives us to the estate. He's gone from exuberant at the bar to almost sullen. Something is bothering him, but I'm not sure I want his answer.

He takes my hand to lead me out of the vehicle and steers us toward my cottage. There's a charged silence between us, but I'm clueless. Whatever Alex is thinking about, I've never felt such deep conflict emanating off him. It's the same energy I've gotten once or twice from other men before they've broken up with me. My stomach flips.

We enter my cottage, and I turn on lights. I grab a glass of water and some aspirin for him.

He waves me off and leans against the island. "What if I quit?"

"What?" I turn to face him. "Quit what?" We're halfway through a conversation I didn't know we were having, but the energy I sensed on our walk terrifies me.

He searches my face for a beat, and there's turmoil in his dark gaze. Whatever is coming next, it's not easy for him to say.

"Quit us?" I manage to get the words out past the lump surfacing in my throat.

"No, no." He comes around the island to frame my face. "The opposite. What if I—" He swallows. "What if I quit the monarchy?"

"Why would you... why would you quit the monarchy?" My throat is dry, and my heart is thudding so loud I'm not sure I'll hear his answer. Is he quitting for me? A minute ago, I was worried he was going to break things off with me.

"If I quit, we can be together, really be together."

"I don't—I—" I bite my lip. Am I supposed to say yes? I want to. But I don't understand what saying yes will do. "If you quit, then what?"

Alex releases me and leans against the island. "Nick would become king, assuming he's agreeable. I would—I would have to leave Bellerive."

"Leave?" My heart isn't just thudding heavily now; it's racing. "You'd have to leave the country."

"The current rules of succession mean I can't live in Bellerive if I opt out of being next in line. It's—it would be too confusing for everyone if I were here." There's a touch of agony in his voice. "I'd have to watch Nick cock it all up. Bad for everyone."

Panic flutters to life in my stomach. This is a huge conversation to be having while he's drunk, and I'm unprepared. "The coronation is almost a year from now. My visa is good for a year."

"I have until Friday to make a decision. There are things that will be set in motion, and once they're moving, I can't stop them." He rubs his face, and his voice catches. "It's now or never."

"You just found this out?" I get out my baking supplies and start mixing. Stress baking. My hands need to be busy doing something so my head can make sense of Alex's words. The year I thought we'd have has turned into days, maybe hours if I say no to him leaving the monarchy.

When he doesn't answer, I glance at him. The other shoe drops. Whatever is happening on Friday, he's known for a while. "Oh, Alex," I breathe out. "Why didn't you tell me?"

"Because I didn't want it to be happening. I have this little corner of my life, this slice of normalcy with you—the most normal thing I've ever had in my life—and I didn't want it tainted."

"You would leave the monarchy to be with me?" I ask, and there are tears in my voice. "You'd give it all up to be with me?" Flour coats the island, but I've abandoned my baking to stare at his heartbroken expression. He doesn't want to make this decision. The truth is written all over him.

"If I must choose, I will choose." He comes close to me and slides his palms along my cheeks. "Once I tell them I'm leaving, it's done. It's a slip of legal paper and an official announcement. But I cannot change my mind."

"This is a really big decision to be making when you're drunk," I whisper, and my words are garbled with unshed tears. I love him. God, I love him so much, but to be the reason he gives up everything else—his country, his family—I don't want that responsibility.

"I'm not sure I could have said it otherwise," Alex admits.

"But doesn't that tell you something?" His T-shirt is clenched in my fists.

"It tells me I have two things I want most in the world—you and Bellerive. I cannot have both. It's impossible. Believe me, I have scoured every royal document I could find."

My stomach rolls with a sudden bout of queasiness, and I step back from him. I shake my head. "We can't talk about this when you're drunk. If you can't say it to me when you're sober..." Do I want him to be able to say it to me sober? Won't he resent me, eventually? What if he gives up the monarchy and six months from now we fizzle out? This is not a spur-of-the-moment choice.

Whatever he decides, the decision is permanent. Whatever I tell him will change the course of Bellerivian history, will alter Alex's life forever. Julia's advice to me weeks ago when I went on my date with Derrick resurfaces. When you love someone, you protect their happiness.

THIRTY-THREE

ALEX

Rory looks like a startled deer caught in the headlights of an oncoming lorry. I never intended to spring this on her tonight while I'd been drinking, but when she said we had an expiration date, the truth settled over me with more certainty than I expected. If I have to choose, I choose her.

"Just because I'm drunk doesn't mean I'm not serious," I say.

"What would our…" She shakes her head. "What would our life even look like?"

Truthfully, I haven't gotten that far in my exit plan. Although it's an idea that's been floating around in the back of my head since the night I told her I couldn't be with her, I haven't put serious thought into it. Now I've left it too late to formulate a good strategy for my removal, for the termination of my contract with Simone, for putting Nick on the throne.

"Those are details we can figure out as we go along. I'm entitled to some money, so we won't be poor." I tip my head while I do some math. "We won't be nearly this rich, though. But we can live modestly anywhere. Do anything."

"It doesn't…"

Her stilted sentences are starting to get to me. But I've sprung this on her, as far as she knows, out of the blue. While I've considered this possibility, I didn't tell her.

"It doesn't sound like you have a plan," Rory says. "You're the type of person who would have a plan if this was what you really wanted." There's so much sadness in her voice.

I press my fingers into my temples. "You want me to talk to you about this tomorrow when I'm sober?"

"I don't know how to answer you when you're drunk. This is sudden and rash and…" She stares at me. "Not like you."

"I've never said anything to you I didn't mean." I close the distance that's crept between us. She turns her face up to examine me. "This question won't be any different in the morning."

She bites her lip, and she smooths her thumb across my cheekbone. "Have you talked to anyone else about this?"

I shake my head. "I don't need anyone else's council to know my own mind." Others are aware this route is a possibility, but I doubt anyone thinks I'll take it. God, if anyone asked me even a few days ago, I wouldn't have been sure *this* choice was possible.

"We're under a time crunch, but I think both of us really need to be sure we understand what we're doing," she says.

"I understand what I'm doing." Don't I? "I can't give you up." I plant a light kiss on her lips. "I won't give you up." I deepen the kiss. Her nails dig into my hair, and she angles her mouth over mine. Just as long as I don't dwell on what leaving Bellerive will do to me, I'll be fine.

"I don't want to talk anymore," she murmurs against my neck. "I just want to be close to you."

So I give her what she wants—me as close as I can get. We're going to have a lifetime together. We don't have to talk right now.

Rory woke at the crack of dawn to head to the palace kitchen. We agreed to talk tonight when I'm done work. She seemed distracted when she left, and I hope she's getting her head around the idea of us leaving Bellerive together. When I consider my life in that context, my stomach doesn't clench so hard with uncertainty. Maybe I'm not one hundred percent sure about leaving the monarchy, but I'm sure about her.

I've summoned Nick and Jules to my office again on a Sunday. They're probably both hungover and wanting to murder me. But I need to give Nick the heads-up before I contact the law firm we use. Leaving is a relatively simple process, at least legally. By Monday night, I could be out of the line of succession.

My stomach clenches.

But I'll have Rory.

The tightness eases a fraction.

That's what I'll have to do until this is over—close my eyes and think of Rory. Her image can guide me through this, what we can have together. Giving her up isn't an option. If that's my truth, my heart, then I can't let what I'm losing secure a foothold in me.

When Nick arrives, he doesn't knock. He enters, swings around the armchairs, and drops into a seat. Jules trails behind him, and rather than taking her own chair, she curls up on Nick's lap, and he hugs her to his chest.

Instead of being annoyed at their closeness, my mind drifts to Rory. *I get that. With her, I get that.* The realization causes the tightness in my chest to disappear.

"You summoned us?" Nick sighs and strokes Julia's hair. "Is this going to become a thing on Sundays from now on? 'Cause I expect to be even more hungover after our wedding next Sunday."

"No, I don't intend to make it habit," I say. "Mostly because I don't intend to be here."

Nick frowns, and Julia uncurls herself from Nick, but she doesn't leave his lap.

"What?" she asks, and I can tell by her wary tone, she's wondering if she's interpreting my comment correctly.

"Rory and I are talking about it in more depth tonight, but I intend to remove myself from the line of succession tomorrow."

Julia gasps and scrambles off Nick's lap. She perches on the armchair next to him, and she grabs his hand. "Alex, this is insanity."

Nick rubs his face and seems to be a step behind. "You're—you don't *want* to be king?"

I swallow, and I can't meet his gaze. This is the moment where I should be showing absolute strength and certainty, but there's only so much I can fake. "I can't have Rory and become king. That much has become clear. While I have struggled with this decision, I can't let her go." I shake my head and give Nick an imploring gaze. If anyone should understand, it's him. "I can't."

He and Jules share a long glance, and Nick stands up to pace between the chairs and the desk. "Okay. Okay." He spins on his heel to face me. "You're breaking your contract with Princess Simone. Stepping down. And leaving the country? Before we started hunting for a Rory-sized loophole, I didn't know the rules of succession quite so well. But I do now. You'll be expected to leave the country. Leave the family. As the rules stand now, you won't be allowed to return to Bellerive—ever."

To hear the consequences laid so bare causes a cold sweat to rise along my back. I rub my face. "Right. Yes. That's my understanding too." To never again set foot on Bellerivian soil...

"Alex, you *cannot* mean this." Julia slouches into her chair. "Nick, am I still drunk? Is this a fever dream? Am I dead?"

Nick swallows. "You are not dead, and unfortunately, this is no hallucination." He sits beside Julia again and laces his fingers with hers. He huffs out a breath. "Have you really thought about this? Do you have a plan?"

Julia shakes her head. "Every decision you've ever made has had a 'if this, then' chart involved. Where is it?" She cranes her neck toward my bare desk. "This feels *very* impulsive."

A heavy silence settles over the room. It's the same impulsiveness Rory accused me of last night. There are three women in the world who know me, really know me. I suspect my mother would be equally horrified if she were sitting here right now. Her judgement cannot be trusted, unfortunately. Her priority has become the monarchy and not her son's happiness.

"It may be a tad impulsive," I admit. "That doesn't mean this isn't the best course of action for me."

"Why don't you call off the wedding to Simone and buy yourself time? You and Rory can be together longer. What if whatever is happening between you and Rory doesn't last? It's been—what?—three months?" Julia gives me a helpless look. "I realize you might not want to hear that, but you need to consider every angle of this decision. If you won't, someone has to. You would be giving up your entire life for her after knowing her for *three months*."

"Jules," Nick says. "Come on. If he loves her, he loves her."

"Does she love you?" Julia turns to me. "Does she love you enough to accept the weight of this decision too?"

My heart kicks at the implication Rory might not be on board with my decision. She did seem reluctant last night, but I sprung the idea on her. I'm sure after she's had today to think it through, she'll be on my side of this. The only option for us to be together is for me to step down. I love her enough to do it. Surely she loves me enough to accept? Even if we haven't said the words, the air is alive around us when we're together. She loves me. I'm sure of it.

"She understands that our choices are limited."

"Alex, that's not an answer." Julia lets out a frustrated wail.

"If you and Nick aren't keen to lead the monarchy, I'll speak to Brice. Obviously, he'll then have the same wife issue I did."

Julia points a finger at me. "That is not why I'm saying these things right now. Of course we'll step up if we need to. Right, Nick?"

Nick stares at me. "That's a big step," he mutters.

"I called you here to tell you as a courtesy, not to be talked out of it."

"I'm not talking you out of it," Julia says. "I want to make sure you never regret your choice."

"I wouldn't. You don't know Rory." My immediate instinct is to defend her.

"I do know Rory," Julia counters. "She's lovely. I just—" Julia throws up her hands and glares at Nick.

"I need to get some air," Nick says. He rises and runs a hand down his face. "I think we all need some time to think this through. I'll be back in a while." He opens my office door.

When it clicks closed behind him, Julia and I stare at each other.

"Are you sure about this?" Jules whispers.

"The only thing I'm sure about is that I have to make a choice." I rest my elbows on the desk and put my face in my hands.

"Hit pause with Simone."

I let out a long groan of frustration. "What changes if I hit pause? Do we magically find a loophole for Rory? Do I suddenly get her and my country?" I push back my chair in a surge of frustration. I shove my hands into my pockets and stare out the window. "Pressing pause delays the choice. It doesn't change it."

"You'll get a tremendous amount of pushback without a plan." Julia comes to stand beside me at the oversized window.

"My plan is to let Simone down easy and rip up my contract with her. Get the lawyer here to prepare the paperwork for me to step aside in the line of succession. Everything else I can figure out after that."

"Except as soon as you step away from the family, from being king, you're supposed to leave the country. Where will you go? To Rory's parents' farm? The parents she hasn't spoken to in a year?" Julia huffs out a breath. "What worries me about this decision is that you haven't thought it through."

"Rory and I are talking tonight," I say, but there's a sinking sensation in my gut at these home truths Julia is serving me. While I didn't expect them to be delighted by the news, I didn't anticipate so much resistance from *her*. "I won't sign anything until she and I have a plan."

Julia runs a hand through her long hair. "Be honest with her, Alex. Be honest about everything you're giving up. She needs to go into this decision with her eyes wide open too."

I nod. As much as I want Rory, I won't force her into a situation she doesn't want. We both need to be okay with the choices we make.

Thirty-Four

RORY

When my shift in the kitchen finishes, I sneak down the hallway where the royal offices are located. All day, Alex's words and intentions have been playing on repeat in my head. This swing from "I cannot be with you" to "I'll leave everything behind for you" has tipped me sideways. Tonight he'll expect an answer from me, and I'm playing catch-up on the details. Since he's never once led me to believe a future for us was possible, I don't know how to process this change in him.

Part of me, a big, selfish percentage, wants to throw caution to the wind. Alex can quit the monarchy, and we'll roam the globe together doing who knows what who knows where. It's a romantic notion though, the kind meant to sweep someone away. It's the kind of idea that led me here in the first place with Derrick.

I was lured by the romance.

I was met with the reality.

If someone is going to offer me a romantic vision again, no matter how much I want to seize it, I need to understand the reality. There's too much at stake for me to go into my conversation with Alex without a complete picture.

At the king's doorway, I raise my hand to knock. I haven't booked an appointment, and I'm not sure if he keeps the same insane hours as Alex or if he's likely to be upstairs in his suite of rooms in the middle of a Sunday afternoon.

I knock.

There's a shuffling behind the door, and when it's pulled back, King George is standing there in jeans and a T-shirt. I've never seen him so casual.

"Oh, Rory," he says, and he smiles. "I came down here to get something." He shakes his head. "And I can't—whatever I intended to get has slipped my mind." He peers at me with the same hazel eyes as Nick. "Do you need something?"

"I was hoping to speak to you actually, if I can, if that's all right. If you're too busy, that's okay too. It's Sunday, and maybe you don't talk to people on Sundays. I know I'm supposed to book an appointment, and I didn't do that, so..."

He gives me a kind smile and steps away from the doorframe. "Enter at your own risk. It's a mess in here. My wife and I have been sorting through old documents and papers."

He closes his door, and I perch in one of the seats across from his desk. When he eases into his chair, he stares at me over a desk strewn with letters and legal paperwork. He wasn't lying about the mess.

"So, Rory. Do you mind if I call you Rory? I took my cue from Alexander, but if you'd prefer Aurora, I can do that."

"Rory is fine." I give him a fleeting smile and try to gather my thoughts. How does the future king's girlfriend go about telling the present king that his son might quit? It occurs to me I should have thought this through better.

"Um," I say. "I heard that Alex's association with me might have caused a rift between you and him. I just wanted to tell you that he's never led me on or promised me anything that he can't deliver." Oh God. That's going to make what I say next sound even worse, like I've been trying to convince him to leave the monarchy. My cheeks heat.

"Alexander has always been strong-willed with a mind of his own." He gestures to his desk. "Queen Helen and I have been sorting through all of this in hopes of finding something to assist Alexander."

"Oh," I say. "With the coronation?"

"Hmm." The king eyes me. "What can I do for you, Rory?"

I clench my hands in my lap. If I came here for guidance, I need to spit it out. "Last night, Alex, while he was very intoxicated, brought up the idea of..." Oh God. I can't say it. Am I betraying Alex? I need to protect myself and protect his happiness. If I don't understand the decision we'd be making, how can I do that? An hour ago, speaking to the king seemed like the best way to do that. Now that I'm here, I'm fumbling.

The king searches my face. "You know, in thirty-three years, I've never seen my son look at anyone the way he looks at you.

There is nothing you could tell me that would be a surprise about what drunk Alexander might have said or implied."

"He said he might quit." The words come out of me in a rush. The king's declaration that Alex has never looked at anyone the way he looks at me is a swell of warmth across my chest. Does that mean I should let him quit? Why would he tell me that?

The king gives a slow nod. "We have come to this, have we?"

"I—I don't know." I give a helpless shrug. "He was very clear, has been very clear all along that we couldn't be together. Last night was a surprise. But he wants to talk about it tonight, and I don't know what to say." I run both my hands down my hair and then tuck the strands behind my ears.

The king rocks back in his chair, and the move reminds me of Alex. He doesn't speak for a long stretch, and I wonder if I made a massive mistake in coming.

"What do you want to know?" The king's voice is hoarse.

"As much as you're willing to tell me about what it would be like if Alex stepped away from the family."

"Do you love my son?" His shrewd gaze sweeps over me.

Instead of shrinking under it, I sit straighter in my chair. An easy question. "More than I've ever loved anyone. It's impossible for me to put the depth of my feelings into words. But this isn't a situation where I can lead with only my heart. I have to keep my head involved too. There's too much at stake." I've been repeating those words to myself all day, every time I've been tempted to go to Alex and tell him to do it.

"You may be young," the king says, "but you are not naïve." He sets his elbows on the desk. "Ask your questions."

I'm a misstep. That's the thought that keeps running through my head while I sit in my apartment, tears streaming down my face. When Alex implied it that first night we slept together, he meant it.

He's engaged to someone else.

Talking to the king was a car accident in slow motion. He answered every question I asked without any hesitation. Each truth was a blow, from understanding Alex's birthright to his grooming to be king to the arranged marriage he signed to fulfill coronation rules. How I managed to get out of his office without having a monumental breakdown I'll never know.

I didn't make it back to my apartment in one piece. Instead, I stumbled and sobbed along the gravel path, littering the route Alex and I have walked so many times together with fragments of my heart.

At every step, every hurdle, Alex has chosen the monarchy and his country over everything and everyone else. Becoming king is Alex's destiny, but it also appears to be the thing he's wanted most in the world.

Until last night, he never led me to believe otherwise.

Last night isn't a true reflection of Alex's desires. Maybe he wanted to convince himself I meant something to him, or maybe he got cold feet about marrying Princess Simone of Denmark, but I don't for a second believe his speech about quitting was genuine.

For weeks I've turned a blind eye to the truth staring me in the face. We've been so happy in our little bubble together that the idea of bursting it with any piece of reality didn't interest me.

Even if I believed Alex might have been considering quitting, the consequences are widespread and life changing. He's not rejecting the crown; he's rejecting his entire life. Every aspect of it. Making that sort of choice on a whim is wrong.

If Alex steps out of the line of succession, he has to leave the country immediately. As in escorted off the island on a private jet to a location of Alex's choosing. But, as the current rules state, he'll have no access to any of the royal properties. A small monthly allowance would sustain Alex, but the king was clear it would never support a family. He did say that, if Nicholas chose to change the rules when he became king, he could. Until then, we'd be adrift on our own.

Alex must know all this. He must. So, if he shows up here tonight without a concrete plan of where we'll live and how we'll sustain ourselves financially, I can't let him leave the monarchy. If he truly wanted to be with me, if I wasn't a misstep, he wouldn't have been planning this alternate future where I had no place.

There's no room for me. I'll never be his mistress, and he can't be my husband.

The TV, which I turned on in an effort to clear my muddy thoughts, flashes to a full-screen view of Alex giving a speech on the steps of the Advisory Council building.

The sight of him sends a torrent of emotions ripping through me. Hurt. Betrayal. Sadness. Love.

Love.

Unable to resist, I turn up the volume.

Earlier today, there was a horrific car accident on West Shore Road which robbed two families of their children. Since Bellerive is small, the tentacles of grief are wide reaching.

Alex is speaking from a podium at a press conference on what the monarchy's response will be to the plight of both families. In his usual suit, he's regal, and his posture is the same as it was at the ball. Through sheer force of will, he'll hold up the nation. The speech is stirring, and in my already emotional state, I'm sobbing by the end.

Watching him speak to his country, speak to a common grief, solidifies my belief that agreeing to Alex's wild, ill-thought-out plan won't bring either of us happiness. Not really. Temporary joy, and a lifetime of regret.

He was born for this role, and he's spent his life preparing for it. He's made no secret of how much he can't wait to be in control of the country, how he longs to have a seat on the Advisory Council, how hard he's been working to learn everything he can from his father. For him to toss all of that aside for me doesn't sound like an Alex-level decision.

I'm drawn back to Julia's assertion that when you love someone, you protect their happiness. If Posey asked Brent to quit his next Olympic run, he would because he loves her that much. Posey would never do that. When you love someone, you don't ask them to sacrifice their own happiness to achieve your own.

My decision, the one I have to give Alex, comes into sharp focus. Another sob clogs my throat, and I collapse on the couch, listening to him console a country while my own heart shatters into a million pieces.

Thirty-Five

ALEX

When I arrive at Rory's door, I'm already emotionally wrung out. Right after Julia left my office, Desmond came to deliver the news of the brutal car accident on West Shore Road. Dealing with the aftermath and the web of grief that seized the island took all my time and focus. I'm headed into Rory's cottage without a concrete plan and without all the answers I was planning to give her. I'll have to hope she wants to be with me badly enough that the finer details can be worked out later.

I knock on her door and wait. There's no shuffling or movement behind her door to let me know she's on her way to answer. Panic grips my chest, and I knock again with more force.

I've been on the knife's edge of grief all day. At the crash site earlier, my mind kept straying to how different my life would have been if I hadn't turned down West Shore Road and met

Rory. One impulsive turn altered my life, changed the course of hers. Losing her is my worst fear, and the irrational thought that something has happened to her flutters at the edge of my consciousness.

She always answers.

The apartment isn't that big.

I'm poised to knock again when heavy footsteps approach. Normally, she flies to the door, a whirlwind of happiness. She'll rattle off all the details of her day while offering me whatever she's baked in her free time. Coming here, whatever my mood, is like having helium balloons attached to me, lifting me up and out of myself. No matter how terrible my day has been, being with Rory always makes it better.

I really need that to be true today too.

From her approach, I can tell the conversation we're about to have isn't going to be easy. For the first time since I mentioned quitting to her last night, my gut twists with the realization she may not want what I want.

When she opens the door and I see her swollen, tear-stained face without a hint of a welcoming smile, there's no doubt I'm in for an uphill battle. My arms ache with the desire to comfort her, to hold her close.

"Hey, come here." I take a step toward her, and she steps back.

She draws even with the edge of the door and out of my reach. "I wasn't sure I should answer."

"Did something happen I don't know about?" I ask.

She shrugs and doesn't meet my gaze. "No, I'm certain you know it all."

That sounds ominous. "May I come in? We have a lot to talk about."

She leaves the door to put the kitchen island between us. Instead of speaking, she takes out baking supplies. There's flour everywhere, and three Tupperware containers are brimming with various baked goods on the counter.

"This is crisis baking," I say slowly. We've spent enough time together that I recognize the signs. Whenever she's emotionally overwhelmed, she bakes—a lot.

"What did you want to discuss?" Rory asks, and she raises her eyebrows in challenge.

"Exactly what I told you last night." Despite her appearance, I'm approaching this conversation with confidence. "I'm planning to quit the monarchy tomorrow."

"Don't quit for me," she says in a rush. "I don't want that. I haven't asked you to do that."

I'm struck dumb for a beat, and a cool sweat breaks out under my armpits. "Of course you haven't asked me, but I want to be with you."

"More than you want to be king?"

My answer has to be swift and certain, and reminding myself how definite I need to be leads to a hesitation. "Yes."

"Tell me your plan." She coats the island with more flour. "What are your steps to a successful extraction from your family?"

"I sign the paperwork tomorrow, and we leave the country."

"Where would we go?" She bangs a plastic bowl onto the counter.

"Anywhere we want."

"You realize that's not a plan, correct?" She raises her eyebrows.

"I don't care where we go." Frustration leaks into my voice. Given how emotional she looks, she's being very cold and calculating about this conversation.

"What would life be like in this mythical place on Tuesday?" She cracks an egg into the bowl. "What do you plan to do? Your whole life has been about serving Bellerive. Public service. Where would you work?"

I rub my face and wish I'd had time today to come up with any sort of plan. "I don't know," I admit. I've never worked for anyone other than my father. There's never been an opportunity to choose my fate. "But none of that matters right now."

"It matters to me." She dumps flour into the bowl.

Fed up, I circle the island and take her hand in mine. "Do you want to be with me? If there's a way we can be together forever, do you want it?" What angle do I need to work to get her to go along with me? While I didn't expect this conversation to be easy, I didn't expect so much obvious resistance.

She won't meet my gaze, and when I tip her chin with my finger, tears tip over her eyelashes and onto her cheeks. My heart cracks at the sight.

"No," she whispers. "I don't want any of that."

An ache blooms across my chest and ribs, the same one I experienced the night I saved her from going over the cliff. Unlike before, it's not her that's in mortal danger, it's us. "I don't believe you."

"I don't believe you either, so I guess that puts us in a difficult spot." She juts out her chin, but tears trickle down her face.

I feather a kiss along her cheek, and her fingers curl into my shirt. She's lying to me, and there's going to be flour on my shirt as proof. I frame her face and brush her tears away with my thumbs. "I love you, Aurora Wilson, and I think you love me too."

More tears pool in her eyes, and her chin trembles. "Even if it's true, it's not enough." She takes a deep, shuddering breath and draws away from me. "Don't quit because of me. I don't want you to quit because of me. You think it's enough right now, but it's not."

"Rory," I murmur, and I try to draw her back to me.

She shakes her head and steps away to the corner of the island. "Even you don't really want this, Alex."

"I wouldn't be here saying these things if I didn't want this outcome," I say in a burst of annoyance. "I don't do things I don't mean. No one can make me do something I don't want to do."

She purses her lips and nods her head. Her gaze is on the ceiling, and whatever is going through her head I won't like.

"What we've built in this cottage isn't real." Her voice is thick.

"Don't say that." My chest tightens. How has this conversation gone so off track?

"We've created this bubble in here." She throws out her arm. "But this isn't real. *We* are not real. Whatever you think you feel for me today—it's not real."

Where is this coming from? How can she say that?

"Not real?" I stride toward her and grab her hand. "You want to know what's real?" I place her hand over my heart. "Whenever I worry about you, or I think I might lose you, there's this ache in my chest. Our connection is so powerful that the night we met, I thought I cracked a rib. There's a tether between us, invisible but undeniable. The thought of not being with you, of anything happening to you, is physically painful." I search her tear-stained face. "There is nothing in the world more real or permanent than my love for you."

More tears spill onto her cheeks, and I tug her against my chest. She sinks into my arms, and she breathes me in. A sob escapes her, and she buries her face deeper into my shirt.

I rub her back in soothing motions and scramble for whatever else I need to say to put her fears at ease. This has to work between us. The alternative, any life without her, is a slow march to death. I cannot lose her.

She grips my shirt and tugs on it. A moan of frustration rises, and she releases me with a gentle push. "I know about Simone." Her voice shakes.

The blood in my veins runs cold. "What?"

Of all the arguments I expected her to make, this was never one of them. Given how many people are involved in Simone's arrival for Nick and Julia's wedding, it's not a surprise someone put two-and-two together, but I never wanted it to be her.

"When you love someone, you don't build a second life, construct a more suitable path." Her lip quivers. "You don't have a plan right now, Alex. There is no real plan for *us* because *I* have never been the plan." Her voice thickens. "The only plan you've had for weeks is the one where you marry Princess Simone of Denmark and assume the throne. *That* is the plan."

Words are failing me, and I need them right now. Badly.

"You've spent the last three weeks fucking me while you intended to marry her." Her sadness has been overtaken with anger. "That's not love. I don't know what that is, but it *isn't* love."

"You were unexpected," I whisper. Those are not the right words. She's slipping away, and I don't know how to drag her back.

Tears fill her eyes again, and she tilts her head. "I'm a *misstep*. But even if I wasn't, I don't want to be with someone who could do this to me, who could do this to Simone. Neither of us deserve it. If she wants to marry you, that's up to her." She swipes away the tears streaming down her face again. "But I won't be leaving the country with you on Tuesday, and I don't want you coming here anymore."

"Give me a chance to explain." Panic grips my chest, but I keep my tone even, reasonable.

"I need you to leave."

"I don't want that life you described, the one that's been planned for me. I don't want it. I want you. I want us." Desperation has leaked into my voice, but I don't care.

"Alex." Her reprimand is sharp. "I need you to go." She tries to guide me toward the door.

"I have until Friday, and I'm not giving up on us. I've never felt about anyone the way I do about you."

"Alex."

We're at the door, and she's opened it, but I'm not stepping through.

"You're upset," I say. "And I get it. I should have told you or been better prepared for this conversation, but none of that means I don't want to be with you. None of that means my choice isn't sincere."

She's holding the door and staring at her feet. "I have a choice too." When our gazes meet, there's so much anger and pain in her green eyes that I suck in a sharp breath. "You might choose me, but I *don't* choose you."

Her words are a dull knife across my heart, wrenching and painful. "Rory." I clutch my chest.

She shoves me out the door and slams it, clicking the lock into place with force. She thumps against the door, rattling it, and then she slides to the floor.

I press my palms into the wood. How did I fuck this up so badly? After all these weeks, all these years, I finally have something other than the Crown, other than servitude and solitude, and she's seeping through my hands like water. Impossible to hold onto but life sustaining.

Maybe I wasn't completely sure about leaving last night, but I am now. How do I survive this life without her when I know how much better it is with her?

A gut-wrenching sob penetrates the door, and my heart cracks in half.

"Rory. Let me back in. I love you. I'm sorry. I'm sorry. I can fix this. I can fix it."

But I don't know how to fix what I broke between us, and she doesn't let me back in.

THIRTY-SIX

RORY

Every night, he comes.

The exact time varies, but he's knocked on my door each night since Sunday. He arrives, a rap of knuckles on the wood, calls my name, and then he waits. Sometimes it's five minutes, sometimes I hear him out there for hours pressed against the door. The chime of his email and the bing of a text are the soundtrack of our heartache.

On Tuesday, he came to the kitchen, and I locked myself in the pantry. Joyce ran interference by telling Alex I was delivering a cream tea to the queen.

Avoiding him is killing me, though. To have him so close, to have him want to be closer, and to not give in. Each knock on the door dents my resolve. I can barely eat, and I'm exhausted all the time. Sleep comes and goes in fits and starts. When I dream, I dream of him. Vivid, visceral dreams like I had as a kid about this cottage. Waking up is the most exquisite torture. When I sleep, I'm happy, and each morning when the dreams end, I'm faced with a life stretched out before me with no Alex in sight.

My heartbreak feels limitless, expansive, as though it's eaten my whole life.

Whatever heartbreak he's experiencing is temporary. I was a misstep in an otherwise smooth existence. He has another life, one without me, all planned out. A life he's been prepared to live since the moment he met me. My presence and absence will change nothing for him, whereas his has changed everything for me.

My heart is a palimpsest. My love for him might be scraped away with time, but traces of him will remain dotted across my heart for the rest of my life. I will never be rid of the impression he's left.

Posey has texted to visit after work a couple of nights, but I begged off as either tired or too busy with the upcoming wedding. Tomorrow when Princess Simone arrives, Posey will understand why I've been avoiding her.

Did she know about Alex's betrothed? She's loyal to the royal family, but I can't imagine her keeping this from me.

How many people realized I was being played for a fool?

The first few days, I was hurt beyond belief, but a part of me understands that, even if he told me the truth, it wouldn't have made any difference. Going into this affair, I realized we'd never get our happily ever after, and I did it anyway.

With each day, my sadness fades and morphs into anger.

If I'd known the affair would be weeks instead of months, if I'd known a marriage stood between him and the crown, if I'd known Princess Simone would call him husband within the year, I would have left this estate once my concussion was healed and never looked back.

The what-if or if-only games never lessen the hurt, but remembering the ways he wronged me fuels the anger I need to stay away. My resistance is a thinly constructed wall of rage. One caress from him would wipe it away as though it never existed.

Saying no was the right thing to do, but my heart, my traitorous heart, longs for a different outcome.

On Thursday, it's dusk when he knocks on my door. Tomorrow Simone arrives. Will he try to persuade me even once she's here?

"Rory, we need to talk." His voice is deep and sure of itself. A king in command.

My stomach stirs, and against my better judgement, I go to the door and place my palm against the wood. The timbre of his voice burns off the fog of my anger and hurt.

"Simone arrives tomorrow, and if I am making a different choice, I must make it tonight." He takes an audible breath. "It must be tonight."

I press my forehead against the cool grain, and I picture him on the other side. My heart strains toward him, and my hand lands on the doorknob against my will. How easy would it be to turn the handle, to let him in again?

"You made your choice weeks ago when you signed the contract and didn't tell me. Your heart belongs to Bellerive, not to me." I manage to get the words out around the lump forming in my throat. How many tears does a body hold? I've been crying for days.

The door rattles on its hinges, and Alex huffs out a breath of frustration. "When I agreed to the arranged marriage, I didn't know you."

"That's not true, Alex. Stop lying to me!" I bang on the door.

There's a deep sigh. "I signed the contract after I met you, but the arranged marriage was in motion *before* I found you in your car. I didn't—I had no idea how much you'd change my life." There's a beat of silence. "How could I have predicted that the woman I dragged out of the car wouldn't just curl into my arms but into my heart too?"

Tears pool in my eyes, and I cover my mouth to keep from crying. The memory of being cradled in his arms is solid and warm.

If I say yes to leaving with him, how long until he resents me? We've known each other for three months. Right now, I can't imagine breaking up, but what if we hate each other six months from now? Relationships are unpredictable. When I followed Derrick to Bellerive, I never expected our outcome either.

What if something big happens in Bellerive and Alex longs to be here? His father is sick, and the referendum could require a rapid decision from the king. How would Alex handle missing valuable time with his dad? Could he return for his death?

There are too many variables; too many things we haven't worked out. We'd need months to be sure this is the right choice—not hours.

But I so badly want to open the door.

I said yes to the romance with Derrick, and I hated the reality. I can't do that to Alex too. He wouldn't just lose his family; he'd lose everything.

"I can't," I cry. "I can't."

"If you can't—" His voice hitches. "At least let me in for a proper goodbye."

I bite my lip and turn to press my back against the door. Letting him in again would be a mistake. I've barely survived this week, and if I have him tonight, and he's with someone else tomorrow, I'm not sure I'll recover.

I can't cling on and let go.

"You should go, Alex," I call to him, and I pray my voice stays steady. "You've got a big weekend ahead of you. My time in your life is done. You've just—" My voice quivers. "Got to let me go."

He hits the door, and it jars my shoulders.

"We don't end this way," he says. "We're not ending this way, Rory."

I can't stay at this door. The pain in his voice and my own longing to see him one last time are going to pierce what's left of my resolve. If he picked the lock, I'd take him into my bed and bolt him into my heart. I would never let him leave.

In the bathroom, I lock that door too. The murmur of his voice penetrates the cottage, but the words are lost. Whatever he's saying, I can't hear it.

I cover my ears and collapse on the bath mat with a sob. This is the right thing to do. He can't give up his whole life, no matter how much my heart roars its protest.

The limo is visible from a window in the kitchen. I could pretend the shiny black drew my eye, but I've been on pins and needles, waiting.

The flour container is by the window. I grab some measuring cups and go to the workstation that lets me look out without appearing too interested. While I scoop from the industrial-sized container under the wooden counter, my heart beats an unsteady rhythm. This must be her. Panic is a vise across my chest.

I want to see her.

And I don't.

She needs to seem real for me to resist going to Alex, for me to stop myself from changing my mind. Would it even matter if I had a change of heart now?

How long did Alex stay outside my cottage last night? I lay waiting for him to leave long enough for sleep to drag me under.

When I woke, I was curled on the bath mat in a tight ball, but his voice no longer echoed through my empty apartment.

Out the window, I catch a glimpse of a dark-blue suit and shoulders I've traced a thousand times with my fingertips, dug my nails into on the brink of tumbling over a cliff.

The back door of the limo opens, and when she steps out, there's a wide smile on her lips. Tall. Slim. Dark hair. Little black dress. So much makeup. She kisses both of Alex's cheeks, and the blood drains from my body.

She's beautiful, and she'll be his wife. Sleep in his bed. Have his children. Be with him forever. She'll map his body with her lips and fingertips the same way I did.

I grip the side of the workstation to keep from collapsing in a heap on the floor. Their silhouettes grow hazy out the window with my unshed tears.

A rough palm eases across my back, and when I glance beside me, Joyce is watching with me. "He's taking her to the wedding?"

I cover my mouth with a floury hand and nod. Tears slip down my cheeks, and I brush them away quickly.

"So that's it then, is it?"

"That's it," I whisper, and the thickness in my throat makes it hard to speak.

She hugs me to her side. "Take the rest of the day off."

I shake my head. A few other tears slide down my face, and I sweep them away with my fingers. "No, no. Going to my apartment would be worse. There's a lot to do with the wedding tomorrow."

Weeks ago I signed up for overtime to work the wedding alongside the catering company. At the time I thought it would be fun to catch a glimpse of Alex while I served tables, but now I hope I don't see him at all.

"You sure?" she asks, and there's so much kindness in her weathered face. "You've got a support system?"

I brace my hands against the counter. I've got Posey. At least this time, I've got someone. "Yeah," I manage to get out. "I have someone."

She squeezes my arm and returns to managing the rest of the kitchen. When I glance around the huge space, everyone else has their gaze averted.

Their pity threatens to drag me deeper, and I can't afford that. I already feel like I'm drowning. Running my hands over the top of my hair, I suck in an unsteady breath.

Just keep moving forward. Keep moving forward, and soon this will all be behind me.

THIRTY-SEVEN

ALEX

I stare at myself in the bedroom mirror. My black eyes have never been so hollow, and there are dark rings under them. The wedding isn't until tomorrow, so at least I have another night to try to sleep before the press makes up some narrative about why I appear so awful. Not that I've had any luck sleeping this week. Will one night be enough?

Every time I drift into unconsciousness, I dream of her. Visceral, vivid dreams. The kind that only leave disappointment and deep despair in their wake. An alternate reality where she didn't reject me and the life I wanted us to have.

Simone arrives in an hour, and I should be making myself presentable. Since I woke up, I've been sitting on the edge of my bed scrolling through photos and videos of Rory, trying to recapture the elusive *rightness* those dreams inspire.

But I've also sat with my thumb hovered over the trash can icon on my favorite photos and videos. Keeping them doesn't make sense, but deleting them is another form of agony I can't handle.

I've won and lost in my life, but I've never been this defeated.

She wouldn't let me in last night, so I sat outside her door, and I laid out my exit plan. I'd hoped to do it in person. One last push to prove to her that she matters to me more than anything. While I sat there, I listed where we'd live, what I'd do, how we'd survive. I set my fucking heart at her feet, and she never opened the door.

All week I've held out hope she'd change her mind. Time I should have spent on diplomatic relations, referendum advocacy, or coronation business, I used to call real estate agents in other countries, to explore visa requirements and tax treaties. I built us lives in three other countries, and all Rory needed to do was pick one. Say yes.

Silence. A void of silence on the other side of the door so dark and deep I'm not even sure she listened. Her indifference was deafening.

Tonight I'll be forced to sit around an oversized dinner table with extended family and introduce Simone as though she means more to me than I've let on. The duplicity I once could have handled without a second thought stings.

I rub the heel of my hand against my chest, and then I straighten my tie.

My phone buzzes with a reminder to double-check the details in place for Simone to assume one of the rooms in my wing of the palace. I'll have to find Stella.

If this is to be my future, the sooner I accept it, the better. Once Simone steps out of the Summerset limo, Rory can never be more than a memory. My family, my country, my future wife, deserve my complete attention.

When Simone's limo arrives, I resist glancing toward the kitchen. There's a window, near where I used to eat lunch, with a clear view of the front entrance.

Is Rory watching? Do I want her to be?

The night she broke things off with me, I stayed outside her door listening to her sob, and it killed me. To realize my poor planning gutted her was the worst pain I've ever felt. I would have done anything to make it right, to make it up to her.

She asked for a plan, and last night, I gave her three.

Waste of time. Turns out, she didn't want a plan, she wanted a reason to say no.

From today, I'm embracing the sting her indifference left behind.

Fuck heartbreak. Anger is easier.

The rear door to the limo opens, and I step forward to help Simone exit the vehicle. When she emerges, she offers me a beaming smile and kisses both my cheeks. Like me, she's learned when she needs to switch herself into royal mode. We're not on beaming-smile terms with each other. I'm surprised she didn't call the wedding off.

My communications skills were awful this last week. Instead of answering anything, I foisted every exchange onto Desmond's plate. Up until last night, I was still hopeful I wouldn't be in these shoes this morning.

"I hope your flight was good," I say, and I guide her into the house with my hand on the small of her back.

"Very relaxing," she says, and she glances behind us to check on her luggage.

"Kane will bring your things to my wing of the palace."

"I'm staying in your wing?" She eyes me, but I'm not versed enough in her expressions to figure out if she's happy or annoyed.

"In one of the guest rooms." We're in the front entrance, and for the first time in my life, I'm not sure what to do with a visitor. A blind date gone wrong. Comical, really, if she wasn't to become my wife.

"A tour?" she suggests. "Start in the kitchen? I hear the pastries are sinful."

I raise my eyebrows. There's no way I'm taking her to meet Rory. The only reason she'd want to go there is to stake her claim or get a handle on her competition. Since neither is necessary, she won't be getting her kitchen tour.

"Excellent idea," I say. "We'll start the tour in my suite of rooms so you can be sure the accommodations are to your liking."

There are ears everywhere in the palace, and if she wants to read me the riot act for behaving like an idiot since I signed the marriage agreement, she can do it there. Stella will be the only one within earshot there, and she's an exceptional secret keeper.

"Hmm," Simone agrees, and her brown gaze assesses me. "To your wing of the house it is."

While we make our way there, I maintain a running commentary of the various rooms, offices, and functional areas. Boring, mindless chatter that I can rattle off without engaging my brain.

Stella opted to place Simone down the hall and around the corner from my bedroom suite. The logical choice would have been across from my room, but since that's the room Rory used when she first arrived, we seemed to agree Simone couldn't go there. No discussion needed.

Stella is positioned outside the guest-room door, ready for an introduction and to make herself of service to my guest.

Simone peeks in. "This is the room closest to His Royal Highness?"

"No," Stella admits. "The other is due for a renovation. I thought you'd be more comfortable in this one."

Simone nods. "It's lovely."

Kane appears behind us wheeling her two suitcases. "Where would you like these, Your Highness?"

"In the back corner," Simone says, pointing to the farthest space in the room. She turns to me. "Is there somewhere we can speak privately?"

"Of course," I say, but inside I'm grimacing. This is not a conversation I'm looking forward to, but it's best to get the awkwardness out in the open. She's not dancing around what I've been doing, and I respect that. I lead her along the corridor and around the corner to my bedroom suite.

The room is massive, with a king-size bed, sitting area, fireplace, giant walk-in closet, and an en suite that's bigger than many bedrooms. There's even a small corner dedicated to drinks—alcoholic or caffeinated. The one blessing to my heartbreak is that Rory has never been in here. Everywhere else but here.

"Would you like a drink?" I ask as I stride over to make myself a coffee.

"No, thank you. It's too early for alcohol, and I don't indulge in caffeine."

I let out a chuckle which rings false to my ears. "I indulge quite a bit."

"So I hear."

Maybe not quite as direct as I was hoping. Does she expect me to bring up Rory? She'll be waiting a long time.

She wanders around the room while coffee trickles into my cup from the pod machine.

"Desmond seems quite good at his job," she says.

"He is. Yes." Can't disagree with that comment. He's been rescuing me from myself for weeks.

Her deep breath is audible.

Here we go.

"I've been trying to work out whether she was your last hurrah or if I need to be more concerned. Hearing rumors through my staff hasn't been an ideal start." She whirls on me and pins me with her stare. "So tell me, Alex. Am I arriving to the wedding on your arm tomorrow or are we tearing up the marriage contract? There's still time to back out, even if you wouldn't respond to my emails this week."

"I apologize that my communication skills were lacking this week."

"Lacking?" Her tone is brimming with scorn. "Non-existent. At one point, I wondered whether I was actually marrying Desmond."

Desmond has a wife, but I suspect that comment would fall flat. "From now on, you'll have my full and undivided attention." I take my coffee from the machine and turn to face her.

"Full and undivided?" Her gaze narrows. "A last hurrah, then?"

"As far as I'm concerned, if you will allow it, today is a clean slate. A fresh start."

She runs a hand through her long dark hair. "Is it over?"

"It's over." I manage to say it with conviction, but inside a protest mounts. The words are bitter on my tongue. The truth—that my heart might never let Rory go—isn't one I can admit.

She approaches the corner where I'm standing, and she surveys the layout of beverages.

"Vodka?" I suggest. God knows I could easily get drunk right now.

Her red lips tip up, and she glances at me. "Close. Water."

I set down my coffee and pour her a glass from the pitcher in the mini fridge. When I pass it to her, our gazes connect.

"Just don't make a fool of me. That's all I ask."

"I don't intend to," I say. "I promise I won't." For the last three weeks, I've been so caught up in other things, I haven't asked myself or her the simplest question. "Why did you agree to this?"

"You need to be married to become king?" Her dark eyes are calculating. "That's what my family has speculated. A marriage clause in the coronation documents."

"Yes," I admit. She signed the paperwork without an explicit conversation about my reasoning, and she doesn't seem to want to back out, even though I've been parading around with Rory for weeks. If the situation was reversed, I'm not sure I'd be so generous.

"I want to be a queen. In Denmark, my older brother will become the king. My potential is squandered by birth order. Here," she says with a wave of her hand, "I get to be your partner. Power, influence, and a gorgeous husband. I know a good deal when I see one." She gives me a rueful smile. "Or I thought I did."

Power and influence. I'm familiar with that pair, and I can't fault her for wanting something I've also craved. They're both a bit hollow now that I understand what else life has to offer. *Love. So much love.*

The anger I've been trying to cling to just won't stick.

"Let me give you that tour," I say.

Simone drains her water and sets the glass on the small granite counter. "I'm excited to see what our home has to offer."

Her comment reminds me of the conversation I had with Rory at the wine bar. *Home.* Our home.

My chest constricts, and when Simone runs her hand down my back, I let her touch linger, even though everything in me longs to step away.

There is nothing quite like the whirlwind of a royal ceremony of any sort, but the wedding rivals a coronation in the number of staff members frantically running around and shouting orders into their walkie-talkies. It's a military grade exercise with civilians at the helm.

Simone straightens her dress beside me while we wait for Nick and Jules to arrive and for the church balcony doors to open. The ceremony is done. It was streamed across Bellerive in every conceivable public area as well as to the world via news stations and the royal social media accounts. Family photos are complete, retouched, and posted.

Outside the church, the majority of Bellerive waits for their first glimpse of Prince Nicholas and his bride. But I'm also keenly aware, thanks to our social media manager, that the country waits for another opportunity to scrutinize Simone on my arm. Our arrival to the church together caused quite a stir, as we realized it would.

What I didn't anticipate, and I doubt anyone else did either, was the public's response. Along with all the usual wedding nonsense involving Nick and Jules is my very own hashtag. *#AloraDead*. A lump sprung into my throat when I happened to check the reaction to Simone earlier and spotted the trending moniker. Were people happy or sad about the newest development? I couldn't allow myself to click. Either would crush me.

To maintain my sanity, I switched off my phone.

"Here they come," Simone says in my ear as frantic activity swirls increasingly louder behind us.

I half turn to find Julia resplendent in a white gown that is stunning in its simplicity. A scooped neckline, three-quarter-length lace sleeves, and enough royal jewelry to sparkle off the glare of the sun. The tiara, long train, and turned down veil are all staples of the royal look, but on her there's something relatable about the glamor. She might have grown up one step removed from royalty, but like my mother, the people see Jules as one of them.

How would they have viewed Rory?

I close my eyes and rub my forehead. How will they view Simone? That's the question I need to be concerned about. *Simone.* I drill her name into my brain and hope it sticks.

"Headache?" Simone murmurs in my ear.

"Yes," I say, and the lie comes easily. There's definitely an ache, but it's not in my head.

"I have pills in my purse. I'll grab them for you after this."

"Thanks," I mutter. Medicine for an ailment that cannot be cured.

Across the hallway, my gaze connects with my father, and he's frowning while he scans my features. How broken do I appear to him? There's only so much I can hide from anyone who knows me well. Simone has sailed through the day as though I've been excellent company, but I understand my performance, outside the glare of the press, has been lackluster.

None of this is her fault, and I need to rein in my poor attitude. We all made choices, and this is where we've landed. Leaving the monarchy when Rory told me not to would have been beyond foolish. While I'm convinced she loves me, she didn't believe it was enough. To me, it became everything. Now I need to cut those feelings out and staunch the bleeding.

Staff rattle off a list of instructions to all of us while Jules and Nick take their places in front of the double doors which open onto the huge balcony overlooking the center of Tucker's Town. For centuries, royalty has been married in this church, greeted by citizens below.

"It's nice to see how this will work for us, isn't it? A dry run." Simone smiles and glances at me. "Oh, you poor thing." Her fingertips graze my brow. "Is your head that sore? Are you going to be okay?"

I stare at her, willing myself to invest in this moment with her. "I'll be fine," I say.

Before the double doors open, Nick raises Julia's hand to his lips, and when their gazes connect, there's little doubt how they feel about each other. Love pours out of them, an endless well. Jealousy of *that* has consumed me for years. Until I met Rory, I never realized what bothered me about Nick and Jules, but it's their closeness, the connectedness that they've had since we were kids. I've longed for it—with him, with her—and I could never get there. Nick and I are too different. Julia loved Nick too much.

These last few months, I've experienced the kind of endless love they have. A love that wasn't tied to being next in line to the throne, wasn't tied to a lifestyle someone wanted to achieve, wasn't tied to power or influence. Rory wanted *me*. Welcomed *me* into her home, her bed, her heart.

The doors ahead of us open, and Simone slides her hand into mine. A break in royal protocol, but after my shitty attitude all day, I don't have the heart to extract myself.

"Smile," she reminds me as we follow Nick and Jules onto the balcony.

The roar of the crowd is deafening, and there's something in the noise, the joy of the people, that buoys me up. My country is thrilled, and I should be too. With Simone's hand grasped in one of mine, I wave to the crowd with the other.

I need to accept what can no longer be changed.

We're ushered into the hall with a crowd of other people. The public appearances in front of the majority of Bellerive are done. Now we need to deal with five hundred or so guests from diplomats, to celebrities, to other royalty, to Bellerive's elite for drinks and mingling before dinner begins.

When Simone disappears to the washroom, I breathe a sigh of relief. She isn't poor company, but since our appearance on the balcony, I've been trying harder to be upbeat. It's fucking exhausting to pretend an emotion you genuinely don't feel.

"Are you to follow suit next?" Lawson, the mayor of Tucker's Town, claps me on the back while he extends his Black hand for a shake. "Get another wedding in the books before you become king?"

We've known each other since high school, and his familiarity isn't out of place, but hearing what people are speculating stirs a hint of unease. "Local gossip is out in full force, is it?" I tease and sidestep his question.

He grins and surveys the busy room with me. "My wife is a royalist. She ordered one of those coronation bibles. Found a clause about you needing a wife." He waggles his brows.

I suppress a grimace. "She find anything else useful in there?"

Lawson chuckles. "What else are you looking for?"

A loophole big enough to fit a petite blonde with the prettiest green eyes. If one existed, Jules or Desmond would have rooted it out. Besides, I'm past the point where a loophole would help me. Appearing on the balcony with Simone was as good as declaring an engagement. Our linked hands are probably screenshotted across the internet.

"I've been meaning to speak to you," I say. A subject change is the best remedy here. "I have some ideas about how to increase tourism around Tucker's Town and perhaps a new recreation idea for Bellerive."

"Do tell," Lawson says, grabbing a drink off a tray that passes us.

"The old railroad trail that's been abandoned, I'd like to turn it into a riding path."

"A riding path?" Lawson rotates the liquid in his glass. "Who'd manage the horses?"

"My friend, Edward, he's game. His property connects with a portion of the trail. We'd have to work on permits and such. The trail goes through Tucker's Town main park, so we'd have to analyze the logistics."

Lawson nods. "I'm open to that discussion." He tips his chin at me. "What else?"

"A rink. For skating and ice hockey. Perhaps curling or broomball."

Lawson chuckles and eyes me. "Sounds like you've been speaking to a Canadian."

Warmth spreads across my chest, and on instinct, I search the crowd. She's not here, but even the mention of her causes me to seek her out.

The warmth coursing through me freezes when I catch sight of a blond braid in the crowd. At the same time, a hand glides across my back, and Simone reappears at my side. She extends the hand not on me toward Lawson and introduces herself.

The two of them fall into easy conversation while I search the crowd. But the blonde has disappeared, and the sucking wound in my chest has returned.

Lawson takes his leave, and Simone fishes in her purse before passing me two aspirin.

"You've gone pale again," she says. "Must be a bad one."

"It is," I say, and I take the pills. In my closed hand, I rotate them. Not going to make a lick of difference, but I toss them back and chase them with my wine. "Thank you."

It's going to be a long fucking night if my mind is slotting Rory into the crowd. She is nowhere, and she is everywhere.

I have no idea how I'll cope over the next nine months before her visa expires, and I'm not sure I'll cope at all once she leaves Bellerivian soil. How do I let go when everything in me is determined to cling?

Thirty-Eight

RORY

I've always loved weddings. As a kid, I spent hours visualizing my dress, and little else. The groom? The venue? Secondary to the dress. Julia's does not disappoint. Not that I'd expect a royal wedding to have a lackluster dress, but it's gratifying to see a gown that not only feels like Julia but that flatters her so well. Posey told me it was gorgeous, but the details were hush-hush.

When I appear in front of Julia with a tray of drinks, she glances in my direction and then does a double take.

"You're working?" Julia's gaze slides from mine to search the room. "Why are you working?"

"Overtime," I say. "You look gorgeous. Congratulations."

Nick turns from whoever he's been speaking to and scoops the last glass of champagne off my tray. He frowns at me, and then he seems to search the crowd.

"I didn't realize you were working the wedding," Nick says.

"I should—" I start to say.

"Come with me," Posey says into my ear. She takes my elbow, and I follow her.

"I'm working." I flash my empty tray.

She leads me into a side hallway, and she glances around her for reporters or other people who might take an interest, but we're alone. "Please tell me you knew about Simone and that Alex isn't a complete shit."

I swallow. "I'm working," I say again. As long as I keep moving, serving drinks and food, blending into the crowd, I can get through tonight. She might think she's helping, but she's not.

Her shoulders slump. "He didn't tell you?" She wails the question.

"It's—it's complicated. I can't do this here." The door behind us opens, and someone glances around.

"Not the bathroom," they mutter before ducking inside again.

"Tomorrow," I say. "Come by tomorrow, and I'll tell you everything. But don't—" I take a deep breath. "Don't say anything to Alex."

"It's one thing to tell you he can't ever marry you. It's another to be planning some sort of secret wedding to someone else behind your back." Her jaw is tight with tension.

Tears fill my eyes at having her condense my pain. "I'm working."

"Right. Shit. Sorry. Okay. Sorry." She gives me a quick hug and then tugs open the door to the hall. "Tomorrow we'll get drunk and bitch about men."

"Isn't Brent here?" I ask.

"He leaves tomorrow afternoon," she says. "We'll be bitching about Alex, but I'll find something to complain about with Brent if it'll make you feel better."

Only two things seem to make me feel somewhat normal: sleep and work. "Sure," I say. "Tomorrow."

When I step into the hall, I'm unprepared for the sight of Alex only a row of people away from me in conversation with the mayor of Tucker's Town. Whatever they're talking about seems to have made him happy.

A twist of the knife. He's in his element. A reminder that as much as it hurts me, he'll be okay. He glances up and searches the crowd, a frown on his face. I slip between rows of people before stopping to stare at him again. I can't help myself.

Simone appears behind him. Her hand slides across his shoulders, and she leans across his body with an unexpected familiarity. Has he kissed her? Slept with her? Will he? Each question is a punch to the gut.

According to palace gossip, she's staying with him for a week in his wing of the house. He's going to marry her. Of course they'll do all those things.

My stomach rolls, and I turn away from them, my empty tray clutched in my hand. Without looking back, I weave through the crowd to the kitchen. I'm supposed to collect empty glasses on my return, but I keep my tray down, determined to put distance between me and Alex. Until dinner starts, I'll switch with someone and work the back of the crowd, but I won't go near the front again. I congratulated Nick and Jules, and I have no desire to speak to anyone else.

The rest of the night passes in a blur of entering and exiting the kitchen, first with drinks and then with dinner. The head caterer gives me a table near the back of the hall with a group of foreign diplomats, and I'm grateful I won't be anywhere near Alex and Simone.

By the time dessert rolls around, I'm not quite as thankful.

"Prince Alexander seemed to be making a statement with Princess Simone on the balcony. Unless my eyes deceived me, they were holding hands," one of the male diplomats says while he eases back for me to slide his dessert in front of him.

"I heard they've been dating in secret for months," the woman next to him chimes in. "You know how these royal things work. Date in secret until you're sure. The opposite of how the rest of us behave."

Frustration and jealousy war in me while I set another dessert in front of someone else at the table.

"I thought we might get a scandal with the American girl he rescued from the car crash," another one said, paying no attention to me while I serve their table.

Sometimes being an invisible worker isn't a perk. The longing to correct my nationality rises to the surface.

"Can I get you anything else?" I ask.

They all peer at their plates, and then the one who isn't facing me says, "No, I think we're good. We're good, right?" He glances around the table.

Everyone else is already picking up their forks and digging in.

When I return to the kitchen, I'm on the verge of tears. With a hand on my diaphragm, I take several deep, steadying breaths.

"You all right?" Bethany, someone I work with in the royal kitchen on Thursdays, peers at me while she rushes around the kitchen putting finishing touches on desserts. "You're due your break. Tell Claudio you're taking your break." She nods toward the head caterer.

Without speaking to him, I rush out of the kitchen into the hallway where the staff bathroom is located. Ahead, out a side exit, Alex appears. The guest bathrooms are in this hallway but farther down.

My steps falter, and we stand staring at each other from a distance. His weight shifts, and I realize he's coming to speak to me.

I can't. I can't. I can't.

With my head down, I dash into the women's bathroom. At the mirror over the sink, I glare at myself. My breathing is heavy, and my stomach is queasy. Cornered. Wild with longing. The sight of him is enough to undo every other sensation except love. Zoomed in, enlarged, crowding out my anger, my hurt, my disappointment.

I splash water on my face, and I wash my hands. Go out. Finish my shift. Go home. Fall apart in my apartment. Count my money to see if I can afford a plane ticket and an apartment back in Canada.

Soon. Soon.

If he is marrying her before his coronation, I cannot watch it happen. Seeing them together, imagining their future, is a million times worse than walking in on Derrick with Janessa.

Deep breath. Out you go. I stride out of the bathroom, and a hand snags my elbow.

"Rory." Alex's voice is raw and husky.

I whirl toward him, and he drops my elbow as though the contact has scalded him.

"I'm sorry. I just—I..." He trails off, and we stare at each other.

What do we say? What can we say?

Words won't move past my lips. Not that I'd want them to. *I'm sorry. I made a mistake. I want you. Please don't marry her. Run away with me.*

Run away with me.

Run away with me.

My heart aches. "I—"

The side door behind Alex pops open, and Simone's dark head peeks out.

I snap my mouth closed, and I cross my arms, avoiding eye contact. Earlier *#AloraisDead* was trending on social media. One of the other workers was talking about it within earshot.

Simone must know about me. Everyone knows about me. My first instinct is to apologize, but I didn't know about her, did I?

And I'm not actually sorry.

She wanders over, and out of the corner of my eye, I catch her possessive hand sliding across his back again.

I want to slap her hand away. I want to curl up in a ball and never unfurl. I want him to tell her he picked me first. My jaw throbs with the things I want to say and cannot.

"Are you still not feeling well?" she asks him without acknowledging me.

"No, I'm—" He glances at me, and he grimaces.

His expression, as though I'm something sinful, is enough to cause tears to well in my eyes. I've become his dirty secret. Without waiting to see how the rest of the conversation will play out, I spin on my heel and disappear inside the kitchen.

After crying myself to sleep last night, I woke up this morning and counted my money. I'm three weeks of pay away from being able to secure a flight as well as first and last month's rent for an apartment in the town where I grew up. Not ideal, but I'll have to restart somewhere. Might as well go with somewhere familiar.

By the time Posey arrives in the afternoon, I've just about gotten myself together.

When she enters, she takes one look at the Tupperware containers littering my counter, and she shakes her head. "This is worse than I thought."

"I've been a little stressed," I admit.

"Why didn't you tell me what was going on?" She collapses into the couch with a sigh. "I would have neutered Alex for you."

While I wipe down the counter, Posey picks at her nails.

"Do you want to know what I got from Jules?" she asks.

"You didn't grill her at her wedding, did you?"

Posey scoffs. "Give me some credit. I followed her and Nick to their suite and grilled them when they were both drunk."

I shake my head. "On their wedding night."

"She's my sister. And she and Nick have a lot of sex. It's not like their wedding night is something special."

With a shaky laugh, I run my hands through my hair. "He didn't tell me, but I knew about Simone. I knew."

"When?" Posey asks.

"I wondered if you knew, actually." My voice wobbles.

Posey springs off the couch and comes to the island. "I had no idea. I swear." She takes a deep breath. "If I'm totally honest, I suspected something was up, but I thought he was searching for a loophole for *you*."

"Why?" I ask.

"I caught Julia, Nick, Desmond, and Brice in some big conversation in the library one day. They had old coronation and wedding documents spread out across the table." Posey frowns. "Then I flat-out asked Desmond if the Bellerivian or royal mumbo-jumbo was true. Which he confirmed without hesitation." She sighs. "I didn't realize Alex was fucking around behind your back."

Her last claim catches my breath in my throat. He only went to Europe the one time since we met, and Simone never came here before this weekend. "Was he fucking around on me?" My voice is barely above a whisper. That would be so much worse.

"Oh, shit. No. Poor choice of words. He just—he just wasn't honest. The whole arranged marriage thing." She bunches her hair into a fist and tosses it over her shoulder. "Alex is a lot of things, but I've never considered him dishonest."

I fold the cloth in my hand and stare at the counter. How do I argue that? Had anyone asked me, I would have told them Alex was brutally honest. The honesty had been brutal, but it wasn't his.

"Are you okay?" Posey asks, her voice quiet.

Tears pool in my eyes, and my chin trembles. "I don't think so," I whisper. "I think I made a mistake." When I glance up, tears tumble down my cheeks. "He asked me to leave with him. He offered to quit, and I told him not to." My words are garbled by the lump in my throat.

"Nick said Alex considered stepping down." Posey's eyes are soft with sympathy.

"Do you think he meant it?" I ask.

Posey bites her lip. "What do you want me to say here, Rory?"

"The truth," I say, and my voice hitches on a sob.

"Yeah. Yeah, I think he meant it."

"Oh God," I wail, and a sob climbs up my throat. "I didn't think he meant it. I didn't think he meant it. Why would he have waited till the last minute? He didn't have a plan."

"Knowing Alex? He was scared. Too scared to admit he was scared." She runs a hand along my arm. "Life doesn't always come with a plan. Sometimes it just happens. We jump or we stand on the edge of a cliff wishing we'd jumped."

Tears stream down my face, and I press my fingertips into my temples. "I love him so much. I'm sick with it. So sick." Posey drags me into her arms when the first sob releases. "I should have jumped. Why didn't I jump?"

Thirty-Nine

ALEX

Simone left yesterday, and I can finally breathe. The crushing weight across my chest hasn't eased, but at least I can be in my office, in my suite of rooms, without gasping for air. Having her in my wing of the house for a week was a slow suffocation. Although I gave her room to conduct any business related to Denmark, she shadowed me to learn Bellerive's operation.

Under almost any other circumstance, I would have welcomed her involvement, her thoughtful questions. Admirable, even. She cared enough to understand what she could and to ask questions about what she couldn't. Royal politics aren't a mystery to her, and quite often I would be halfway through an explanation before I'd realize she didn't need it.

My head can grasp she might be the wife I need, but my heart is across a field, tucked inside a cottage, surrounded by the smell of sugar and vanilla.

My heart is a fucking liability.

My heart is walking around this estate with no clue that it's been detached from my body.

The most surreal experience to be present and absent at the same time. I'm here, living this life, and far away, living another.

Simone was patient with my aloof demeanor. Other than a lot of back rubbing and casual touches, she didn't press for a more physical connection during her week here. She seemed content to sit close, observe, offer opinions, and get to know my family. Perhaps she was also happy I wasn't jumping from Rory's bed straight into hers as though I had no self-control.

I fear she may not be pleased with how much control I possess. Will she be okay with a glacial pace? I'm not remotely ready to move beyond Rory, despite what I claimed to Simone.

The referendum takes place this week. The day after, regardless of the result, Nick and Jules are flying to Tanzania for their working honeymoon. I'm supposed to head to Denmark. If we get voted down, I'm staying here. My parents and Brice will need the support, especially with Nick and Jules gone.

My phone beeps with a reminder to meet Brice at the front entrance for one last public appearance at an Alzheimer's clinic in Rockdown, the other major city, located at the other end of the island.

My "on" switch has been flipped from the minute Simone stepped out of the limo, and I'm exhausted from pretending to be okay when I'm not. Not even close. At least I'm attending this public performance with Brice. His problem is switching his "on" to "off."

I grab my phone from the desk and head out of my office. Desmond meets me in the corridor, and he passes me the talking points to go over with Brice in the vehicle. For a king, appearing to know your subjects is key. Everyone we'll be meeting today is in this folder, along with key details of their lives and careers. Remembering them all when my brain is in a fog might be a problem.

"I'll check in with you upon your return," Desmond says. "I have a meeting with Prince Nicholas and Julia about their plans for Tanzania."

"Sounds good." We approach the front entrance, and Desmond leaves me to circle toward Nick's section of the palace.

Outside the front doors, I wait for Brice and the car to arrive. I'm early, and Brice waffles between being right on time and five minutes late. Today he'll be late because I'm anxious to get out of here.

I'm riffling through the folder of information when a tinkling to my right catches my attention.

"Oh, um," Rory stutters. "I was expecting Brice."

Her voice is a knife to my heart, and I turn to face her. She's pale and drawn, exactly as she appeared after the car accident.

The sharp, shooting pain I'm coming to associate with having her close and not being able to protect her, protect us, spreads across my ribcage. In another life I loved her, and I lost her. That's the only explanation for how I've felt since I caught a glimpse of her in the wreckage—the dreams, the complete certainty, the peace that lives in me only when she's close by.

Had anyone told me I'd be standing here with thoughts like these one day, I'd have laughed in their face. Past lives. Fate. Destiny. Love. Not an ounce of it lived in me until I caught sight of her unconscious on the edge of a cliff. Then something in me roared to life, and I haven't been able to quiet it since.

The cups rattle again, reminding me where we are. I break eye contact with her startled green eyes, and I realize she's carrying a full cream tea on a tray.

Fucking Brice.

"My brother ordered this?" I ask. Kane isn't here yet with the car, and I've got this stupid folder in my hands. Seeing her balance the tray when she appears so exhausted is causing a riot of emotions to erupt inside me.

"Yes," Rory says, and there's a sheen of tears coating her eyes. "Sorry."

"No need to apologize." Brice, on the other hand, is getting an earful. I stuff my folder between my knees, and I offer to take it. "Let me."

She shakes her head, and the cups rattle again. "I can't let you take it. It's a violation of protocol. I have to deliver it to the vehicle. I didn't realize Brice would be late."

I want to shout, "I'm going to be the fucking king, let me take the tray!" Fuck protocol. Fuck the whole thing. I press my lips together to prevent the words from bursting out.

There's suddenly so much anger in me, I'm not sure what to do with it. She didn't say yes, and now it's too late, but she's miserable. There is an air of despair coating her that breaks my heart all over again.

Kane drives the car up to the entrance, and a second security vehicle appears behind him. He opens the driver's door and hustles to the rear passenger door to arrange the middle console for Brice's cream tea for two.

My brother is so bloody infuriating. His cream tea is here. Rory is here. I am here. He's nowhere to be found. Even later than he usually is. It screams setup, but to what end? So I can see how miserable Rory is? So I can drown in my own sorrow over what we might have had?

Kane takes the tray from her, and once she's empty-handed, our gazes connect. I want to ask if she's all right, but it's clear she's not.

"Thank you," I say. It's all I've got. An inadequate response. What do I say when everything I want to say can no longer be said?

"Alex, I—"

"Wahey!" Brice crows from the doorway. "My cream tea for the road." He throws an arm around Rory's shoulders and kisses her temple. "You're a gem."

I clench my hand around my folder at the casual contact, at her surprised expression. Never again will I touch her like that. It would kill me to be that close and not have her be mine.

"Ready to go, brother?" He slaps me on the shoulder before rounding the trunk to climb into the car.

Rory and I stare at each other, and the sharp, stabbing pain is a constant reminder of what I no longer have.

"Were you about to say something?" I ask.

"No, I—" She runs her hands down her cheeks and takes a deep breath. "Good luck with the referendum. I hope you get the result you want."

"Your Highness," Kane says from beside the driver's door. "If we don't leave now, we'll be late."

"Right. Yes." I search Rory's face for one more beat. It's been a week since I've seen her, but it feels like years.

"This is delicious, Rory!" Brice calls from the car. "Thank you."

Right now, I hate him. Fratricide might happen before we reach Rockdown. He is not this clueless.

With that, I tear myself away from her at the front entrance and duck into the back seat with Brice. He's slathered clotted cream and jam on a scone. I tug the door closed behind me, but I can't help glancing at Rory as we pull away from the curb. My chest is a wildfire of pain. I would have done anything—everything—and it wasn't enough.

"What the fuck was that?" I turn on Brice as soon as we're out of the gates.

"I felt like a cream tea." He picks up another scone. "Rory makes the best ones."

"You knew I'd be there early."

"Of course. You always are. I gave her the right time." He eyes me as he takes a bite. "I was a wee bit late."

"You cannot be this clueless."

"That you're in love with her and you're pretending you're not? Nope. Not that clueless."

"The time for matchmaking, as terrible as you were at it in the first place, is over. I'm engaged to Princess Simone of Denmark."

"I can't believe you're going through with it." Brice shakes his head. "I really thought you had the balls to go after what you want."

A surge of fury rises in me so fierce, I crumple the folder still in my hand. "I did go after what I wanted. I gave her a plan. Three exit plans to leave it all behind. She told me none of it was enough." Not exactly true, but the result is the same. Her silence spoke volumes. Me and my plans weren't enough for her.

Brice frowns. "Doesn't seem right."

"Well, it happened." I stretch the folder out, smoothing the creases, and I open it. "Whatever was going on between us is over. I promised Simone I wouldn't embarrass her. As the future king, my word must mean something. I promised her. Your interference at this point isn't helpful; it's acidic." My jaw is so tight it's aching with all the things I'm not saying.

"You both seem miserable."

"And maybe we are," I say. "But it's a misery she chose, and now we're on different paths. There's no going back. I made a commitment to Simone, to my country, and I will honor both." Even if it kills something inside me to do it.

"When we played Truth and Tequila the night of Nick's bachelor party, you told me you planned to give Rory the one thing she wanted above all else."

"I tried," I say, and weariness creeps into my voice. "I tried. Turns out what she thought she needed most in the world wasn't something she wanted from me." I'm staring at the folder in my lap, but the words are swimming together. To stem the emotional tide, I pinch the bridge of my nose. "Where's your folder?"

"Locked in my brain. Desmond gave it to me first thing this morning, and I had nothing better to do. So I memorized it." He shrugs and stuffs another scone in his mouth. "Youngest child problems."

"Must be nice," I say.

"How so?"

"To never have to worry about anything except what's in front of you." That's never been my life, and it never will be.

Forty

RORY

Sometimes being in the royal kitchen is a lot like being transported back in time. There's no television in here, but since the referendum vote closes at the end of my shift, Joyce has the national radio station blaring. They're providing up-to-the-minute results. Unless there's a last-minute surge, it's a lot closer than I expected.

Given how hard Brice, Alex, and Nick have been working on community outreach, media blasts, and framing the narrative as both personal and for the people, I anticipated a landslide win. Or at least not a victory or loss this narrow.

Each update ratchets up my stress level. Since I understand how much this result means to Alex and his family, I'm brimming with anxiety. None of this directly impacts me anymore. I won't be living here. Alex and I are over forever. Tears well at the brutal reminder.

"You all right?" Joyce murmurs next to me while I form dough for my scones.

"Fine. Why?" The next update blares from the speaker, and I avoid eye contact.

"Haven't seemed like yourself for a few days. Bethany said you were unwell at the wedding?"

Days? When was the last time I felt like myself? Years? Time is marching on, but keeping track of it drags me further away from Alex. I count my time in dollars and cents now.

Of course Bethany told Joyce about my breakdown in the kitchen after my run-in with Alex. Claudio sent me home in a huff and said I wouldn't be receiving my full pay because he couldn't allow someone emotionally unstable into the wedding fray. What would the guests think?

I had no desire to return to serving, anyway. One taste of the gossip circulating the crowd—about Alex, Simone, and me—left bitterness on my tongue.

The reduced pay puts me behind on my escape from Bellerive. Another half week of regular work has been tacked onto my exit plan.

"Rory?" Joyce tugs me out of my thoughts. "If you're not okay, I wouldn't blame you. I'm on your side."

While she's been careful not to say anything disparaging about Alex, she's been attentive to me in the kitchen, alert to any changes in my mood. She's become better at reading me than my own mother ever was. A deft touch is what Alex told me about her once. Not just in the kitchen, apparently.

The reminders of Alex cause my stomach to swoop low. Everything in Bellerive circles to him. Even when I venture off the estate for groceries or to meet Posey for a drink, people snap furtive photos, whisper words I can't hear. The only way to return to obscurity is to leave.

"I wasn't okay at the wedding," I admit. "But I'm feeling much better. My departure is set back, though. I was counting on that money."

Joyce purses her lips. "I'll see what I can do with the schedule. Did you want some overtime?"

"Do you have any?" I'm exhausted, but if she can get me the hours to leave earlier, I'll take them.

"Let me check. I might be able to move some people around as long as you're not particular on the type of work."

"Thank you," I breathe out. The weight that's been crushing me since Simone appeared out of that limo eases slightly. As soon as I have some distance from this place, I'll start to feel better.

"Are you eating? You've lost weight, and you didn't have it to lose."

I carve out a scone and place it on the cookie sheet. "I'm eating." A little. Heartbreak has robbed me of sleep and my appetite.

Joyce tries to catch my gaze, but I stay trained on the task at hand. "I'll let you get back to it, but if you need anything, you ask. There's no shame in seeking help."

"Thanks," I say, but the only help I need is an influx of cash so I can leave this all behind. Having a front row seat to Alex falling in love with another woman is my worst nightmare. My stomach rolls at the thought, and I grip the wooden counter to suck in deep breaths.

Joyce has gone off to talk someone else through the dinner menu for tonight. Win or lose, the meal is the same. But Julia and Nick leave tomorrow for Tanzania, and Alex is headed to Denmark for a long weekend. Learning their schedule secondhand through the kitchen staff, when I've been privy to these details before anyone for months, is an unexpected injury. To be so close and now so far.

I check the clock and realize the final results should be out any moment. Anxiety kicks my heart into an unsteady rhythm, and I finish prepping the scones and slide the pan into the fridge for tomorrow morning. The door clicks closed, and the announcer cuts out the song playing on the radio.

Well, folks, the final totals have just arrived, and the result has been officially declared. The percentages remained tight throughout the day, but in a vote of 51 to 49, Bellerive has opted to create a law in favor of assisted suicide.

Relief rushes through me so hard, black spots appear on the edges of my vision. It's swiftly followed by the realization that Alex will likely lose his father even sooner than he wants. My vision blurs, and I need to get out of here before I embarrass myself.

Lately, I'm an emotional wreck.

"I'll see you tomorrow," I say to everyone before I shove myself away from the workstation I've been learning against. Out the door. Back to my cottage.

As soon as I take a step, the black dots at the edge of my vision reappear, and the room swirls. I scramble to grab onto something as my knees give out.

"Rory!" Joyce calls.

But it's too late. My legs give out, and the buzzing kitchen falls dark and silent.

Joyce is hovering over me when I come to. I blink and blink again trying to put the scene together. Am I on the floor?

"Rory, love, you've fainted," Joyce says. "I've sent for Doctor Bennett."

"Dr. Bennett?" My confusion hasn't quite cleared. "Why?"

Joyce's worried gaze searches mine. "When was the last time you ate?"

Heat creeps into my cheeks. "This morning." Last night, and then I thought of Alex with Simone and promptly threw it all up again. Seems to be my pattern. Eat. Consider Alex's future without me. Lose whatever I've eaten into the toilet.

Joyce frowns, and the side door to the kitchen creaks open.

Dr. Bennett crouches beside me and starts taking my vitals. The deep crease in his brow isn't helping my mounting anxiety.

"Is there something wrong with me?" I whisper.

He meets my gaze. "I need to run some tests at the clinic. Bethany is behind me with a wheelchair."

"I'll come with her." Joyce clutches my hand. "She doesn't have any family in the area."

At one time, Alex was all I needed. Dangerous to pin my life on one person. A lesson I should have learned with Derrick and didn't. Posey or any of her friends would come to my rescue, if I called.

It's still Alex I long to see. The realization causes my stomach to clench again.

Joyce and Dr. Bennett help me into the wheelchair. The room spins as I settle into the seat.

"I didn't eat," I admit as I'm wheeled along the gravel path. "I've been having trouble eating."

"That might be all it is," Dr. Bennett says. "Fainting often happens under extreme emotional distress. Blood pressure drops, and boom, you're out."

I rest my head in my hand and try not to let self-pity drown me. Will Joyce let me work my shift tomorrow? There will be protocol to follow. There's always a precedent somewhere.

At the clinic, a nurse draws blood, and Joyce keeps my hand in hers.

"Explain to me how you've been feeling." Dr. Bennett's pen is poised over his notepad.

I swallow, and I sneak a furtive glance in Joyce's direction.

"Would you rather be alone?" Dr. Bennett asks.

"I'll go," Joyce says, and she squeezes my hand. "Before I do, I want to add my two cents. Rory has been in a right state the last few weeks. Tired. Not eating properly." She purses her lips. "Depressed. Not herself. I'm not telling you what to do." She meets my gaze and then stares at Dr. Bennett. "But she needs help."

My heart squeezes in my chest. God, is this what everyone has been thinking about me since Alex and I ended?

"She's not been herself," Joyce says. She gives me a half hug. "Dr. Bennett is bound by doctor-patient confidentiality. You be honest with him so you can get the help you need."

There is no medicine for heartbreak, and I'm not sick enough for antidepressants, am I? My emotional breakdowns, my inability to sleep, the food I've thrown up, come back to me in a rush. A crushing heartbreak, that's all.

"I will," I say.

She gives me one last squeeze before slipping out the door and heading to the kitchen. As my shift supervisor in the kitchen, she's been an unexpected gift.

Dr. Bennett adjusts the notepad on his lap, and he searches my face. "Tell me the truth."

"You won't tell Alex?" I ask.

He meets my gaze. "Joyce is right. I'm bound by doctor-patient confidentiality if you want it. He won't hear anything from me. Your well-being will stay between us."

I nod, and I gather my thoughts. Apart from my conversation with Posey after the wedding, I haven't given anyone the complete picture of how I'm coping. Joyce's assertions before she left make me realize I haven't been doing a very good job of hiding anything. But if I do need help, if whatever I'm feeling isn't just extreme heartbreak, I need to be honest.

I take a deep breath, and I tell him everything.

Dr. Bennett is quiet while I speak, and other than taking a few brief notes, he doesn't write much on his paper. It's comforting that he isn't keeping a record of what happened between me and Alex and how I haven't been coping well. I'd prefer not to become a footnote of Bellerivian history.

Once I'm finished, he releases a deep sigh. "That's a lot for anyone to handle, Rory. There's no shame in needing help, whether it be emotional or physical. We'll wait for the bloodwork to come back, and then we'll go from there. If something is off, we'll order more tests. If that's clear, I can refer you to a counselling service."

"Oh, I can't afford—"

"It's covered. The royal insurance is all-encompassing. Best on the island. But if you're feeling as low as you say you are, I might recommend an antidepressant as well. We can discuss that once we've got the bloodwork."

"Do you really think that's necessary?" I whisper.

"It's entirely up to you." His eyes are soft with sympathy.

There's a knock on the door, and Dr. Bennett calls for whoever to come in. The nurse who took my blood passes him a slip of paper and retreats out the door.

Dr. Bennett grimaces.

"What is it?" I ask.

"Something is showing up in your bloodwork." His sympathetic gaze turns pained. "Explains all your symptoms."

My heart races, and I search his face for a clue about how bad it is. "What's wrong with me?"

"When was your last cycle?"

The blood in my veins slows at the question, and a loud whooshing enters my head. "I—I don't know. I took my pill packs back-to-back because I didn't want PMS on top of how I'm already feeling."

He purses his lips. "After you had food poisoning, did you use an alternative method of contraception?"

Heat rises to my cheeks, and a cool sweat breaks out under my arms. "No."

"You're pregnant," Dr. Bennett says.

"No," I cry. "I took my pills on schedule."

"Most women don't use the pill one hundred percent correctly, which reduces its effectiveness. Prince Alexander is well aware of this, and I'm assuming, though perhaps I shouldn't, that he's the one who opted to take the risk with you."

Because I told him he could trust me. Is he going to think I've tried to trap him? Trick him?

"The pill is 99.7% effective in women who follow the instructions to the letter. It's only 91% effective when you deviate in any way for any reason, which most women do.

That percentage goes down further when you take certain medications or vomit up pills."

I rub my face, and my stomach swoops low. "What do I do?"

"Do you want to keep the baby?" Dr. Bennett asks.

"Yes." The confirmation is out before I even have a chance to think. Do I want to keep the baby? Does it make sense to keep the baby? *How* can I keep the baby?

"You should speak to Prince Alexander. While the situation is understandably complicated, he would want to know, and he would make sure you're taken care of."

My heart thuds heavily. *Taken care of.* Dr. Bennett would never make promises for Alex, but his phrasing reeks of the notion I'd be the other woman. The one with the unacknowledged bastard child. He'd never be able to be a real father to our child, a real partner to me.

I close my eyes and rub my face. "I need to think. I... am I okay to go back to my apartment?"

"Yes, of course. Before you go, I'll get you some resources. Prenatal vitamins. I can still give you the information for the counselling service, if you'd like?"

I shake my head. "That won't be necessary."

He disappears out the door, and I sit in the empty examination room with a hollow heart.

What do I do now?

FORTY-ONE

ALEX

As soon as the results of the referendum are announced, my father and I speak to the cameras and public on the steps of the Advisory Council building. We both talk about hope and choice, and we treat the victory as though it wasn't an inch away from tumbling in the wrong direction.

In the car on the way to the palace, my father laments the lack of voting power on the Advisory Council. Though neither of us says it, we realize the letter of the law still might not fall in his favor.

No one ever likes the idea of death being too easy, which is ridiculous. Anyone in proper mental and physical health would choose life over death. Predicate the rules on that central premise, and the law will come out fair. Not convinced that'll happen with a fifty-fifty split within the council itself. We really need our voting power back. Once I'm the king, I can wield some influence and try to bring the two sides together.

We're driving up to the estate gates when my father eyes me. "How are you doing? I understand you've made some difficult choices lately."

Since I capitulated to Simone and the arranged marriage, I haven't spoken to my parents about my almost rebellion. Much like the referendum results, we've behaved as though I didn't almost tumble out of the line of succession. Things between the three of us have resumed as though I never had an affair with our pastry chef. They've erased her, and I've allowed it for the sake of family unity.

"You're actually bringing her up?" I ask.

"I am," he says. "You seem very..." He struggles to find the word. A flash of annoyance crosses his face. "Unhappy with the choice you've made."

Christ, I hope I haven't been that obvious to Simone. She doesn't deserve my misery. I did this to all of us with my lack of willpower. In seeking a corner of my life free of the monarchy's restrictions, in trying to ease my loneliness, I almost blew the whole thing up.

"Are you suggesting I should have made a different choice?"

He purses his lips. "I was prepared for you to make a different choice."

"It's too late now," I say. My chest compresses with the crushing weight of the path I've gone down.

With both hands, he rubs his cheeks. "I wish I could tell you it wasn't too late. But you're right. It is. Public opinion, our relationship with Denmark, and Simone's reputation are at stake now."

"I promised her I wouldn't embarrass her. I don't need a reminder about what's on the line. I won't let anyone down." He's not lecturing me, but I'm anticipating one.

"I wish you'd spoken with your mother and me. We tried to discuss this with you, but you wouldn't see us."

"Any messages you had could have been passed through Desmond."

"As a king to his successor, yes. As a father to his son, no."

Is that why they didn't send communication through Desmond? It's an easy excuse when faced with my unhappiness. What would they have done? Warned me again? Offered to find me a different arranged marriage? Rory is not a native Bellerivian or a royal, and neither of those will miraculously happen. Another marriage wouldn't have mattered because the only one I want, I cannot have.

"What's done is done," I say. Even if he told me I fucked up somewhere along the way in my efforts to be with Rory, we can't go back. Some decisions, once made, cannot be undone. Playing the what-if or if-only game leads to madness.

"Your mother and I are capable of acting in your interests as your parents."

"Yes," I agree. "But you're always the king and queen of Bellerive first." A truth I've rarely thrown in their faces, but I'm not keen to play nice.

"Someday," my father says, "you'll comprehend what it's like to walk this tightrope."

"I will always put my children first." Whenever children cross my mind, Simone isn't in the picture, and I'm not sure how to slot her in. She'd have to push someone else out, and I'm not ready. What will it take for me to truly move on?

My father chuckles, but the sound is sad. "I wish I could be around long enough to remind you of this conversation. As admirable as that is, that'll be an impossible vow to keep."

We arrive at the front entrance, and Nick, Jules, Brice, Mother, and a slew of workers greet us.

I search the crowd. A blonde near the back. The crowd shifts, and disappointment squeezes my chest in a vise. Not her.

A foolish hope.

Dinner is a strange affair. We celebrate choice, but in essence we're rejoicing at our father's right to take his life. Fucking depressing.

Nick is sullen through most of the meal. Does he expect the law to come into effect tomorrow? He understands so little of government politics because he's never had to. A small comfort, in a slew of disappointments, that Nick won't ever sit on the Advisory Council to demonstrate his ignorance and lack of preparation.

Ditto Brice. He's jubilant that we've succeeded. He believes our father has options. Many, many people will, but I'm not sure my father will make the cut. The referendum isn't a law, and until we have one of those, we're not much further ahead.

During dessert, my phone beeps beside me. When I turn it over to find Simone's congratulatory text, I can't bring myself to respond, and I turn it off. I'm in no mood to speak to anyone. Tomorrow I fly to Denmark.

My disposition has soured since the referendum win was announced. While I've campaigned for this outcome, it doesn't seem like something to be celebrated. My father is dying, and today may have brought us one step closer. To say I'm not ready is an understatement. For the power and responsibility? Yes. To lose my father? Never.

If I'd left the country with Rory, would I have been able to visit my father again? Could I have been at his death bed? I'd have missed what's left of his good health. If I could have returned, what would I have returned to? How would I have come to terms with the lost time?

The decision to leave came to me so swiftly, and the timeline for a decision was so tight, I didn't factor my father's health into my decision. Incredibly selfish. I sought happiness at any cost.

Misery has found me instead.

At least I'll get whatever time I have left with my father, and if I'm honest with myself, I would have mourned the loss had I run away with Rory. Perhaps I should be thankful she didn't love me enough to take the leap.

Conversations zip around me, and my foul mood is threatening to infect the table with my non-answers and refusal to participate in their various conversations. I push back my chair and grab my phone.

"It's been a long day. Good luck in Tanzania, Nick and Jules. I'll see the rest of you in the morning before I leave for Denmark."

I don't stick around for the usual preamble whenever anyone leaves a family dinner. Instead, I make my way to my suite of rooms. Where I used to seek out Rory on nights like this—who am I kidding? I sought her out every night—her comfort is no longer an option.

At least in my sleep, my subconscious might give me a glimpse of what I once had. Dreaming of her is the poison and the elixir.

When I reach the entrance to my wing of the palace, Kane is there.

"I tried to get you on your phone, Your Highness," he says. "Called the internal line as well, but you'd left the dining room."

"What's wrong?" Whatever it is, I'm in a poor state of mind to deal with yet another crisis. My temper is barely in check. Press the wrong button, and I'm likely to detonate. "If it can wait for tomorrow, that's best."

Kane rubs his face. "Aurora Wilson is in your bedroom, Your Highness. She's still on the list of approved visitors, and when I couldn't get in touch with you, I made the decision to let her in."

"Rory's here?" My mind has turned sluggish at her unexpected appearance. The last time she was willingly in the same room with me was three weeks ago.

"Yes, but I'm happy to tell her you've been called away elsewhere if you'd prefer not to see her." He hesitates. "Or I can keep her visit to myself if you'd prefer."

A flare of pettiness sparks. What could she possibly have to say to me after avoiding me for three weeks? After rejecting my plans for us?

I'm on the cusp of telling him to send her packing out of spite when Kane says, "She seemed upset. Looked like she'd been crying."

"Oh," I say, and the pettiness in me vanishes. "No, I'll... I'll see her. Of course I'll see her." I open the door to my wing and turn back to him. "Between us, yes?"

Kane purses his lips and nods.

The door to my room is closed, and I hesitate before seizing the handle. My bedroom has been my sanctuary. It's the one place in the palace that bears no memories of Rory, but once I step through the door, that'll no longer be true.

Maybe I should have sent her home or had Kane move her to another room, a more neutral location.

With a deep breath, I open the door. She's in one of the chairs by the fireplace, pale and puffy faced. The door is still open behind me, but I can't help taking a beat to drink her in. This conversation might haunt me, but I won't forget this mental picture of her in my room as though she belongs here.

She wipes her tear-stained face and stands. "I'm sorry."

I ease the door closed behind me, and I shove my hands into the pockets of my suit pants to stop myself from trying to physically comfort her. We're not those people anymore, the ones she claimed weren't real in the first place. In her cottage is the closest I've ever been to *Alex*, whoever he is. Perhaps she was right, and he was a mirage. Who I was then feels impossible to reclaim.

Words are failing me, so instead of saying anything, I stand behind the chair and try to memorize every inch of her to take out like pieces of treasure to admire later.

The sharp stabbing pain is back in my ribs. A piece of me is carved out and belongs to her. The pain used to bring me pleasure, too—to realize I was capable of such a big feeling for someone else was a revelation. She's the first woman I've ever been one hundred percent certain I loved, and it wasn't enough.

"What are you doing here?" My last thought has tinged my voice with annoyance.

She swallows and more tears leak down her cheeks. I clench my hands in my pockets to keep myself in check. I'm engaged to someone else, and I made a promise to Simone, to my father, to my country.

"I'm not sure what to say or where to start," she whispers.

My frustration and anger from earlier resurfaces. She's here, and there's nothing I can do to soothe her. Aurora Wilson isn't mine anymore, and the cold realization makes me want to roar with rage.

"If this is a kitchen matter or if someone on palace grounds hasn't been treating you properly, you'll have to speak to HR." My tone is clipped with frustration. I won't stand for anyone being unkind to her. While I can no longer have a direct hand, once HR is aware, I'll ensure whoever it is loses something in return for hurting her.

She stares at me, and I can't read what's being processed behind those green eyes. Some calculation I cannot possibly fathom is happening.

"What if I..." She takes a deep breath. "What if I wanted to change my mind about us?"

"About us?" I frown and search her face. Am I understanding this right?

"Yes." She doesn't elaborate.

I run my hands through my hair in rough movements, but I keep the chair between us. My resolve around her is paper thin, and I've made promises to other people now.

"It's too late." The words come out a dull rasp, as though nothing in me wants to form them.

"You're not married yet," she says. "We could run away together. I don't care where or what we do or anything." She rises from her chair and takes a step toward me.

I step back and shake my head. "I spent the better part of a week trying to get you to open your door to me. I even sought you out in the kitchen. Now—*now* is when you change your mind?"

Her bottom lip quivers. "I should have said yes."

"But you didn't say yes. On that Thursday night, I sat outside your door for over an hour laying out three very detailed plans of places we could go, lives we could live together. Three! And you didn't open the fucking door. I told you, come Friday, the course would be set, and you kept me locked out. I needed your yes then." My voice cracks, and the pain in my ribs is almost unbearable.

"Three?" she whispers.

"Come on, Rory." I let out a huff. "You made a choice."

"I didn't make the right one because I didn't hear you," she says, and she takes another step in my direction. "I locked myself in the bathroom to stop myself from opening the door." Her tone is pleading.

I cover my face with my hands and run my fingertips over my temples. My stomach rolls with the realization of how fucked up everything has gotten. She didn't hear me. Explains so much, but it's still too late. My word has to matter, and I gave it to my father. I gave it to Simone, and when I stepped out onto the balcony with her at Nick and Julia's wedding, I gave it to my people.

"It's too late," I rasp.

"You're not married yet."

"I gave my word," I roar. "I've gone down this path now. Whether or not you heard me that night, you made a choice not to let me in."

"I made a mistake." The words are garbled by her tears.

When I turn to her, her face is streaked with the evidence of her sadness. She's breached the gap between us, and if I reached out a hand, I could scoop up her tears, drag her to me, tip my life on its axis. Three weeks ago, I wouldn't have hesitated.

But now? I've had time to consider what else I'll lose beyond my word.

Whatever time is left with my father will vanish. His opinion of me will sour. There isn't time to repair that sort of rift.

"I can't." I close my eyes and press the heels of my hands into my cheekbones.

"Alex." Rory curls her hand into my jacket.

When I open my eyes, our gazes connect, and a deep well of despair opens in me. How do I go back on my word? How do I turn my back on my father? How do I say no to her when everything in me is screaming to say yes?

"I love you," she says. "I don't want to be without you."

I frame her face, and I bend down so our foreheads are touching. My jaw aches from keeping myself in check. "Do you remember when I asked you what you wanted most in the world?" I ask. "You said you wanted to be loved, and you wanted to be put first. I laid those things at your feet that night, and your silence told me I wasn't enough."

"Oh, Alex, no," she breathes out. "No."

I let her go and step back, desperate for some distance. If I keep letting her suck me in, I'll make an impulsive choice. Three weeks ago, the situation was complicated, but it didn't feel impossible. In the time that's passed, too many things out of my control have become tangled.

"Tell me what I can say," she says. "Tell me what you need me to say to change your mind."

"I can't—" My voice cracks. "I can't leave now, Rory." Once there's some distance between us, I sit on the bench at the end of my bed. Nervous energy buzzes off me.

"There's nothing I can say?" Her voice is distorted by tears.

"I told you the window was narrow, and you let it close." I throw out my hand. "I would have left it all for you, but it is *too late*." Anger is raging in me that she's come here after *three weeks* to tell me she loves me, misses me, wishes things were different. "What's changed?" I ask. "Three weeks ago I wasn't enough for you."

"That is *not* true," she says, and there's a hint of anger in her tone. "I didn't want you making a mistake you'd regret for the rest of your life. You proposed your non-plan to me while you were drunk, Alex. What was I supposed to think?"

"But now it's okay for me to throw it all away? Now that we're on your timeline, it's perfectly acceptable for me to have a lifetime of regret?"

She stares at me, and she shakes her head.

"For five nights, I stood outside your apartment door, and I pleaded with you to let me in. I fucking begged you, and now you come here asking me to betray people who've put their trust in me?"

"Is there..." She bites her lip, and she wipes her tears away with impatience. "Is there any way we can be together?"

"Three weeks ago there were three of them. Now the best I can offer you..." I rub my face, and I can't meet her gaze because whether she turns me down or accepts this, no one wins. "The only thing I can offer you—" The words gets stuck in my throat. "You could stay in the apartment. I could see about extending your visa... but we would never be, could never be, more than that."

There's a heavy silence from her side of the room, but I don't glance up. Whatever expression is on her face, I don't want to see it.

"I would never do that to another woman," Rory whispers. "And I'm ashamed that you even suggested it."

The bedroom door opens with a click, and I still don't look up. Once the door closes again, I stride over to the minibar and grab one of the crystal tumblers. With all the pent-up rage and frustration storming through me, I hurl it at the wall.

It shatters into a million pieces, and I fall to my knees on the floor.

Forty-Two

RORY

I should be at work in the kitchen, but Joyce texted and told me she'd send me home if I showed up. Instead, I'm standing at my kitchen island, staring sightlessly at a pamphlet and information package Dr. Bennett gave me yesterday before I left his office.

So many options, and none of them the one I want.

After my confrontation with Alex last night, I came home and lay in bed staring at my ceiling, stuck in a pit of guilt and despair. I didn't tell him about the baby, and I can't stop thinking about how he couldn't even look at me when he proposed I become his mistress.

His absolute certainty we're beyond any avenue to be together crushed me. If I told him about the baby, would he try to convince me to get an abortion? Hide the child? *Take* my baby? If I give birth here, he'll never let his child leave the island, which will mean I'll be tied here forever too. Doomed to watch him fall in love with Simone, have children with her, declare them the rightful heirs to the throne. What sort of life is that?

When I went to his room, I hoped he'd agree to run away with me, and then I'd tell him I was pregnant. As long as he was leaving, I could share the news with him. He wouldn't be angry. He'd be happy. We'd be together and a family. In my head, it made perfect sense.

But the longer we talked, the more the reality of how far apart we've drifted, how firmly entrenched he's become in another path, set in. He won't leave, so I can't tell him.

There's a knock on my front door, and I glance at the clock. Alex is long gone to Denmark. At the door, I check the peephole.

I crack open the door, and Posey's brown eyes scan me.

"Shit," she says. "Why didn't you call me? Joyce said you were in rough shape, but you've been avoiding me."

"I've been avoiding everyone," I admit, and I leave the door to let her in. Between puking and fits of crying, I haven't been good company. At the couch, I collapse into it.

Posey closes the door and comes to sit beside me. "Is this..." She bites her lip. "Is this because of Alex?"

I let out a harsh laugh. "In a nutshell? Yes. I'm just so miserable, and I can't seem to haul myself out. I think I need to go home, but I'm wrestling with that because it's not what I really want."

Posey sits with her arms crossed and purses her lips. She claps her hands. "Tea. We need tea. Big decisions are best made with a cup of tea."

She sounds like Alex with his love for British tea, and the thought makes my stomach roll. Posey heads to the kitchen, and I jump off the couch to run to the bathroom. I make it to the toilet in time to lose the little breakfast I managed to eat, but I didn't get a chance to close the door.

Posey appears at the edge of the bathroom, my pregnancy pamphlet in her hand. "It's not just heartbreak, huh?"

I wipe my mouth with toilet paper, and tears well up in my eyes. How could I forget I left those on the kitchen island? I sit on the edge of the bathtub and cover my face with my hands.

Posey sits on the tile floor cross-legged. "Are you going to tell him?"

Such a simple question with an impossible answer. "You won't tell him, will you?"

"What are you going to do?"

"I don't want an abortion."

"But you're not going to tell him?" Her voice is gentle, and there isn't even a hint of accusation.

I take a deep breath and ease my hands down the sides of my face. "I went to see him last night. I asked him." My voice cracks. "I asked him to run away with me. If I wasn't pregnant, I'm not sure I would have gone even though I'm so miserable. My heart is so heavy. I wouldn't have wanted him to be unhappy or resent me or anything. But now, it's not just me."

Posey presses her fingertips into her temples. "Oh, wow."

I let out a mirthless laugh. "Close. His reaction was more like 'oh, hell no' in response to running away." My hand shakes when I tuck a strand of hair behind my ear. "I didn't tell him about the baby. After he said no, I was afraid of what he'd say or do or try to make me do."

Posey draws her knees to her chest. "I don't know what to tell you."

"If you were me, knowing Alex like you do, what would you do?" I ask.

She purses her lips. "If you tell him you're pregnant and keeping the baby, he'll never let you leave Bellerive."

Given that he'll be the king, I can't imagine I'd have much control over anything in that situation. My mind has been overloaded since I left his wing of the palace. A constant stream of unhelpful thoughts. "His reaction last night makes me think I was right to tell him no in the first place. If he really wanted to leave, to be with me, he would have said yes, wouldn't he? Even if it was complicated? Even if my yes was three weeks late?"

Posey seems lost in thought for a moment. "He's not normally impulsive." Her lips twist. "I don't suppose you'd let me call my sister?"

"No! No. You cannot tell Julia. I shouldn't even—you shouldn't even know. I don't want anyone to know."

"You're carrying the heir to the throne."

"No," I say. "I'm not." I swallow the bile that threatens to rise out of my stomach again. "If he can't marry me, this child is illegitimate. The heir—" I take a deep breath. "The heir won't be *my* child." I can't bring myself to say her name or to consider Alex muttering "Oh, Simone" in her ear the way he used to say "Oh, Rory" in mine. Tears prick at my eyes. "He'll make me stay, Posey. But do you honestly think my child will ever be acknowledged as royal by anyone? What do I get by staying here? Certain heartbreak. He'll marry her. Have children with her. *Love her.*" A sob gets lodged in my throat. "And I'll get to watch it knowing what she has could have been mine if only I'd had the courage to say yes."

Posey sinks onto the edge of the tub beside me, and she wraps her arm around my shoulders, tugging me against her side. "You want to leave?"

I shake my head. "I want him to say yes." I choke on a sob. "I understand now how badly he must have wanted me to say yes." But he doesn't want that anymore. In three weeks, I've become no longer worth the sacrifice. How can this desperate feeling, one he must have felt at the time, fade so fast?

"Oh, sweetie." Posey wraps me into a hug, and she holds me while I cry.

"I don't want to feel this way anymore," I say against her shoulder.

"Tell me how I can help."

The tissue box is on the sink, and I leave Posey to grab a handful, wiping my tears and blowing my nose. No more tears. I'm done crying over something I can't change. I asked him to leave, and he won't. Instead of dwelling on what I can't have, I need to look after myself and this baby.

"Alex is gone until Monday night," I say. The thought of what he's doing in Denmark causes my stomach to heave again, but I close my eyes and wait for the sensation to pass. "I need to be packed and gone before he gets home."

"Where will you go?"

"Home?" I give her a hopeful look. "My options are limited on such short notice."

"I have friends in Toronto, and I'm sure they'd let you crash in their spare room until you got yourself together."

I shake my head. "My parents might be angry with me, but they won't leave me out in the cold if I show up on their doorstep." I run my hands through my hair. "And I'm going to need help with the baby." My voice catches, and I clear my throat. I'm not naïve enough to believe I can raise a child and earn a living without some sort of assistance.

Posey takes a deep breath. "You're sure this is what you want to do?"

For a beat, I consider my options again, but I've been over them so many times, and they never change. I want to rewind time to tell Alex yes, to have never gone to his father and asked for guidance. If I'd been selfish then, I wouldn't be so alone now. I wouldn't have a child who'll never get to know their father.

Another sob threatens, and I shake my head. "I can't stay."

"I'll get you a flight, and I'll arrange for a car to take you to your parents' farm from the airport."

"I can't let you do that."

Posey chuckles. "I'm doing it anyway. Just try to stop me." She winks at me before her expression turns serious, and she takes a deep breath. "If there's one thing I know for sure, it's that Alex would want you taken care of. That's the tragedy in this whole thing. At his core, I really believe he loves you. Offering to leave in the first place was huge, even if he can't or won't see it through now. His dad is sick, and his appearance on the balcony with Simone—"

"You don't need to justify his refusal to me, okay?" My tone is sharp.

Up until last night, I believed he loved me too. Now I don't know what to think. For him to get over me in three weeks when I'm still so desperately in love seems impossible. Everything is more complicated now, but it's not any more unfeasible than it was three weeks ago, is it?

"Sorry," Posey says. "Obviously Alex is a total shit."

I give her a wry smile. "You don't need to make him worse than he is either." Emotionally, I'm a wreck, and I'm grateful Posey is here, even if neither of us understands how to make me feel better. Wine is out of the question.

"Tomorrow?" Posey suggests. "Do you think we can have you packed up and on a plane by tomorrow?"

I nod, and tears well up in my eyes again. "Yeah," I say. "I don't have much."

"You and I are going to stay in touch," Posey says. "That's my one caveat to helping you."

"As long as you never tell Alex about the baby, I would love that." She's been a gift to me the last few months. A pinch of humor when I needed it, and a shoulder to literally cry on today.

Her brown eyes are sad when she pretends to zip her lips. "Your secret is safe."

Forty-Three

ALEX

Forty-eight hours after Rory blew back into my carefully reordered life, I'm sitting at a dinner table in Copenhagen surrounded by Simone's family. The part of me that's been royally trained is able to maintain a façade of politeness and interest in the conversations of others. My mask is firmly in place. Beneath it, the expression on Rory's face as she pleaded with me to make a different choice is torturing me. The conversation has been playing on repeat since she left my room.

God help me. When I asked, she said no. When I gave her three plans, she didn't hear me.

She didn't fucking hear me.

If she had, we'd be gone. I wouldn't be sitting at this table. My sham of an engagement wouldn't have gone ahead. I'd be holed up in some midscale apartment or house in another country with Rory, and I'd be *happy*. Or happier, anyway. I think.

But my father.

My father.

He's dying, and his decline is already becoming more evident. Word finding is an ongoing issue. The other day, he couldn't remember how to button his suit jacket. Soon, I won't be able to pretend or ignore what's happening right in front of me. Memories are trickling out, fading away, and if I'm gone from the island, I may miss the last of his lucid days.

Simone's hand squeezes my thigh, drawing me into the conversation happening around me.

I fall back into polite conversation while we finish dessert and drink a nightcap. As people take their leave from the table, Simone and I stay seated.

Once everyone is gone, and the staff have cleared everything but the drinks we're still sipping, an edge of discomfort lodges in my chest. During her stay in Bellerive, she didn't push for more than I was prepared to give, and yesterday she was attentive but not demanding. I have no idea how long she'll be content to be together and not together at the same time.

"Desmond gave you the itinerary for tomorrow?" she asks.

"Yes, I've got a copy on my phone." With the referendum result pending, my week was busier than normal, so Simone communicated the final agenda to Desmond. "Sorry I wasn't more available to you last week."

"I do understand you lead a busy life." Her lips twitch. "Sometimes dealing with your secretary instead of you is unavoidable. I'm sure once we're married, there will be times like this as well."

The casual mention of our marriage, our future, twists my stomach into knots. At the edge of my consciousness is Rory with her tear-stained face telling me I'm not married yet.

"Your family must be pleased with the referendum result." She fiddles with her coffee mug.

Pleased doesn't feel like quite the right word, but it's such a complicated vein of feelings that any word she used wouldn't have suited. "Bit closer than I expected."

"Not sure anyone can understand what might lead someone down the assisted-suicide path until they're staring it down themselves." She shrugs. "If we're lucky, most of us remain ignorant."

Ignorance about a few things would be great right about now. I flick my watch around to check the time. It's not overly late, but I'm going to claim jet lag anyway. My excuse for retiring early last night was travel fatigue. Tonight will be another bullshit reason to keep my distance.

"Looked like a full day tomorrow. I should get some sleep."

Simone rises when I do. "I'll walk you to your room."

I'd prefer she didn't, but it's not something I can say to my host and definitely not something I should say to my fiancée, even though it's more of a paper arrangement than an actuality. We haven't even kissed, and I'm not keen to change that.

Her suite of rooms is on the second floor, and she leads the way to my bedroom, making small talk about tomorrow's agenda while we wander. When we get there, she leans against the wall as I turn the handle.

"My room is just"—she points across the hall—"there, if you wanted to come for one more drink."

I lean against the other side of the doorway, and I scan her features. She's pretty, and maybe, had I never met Rory, she would have been enough for me. But I understand how big love can feel now, how completely someone can consume me. My first glimpse of Rory through a smashed car window was a sucker punch I've never recovered from. Will I ever?

"Not tonight," I say.

She closes the distance between us, and I fight the urge to step back. This path might not have been my first choice, but it's the one I've taken.

"It's been three weeks, Alex. I've tried to be patient. Part of me was pleased you weren't like your brothers, bed-hopping from hers to mine." She searches my face. "But now I'm starting to wonder whether you'll ever climb into mine."

I wince and break eye contact to stare over her shoulder. Could I sleep with her? I rub my cheek with my palm. Sex was always just that before Rory—a physical act. No need to attach emotion to something that could be mutually pleasurable. But with her, it was... so much more.

"I have enough vanity that I'm not willing to cajole you into sleeping with me." She gives a little laugh, but it's devoid of humor. "We're getting married, and I think it's important we're compatible in every way. That's where I stand. When you're ready, I'm yours."

She presses herself against me, and she kisses my cheek. Her action doesn't inspire even the tiniest twinge of desire. Instead, the brush of her lips against my cheek reminds me of when Rory did it, and I long for so much more.

She draws away and frames my face. "If you don't let yourself get over her, you never will. It's a choice, Alex." She draws her hand down my chest as she crosses the hallway to her room. It's a move designed to seduce, and if I'd been on the cusp of giving in, it would have been enough. But there's not a single fiber in me tempted to follow her. After she opens her door, she peeks over her shoulder, but I'm glued to my place.

"I'll see you in the morning," I say. I roll off the wall into my own room, and while I strip for bed, I consider Simone's claim that it's possible to choose to fall in or out of love. In any of my other relationships, I might have agreed with her.

What I had with Rory isn't like anything else I've experienced. Falling in love with her was never a choice, something I could avoid or stop. From the moment I saw her in the car, she ran through my blood like a virus, infecting everything. There's no cure for that kind of love, and I'm not convinced it ever runs its course. It'll live inside me, dormant or wreaking havoc.

Last night I took one of the sleeping pills Dr. Bennett prescribed in the lead-up to the referendum. Between worrying about the result, missing Rory, and being sure I was somehow fucking up my life, sleep was eluding me. The beauty of the sleeping pills is that they provide a dreamless sleep. Rory doesn't make an appearance, so I don't wake up disoriented and depressed. A blank slate to start my day until my first thought of Rory hits me, two minutes, five minutes, or ten minutes into my morning, and the piercing ache across my chest resumes.

Unlike other nights, I don't want to be dragged under or pass out. Instead, I lie in the dark, staring at the ceiling like I've done for the last three weeks when I didn't take a pill to ease my misery.

Except this time, I'm not trying to puzzle out why none of my plans were good enough for Rory or why she didn't love me like I loved her. When I asked her to leave with me, I never doubted she was right there with me—desperate to be together. Her refusal to let me back in was frustrating and infuriating and fucking heartbreaking.

If there was one thing crystal clear in her appearance and her pleading the other night, it was how much she loved me, how hard the last three weeks have been on her too. She didn't come to my room looking for Prince Alexander or the future king of Bellerive. She came for Alex. But I've spent so much time suppressing him since she turned me down, that I couldn't get to the yes she needed. Didn't understand *how* to get there.

I might be there now.

For the last two days, my mind has been humming with potential scenarios. Simone's comment that I should let myself get over Rory has brought my choices and decisions into sharper focus. What I'm willing to sacrifice and what I'm not.

I can get over losing my country.

I can get over starting somewhere new.

I can negotiate with my brother to get more time and access to our father once Nick's the king.

I can't get over losing Rory.

I can't.

More than that, I don't want to. She's out there, as miserable as me, and I've got it in my power to make both our lives better.

It's going to be hard, and really fucking messy, but I can't let her go.

Climbing out of bed, I throw on some clothes. At Simone's door, I hesitate, and then I knock.

When she opens the door, a smile spreads across her face. "Decide to take that drink after all?"

I take a deep breath. "I haven't been honest with you, and I think it's about time that changed."

She waves me in, and I prepare myself to do the first hard thing that'll lead me back to Rory.

Forty-Four

RORY

True to her word, Posey booked me a flight—in first class no less—and hired a driver to get me to the farm. She also instructed him not to leave the house until it was clear my parents were going to let me in. If they didn't, she'd given him instructions to take me to her friend in Toronto. When he'd told me the secondary plan as he removed my suitcases from the trunk, I'd almost burst into tears. I've never had a friend quite like Posey Jensen. Pregnant and alone isn't a good look, but at least I've got her in my corner.

I glance at the driver, who is leaned against his car door with my suitcases beside him in the gravel. He said he'd wait to make sure delivering them to my side was the right call.

Out in the pasture, cows moo, and the two horses my parents keep to ride are off in the distance. If I whistled, they'd come running and expect a slice of apple or a sliver of carrot as their reward. In some ways, being home is already a comfort.

Except for my parents' reaction to my return, nothing is unknown. Tomorrow, I'll wake up and understand exactly what's expected of me. Hard work, and not another murmur of leaving this behind for something else.

If I ask for their help, this farm will be my future.

Whatever life I might have made elsewhere with Alex is nothing but a dream. Not for the first time, the reality of where we've landed hits me. He's the father of my child, and I'll never be able to see him again.

Tears pool in my eyes, and I stare at the porch overhead, willing them away. Crying won't get me through this.

With a deep, steadying breath, I knock on the screen door of the sprawling two-story farmhouse. I'm surprised they aren't already peering out a window after the car's tires crackled down the gravel drive.

Inside, my mother calls to my father as she makes her way to the front entrance.

The metal door swings back, and my mom and I stare at each other through the screen door.

"Rory," she breathes out my name, and it hits me that maybe she's not mad at me after all.

"Mom." Her name is garbled. When a sob breaks through, she yanks open the screen door and drags me into her arms. I cry while she makes soothing noises, and I breathe in the familiar scent of jasmine.

"You're home," she says into my hair. "I'm so glad you've come home."

"Who is it?" My father calls from the other room.

"Rory's home." There's a wariness to her response, as though she's worried my dad might not be quite as relieved as she is.

He comes through the farm kitchen, and he stops on the other side of the door. He's tall and broad and still fit from the work he does around the farm. "Your big adventure has come to an end, has it? That fancy boy let you down just like your mother said he would."

He's talking about Derrick, but the words sting given my recent conversation with Alex. They don't even know about Alex. They aren't the type to follow social media, so they'd have no idea #Alora was ever a thing, that the future king of Bellerive took more than a passing interest in their daughter after saving her life. That three weeks ago he offered to abdicate the throne to run away with me.

Was it months or years since I woke up to find Alex at my bedside? I've aged a hundred years in a few days. Each time I consider the choices I'm making, a crushing weight settles across my shoulders. Would my life have been any worse if I'd told him?

But I know it would have been. Seeing him with Simone, understanding what would have to evolve between them, how I'd never be his priority again, and our child would be a dirty secret, wasn't something I could accept.

I don't even know if he'd be okay with me keeping the baby. Hidden children have ways of being discovered. He'll build his family with Simone.

The argument that I'm *only twenty-three* is also one of his favorites. Lots of time for me to try again, start over. Would he ask that of me? I couldn't risk it.

"Where's your stuff?" my dad asks.

I gesture behind me, and he waves to my driver before ambling down the porch stairs. My mother leads me into the kitchen and sits me at the table. She scooches her chair next to mine, and she keeps her arms wrapped around me. It's a level of comfort I forgot she could provide and didn't realize she'd want to give. She sent me a text message when I almost went over a cliff.

"I've been so worried. After that car accident, I almost flew out there, but your father talked me out of it."

"Why?"

She's quiet beside me for a long time, and she gives me another squeeze. "Said you'd ask us to come if you needed us. And you've come home now, so maybe he was right."

I bite my lip to keep from unleashing the anger that's been simmering in me over their indifference. They taught me, often forced me, to be independent, and they convinced themselves I'd tell them I needed their help?

"I thought you might come home once it was clear that boy wasn't any good," my mother murmurs into my hair. "Did you two try to work things out?"

There's no judgment in her tone, but I'm not sure where to start since Derrick hasn't been on my relationship radar for months.

"No," I say. "I got a job somewhere else. An apartment."

"Oh." There's surprise in her tone. "Okay." She draws away to search my face, and my father bangs in the door with my suitcases.

"Want these in your room? I'm assuming you're staying?" he says.

"If that's okay," I say.

"We never wanted you to leave," my father says in a quiet voice. "I'll take these up." He juggles my things and heads for the stairs.

I've come home with my tail tucked between my legs, and that's good enough for him.

My mother rotates in her chair, and I get my first chance to take in the changes in her. A few more lines around her eyes that are a light shade of green. Her blond hair has more highlights to cover the gray. Otherwise, she looks like I remember her. A year that feels like a lifetime has passed between us.

She leans her elbow on the table. "Tell me everything."

I'm not sure where to start or even what to say. She hasn't asked me why I've come home, and I was prepared to announce my pregnancy and fall on their goodwill. But my mother wants to have a gossip session as though we haven't been at a lengthy impasse.

"You must have been shocked to discover the future king was the one who rescued you from the car wreck."

"Yeah," I murmur. "Definitely a surprise."

"Did you get a chance to meet him?"

"Yes." I squirm in my chair.

"What was he like?" Her eyes are alight with curiosity, and it's strange to see her starry-eyed over Alex. A glimpse at how other people see him. So many of our interactions were with people who knew him well, and other than social media storms, I rarely caught a glimpse of how the world saw him.

"What do you think he'd be like?" I ask.

"Definitely handsome. Too old for you, though."

Warmth floods my cheeks. Ten years never felt like anything to me. A blip. Another perception people would have that I've never bothered to consider. Our age gap would have occurred to Alex since he's hyper aware of how things appear. All these thoughts of him are turning my stomach.

She smiles. "He must be heroic to risk his life to get you out of that car."

Alex told me once that he couldn't help himself. He saw me lying there, and he had to get me out. Wouldn't have mattered what he had to do. Tears prick at the back of my eyes. Three weeks ago he loved me enough to turn his life upside down. Or maybe he didn't. Maybe when it came down to leaving, he wouldn't have been able to do it after all.

"Oh, I'm sorry, sweetheart. Is it still hard to talk about the accident?" She places her hand over mine and gives my fingers a gentle squeeze.

The stairs creak, and my father wanders into the room and draws out another chair from the kitchen table. He eases himself into it, and he takes in my appearance.

"You look like hell," he says.

"Arthur!" My mother hits his arm with the back of her hand.

"You get your fill of adventure or is something else going on?" my father asks.

Trust him to cut through the bullshit. This is my chance to come clean to someone on my own terms. The narrative I decided I'd have to tell on the plane starts here.

I run my fingertips over my eyebrows and take a deep breath. "I'm pregnant."

"What?" My mother jumps out of her chair. "Derrick? Oh God. What a mess."

Bile rises into my throat, and I swallow. "No."

"Does the father know you're pregnant?" my dad asks.

"No," I admit.

"Why not?" my father asks. "He's got a right to know, especially if you're keeping the baby. At the very least, he needs to be paying something toward raising his kid."

I bite the inside of my cheek. More than telling them I've come home pregnant, I'm dreading the next thing I'm going to say. "I don't know who the father is."

"What?" My mother pales. "How can you not know?"

"A rebound after Derrick and I broke up. He was in Bellerive on vacation. I didn't get his name."

My father lets out a scoff of disgust, and his chair scrapes across the floor. He's gone from the kitchen without another word, and the front door slams.

This time when my stomach rolls, I realize I'm not going to be able to keep my sickness at bay. I press my hand over my mouth, and I run to the two-piece bathroom in the hallway. Just in time, I kneel over the toilet to lose my meal from the plane.

When I glance up, I half expect to see my mother in the doorway with a sympathetic expression or another warm hug. Instead, the front door slams again, and I'm alone in the house.

Out the window, a breeze whips through the trees. Winter will be here soon. A chill in the air to match the ice in this house.

Coming home was a gamble, but I thought facing my unexpected circumstances with my parents would make me feel less alone.

In my pocket is Posey's name and number written on a slip of paper. A scrap of the life I've left behind. My phone, wiped clean, sits on the kitchen island next to a final Tupperware container of midnight brownies with a note telling whoever cleans the apartment to enjoy them as a parting gift.

I slouch against the bathroom wall, and I stare at the familiar floral wallpaper. Other than my mother's tight embrace, nothing in this house fits anymore. The list of things I'm longing for is a mile long. Home isn't here. It's in the muscled embrace of a six-foot royal who told me the other night I could never be more than a mistress to him.

I miss him. I miss him so much, and I fear this deep despair will never end.

The tightness across my chest threatens to squeeze me in half. I've been alone before, but I'm not sure I've ever felt this lonely.

FORTY-FIVE

ALEX

By the time I get back to Bellerive, it's Sunday afternoon. Earlier than expected. But there's a knot of dread in my stomach, as though I'm already too late.

My car from the airport has barely come to a stop before I'm out the door and headed across the field to Rory's apartment. Her shift in the kitchen will be done, but she might not be home. She used to grocery shop on Sunday afternoons while she waited for me to finish whatever royal business I needed to take care of.

For some reason, her less-than-subtle points about my work-life balance come back to me. If Nick and my father go for my plan, I'll spend the next few months getting my brother caught up on the political side of Bellerive while Rory and I keep our relationship under wraps. At the eleventh hour, I'll abdicate, and Nick will become king of Bellerive. More time with my father, less concern about Nick's incompetence, and I get to be with Rory.

Now, I just need to find her.

Last night I dreamt I arrived home to discover her apartment empty, and I haven't been able to shake the sense that something isn't right since. At her door, I pound on it, and I call her name. When I press my ear to the heavy wood, I don't hear any movement.

Unlike the week before Simone arrived, I'm not taking a chance Rory won't let me in. The groundskeeper has a set of keys to every building and room in the palace, and I head to his office, which is near Dr. Bennett's medical clinic.

Is what I'm about to do a breach of her privacy? Yes. But after our last two disastrous conversations, I want to ensure we talk calmly and rationally. Sort this whole thing out like adults who know how to speak to each other. We used to be able to do that easily, and maybe we can again now that we both want the same thing.

When I rap on the groundskeeper's door, he calls for me to come in. Inside his office and workshop, Juan is puttering around. A young guy in his twenties, he has a key in one hand and a brownie in the other when he glances in my direction.

"Oh, Your Highness." He drops the key on a table and stares at the brownie before shoving it into his mouth. "Sorry." He points to his mouth. "These are incredible."

It's then I spot the Tupperware container on his desk, which is brimming with midnight brownies.

Rory.

"Are you here about Ms. Wilson's apartment? I'll have the locks changed by tomorrow. It's being cleaned today."

"Locks changed?" I rock back on my heels.

Juan nods. "Policy when someone moves out." He shrugs. "I had a look through. All she left behind was the container of brownies and her disabled phone." He holds it up.

Waves of hot and cold are rushing over me. "She's moved out?"

"This morning, as far as I heard, yeah." He holds out the brownie container to me. "Want one?"

I swallow the panic creeping across my chest. "No note or anything?"

"Just one saying anyone could eat the brownies." He takes another one out and bites into it. "I can't believe she left them behind."

As far as things left behind, her brownies are the least of my concerns. "Thanks, Juan."

As I make my way to HR, I tamp down my fear. Maybe she moved off the property. Gone from here doesn't mean gone from the island. She's been working for us for months, and she could have easily saved up enough money for a deposit on an apartment in Bellerive.

She's not gone. She's just not here.

Since it's Sunday, there's no one in HR. I stand outside the office door, and I curse their Monday-to-Friday hours.

My next stop is the kitchen, and as soon as I walk in, Joyce's back straightens.

"Your Highness, what can I do for you today? A sandwich? Cup of coffee?"

Sundays have a smaller staff, but there are still several people listening in. I'm all out of fucks to give about who hears what. "Where's Rory?" I ask, my tone sharper than I intended.

"She's all done," Joyce says with a shrug.

"All done for today, or all done forever?" I ask. "Juan tells me her apartment is empty."

"Yeah, I expect it would be," Joyce agrees, but she hasn't really answered my question. There's a coldness in her tone she's never used with me before.

"I need to speak to her."

"I apologize, Your Highness, but I can't help you." Joyce meets my gaze. "It's best for you to leave her be, I think."

I shake my head, and my jaw tightens involuntarily. "Is she still in Bellerive? Can you at least tell me that much?"

Joyce's expression hardens, and she stares at me without speaking.

"She's not," Bethany says from near the pantry. Joyce turns her glare on the younger woman. "She's gone back to Canada. Joyce is right, though. It would be better if you let her go."

That gives me something at least. "I'll take your suggestion under advisement. Good afternoon, ladies."

I've kept my phone off since I sliced and diced Bellerive's relationship with Denmark. A verbal dressing down from anyone isn't on my agenda for today. I make a beeline for my office, and while I walk, I wrack my brain for any details Rory gave me about where she was from. If I look up Wilson Dairy Farm, will I find her?

Her parents have been so awful to her, there's a chance she didn't even go home. She could be staying with a friend. Every friend she mentioned was from her town or from college. The college friends are spread out across Ontario, and if she's gone to one of them, I'm not sure what I'll do.

When I make the turn for my office's corridor, Posey is leaning against the doorway outside with her head bent over her phone. She glances up at my approach. Here to help me or berate me?

"You pulled the pin, did you?" Posey asks. "Detonated your neat, ordered life in favor of absolute chaos with our favorite Canadian?"

The heaviness that's been plaguing me eases at Posey's grin.

"Julia?" I ask, and I unlock my office door. "She told you?"

"She texted me to say Simone texted her to say the engagement and wedding were off. Your heart belongs to someone else." She makes the last sentence sound ooey-gooey, and I cringe.

"Except my heart," I say, giving her a pointed look, "appears to have fled the country."

"Yeah," Posey agrees. "She has. In tears, no less. Quite a sight. When you go to the farm, you should take flowers. Maybe a truck full? No such thing as too many 'I'm a dick' roses, just ask Brent."

"You've got the farm's address?" Hope is stirring in my gut. I'll take fifty fucking truckloads of flowers if Posey can direct me to the right place.

"I do." Posey's smile fades. "But I'm not giving it to you unless you're one hundred percent committed to making it work with her."

"I have three separate plans to get us off the island, but better than that, I have a six-month plan to get Nick ready to become king. I would have left with her three weeks ago." I run my hand through my hair. "But Rory had a point about my impulsive decision. I would have regretted that exit. Deeply regretted aspects of that exit. This one? This one I can do." Will a part of me always carry some sadness over losing my country, losing my title? Yes. But I can live with that as long as I've got her.

Posey draws a slip of paper out of her pocket and passes it to me. "Go get your girl."

Kane is navigating the country roads in the luxury rental vehicle. Behind us is another car with more security. For the first time in my life, the security detail feels both excessive and invasive. The conversation I'm about to have with Rory isn't one I'd like to have an audience for. Especially since they'll want to sweep the house and the buildings, and I'd prefer to surprise her.

This is romantic, isn't it? Having me track her down?

God, I hope this is romantic. I don't have a fucking clue anymore. It's been three days since I've seen her, but it could be a hundred years with how I'm feeling.

Once I see the expression on her face, I'll be sure coming after her was a good idea. Posey seemed convinced Rory would want to see me despite how we left things the other night.

We turn down a gravel laneway, and I'm glad our vehicle is out in front.

"Tell them I don't want a sweep," I say to Kane.

He catches my gaze in the rearview mirror. "Your Highness, protocol—"

"Well aware. Tell them."

He calls the other car on speakerphone so I can hear their protests for myself. When he allows them to go on a little too long, I interject. "It's what I want, and it's what we'll do."

The line goes quiet. Guess they didn't realize I could hear. Suppose I'm lucky they didn't outright call me an idiot.

We round the corner that leads us to the front of the two-story house. To the right are the horses Rory told me about. The cows are out in the pasture, but I remember her saying they're milked at regular intervals. This must not be one of them. There are a lot of cows.

I grab the flowers off the seat next to me. Rory's favorite flower is a daffodil, which ended up being shockingly hard to locate. Out of season except at a greenhouse Desmond managed to locate. Kane opens my door, and I slide out.

"I'm coming to the door with you, Your Highness, and if you decide to go inside, I also need to be present," Kane says as the gravel under our feet crunches.

There's only so far I can push my security detail without appearing grossly incompetent. Are there likely to be kidnappers or murders in rural Ontario, Canada? No. But as we're taught in one of a thousand courses during childhood, an unnecessary risk can easily lead to unexpected consequences.

At the entrance, I hit the doorbell. Almost immediately, the door swings back, and a tall, broad man whose scowl reminds me of Rory is eyeing me. Must be her father. He takes in my flowers, and then he glances over his shoulder toward someone I can't see.

"Huh," he says when he turns back to me. "Suspected she was lying. You brought flowers and everything." He smirks.

"Mr. Wilson, I'm—"

He waves me off. "I know who you are."

"Dad!" Rory calls from inside the house. "Dad, don't."

Something is going on here, and I'm not sure what. There's an edge of panic in Rory's voice that's making me want to bulldoze my way past her father.

His gaze narrows, but he doesn't turn toward Rory. "Maybe she was honest about that part. Did she tell you she was pregnant before she left Bellerive, or is that a surprise to hear?"

I clench the flowers in my hand. Rory appears at her father's side. Instead of drinking in her appearance like I expected to, I'm dumbfounded, searching her expression for whatever truth might exist there.

"You're pregnant?" My tone brims with the stunned confusion I feel.

Her green eyes tear up, and her chin trembles. "Yeah," she says. "I'm pregnant. I'm so sorry."

FORTY-SIX

RORY

My father put the situation together faster than I expected. As soon as I noticed the two-car convoy coming along the long gravel drive, I knew it was either Alex or someone from the royal family. The mere thought of seeing Alex caused my stomach to riot. When Alex arrived at the door, I was in the bathroom puking, and then I wasted precious seconds rinsing my mouth with mouthwash before I arrived at my father's side. Alex's expression when he asked me if I was pregnant will haunt me for a long time. Shocked betrayal.

Now we're in the milk barn to "sort out what the hell you're going to do," according to my father. He didn't invite Alex in, and he didn't even offer to shake his hand. Does that mean he's on my side or just dislikes what he perceives to have happened? He made a grumbled comment about a man knowing better. My overconfidence led us here.

For Alex's part, he hasn't said a word since we left the doorstep. He's sitting on an ornamental hay bale in the barn, and my daffodils are perched beside him. His head is in his hands.

Since I have no idea what to say, I'm leaned against the cool cement wall with my arms crossed, praying that another rush of vomiting doesn't seize me.

He runs his hands down his face, and he meets my gaze. His expression is weary. "Because of who I am and what this means, I have to ask. I'm not judging you, but is the baby mine?"

"Yes," I say.

We were together for three weeks, apart for three, and some version of friends before we ever had sex. I understand enough about Alex's life to realize he can't assume. Still stings to have him ask.

When I'm brave enough to make eye contact with him again, there's a glassy sheen to his eyes, and my heart sinks. I expected his anger, but he looks as though I've ripped his heart out of his chest and left him to die.

"You weren't going to tell me?" His voice cracks. "You had so little faith in me you weren't even going to tell me?" He runs his hands through his hair. "You're having *my baby* and you didn't think you could tell me? Jesus, Rory. How did we get *here*?"

"I wanted to tell you." I'm on the cusp of crying again, and I'm so tired of being weepy.

"No." Alex shakes his head. "No. If you wanted to tell me, you'd have told me. Or you'd have stayed. You didn't want me to know. Whether to punish me or if it's some indictment on my character…"

"You're engaged to someone else. You kept your engagement from *me* for months. How was I supposed to know how you'd react when I told you?"

"You also knew I was *desperately* in love with you."

"You're also desperately in love with your country."

"Not like I am with you. I've never felt about my country the way I feel about you."

His claim softens the anger I need to shield me from his hurt. I don't want to be the bad person in this scenario. Telling him was a risk I couldn't take for my own sanity. The last selfless act I did for him nearly killed me.

"I asked you to leave," I say, "and public perception was more important to you than me."

He scoffs. "You're boiling an incredibly complex situation down to nothing. Simone knew about you, Rory. She asked me not to embarrass her. Publicly declaring that I was with her at Nick and Julia's wedding meant a lot in my circle. A lot. If I thought there was even a chance you'd change your mind, I never would have allowed that situation to happen. Having you come to me weeks later to ask me to change my mind after our public performances is tantamount to political and social suicide. That's not *nothing* when you're a future king. Public perception matters." He lets out a frustrated noise. "None of that is *more* important than you, but it all has weight." He rubs the back of his neck. "On top of that, I finally gained some perspective about how much time I'd miss with my father if I left."

When he meets my gaze again, my heart constricts.

"That's not nothing either," he admits. "Add Nick's lack of preparation to become king, and I was..." He grimaces. "Overwhelmed."

"Welcome to my life the night you decided we should run away together while you were drunk."

"Not my finest hour, but I meant every word then. There was a window to make my exit, and I understood how to do it. Messy, but not impossible. I would have done it. Were you right that I'd have regretted aspects of my hasty exit? Yes."

There's nothing vindicating in his admission. A choice riddled with regret leads to resentment.

"When you came to me the other night, I didn't see a way out anymore without hurting Simone, and she didn't deserve that. My father's decline is also becoming more noticeable, and he's my—" He shakes his head. "He's my dad, and he's going to need me."

He's killing me with his honest reasoning. Posey already laid the reality of his circumstances out to me, and I had an inkling already. Those factors would make me a single parent, so I tried to pretend they didn't exist when I went to see him.

"I don't know if it was Dr. Bennett or Posey who told you about the baby, Alex. But I'm not asking for anything from you. You don't have to give anything up," I say. "Time with your dad or, or..." I can't say her name, and my stomach rolls. "Anything else."

He lets out a dark chuckle. "You want to know who told me?" He points toward the farmhouse. "Your father, just now. I didn't have a fucking clue when I arrived."

My knees go weak at the realization he's not here because of the baby, and I scramble to grab onto something. Alex is at my side in an instant, and he sweeps me into his arms. He takes me to the hay bale, and he keeps me cradled in his lap.

The room contracts around us, and a frisson of awareness runs down my spine. We haven't been this close in weeks. "You came for me."

"I came for you. The baby is a bonus."

I cup his cheek and graze my thumb across his cheekbone. He rubs his stubble against my palm, and the skin-to-skin contact releases the knot of anxiety I've been carrying for weeks. I can breathe again.

He closes his eyes and releases a deep sigh. "I didn't even realize it was possible to miss someone this much."

"Me either." I wrap my arms around his neck and plant a kiss on his cheek. "You brought me flowers."

"Daffodils. Your favorite."

Neither of us speaks for a while, and I realize I should ask about Simone, but I can't bring myself to phrase the question. Her presence was a painful symbol of what I thought I'd never have, and the thought of them together still makes me queasy.

"What happened in Denmark?" I slide my hand into his suit jacket and along his pecks. He hasn't said it, but he must be mine again. His arrival here, unattached to our baby, back from Denmark early, can't be for any other reason.

He swallows, and he places his hand over mine to still my exploration. "I broke my contract with Simone. I told her I wanted to be with you more than I wanted to be king."

The explanation causes a brief bout of dizziness, and I'm glad I'm in his lap. To pick me over a kingdom was inconceivable a few weeks ago. "Are you in trouble?" I ask.

He chuckles. "I have no idea. I haven't made myself available to anyone. Agreeing to the engagement and then changing my mind is a massive error in judgement, but I think my father might be more sympathetic than he was before."

"I talked to him," I admit. "Before I told you no, I had a long chat with him."

Alex's posture stiffens. "Did he convince you to say no?"

"No," I say. "No. He didn't try to sway me at all. He was really kind, but he was also really honest about his disease, about Nick's preparedness to take over, about how you've always been keen to rule." The heaviness of that conversation weighs on me again. "After I talked to him, it made me realize you hadn't thought your decision through very well. Maybe being with me forever was an impulse. Something you'd regret. Then you showed up without a plan."

"The car accident on West Shore Road—"

"But if you were really going to let Nick take over, you could have sent him," I say. "If you intended to step away, you could have let Nick handle the public side, and you didn't. You didn't because *you* wanted to be there. That's not an accusation, but it was another sign you weren't ready to let Bellerive go."

Alex is quiet for a long time, and when I glance up at him, he eases my hair behind my ear. "That's incredibly insightful."

"I love you a lot," I say. "And it was really important to me that your choice was the right one for you, not just the right one for me." Tears fill my eyes. "I had no idea how hard it would be to watch you with her. It was like... it was like—"

He draws me tighter to him and kisses my temple. "Would have killed me too," he says. "If the situation was reversed, it would have fucking killed me. Being without you was already unbearable." He gathers me closer, and we sink into each other for a beat. "Have they been all right to you? I don't have a lot of faith in people who send their daughter a text message when she almost dies."

His scornful tone makes me smile, and I bury my face in his chest. "They let me in the door, and my mom gave me a really great hug."

"We're going to be much better parents."

Parents. The realization we're in this together, and I won't be trying to manage on my own, spreads a layer of warmth across my body.

"What now?" I ask.

"We go into the house to gather your things. Spend the night in a hotel. Back to Bellerive tomorrow braced for the storm we'll have unleashed. You in?"

"I'm in," I say. "I'm all in with you."

Forty-Seven

ALEX

Although it killed me to say it, I told Rory's parents they'd be welcome to visit Rory and me wherever we landed. Their reception, both when I arrived and after we'd gotten Rory's things together, wasn't exactly warm, but Rory values her parents despite their shortcomings. I understand all too well the complex parent-child dynamic.

We're sitting outside the hotel near the Toronto airport while half my security team sweeps the premises. Rory's hand is locked in mine, and she hasn't let me go for more than a moment or two since I stopped her from collapsing in the barn.

"If you were..." She hesitates. "If you were becoming king, this is what our life would be like?"

I chuckle. "Probably still what our life will be like. Until we can be sure we're not under any threat, we'll have a team of security that Bellerive pays for. We'll have to negotiate all that into the exit plan."

She sighs. "I'm sorry you have to do all this."

"Bellerivian draconian royal laws. Who I marry shouldn't matter, and I'll be telling Nick to get rid of this law as soon as he's got the crown on his head." My chest constricts at the thought, but I keep my tone upbeat. "Not your fault. I'm going into this with my eyes wide open. I promise."

She squeezes my hand.

Kane opens the door, and we're led through the lobby straight to our room. Rory's bags are already there, and so is my small suitcase.

Kane does one last sweep of the rooms and then closes the door behind him. He'll be just outside in the hallway, and the others will be in the adjoining room.

Rory takes in the large suite with a sitting area, massive bathroom, and king-sized bed, and she laughs. "I never in a million years thought this would be my life."

"No?" I draw her toward me and smooth the tendrils of her hair that have escaped her loose braid.

"Maybe once or twice I let myself hope." She gives me a small smile. "Feels like I've loved you forever."

I frame her face, and I kiss her. She meets my lips, but there are still tinges of the sad desperateness that's coated us for weeks. We've spent so much time believing we can never be that even now this isn't quite real. I want to wipe away any lingering doubts the only way I know how, and that's to be as close to her as humanly possible.

Her kiss becomes more insistent, and she shoves my suit jacket off my shoulders. The frantic can't-get-close-enough pace I'd been half expecting comes to life between us. We're shedding clothes and walking toward the bed, our lips breaking contact only long enough for a gasp, a moan, or a pant of frustration when a piece of clothing doesn't come off quite how we expected.

How did I ever convince myself I could survive without her? This time when we go over the cliff together, there'll be no breaking or drowning. The depth of the water might still be unknown, but it's deep enough to last a lifetime. We'll be swimming and floating, and when the swells come, we'll cling to each other. The rest of the world can come tumbling down around us, and as long as I've got her, I'll be just fine.

"I need you, Alex," Rory says when we get to the side of the bed. "I need this."

The panicked edge to her voice makes me slow down, and I draw back to search her face.

"Please," she whispers.

"Nothing's coming between us anymore, Rory. I promise."

I lift her onto the bed, and I follow her down to worship her body in ways I've been denied for weeks. Having her on the royal estate and not being able to go to her, to catch glimpses of her, and to realize she'd never be mine again has been a vise around my heart. With my lips, hands, and tongue, I try to show her how much I've missed being with her. She's the only woman for me, and knowing she'll be mine forever offers a level of comfort I never believed I'd get.

I slip one hand under her head, and my other is on her hip as I ease into her. Her pupils are heavily dilated, and she breathes out a sigh of contentment once we're locked together.

"Yes," she whispers. "Yes."

"I love you," I murmur, and then I ease out to start the rhythm she needs to get where we both want her to go.

"I missed you so much," she moans, and she arches her back. "Oh God. Why does this feel so good?"

I let out a strained chuckle. "If it didn't feel good, we'd be doing it wrong."

"Yeah," she pants. "But it's just—it's always been so much more with you."

Me too. For me too. To think we almost threw this away.

"A little faster," she says, and I can tell by the way she's tightening around me that she's close.

I cradle her, and I increase the pace. "Oh, Rory," I mutter. "God, you feel so good." My orgasm is hovering around the edge of my consciousness, and I grit my teeth to keep myself from losing it.

"Alex," she gasps, and then she lets out a moan of satisfaction, and I follow right behind.

With her tucked against me, I lay out my three plans for us once we leave Bellerive. Western Australia, Cayman Islands, or Ontario, Canada. She listens and asks questions while tracing figure eights on my chest. It's hard to concentrate on the details when everything inside me is singing. That's how it feels—as though my body has woken up to extreme joy. I was the Grinch in his cave, and now my heart has grown ten sizes.

"You seem happy," she whispers.

"I am." I chuckle. "Why wouldn't I be?"

"I thought you'd be angry with me," she says. "I promised we'd be okay, and we weren't."

I frown. "You mean the baby?" The sting of realizing she didn't intend to tell me hasn't quite faded. We fell pretty far from each other if she honestly thought I'd turn my back on her and our child.

"Yeah," she says. "I swear I took my pill."

I'm self-aware enough to understand the choices I made and their consequences. If there was one thing drilled into us as kids it was how closely those two things were tied together. Whatever choice you made, you had to be okay with *any* potential fallout.

"If this was anything other than an accident, you would have left with me when I asked or told me the other night." I hesitate for a beat because what I say next might surprise her. "But more than that, I understood the risk and consequences. I was okay with them then, and I'm okay with them now."

She props herself onto her elbow. "No. I don't believe you. You're fine with this?" She lets out a laugh of disbelief. "That's a tough sell, Alex."

"Look, if I was really that worried about you getting pregnant, I might have let the first time go, but after that? I'd have been more careful. I knew the risk, and I took it more than willingly *every* time." I take a deep breath and dip into territory I'm not sure I want to go. "What about you? Are you okay with having a baby? You're only twenty-three, and—"

She smacks my chest. "God, would you stop with the 'you're only twenty-three' nonsense? Or else I'll start leading conversations with, 'Well, you know, you're *already* thirty-three.'"

"That's a threat? Everyone knows men get better with age."

She grabs my nipple, and I laugh before linking her fingers with mine.

"Answer my question," I say.

"None of this is how I would have opted for it to go, if I'm honest," Rory says. "But I want to be with you, and I want our baby. If there's one thing our time apart taught me, it's how fiercely in love with you I am. I've been barely functioning. So unhappy and not myself."

Our baby. I scooch down her body and kiss a line across her stomach. She runs her fingers through my hair and lets out a sigh of contentment.

"Everything I've ever wanted is right here in this bed." I prop my head onto my hand. "But tomorrow is going to be rough," I say. "But no matter what, you and I come out of the discussions together. Every department will be in crisis management, and those people speak very frankly when we're trying to protect the Summerset brand or the country. But nothing anyone says has any bearing on where we're headed. From now on, you come first. Always."

"You and me," she says. "No matter what." She kisses my jaw. "I like the sound of that."

Me too. But I'm not sure she can really comprehend what it'll be like to go back to Bellerive after what I've done. She won't be on the outside looking in anymore, she'll be right in the center of the storm.

My father's office is packed with my brother, my mother, Nick and Jules via video chat from Tanzania, secretaries, social media managers, diplomatic relations experts, and HR.

As soon as we arrived on the property, our HR manager whisked Rory off for the exit interview she should have had when she quit so abruptly. Rory told me just before this meeting that every question was centered around my relationship with her. They're worried about a sexual harassment lawsuit or public perception that I abused my privilege as a prince to cajole Rory into a relationship. No one even knows Rory is pregnant—yet.

Currently, the room is buzzing, and questions are being hurled in my direction rapid-fire. Rory has a death grip on my hand, and I have to admit as an introduction to the machinery of royalty, this is a baptism by fire. I've basically thrown the monarchy to the wolves for breakfast, and each department is trying to triage the bite marks to our brand and family.

"What have you promised Denmark in exchange for the canceled contract?" Carol, our diplomatic relations expert has a notebook in front of her.

"Keep my relationship with Rory quiet for a few months to distance Simone from the fallout. That may be more complicated than I anticipated." Seemed like an easy promise at the time. "Ease visa restrictions for Denmark citizens who want to live, work, or visit here. I'll need to speak to Brice privately about the final piece."

"Please don't tell me you volunteered me as marriage tribute," Brice groans. "I am capable of finding my own wife." He glances around the room for confirmation, but no one is playing along with his ridiculous schtick.

Rory's grip on my hand tightens to an almost unbearable pressure. Any time Simone's name comes up, Rory white knuckles through it. Can't blame her. I'd be the same if the roles were reversed. The thought of her with anyone else sours my stomach, and she had a front-row seat to that show for weeks.

"It's not marriage related," I say. "But I did make a promise on behalf of the family, and you're the best one to fulfill it."

"Well," our social media coordinator says, "given what you've done, this doesn't seem too complicated on the socials side. We can spin this. Harken back to your heroic actions at the car accident. Cinderella it up."

"Right." I glance at Rory. She knows we're telling them, but I'm not sure she's prepared for the roar that's about to hit this room. "Just one last complication there. Rory is pregnant, and the timeline will be obvious for anyone who knows how to count."

The room falls into a deathly silence for two beats before everyone lobs questions at us and frantically takes notes.

Brice crows from the back of the room. "Holy shit, you knocked her up. Nick, he beat you to it."

Beside me, my father rises from his desk chair. It takes him a moment to say anything once the room quiets. He glances at me, and I can't decide if he needs my help to find the words or if he's contemplating murdering me. His frustrated expression is familiar for too many reasons lately.

"George?" My mother's tone is uncertain on the other side.

"Everyone but family out. Desmond, stay."

Perhaps I should have broken the grandparent news to them ahead of the full staff meeting. My parents might not be the only ones who sometimes blur the personal with the professional. It'd be something to work on if we were living this life. All these meetings are a formality. We're not staying in Bellerive long-term. We won't be tied to the fallout of my abrupt choices beyond Nick's coronation. We're in Bellerive to salvage what we can before we leave.

The various staff members file out in silence, but it just means the buzz has moved to the corridor outside. Whatever they think, I could care less.

"A little warning would have been nice," my mother says as soon as the office door is closed. "Pregnant?"

On the video chat, Julia clears her throat. "First of all, congratulations! On a personal level, I'm very happy for you both. A baby is such a blessing. However, I don't want to be the one to point this out, but, Alex, have you considered the public response to this?"

It'll appear as though I've been playing both women. "As long as the poor perception lands on me, I'll be fine."

"There's no guarantee," Julia says. "I realize the two of you had your own hashtag, but we need to get out in front of this. Do you think Simone would agree to step out with someone else at the same time you and Rory go public? With the pregnancy, you've got to do that fast."

I rub my face with the hand that isn't in Rory's death grip. "Our conversation didn't go overly well." Rory hasn't asked for details, and I wouldn't be keen to share anyway. The whole thing makes her uncomfortable, and Simone's anger was justified. "Whatever impression the public has of us, it'll be temporary since I won't become king."

"No," my father says from where he's standing by the window.

"No, what?" my mother asks.

"Alex may not have to step down," my father says. "Helen, didn't we find something in King Henry's documents that mentioned a marriage because of an heir?"

My mother's brow knits. "Henry married a foreigner, but it was a second marriage because his wife died."

"Died without any children," he says. "But this particular paramour was pregnant."

"I—" My mother shakes her head. "I don't remember what we read that well. We were reading so much trying to find something. None of the scenarios we found fit."

"King George is right," Julia says, and she holds up her phone. "I have a note here about a pregnancy exception during King Henry's reign." She chuckles. "I even wrote here—only valid if Rory were pregnant."

Nick raises his hand. "Rules change from one king to another, right? Like if Alex takes over or if I take over, we can change the marriage rule. Is it possible the rule was created during Henry's reign and then declared void somewhere else?"

Julia must have been preparing him in case I changed my mind. There's not a hint of unease in his tone, unlike the day he walked out of my office when I proposed this.

"Yes," my father says. "It's possible."

"I'll trace it," Desmond says. "It may take me a few days."

"I'll help," Brice says. "Reading almost indecipherable handwriting sounds like an excellent way to kill some time. Or kill me. Why hasn't anyone digitized our history?"

"That hasn't been a priority item," Julia says with a huff.

"You might still be able to become king?" Rory whispers beside me. The death grip on my hand has eased.

"It'll take a while to verify in either direction, but a window might be cracked." At her panicked expression, I kiss her forehead. "Whatever happens, you're my priority."

She curls her fingers into the lapel of my suit, and I drop her hand to loop my arm around her shoulders and draw her to me. Everyone is talking around us about the sliver of hope that's sprung up, and while there's a frisson of excitement in me, Rory and I have never talked about an "us" where she becomes queen of Bellerive. Not exactly what she thought she was signing up for.

"All right," I say, cutting off the chatter. "Priorities. Desmond and Brice—you're tracing the marriage and heir rule through the generations. In the meantime, I have to meet with the Advisory Council about the referendum and subsequent law that needs to be crafted. Nick, we should probably keep in touch over that process."

"I'll talk to Simone," Julia offers. "If the marriage and heir rule stands, you need positive PR around you and Rory. You had that before, and maybe we can get it back. You think you don't care right now, but I know you, Alex. At some point, you'll care. And Rory has no idea how vicious this could get if we don't manage it properly."

Rory's grip on me tightens again. *Thank you, Julia, for such a great reminder.* While Rory "trapping" me into marriage never once crossed my mind, public perception could be very different. They'll have no idea I offered to leave everything for her and she said no. If the reveals around our relationship get ugly, we might have to leak real details to protect Rory. I'll throw myself to the wolves to save her from being bitten.

In spite of the uncertainty over how everything will turn out, I'm feeling hopeful for the first time in months. There's a chance, however slim, that I might get everything I've ever wanted. Now, I just need to make sure Rory feels secure with either outcome.

Forty-Eight

RORY

The next day, Alex leaves me to get settled in his suite of rooms while he makes phone calls in his office. Slotting my clothes into his massive walk-in closet is surreal and exactly right. Although Alex and I have spent plenty of time together over the last few months, it was always in my cottage. Our bubble. Our safe space.

Here in his suite of rooms in the palace, the enormity of who he is and the life we might lead is causing me a tiny bit of panic. Or maybe my hormones are inciting panic, but either way, I'm on the edge of a freak-out. The bubble has popped.

After I left Derrick, I said I was never getting involved with another boyfriend's family business. My resolve disintegrated in the face of Alex's love and devotion. He's said he'll make me a priority, and I believe him. While I might be taking on a role in the one of the biggest family businesses in the world, I have a lot of faith in the partner I'll be standing beside. The bubble might have popped, but he won't let me fall.

I end my exploration at the doorway to the bedroom where it all began. It's made up exactly the same as it was when I was here. Stella, who is hovering somewhere unseen, runs a tight ship. Everything has a place, and now it feels like I do too.

On a whim, I lie on the bed and set my hands on my abdomen. There's a baby in there, which is hard to imagine when the only thing that's changed is how often I'm staring into a toilet bowl or garbage can.

Months ago I woke up in a strange man's spare bedroom, and I had no idea our chance encounter would alter the course of my entire life.

Alex appears in the doorway. "Is this some sort of role-play exercise?"

"You be Prince Charming, and I'll be the damsel in distress." I bat my eyes at him. "Oh, Alex. Please, save me."

"We've already played that one."

I prop myself onto my elbow. "It's a good one though."

He comes to the bed and hovers over me, one hand on either side of me. "If I kiss you, does it break the spell?"

"You *are* the spell," I say with a grin.

"Hmm." He scans my face. "Conundrum. To kiss or not to kiss."

"Always kiss."

He smirks, and then his lips brush against mine in a fleeting contact. Before he can draw away, I frame his face and draw him down for a deeper one. My heart can't quite comprehend what my head knows—we've got nothing to fear anymore.

"It's funny. Ever since you stayed in here, however brief that was, I glance in this door each time I walk past. A quick check as though you'll miraculously appear."

I pat the spot beside me, and Alex sheds his suit jacket and climbs into bed. He wraps an arm around my waist and hauls me against his chest. I nestle into him, and I take a deep breath.

"How are you feeling?" Alex asks.

"Overwhelmed and happy. You?"

"Relieved and happy. But we should probably talk about this latest development."

"The one where you get to become king after all."

"The king part I'm okay with—in either direction—but I want to make sure you are too. If you don't want this life, if you don't want to be queen, then loophole or not, I'll step down."

I turn in his arms so I can see his face. Whatever he's feeling, I need to see it. "I want you to be happy."

"And I don't want my happiness to cause you misery." He gives me a pointed look. "What makes me happiest is you. Full stop. No exceptions. Becoming the king is equivalent to sprinkles on a cupcake. Nice to have but not essential."

I brush my thumb against the stubble on his cheek, and when I stare into his eyes, I recognize how serious he is. Although he's already offered twice, even if there was a way for him to have both me and the crown, he'd still choose me. "But I'd be working with you, not for you, right? We'd be partners."

He cups the back of my head and kisses my forehead. "I'll choose you, Rory. Every time. I'd rather be a poor man than a lonely king."

"I love you." I press my lips to his, and when I try to draw back, he deepens the kiss.

"Have I mentioned yet how much I missed you?"

I bury my face in the crook of his neck, and he wraps his arms around me. His familiar sandalwood scent and the firmness of his embrace are the best kind of comfort. Since he came to get me from the farm, my morning sickness has eased as well. Heartbreak and babies were never meant to go together.

"Whatever we do," I say, "I still want to be able to bake."

He rubs my back and draws me a fraction closer. "We'll keep the apartment as our own little weekend hideaway. You can hide out there whenever you need to. Palace Monday to Friday, but Saturday and Sunday are ours unless we have to make an appearance somewhere."

"Is that—is that work-life balance, I hear?"

"Whether we stay or go, I have no intention of being an absentee father or…" He hesitates. "Husband."

"That's weird." I draw back to stare at my ringless finger. "I don't remember anyone asking."

"Hmm."

Alex isn't the type to propose without a ring, and we don't even know what's going to happen with the succession. Probably a silly thing to bring marriage up right now. There's no doubt where we're headed, but after being apart for weeks and believing I'd never get this, the weight of a ring on my finger would make this sharp turn in my life feel solid and not another vivid dream that used to shatter my heart.

"The groundskeeper mentioned you left some things behind in your apartment," Alex says. "Do you want to come with me to get them?"

"Brownies and my phone." Snuggling with Alex in this bed is a far better idea. But if he's leaving, I'd rather go with him. "Why not?"

He takes my hand and leads me out of the room. We weave our way through the palace to a side door. Since we've returned, he's always taken me out the front entrance to help orient me.

"Is this the door you used to visit me?"

"You mean the one I used to sneak out every night?" He raises his eyebrows. "As a matter of fact, it is."

"Who knew that night would lead to all this."

Alex squeezes my hand. "I shouldn't have been there that night. Kane planned to take Lighthouse Street because of the fog. This incredible compulsion or instinct or whatever you want to call it to turn down West Shore Road seized me. Fate. Destiny. Neither of those things are words I could say in the past with a straight face. But how I felt was like"—his other hand stretches across the center of his chest—"we were connected, before I even met you, in a way I've never experienced with anyone else."

"I felt it too," I say. "When I woke up in the hospital room, you were so familiar. Later, I convinced myself it was because you were famous. But the familiarity didn't end there. It was everywhere, constant." I let out a self-conscious laugh. "Since we stopped seeing each other, I've been having such vivid dreams of you, here, us."

We reach the apartment door, and Alex smooths my hair that's been caught by the ocean breeze. "I had similar dreams. I don't know what to label us, but whatever it is, it's powerful and real, and I have faith it'll never end."

I rise on my toes to kiss him, and one of his arms circles my waist while the other takes something out of his pocket. He tucks me against his side.

He slides the key into the door to my apartment. "I wasn't making phone calls this afternoon."

When the door swings wide, the apartment is crammed with daffodils, and I let out a gasp of surprise. "Alex, what is this?"

"A promise," he says. "That I'll pay attention, and when I screw up, I'll make it right. I'm sorry I wasn't as honest with you as I should have been. I'm sorry I didn't give you a plan as soon as you asked for one. I'm sorry I ever made you think there could be anything more important than you or our child." His voice is husky. "Because there isn't, and there never will be."

I wander through the small space, touching petals and marveling at Alex's ability to get something huge done on short notice. There are petals on the bed, and I glance at Alex over my shoulder. "This seems very romantic for you."

He smirks but doesn't say anything.

When I get closer to the bed, I realize the petals spell something. I stare at the words, dumbfounded.

Marry Me.

"Alex?" When I turn around, he's behind me, and there's an open ring box in his hand. Inside is a jade-and-diamond ring that matches the necklace he gave me for my birthday. "Oh my God."

"I made a choice four months ago to take the road less traveled, and I never want to veer off it again. What do you say, Rory? Want to come on the ride of a lifetime with me?"

"Yes!" I throw my arms around his neck and hug him tight. "Yes!" He chuckles in my ear.

My hand shakes when Alex removes the ring from the box and slides it onto my finger. Tears pool in my eyes as I stare at the proof that we'll be together forever. "Thank you."

Alex loops his arm around my shoulders and draws me close to kiss my temple. "I bought the ring before I left Denmark. Same shop as your necklace."

"It's beautiful." I take in the flowers and the message on the bed again. "This was perfect."

There's a knock on the door, and Alex releases a sigh. "Come in," Alex calls.

The door creaks open. "Your Highness?" Desmond calls. "Are you in here?"

"Make your way through the daffodil forest," I say.

Desmond appears at the corner of the kitchen and peers at us. "Ah, I see congratulations are in order."

"Thank you," I say.

"Any news?" Alex asks.

"In fact, there is. The king and queen just finished verifying the last document. King Henry's heir to the throne exception was never revoked by another sovereign. Technically, should you both wish, Aurora Wilson can become queen of Bellerive."

I suck in a sharp breath. While we knew it was possible, most of me didn't expect it to end up being true. "Oh."

"Once you've had a chance to process the news," Desmond says, "the king and queen would like to see you both to discuss next steps. Julia has had a response from Simone, and she's agreed to our proposed PR strategy if we need it."

"Thank you, Desmond," Alex says. "Rory and I will discuss the newest development and then meet with my parents."

"I'll let them know," Desmond says.

The door clicks behind him, and Alex turns to me. "You're not hovering over the toilet, so I'm wondering if this news isn't terrible?"

"What are you talking about?" I laugh.

"You haven't noticed? When you get emotionally overwhelmed your morning sickness is worse. It's why I put the garbage can next to you at the meeting the other day."

Had I puked at that meeting, I would have been mortified. I narrow my eyes. Although perhaps I shouldn't be surprised, I'm impressed he noticed the link between the two.

"In all seriousness, if you don't want to be queen, we'll go. Leave it all behind. Other than your baking comment, you didn't give me a straight answer, and this decision is too big to risk a miscommunication."

There's an unexpected calmness in me at the thought of standing shoulder to shoulder with Alex all over Bellerive and the rest of the world. I have no doubts about him. None. "Do you think I could do it?"

"Be queen?" He raises his eyebrows. "It'll be a steep learning curve. I won't lie. You are definitely capable. But like anything, if you don't want to learn or don't think you'll enjoy learning, then perhaps it's not worth it. As I said before, your misery can't be the price for my happiness."

With my parents and with Derrick, my happiness was the least of their concerns. My parents wanted me to run the farm and accept the life they'd planned for me. Derrick wanted me to sacrifice my family and my free time and to overlook his indiscretions. What Alex is proposing is the opposite. He's open to negotiation, to compromise, to listening to me when I'm unhappy. Above all else, he loves me in a way no one else ever has.

"Cup of tea?" Alex asks. "Big decisions require tea."

He heads to the kitchen, and I wander to the window that looks over the fields to the ocean in the distance. The sun is sinking in the horizon, and it's one of my favorite times of day. The sky is alive with pinks and oranges.

Alex's reflection wavers in the window when he appears behind me.

"I do declare that is a cracking view," I say in my best worst English accent. It doesn't look like someone else's country out there; it looks like mine.

He loops his arms around my waist, and I ease back against him, content to be back in his arms.

"It's a mystery how that accent isn't getting any better," he says.

"Want to hear the good news?"

"There's good news about that accent?"

"You've got the rest of your life to help me improve. Isn't that amazing? You can hear my fake accent every day. Maybe even several times a day."

"Bloody hell," Alex mutters, but I can hear the grin in his voice.

"I want to be your queen," I say. "I don't know if I'll be as bad at it as I am at accents, but I'll do my best."

He nuzzles my neck, and he trails a line of kisses to my ear. "I love you and your terrible accents. Bellerive will love you too. Just, maybe, don't do the accents in public."

I turn in his arms and slap his chest, but I can't help a laugh. He frames my face and kisses me, stalling my laughter. When I try to return it, he draws away and touches his forehead to mine.

"You're sure?"

I let a beat pass while I search for any anxiety or uncertainty, but there isn't any. I trust Alex to guide me through this. He won't let me embarrass myself, and he won't let me become miserable as long as I tell him when I'm unhappy. We can do this, together.

"Yes," I say. "I'm sure."

He kisses my forehead and wraps his arms around me, tugging me into a tight hug. I stare at the fading light over the ocean and marvel at the decision we just made. I'm going to be a queen. The queen of Bellerive.

Alex's chin rests on the top of my head. "My wife, my queen, the mother of my child. I got the best hat trick of all in you."

In his pocket, Alex's phone vibrates.

"Duty calls?" I ask.

"Always," he says. "You ready to go change the course of Bellerive's history?"

"Let's go bring Rolex back to life." I draw out of his arms and hold out my hand. He links his fingers with mine, and we step out of the cottage and into our new life, together.

Order Brice's book here: http://mybook.to/FallenCrown
Get bonus chapters about Rory and Alex by signing up for my newsletter here: www.wendymillion.com

ACKNOWLEDGMENTS

Thank you to everyone who has been reading and loving this series. I've really enjoyed receiving your emails about these characters. It's a world I intend to live in for a while.

A special thank you to my ARC team who read and reviewed for me. Eliza, Smriti, Sigrid, Sarah, Misty, Phyllis, Soumya, Hilary, Faith, Melissa, Anushka, Michelle W, Michelle M, Daniela, Summer, Alya, Karen, Bri, Liana, and CiCi—your support has meant the world.

As always, I couldn't do this writing gig without the support of my family. I am so lucky to have a proud dad, a supportive husband, and two understanding children.

And lastly, thanks to Cole and Avery who are my writing sounding boards for pretty much any decision I make. I appreciate your friendship.

ALSO BY W. MILLION

Bellerive Royals Series – Interconnected standalones

Fake Crown

Scarred Crown

Heavy Crown

Fallen Crown

New Adult Sports

Saving Us

Fake Crown

W MILLION

Donaghey Brothers Series – Romantic suspense

Retribution

Resurrection

Redemption

Adult Contemporary Romance

When Stars Fall
Miss Matched (coming June 2023)

ABOUT W. MILLION

W. Million is a Watty Award winner whose contemporary romances about strong women and troubled men have captivated her loyal readers. She is the author of the romantic suspense series *The Donaghey Brothers,* the NA sports romance *Saving Us,* the *Bellerive Royals* series, and the contemporary second chance romance, *When Stars Fall.*

When not writing, Wendy enjoys spending time in or around the water. She lives in Ontario, Canada with two beautiful daughters, two cute pooches, and one handsome husband (who is grateful she doesn't need two of those).

www.ingramcontent.com/pod-product-compliance
Lightning Source LLC
Chambersburg PA
CBHW061338190726
48288CB00005B/1510